Flame

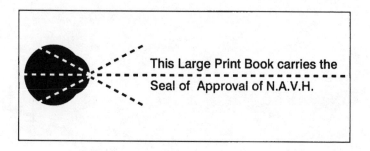

Flame

Connie Mason

Thorndike Press • **Waterville, Maine**

Published in 2003 by arrangement with Leisure Books,
a division of Dorchester Publishing Co., Inc.

Thorndike Press® Large Print Romance.

The tree indicium is a trademark of Thorndike Press.

The text of this Large Print edition is unabridged.
Other aspects of the book may vary from the original edition.

Set in 16 pt. Plantin by Al Chase.

Printed in the United States on permanent paper.

Library of Congress Cataloging-in-Publication Data

Mason, Connie.
    Flame / Connie Mason.
        p. cm.
    ISBN 0-7862-5832-2 (lg. print : hc : alk. paper)
    1. United States — History — Civil War, 1861–1865 —
Veterans — Fiction.   2. Prisoners — Family relationships —
Fiction.   3. Women pioneers — Fiction.   4. Wagon trains
— Fiction.   5. Missouri — Fiction.   6. Large type books.
    I. Title.
PS3563.A78786F58 2003
    813'.54—dc22   2003056430

Flame

As the Founder/CEO of NAVH, the only national health agency solely devoted to those who, although not totally blind, have an eye disease which could lead to serious visual impairment, I am pleased to recognize Thorndike Press★ as one of the leading publishers in the large print field.

Founded in 1954 in San Francisco to prepare large print textbooks for partially seeing children, NAVH became the pioneer and standard setting agency in the preparation of large type.

Today, those publishers who meet our standards carry the prestigious "Seal of Approval" indicating high quality large print. We are delighted that Thorndike Press is one of the publishers whose titles meet these standards. We are also pleased to recognize the significant contribution Thorndike Press is making in this important and growing field.

Lorraine H. Marchi, L.H.D.
Founder/CEO
NAVH

★ Thorndike Press encompasses the following imprints: Thorndike, Wheeler, Walker and Large Print Press.

Prologue

Spring, 1866 St. Joe, Missouri

"Dammit, Captain, you're making life difficult for me. If I don't put you in jail the army will be on my back. Why in the hell did you pick my town to disrupt? The war is over; the South lost. If I can accept it, why can't you?"

Tanner MacTavish rubbed his bloody knuckles against his palm and sent Sheriff Beardsley a sour look. "The war may be over for you, Sheriff, but it will never end for me. After what the bluecoats did to my home and family I can barely stand to look at a Yankee without wanting to kill."

"I was warned to be on the lookout for you even before you arrived," Beardsley said. "The army won't stand for many more of your unprovoked attacks upon their men." His voice softened. "I know you, Captain, and always found you likable. I served under you in the war, but I'm sworn to uphold the law in St. Joe and you know I'm not one to shirk my duty."

Tanner sent Beardsley a look as bleak as his heart. A tall man with hair as black as sin, Tanner had sun-darkened skin, piercing gray eyes and a stubbly chin that gave the impression of a half-wild creature. His shoulders were vulgarly broad; his taut muscles were boldly prominent beneath his mismatched outfit of leather vest and gray Rebel army trousers. One glance was all it took to know that Tanner MacTavish was altogether too physical, too intense, too dangerous.

"Do what you have to do, Beardsley," Tanner said gruffly. "I'm sorry I picked your town but I had no idea you were sheriff when I rode in. Something snaps inside me whenever I see one of those devils in blue coats. I can't promise it won't happen again."

Beardsley snorted in disgust. "You can't take on the whole blasted army, Captain. If I don't keep you behind bars the townspeople will be up in arms, not to mention the army. I promised Lieutenant Pickford I'd keep you out of their hair until the final wagon train of the season departs and they go back to the fort. They don't want a firebrand like you running around attacking men simply because you can't tolerate the color of their uniforms."

Beardsley plucked the keys to the cell off the wall, opened the door and invited Tanner inside.

"You'd better give me your guns," Beardsley said, holding out his hand.

Tanner reached down, untied the laces securing his twin holsters to his muscular thighs, unbuckled the belt containing two

8

.41-caliber, double-action, fancy-cut Colt Lightning models and draped it over Beardsley's arm.

"Is that all?" Beardsley asked.

Tanner's inscrutable dark eyes glinted dangerously as he bent to remove a skinning knife from a hidden sheath in his right boot. "That's it." Since the sheriff didn't search him, Tanner saw no need to hand over the .38-caliber single-action Colt pocket revolver he carried in an inside vest pocket.

"Sorry, Captain," Beardsley said as he closed the cell door with a resounding metallic clang. "Reckon you'll have to cool your heels in here for a spell. It could go bad for you if the army decides to press charges."

"You can drop the 'Captain,' Beardsley; the Yankees defeated us, remember? They took everything of value from me except my life, and they should have taken that too. There is damn little I care about anymore."

Sheriff Beardsley walked away shaking his head. Tanner's hatred for Yankees was deep and intensely personal. Something had happened in Tanner's life that Beardsley wasn't aware of, and he didn't care to know the details, but he recognized a bitter, disillusioned man when he saw one.

Chapter One

"I tell you I'm desperate, Sheriff. I need a husband and I need him now!"

Sheriff Beardsley leaned back in his chair, tipped his hat back and peered beneath the brim at the distraught woman standing before him. He would have considered her a plain and unremarkable spinster if not for her flaming red hair that refused to be subdued beneath her bonnet, and her unusual eyes . . . large, wide spaced and a startling brilliant green. Her mud-brown traveling dress and plain, unfashionable bonnet made her look like a prudish spinster. In contrast, her flaming hair and vivid eyes added a wanton look to her prim exterior.

"You've come to the wrong place, lady. I'm a sheriff, not a marriage broker."

"You're the only person I can trust. You've got to help me, Sheriff."

Beardsley removed his hat and ran his thick fingers through his thinning hair, wishing himself anywhere but facing this intense young woman. "Why don't you sit down, miss, and tell me what's troubling you. I can't help you if I don't know what this is all about. You've gotta admit your request is somewhat unusual. Start by telling me your name and where you're from."

"My name is Ashley, Ashley Webster. I'm a schoolteacher from Chicago." She stared down at her gloved hands, noting with dismay that the handkerchief she held had been twisted into shreds.

"Very good, Miss Webster, that's a start. Now what's all this nonsense about a husband? These days most women prefer to choose their own mates."

Lying in his bunk in the jail cell a few feet away, Tanner MacTavish raised his hat and gave the nearly hysterical woman a slow perusal through eyes turned dark with contempt. Her Northern accent set his teeth on edge. A Yankee, he thought disgustedly. Man or woman, there wasn't a Yankee he didn't hate. This one was particularly annoying. Was she so lacking in pride that she had to beg for a husband?

"I assure you I wouldn't be here if I wasn't desperate," Ashley said with asperity. "I've traveled all the way from Chicago and went to considerable expense to purchase oxen and outfit a wagon in order to join the wagon train leaving St. Joe tomorrow."

She jerked open her reticule and dug out a wrinkled letter. "This is a letter of acceptance from the wagon master that he now refuses to honor. The Cramer company's wagon train is the last to leave this spring. If I can't join it I'll have to wait until next year,

11

and that's too late."

Beardsley stroked his chin. "I know Captain Cramer. I take it you're traveling alone."

Ashley nodded, her green eyes glittering defensively. Anger became her, Beardsley decided. It made her appear almost beautiful.

"The wagon master assumed I was a man," Ashley explained, waving the letter in the sheriff's face. "He accepted readily enough when I wrote asking to join his wagon train. I know my name is unusual but it's not uncommon for women to bear names that could be either gender. After he discovered I was female he refused outright to allow me to travel with his wagon train. The utter gall of the man! He said I needed a husband in order to join his group. Or a family unit consisting of a mother and father."

A low chuckle came from behind her, but Ashley was too angry to turn and locate the source.

"Now I tell you, Sheriff, finding a suitable husband is nearly impossible in a town like St. Joe. So I decided to turn to you for help. I expect you know the townspeople better than anyone. I need a husband to accompany me to my destination, one who won't take advantage of my vulnerable position as a single lady."

Beardsley made a choking sound deep in his throat. "Begging your pardon, ma'am, but didn't you say you wanted a husband?

12

You won't be a single lady if you wed."

Ashley looked at him with growing impatience. "I've been a single lady for twenty-five years and I intend to remain one. I don't really want to get married, Sheriff; I merely want a husband. Let me explain," Ashley said when Beardsley gave her an incredulous look. "I want to hire a man to pose as my husband. He has to be convincing enough to satisfy Captain Cramer. I'm prepared to offer a substantial sum to the right man. I'm not going all the way to Oregon, merely to Fort Bridger. Once we reach our destination he will be free to go his own way."

"Fort Bridger," Beardsley repeated, rubbing his jaw thoughtfully. "What's so dang important at Fort Bridger to make you go to all this trouble? Why can't you wait until next spring? Who knows, by then you may find a real husband."

Ashley leaped to her feet. "No! Next spring may be too late. My brother is a soldier at Fort Bridger. I received a letter stating he was in the stockade. He's been accused of murdering a fellow officer and Lord knows what else. Cole would never kill anyone. He's all I've got left in the world. He didn't do it and I'm going to prove it!" She took off her bonnet and gave her head an angry shake. She had no idea the effect her flaming hair had on people, so she was completely unselfconscious as she raked her fingers through

13

her tumbling curls and jammed the bonnet back on her head.

Beardsley had to give Ashley Webster grudging respect despite her flawed thinking and reckless nature. There was nothing he could do to help her even if he wanted to. Young women had no business harrying off to uncharted territory on their own. The dangers she would face were mind-boggling. Besides, he knew of few men — no, he amended, *no* men — who would accept the kind of offer she was proposing.

Beardsley searched for a gentle way to tell Ashley that she should forget about joining the wagon train, that what she suggested was ludicrous; then his gaze slid past Ashley to Tanner, who was now leaning nonchalantly against the iron bars of the cell.

Having risen from the cot, Tanner had shoved his hat from his face and was now staring at Ashley with piercing intensity. One corner of his mouth was curled upward into a sneer. He had tried not to listen as she explained her dilemma but it was near to impossible to ignore her. The Yankee school-marm was as bold a hussy as he'd ever seen.

Initially he'd thought her a plain little mouse, but when she'd loosed her glorious hair and presented him with her profile, he found nothing plain about her. Certainly there was nothing common about her thickly lashed green eyes or generous mouth. No

14

demure Southern belle would be caught dead looking so flamboyantly brazen, or hatching a harebrained scheme that was doomed from the onset.

Sheriff Beardsley regarded Tanner with speculation. He couldn't help but notice the way Tanner was staring at the Webster woman, and an idea took root in his mind. He knew that if Tanner continued on his rush toward self-destruction he'd sure as hell end up buried six feet under in some nameless boothill. It would be a damn shame for a man like Tanner to end his life still fighting a war the South had lost long ago.

It occurred to Beardsley that the farther away Tanner got from civilization the less trouble he could get into. In his present state of mind Tanner was a firebrand ready to explode. Tanner might be madder than hell at what he was going to suggest, but the sheriff had decided to save Tanner despite himself.

Ashley's patience snapped. Time was growing short. If she didn't acquire a pretend husband soon, she'd be left behind. She knew the sheriff had someone in mind, for his expression abruptly turned thoughtful.

"Well, Sheriff, can you help me? If you don't, I swear I'll march into the nearest saloon and take the first man who volunteers."

Beardsley started violently. As determined as Miss Webster appeared, he feared she'd do exactly as she said. That kind of reckless behavior would get her killed . . . or raped. He spared another glance at Tanner, then made up his mind.

"As a matter of fact, Miss Webster, I do have a man in mind."

Tanner gave Beardsley a look of astonishment. He couldn't imagine what the sheriff was thinking. Abetting the woman's misguided judgment was tantamount to murder. Tanner seriously doubted the schoolmarm would reach her destination alive, with or without Beardsley's help. Didn't she know that any man stupid enough to pose as a husband would demand full husbandly rights? Was the woman so desperate to reach her brother that she'd risk her virtue and her life? Did Beardsley know a man honest enough to follow the rules set by the determined Yank? Certainly not in St. Joe, where men came and went and few stayed long enough to establish a good reputation.

"I'll be forever in your debt, Sheriff," Ashley said with rising excitement. "How soon can you contact him? The wagon train won't wait for me."

"You can ask him yourself, miss. He's right here in this room."

Ashley made a slow perusal of the small room and the two jail cells therein. One of them was empty, but the other — oh no — the other was occupied by a man whose

16

appearance both frightened and fascinated her. Never had she seen such a man! She tried to ignore the way his gray trousers rode his hard-muscled thighs, and the way the sinews of his shoulders bunched and flexed beneath his leather vest. She wanted to ignore the stark planes of his brutally hand- some face and the unrelenting, steely-eyed look of contempt he gave her but could not. His face was too compelling.

His features could have been carved from stone. Gathering her wits, she concentrated on his square jaw shadowed with dark stubble, which was almost but not quite as intimidating as the rest of him. He needed a shave, she thought dimly, and a haircut. The realization that this was the man to whom the sheriff was referring appalled her. She tore her eyes from Tanner to stare with horror at Beardsley.

"Surely you're not suggesting that I . . . ? Dear God, the man is a criminal!"

"That all depends on the way you look at it," Beardsley claimed. "Tanner ain't all that bad."

"The lady is right, Sheriff," Tanner drawled. "Count the times I've been in your jail and add it to jail cells I've occupied in other cities. Now do you get the idea?"

"He's a Reb!" Ashley cried, recoiling instinctively when she heard Tanner's soft drawl. A staunch abolitionist, Ashley had

17

seen firsthand the cruelties inflicted on slaves. Those who reached Chicago during the early years of the war had arrived in pitiful condition, bearing tales of atrocities inflicted upon them by their masters.

"And you're a Yankee." Tanner's eyes turned dark as sin — cold, ruthless, even predatory.

Beardsley looked from Tanner to Ashley, stunned by the animosity that flowed between them. They appeared to despise one another on sight yet seemed unaware of the tension that sparked between them.

"Yes, I'm a Yankee, Reb. I've never owned a slave or mistreated a living soul in my life. Can you say the same?"

"Would you believe me if I said I had not?" He laughed harshly when Ashley sent him a look of utter disdain. "No, I thought not. Fear not, Yank. I'd be a damn fool to involve myself in your reckless scheme. I have enough problems of my own without taking on those of an irresponsible spinster."

Ashley's eyes blazed in sudden anger. She didn't need to be reminded of her unmarried state. "I'd have to be a hundred times more desperate than I am now to ask for your help."

"Well, I reckon that settles it, Miss Webster," the sheriff said dismissively. "You won't have any trouble selling your wagon and oxen. Perhaps you'll have better luck next year."

18

"Next year is too late. My brother is in desperate straits, accused of a murder he didn't commit. I need to go to him now. If there is a way to clear his name, I'll find it."

"That's commendable, Miss Webster, but I've done all I can."

"Is that all?" Ashley asked. A black fog of despair settled over her. "Can you offer me nothing in the way of help? Are there no decent men in St. Joe willing to pose as my husband?"

"None that I know of," Beardsley said blandly. "Except for Tanner here. I've known Tanner MacTavish a long time, miss, and he's a good man. I fought under him during the war and I'd trust him with my life."

"Then why is he in jail?"

"Because I can't stand the sight of Yankee soldiers," Tanner said in his own defense. "Nor am I fond of Yankee spinsters who resort to bribery to find husbands. Even bogus husbands. Go home, Yank. If your brother is a Yankee soldier I have no sympathy for him or his kind."

Her face flaming, Ashley turned away from the bitterness of Tanner's words. His intense, fathomless eyes reflected the emptiness of his soul. Something that was neither pity nor hatred shuddered through her. Something she could not name.

"You're being a mite hasty, Captain,"

Beardsley cautioned. "Think carefully on what the lady offers. To my knowledge you have no money and no job. The army is getting fed up with you attacking their men without provocation. The West is a vast, open country. Miss Webster's money can help you buy land, forge a new life and forget the war. You're too good a man to waste your life holding grudges."

Tanner's face hardened. "Grudges?" He laughed harshly, a hollow echo of despair. "If you only knew."

"I think you oughtta reconsider, Tanner," Beardsley said. "The lady needs help and so do you. Lieutenant Pickford stopped me on the street just this morning and said he was considering taking you back to the fort to be tried. You're becoming a nuisance to the army. Your hatred is going to get you killed."

"I didn't say I'd accept Mr. MacTavish's help," Ashley reminded him. "I want a man who can follow orders, not a firebrand who's likely to desert me before we reach Fort Bridger. If not for Captain Cramer's prejudice against females traveling alone I wouldn't need a man to pose as my husband. I'm perfectly capable of handling my own affairs. It's not as if I'm an inexperienced girl. I'm an independent woman with experience in many areas." That wasn't exactly true but it sounded good.

Tanner guffawed loudly. "I wasn't aware

that twenty-five was such a great age, Yank. But mayhap," he added crudely, "your experience lies between your —"

"Tanner! Dammit, man, where are your brains? You're undoing all my efforts to help you. Miss Webster is a lady; mind your tongue."

"Of course she's a lady." His lip curled derisively as he stared at her, unblinking, hard eyed, mocking. "A Yankee lady. Where is your pride? No ladies of my acquaintance would go begging for a husband, no matter how desperate they were."

Red dots of rage exploded behind Ashley's eyes. "I need a man to pose as my husband, not a bed partner. If all men are like you, I'm grateful I chose to remain unwed."

Determined to prevail, Sheriff Beardsley tried one last time to convince the feisty pair. "Think of your brother, Miss Webster. The stockade can't be a healthy place. I can guarantee that Tanner is honest. Once he agrees to something his word is good. You can trust him to protect you. Admittedly he goes a little loco when he sees bluecoats but he can learn to control that flaw with a little help from you.

"And you, Captain," Beardsley continued, "do you want to spend your life in and out of jails?" When he saw Ashley frown and Tanner turn his back, Beardsley spit out a curse. "Aw, hell, I don't even know why I try."

Ashley was the first to actively consider the notion of accepting Tanner as a traveling partner, though she didn't know how she'd put up with the disreputable Rebel all those weeks it took to reach Fort Bridger. But if the sheriff could vouch for his character she should at least consider him.

He'd need a shave and new clothes, she thought, if he had nothing better to wear than the leather vest and gray army pants. Briefly she wondered if Tanner could convince Captain Cramer that he was her husband, then scoffed at the notion that he couldn't. She suspected that Tanner MacTavish could convince anyone of anything, if he put his mind to it.

Never had Tanner encountered such a determined woman. The flame-haired Yankee spinster was as crazy as she was extraordinary. Her brother must be a special man for her to risk her life and reputation. Did she have no parents or guardian to curb her reckless behavior? he wondered. If he didn't agree to her foolhardy plan, would she find someone even more disreputable than him? Though why he should even care escaped him.

He didn't care, he told himself. If he agreed to her proposal it would be for his own benefit. Beardsley was right, he decided. He should take the money she offered, see her to her destination, then bid her good-bye without regrets. He'd heard they were mining

22

silver in Colorado and a few other western states. With a grubstake he could claim some of it for himself.

Beardsley knew the moment each of them reached the same decision. Tanner wore an expression of bitter resignation and Ashley one of grudging acceptance.

"How much are you offering, Yank?" Tanner asked gruffly.

"A thousand dollars," Ashley said without batting an eye. "Half now and the other half when we arrive at Fort Bridger."

Beardsley let out a low whistle. "That's a lot of money, Miss Webster. You really are desperate."

"Desperate enough to risk everything I own," Ashley admitted. "My aunt, with whom I'd been living, died recently and left me her house and a small inheritance. I sold the house after I learned about Cole. I also had some savings."

"You're a fool, Yank," Tanner said with derision. "But I'm not. I'll pose as your husband and take your money with no qualms. Yankees took things from me that can never be replaced. I'd be stupid not to take your money."

Ashley bit her lip as she considered her options. She felt helpless and utterly at the mercy of an unscrupulous man. But Sheriff Beardsley had pegged her right: she was too desperate to be choosy.

23

Tanner watched Ashley in waiting silence. He thought her outrageously daring, singularly lacking in wisdom and untempered by caution. She looked innocent yet seductively earthy. Except for the sheriff's word, she knew nothing about him. Didn't she care that she'd be entirely at his mercy? He could take her money, rape her and kill her at his leisure and she would be helpless to prevent it. But what in the hell did he expect from a Yankee schoolmarm too long in the tooth to attract a man?

With each passing minute Ashley knew her chances of finding another man to pose as her husband grew increasingly slimmer. Cole needed her; she couldn't let him down. Come hell or high water she intended to leave with the wagon train in the morning. Even if it meant joining forces with an embittered Rebel who hated her guts.

She lashed him with a narrow-eyed look of contempt. "Very well, Reb, I suppose you'll have to do. Sheriff Beardsley seems to think you're dependable, and at this late date I can't wait for someone better qualified to come along."

Tanner gave her a long, level look that made her think she had been too hasty. "Unlock the cell, Sheriff. The Yank and I have a deal."

A pleased smile lifted the corners of Beardsley's mouth as he uncoiled his long length from the chair, reached for the key hanging from a nail on the wall and approached Tanner's small cell. He almost pitied Tanner the next months in the company of the acid-tongued Yankee miss. He could understand why she was still a spinster. What man would willingly wed a woman whose sharp tongue and biting wit cut him to ribbons?

The cell door swung open and Tanner stepped out. He nodded briefly at Beardsley, then turned to Ashley. "We have some business to transact, Yank. Half the money now, if I recall correctly."

Ashley sent him a scathing glance. "You're not lacking in memory, Reb."

Tanner's jaw hardened. "Memory is all I have left and I wish to God I didn't have one."

Unable to make sense of his words, Ashley dug in her reticule and removed a stack of bills. "How do I know you won't take my money and leave town?"

"He can't go anywhere without his horse and guns," the sheriff offered. "And he won't have either until tomorrow. I'll personally hand them over at the departure site in the morning."

"So much for trust," Tanner muttered darkly.

Beardsley shrugged. "I'm protecting my ass, Captain." Suddenly recalling his language, he sent Ashley a sheepish grin. "Begging your

25

pardon, Miss Webster."

Wondering if she'd live to regret it, Ashley placed the money in Tanner's hands, then had the unaccountable urge to snatch it back. But it was too late. Tanner closed his large, callused hand over the money and tucked it into his vest pocket.

"I have some shopping to do before we travel to the departure site," Ashley said. "I suggest you use some of that money for a shave, haircut and proper clothing for the trip. And anything else you deem necessary for your personal needs. I'll take care of the food and supplies. We'll meet at the livery in two hours."

"Let's get one thing straight, Yank. I agreed to pose as your husband, not take orders from you. I'll stick to our agreement but will stand for no interference in my personal life. If you can't abide by those rules I reckon we better part ways now."

Ashley bit her tongue to keep from blasting the obnoxious Rebel with the sharp edge of her tongue. Unfortunately she needed him, but one day she wouldn't, and on that day she'd tell him exactly what she thought of him.

"Do as you please," she bit out. "Just be at the livery in two hours so we can present ourselves as husband and wife to Captain Cramer."

With her chin thrust at a defiant angle,

Ashley whirled on her heel and stormed from the sheriff's office. She treated Tanner and Beardsley to an unintentional display of femininity when her skirts flipped up to reveal a pair of trim ankles.

"Whew," Beardsley said, somewhat dazed by the flame-haired termagant. "That little lady has a mind all her own. I'm not sure I envy you the next few months."

"That little lady is no lady at all. She's a brazen Yankee baggage with a bee in her drawers. Maybe all this talk about her brother is pure fiction. Maybe she wants a man in her bed bad enough to buy one. By her own admission she's experienced, and if I'm not mistaken she's no timid virgin."

"I vouched for you, Captain. You've taken her money. You have a moral obligation to see her safely to her destination."

"So I have," Tanner said thoughtfully. "But she damn well didn't pay for me to service her in bed. The Yank will whistle "Dixie" before she lures me between her legs. Be sure to show up tomorrow morning with my horse and guns," he reminded Beardsley as he walked out the door.

"Stay out of trouble," Beardsley shot back. He watched Tanner walk down the street, wondering if he had made a mistake. He fully expected fireworks to develop between the flame-haired Yankee and the Rebel hothead. Too bad he wouldn't be around to enjoy them.

27

"Back again, Miss Webster?" Captain Cramer asked when Ashley confronted him a little over two hours later. "I haven't changed my mind. Unless you have suddenly acquired either a husband or parents, you aren't welcome here."

Cramer's brows arched sharply upward as Tanner materialized from around the wagon to stand beside Ashley. He was clean shaven and wore a blue cotton shirt under his leather vest. Though his hair was still long, it was secured at his nape with a leather thong. Unfortunately he hadn't seen fit to replace his gray army trousers with something more appropriate, but Ashley decided not to comment on it since he had arrived at the livery at the appointed time.

"This is my husband, Captain Cramer. I'm Mrs. Tanner MacTavish now. So you no longer have an excuse to ban me from joining your wagon train."

Tanner and Cramer shook hands. "Your husband, eh? Sudden, wasn't it?"

"That's none of your concern," Ashley said tartly. "You said I needed a husband and so I have one. What is our position in the lineup to be?"

"Not so fast, Miss . . . er, Mrs. MacTavish. Do you have a marriage license? I'd like to see it."

Ashley blanched. Lord, she'd never

thought he'd ask to see a marriage license. "Of course we do," she answered before she had time to think. "We're to pick it up at the preacher's house later today."

"Show me the license before departure time tomorrow and you and your . . . husband will be welcome to join our company." It was obvious from his words and tone of voice that he thought her a liar.

Ashley watched him walk away, as inflexible as iron. What in God's name was she going to do now?

Tanner's face went slack with relief. Fate had intervened and saved him from making a disastrous mistake. Getting mixed up with the Yankee spinster had been wrong from the beginning. He stepped away without visible regret.

"I reckon you'll be wanting your money back, Yank," Tanner said as he reached inside his vest pocket. "I spent some, but that's the breaks of the game."

"Do you relish the thought of going back to jail, Reb?"

Tanner sent her a ferocious scowl. It was just like a Yank to derive enjoyment from a man's misfortune. "I've been in jail before."

"And will likely end up there again. If not in St. Joe then in some other town." A small, utterly outrageous thought stirred in the back of her mind. She faced him squarely. "I'm willing to show Captain Cramer our marriage license; are you?"

At first Tanner had no idea what she was talking about. As he grasped for rationality, her words finally took on meaning. His eyes widened, his mouth fell open and his breath lodged in his throat. When speech finally returned, all he could do was sputter irrationally.

"What's wrong, Reb; are you afraid to accept a challenge?"

"If you're suggesting what I think you are you've got to be insane, even for a Yankee."

Ashley closed her eyes, looking painfully brittle. "I'm desperate. The marriage would be in name only. Once we reach our destination you'll be free to seek an annulment. Or I will, if you prefer."

"And I'm crazier than you if I agree to such a stupid proposal. I can't stand the sight of Yankees. You and I are antagonists. We feed off of one another in ways that are volatile and potentially dangerous. How long would it be before one of us does the other bodily harm?"

Ashley wondered the same thing, but she was determined. "I'm willing to take the chance if you are, Reb. It's only a few months out of your life."

He remained silent so long Ashley began to despair. It was too late to find another man even if she wanted to, and she wasn't sure she had the courage to ask another man to marry

30

her. Better she stick with the known danger than the unknown.

Tanner searched her face, seeing more than met the eye, far more than he wished. He saw a woman whose youthful prettiness had matured into subtle beauty. He recognized vulnerability and fragility. He saw stubbornness and inflexibility. More important, he saw a Yankee. He knew instinctively that Ashley Webster was dangerous; exactly how dangerous and in what way he'd yet to discover. He smiled mirthlessly, recalling every damn thing Yankees had cost him. But since returning to jail did not appeal to him, he made a decision that would irrevocably change his life.

"What the hell, Yank; let's get married."

Chapter Two

The gold band Tanner had placed on the third finger of her left hand felt suspiciously like a noose, Ashley reflected. Ashley had been surprised when Tanner insisted on stopping at the mercantile and buying the ring before looking up a preacher. She had demurred politely but the damn Reb had insisted. He probably enjoyed her discomfiture; that's why he'd done it, she thought sourly. Then he had taken the liberty of asking Sheriff Beardsley to act as witness. She could still envision the sheriff's shocked expression when Tanner invited him to their wedding.

The preacher had married them a short time later, with Sheriff Beardsley, wearing a curiously complacent smile, acting as witness. When it came time to kiss the bride, some devil in Tanner made him grasp Ashley's shoulders and kiss her roughly, thoroughly, with a brutal lack of tenderness. In a daze she had signed the marriage paper below Tanner's signature and shoved it into her reticule.

"You sure as hell know how to make a man a believer in the hand of fate, Tanner," Beardsley said, shaking his head in disbelief. "Congratulations. I hope the union will prove long and fruitful." He gave a bark of laughter.

"Go to hell," Tanner returned shortly. "Laugh all you want. You started all this; you're responsible for the outcome, though only the good Lord knows how it will all end."

Ashley sent both men a dark scowl. "This is a business arrangement, Reb. As soon as it's feasible you can obtain an annulment and go on your way a thousand dollars richer."

"Amen to that, Yank."

Vastly amused, the sheriff tipped his hat and said, "Good luck, Mrs. MacTavish. You too, Tanner. Something tells me you're both going to need it." He laughed all the way back to his office.

"I'd laugh too if I wasn't so damn sure that I'd just made the biggest mistake of my life," Tanner complained, unable to believe he'd just gotten married, even if it was in name only and unlikely to last more than a few months.

"It's too late now to back out of our deal," Ashley said crisply, though in truth his kiss had given her second thoughts about the wisdom of asking help from a man with a healthy hatred for Yankees. And now he was her husband.

Tanner gave her a smile that did nothing to ease her fears. "I wouldn't think of backing out, Yank. Shall we go?" He offered his arm, which she ignored. He shrugged and walked off, obviously not caring if she followed or not.

"You asked for our marriage paper, Captain Cramer. I hope you're satisfied," Ashley said as she handed the wagon master the marriage license.

Though Tanner thought her headstrong and foolish, he couldn't help admiring her gumption. He hoped her brother appreciated her efforts on his behalf.

The wagon master hurriedly scanned the document, then gave Tanner a look of utter disdain. "I hope she's making it worth your while, MacTavish. You don't look like a man to sell yourself cheap, but appearances are often misleading. Nevertheless, you have produced a marriage license and I did promise your . . . wife a place in our train.

"Had she told me what she intended I would have recommended someone better suited to her needs. We have several unmarried men traveling with the group who would have been eager to take a wife, but I hoped to discourage Miss Webster to the point where she would give up and go back home. I had no idea she'd look for a husband among the riffraff of St. Joe. It's pure foolishness."

"Perhaps my wife chose wisely, after all," Tanner allowed.

"And perhaps she didn't," Cramer countered. "Nevertheless, it's too late to change things. You can pull your wagon in place at the end of the line. And if I were you I'd find a different pair of trousers. There are those among us who take offense at slave-owning Rebels." Nodding curtly, he walked off.

"Yankee bastard," Tanner spit out. Fists clenched, nostrils flaring, he started after the pompous wagon master. Pride would not allow him to let the man walk away unchallenged.

Realizing that Tanner had a low boiling point and that he had reached it, Ashley sought to cool the firebrand's rising temper. She grasped his arm and refused to let go.

"Reb, no! Forget it. I can't allow your antagonism to prevent us from leaving tomorrow. If this is going to work you're simply going to have to control your temper. We've gone this far; you can't spoil it now."

Her words had the desired effect. Exhaling sharply, Tanner turned to stare at Ashley, his sanity slowly returning. "Has the war affected you personally, Yank? I think not. You're brother was tucked safely away on the western frontier, while those of us not so lucky lost our loved ones, our homes, our . . . Forget it," he rasped, "what's the use? You wouldn't understand." Whirling on his heel, he stalked off.

Ashley watched in dismay, already regretting her decision to marry a virtual stranger.

35

She knew nothing about Tanner MacTavish, a man so complex and unreliable she couldn't predict what he was going to do from one minute to the next.

That night Ashley cooked supper over an open fire Tanner had built for her. She wished she had paid more attention to the womanly arts of cooking and sewing, for they were bound to come in handy during the trek to Fort Bridger. She could fry bacon and make corn bread but that was the extent of her skills, as Tanner was soon to learn. The beans she had cooked were hard as stones, badly seasoned and watery. Biscuits were beyond her meager skills, but she managed not to burn the corn bread.

"You'll have to do better than this, Yank," Tanner complained as he tossed the contents of his plate into the fire. "Can you cook wild game? I'll be hunting every day for meat. Biscuits would be a nice change from corn bread, if you can manage it. And I hope you laid in a store of potatoes, onions and bacon." He rose abruptly. "I'll check the water barrels while you do up the dishes. If you leave those beans over the fire all night they might be soft enough to eat in the morning."

Ashley tried to summon a scathing retort but he was gone before she could spit it out. Instead, she grumbled to herself as she

36

worked, calling the overbearing Rebel every nasty name she could think of or had ever heard. Then she burned her fingers on the coffeepot and yelped in pain.

"Can I be of help, ma'am? That looks like a nasty burn."

Ashley started violently, surprised to find a man standing on the other side of the fire. "What? Oh, no, it's not bad, thank you."

"You're Mrs. MacTavish, aren't you?"

"Y-yes, why?"

The man gave her a cheeky grin. "I heard you're a newlywed. Got married today, did you? Where's your man?"

What Pratt Slater didn't say was that Cramer had spoken to him earlier today about the attractive redhead who had been desperate to join the train. Cramer told Slater that he had stuck to his policy of refusing to give unaccompanied females a place in his wagon train. Cramer had said that the woman would need a husband if she wanted to travel with the group. He even suggested that Slater should offer for the woman. Slater had thought on it and decided to go into town, find Miss Webster and offer his assistance.

According to Cramer the woman was pleasing to look at, reasonably young, and appeared strong. Of greater importance, she had a wagon already outfitted and did not lack funds. Slater considered marrying her, then abandoning her at the end of the journey, after relieving her of her money, of course. And it wouldn't hurt having a woman to warm his bed during the long months it would take to reach Oregon. He hated having his plans thwarted. When the woman returned with a damn Reb husband and Slater saw how uncommonly pretty she was, he felt as if he'd been cheated.

"My husband is nearby," Ashley said, hoping he believed her. "Is there anything in particular you wanted?" A frisson of fear snaked down her spine. The man's bold perusal unnerved her.

"My name is Pratt Slater. I've hired on as guard and hunter on this trip. Captain Cramer and I were friends during our army days. I'm surprised a respectable Yankee lady like yourself would marry a Reb." He searched her face, his smile insultingly intimate. "Captain Cramer tells me your marriage was real sudden like."

"That's none of your business, Mr. Slater. If you'll excuse me, I've chores to do." She tried to walk away but he grabbed her arm.

"If you ever want to know what it's like to have a real man in your bed, you know my name."

Recoiling in disgust, Ashley pulled out of his grasp, then turned and fled. She ran into a solid wall of flesh and bone. Tanner caught her against him. "What's wrong?" he asked sharply.

Ashley glanced over her shoulder, relieved to see that Slater was gone. "N-nothing. I burned myself." If she told Tanner about Slater a fight was sure to result, and Captain Cramer would probably ban them from his wagon train.

"Let me see." Tanner led her to the fire, holding her hand to the light. "It's not bad. I'll put some axle grease on it and tomorrow it will be good as new."

A jolt of awareness sent shards of feeling through her arm. He must have felt it too, for he sent her a startled look. She pulled her hand away and hid it in the folds of her skirt. "It's all right; thank you anyway."

"Does my touch disgust you, Yank? I suggest you be more careful around fire. Obviously your experience doesn't lie in the field of cooking."

"I'll try to heed your advice. Now if you'll excuse me I'm going to retire." She climbed into the wagon and dropped the back flap into place.

Tanner stared at the wagon a long time. He was about to turn away and make his bed beside the fire when a lantern flared inside. A woman's shadow appeared against the canvas, titillating his senses. Mesmerized, he watched as Ashley stripped down to her shift and corset. He felt himself growing hard, felt himself pulsing, filling. Damn. He didn't want to feel desire for a damn Yankee school-

39

marm. He made a growling sound deep in his throat when he realized she was preparing to remove her corset. In another minute she'd be . . .

"Dammit, put out the lantern," he hissed through his teeth, "unless you're advertising."

The light went out immediately. Grumbling to himself, Tanner spread out his bedroll and tried to find a comfortable position. It wasn't easy with an erection as hard as stone pressing against his stomach.

Ashley stood beside the wagon, watching from her place in line as the wagons were ferried across the Missouri River. As far as the eye could see, a long line of white canvas stretched out along the banks. Rain threatened but had not yet begun to fall. Sheriff Beardsley had arrived early with Tanner's horse and guns. Tanner had strapped his guns on immediately, patting them as if they were old friends. Armed thusly, Ashley thought he looked more dangerous than when she'd first seen him. He rode along the line now, checking the progress of the wagons. Theirs being last in a line of fifty wagons, Ashley supposed it would be days before their turn arrived.

Tanner rode up from the front of the line and stopped beside her. "The river is swollen but the ferrying is going smoothly. Are you sure you can handle the oxen?"

"Don't worry, Reb. I can handle them. The man who sold them to me gave me instructions on how to drive a wagon and team of oxen. I have experience with a horse and carriage; it can't differ all that much from driving oxen."

Tanner cursed beneath his breath. "I forgot that you're an experienced lady, Yank." His mocking tone set her teeth on edge. "Forgive me for doubting you." Kneeing his horse, he rode off.

"Problems already, Mrs. MacTavish? If I didn't know better I'd think you and your husband were at odds."

"No problems, Mr. Slater." Why did the man always seem to pop up when she least expected it? Ashley wondered dimly. What did he want from her?

Tanner looked over his shoulder, saw Ashley in conversation with a stranger, and the hackles rose at the back of his neck. Turning his mount, he rode back down the line to their wagon. "Something wrong?"

"You must be Tanner MacTavish," Slater said with a smirk. "I'm Pratt Slater. I was just talking with your pretty little wife. Captain Cramer tells me you're newly married."

"Do you have a problem with that, Slater?"

"Not really. Me and some of the others were wondering why a nice woman like Mrs. MacTavish would marry a Johnny Reb when

41

there are plenty of good Yankees around."

Tanner's spine went rigid; his eyes were the only thing about him alive. And they blazed with fury. "The only good Yankee is a dead Yankee."

Ashley exhaled sharply. Slater's hand went to his gun but Tanner was faster. "I wouldn't do that if I were you, Slater. Only a fool would draw against me, and you don't strike me as a fool. Stupid, maybe, but not a fool." He slid his gun back into the holster.

"What's going on here?" Captain Cramer rode up when he noticed a dangerous situation developing, and insinuated his horse between the antagonists.

"Everything is fine, Captain," Ashley said in a shaky voice. "Isn't that right, Tanner?"

"Yeah, just fine," Tanner echoed, eyeing Slater warily.

"Yeah," Slater echoed, sending Tanner a black look. "We were just having a little chat." Slater wasn't dumb. If he wanted to blow the Reb away it would have to be done in a sneaky manner. The Reb could be a dangerous foe.

"Go help the wagons with the crossing," Cramer said to Slater.

"Sure, boss." Slater grinned, tipped his hat at Ashley and rode off. Cramer gave Tanner a hard look, then joined Slater.

"Slater is a troublemaker, Yank. I suggest you don't encourage him," Tanner said.

42

There was a raw edge to his voice, which made his unjust accusation all the harder for Ashley to swallow.

"I did not encourage Mr. Slater," Ashley declared hotly. "I don't even like him. There's something slimy about him."

"You didn't like me either but you married me," he reminded her.

"I was desperate; you know that!" Damn arrogant Rebel, Ashley thought as he rode off without replying. She hated it when he put her down like that. So damn smug, so sure of himself, his face as hard as stone. She knew he hated her, that he was only doing this for the money, but did he have to be so damn disagreeable and swift to condemn?

At dusk of the third day, the MacTavish wagon crossed the Missouri River. They camped for the night along the banks, then started out early the next morning. A week slid by, then another, and each day Tanner used his hunting skills to supply their cookpot with fresh meat. Ashley had learned to cook a tolerable stew, combining the game, dried vegetables and wild onions and herbs Tanner supplied from his hunting forays.

Her biscuits never did reach the degree of flakiness she would have liked but they were edible, if somewhat chewy. Tanner took on the chore of caring for the oxen. He unhitched them, watered them and staked them out where they could graze on the lush buffalo grass. Then, after their meal, he usually bedded down beneath the wagon or beside the fire. During those first weeks Ashley made friends with three women who sometimes joined her in walking beside the wagon.

Nancy Lind, Sarah Phister and Mary Dench were Southerners who no longer found the South a hospitable place to live. It amused as well as puzzled Ashley that these women considered her an ally simply because she had married a Rebel. To her amazement, Ashley found herself admiring these women who had suffered hardships she couldn't even begin to imagine. Together with the women's husbands and children they formed a tightly knit unit, banded together by their need to survive in the predominantly Yankee population of the Cramer company.

The wagons followed the Platte river through Nebraska Territory, unpacking each night and repacking before leaving the following morning. The journey thus far had been tedious, and then the rains came, swelling the muddy river and making a quagmire of the deeply rutted trail. For five days Ashley felt as if she'd been wallowing in mud. She never felt clean. Her hair and clothing and skin were splattered with dried brown splotches, and washing in the muddy river did little good.

At least Ashley didn't have to walk if she didn't want to. Since she had brought very little in the way of household goods her wagon did not overly tax the oxen's capability. Sometimes Tanner drove the wagon and she walked with the other women to stretch her legs and break the monotony. Then the sun came out. The mud dried up and everyone's mood lifted.

One lovely morning Ashley trailed some distance behind the wagon picking wild-flowers, which grew in abundance along the trail, when Pratt Slater rode up beside her. "Don't lag too far behind, Mrs. MacTavish," he cautioned. "We're in Indian territory now."

"Indians!" Ashley gasped, looking warily across the unbroken plains. "Are they hostile?"

"You never know with Indians. They're supposed to be living on reservations but they often leave to hunt or engage in raids. Treaties mean nothing to these savages. Sometimes they demand tolls for crossing their land and after they're paid in cattle or goods they let travelers pass unharmed. Don't worry, Mrs. MacTavish; I'll protect you."

"I have a husband to protect me."

"Ah, yes, a slave-loving Reb." He gave her a sly smile. "It must be difficult to remember that you have a husband when he doesn't

45

sleep with you in the wagon at night. I can't blame you for making him sleep alone; the Reb probably doesn't know how to treat a woman like you. But I do. I'll bet you're hot to trot right now." He licked his protruding lower lip and leered at her. "Too bad I didn't know you were looking for a man when you first approached Captain Cramer. I would have been happy to oblige you had I known how desperate you were to join the train."

Her cheeks flamed. "How dare you talk to me like that!"

"When you're hard up for a real man, look me up. I won't be far." Spurring his horse, he galloped off, leaving Ashley sputtering in outrage.

Ashley had been naive to think that no one would notice Tanner's habit of sleeping outside the wagon each night instead of inside with her. They were supposed to be newlyweds and were behaving like strangers. She wondered what other rumors concerning her and Tanner were being circulated and decided to ask one of the women. She got her chance when Nancy walked up to join her.

They spoke about inconsequential matters for a short time before Ashley broached the subject. "Nancy, I'd like to ask you something and I'd like a truthful answer."

Nancy, a blue-eyed blonde younger than Ashley and pregnant with her second child,

46

gave Ashley a wary glance. "What would you like to know?"

"Are there rumors circulating about Tanner and me?"

Fidgeting nervously, Nancy looked away. "I don't know what you're talking about."

"The truth, Nancy. I know there's gossip; I've heard some of it."

"Very well, if you insist. Talk is that you bought Tanner. Rumor has it you paid him to marry you because you were desperate for a husband. I don't believe it," Nancy defended staunchly. "You're too beautiful to have to resort to such measures. I'm sure there were plenty of men you could have married. I do wonder, though, why Tanner sleeps beneath your wagon or beside the fire at night."

"You and everyone else, apparently," Ashley bit out. "The gossip is partly true, Nancy. I did pay Tanner to marry me."

"Oh." Nancy's hands flew to her cheeks.

"I was desperate, but not for a man, just a husband. Captain Cramer refused to let me join the train unless I had a husband, so I found one. Tanner and I have an arrangement."

"I see," Nancy said slowly, not really understanding. But since Ashley seemed disinclined to offer more, she thought it impolite to inquire further. It did puzzle her, though. Tanner was handsome, well built and young, and she couldn't imagine Ashley not wanting him in her bed.

★ ★ ★

Pounding rain kept the wagon train camped along the Platte the next day. Ashley hated the drenching downpour, hated the mud that sucked at her boots and the hem of her skirt. Slickers gave scant protection against nature's fury, and Ashley stayed inside the wagon most of the day, preparing a makeshift meal of leftover corn bread and cold venison. When Tanner came inside to eat she noted that he was drenched to the skin and more uncommunicative than usual.

They ate in silence by lanternlight, listening to the steady tattoo of raindrops and rumbling thunder as flashes of lightning arced across the sky. After their meager meal, Tanner left. He returned a couple of hours later with his saddlebags and blanket. He took off his slicker and hat, shook them out and spread them over a chair in the rear of the wagon.

"What do you think you're doing?" Ashley asked shrilly.

"Bedding down, Yank," he drawled gruffly. "There's a river running under our wagon and I'm not a fish. You'll just have to put up with me tonight." He spread his blanket down beside her pallet. She wrinkled her nose, recognizing the odor of liquor immediately. He reeked of it.

"You've been drinking! You can't sleep in here with me."

"I can and I will." He pulled off his wet shirt, and before Ashley could protest, he peeled his trousers down his legs. "I had to keep warm somehow and whiskey seemed the best way to ward off the chill."

Ashley yelped and closed her eyes against the titillating sight of Tanner's naked body. "Don't worry, Yank; you're safe with me. Unless," he added, his gray eyes glittering dangerously, "you're hankering for a little loving. I'll wager you've been without a man a long time."

Indignation brought her eyes open with a jerk. "Loving? From you? Never! You must be drunk to think I'd lie with you." She was angry, but not too angry to note that he wore drawers on his lower half, saving him from total indecency. His chest was bare and gleamed damply in the flickering lamplight; she didn't want to stare but couldn't help it. Dark fuzz stretched across his midsection, traveled in a tantalizing wedge down his washboard stomach and ended in a line that disappeared beneath the waist of his drawers. She didn't need to be told what the bulge below his waist was; she was twenty-five years old, for heaven's sake. But this was the first time she had actually seen the result of a man's arousal beneath his clothing.

That thought led to another. Why should the Reb be aroused? He hated her, didn't he? Probably as much as she hated him. She wasn't all that knowledgeable about a man's anatomy but she did know that desire had to be present for a man to react in such a manner. Her aunt had presented the facts of life to her in a forthright and succinct manner so she would know how to protect herself.

Tanner noted the direction of Ashley's gaze and smiled derisively. The little Yank wasn't completely immune to him, he thought. The way she was staring at a certain part of him made him thicken and harden. He recalled telling Sheriff Beardsley that no amount of money could persuade him to bed a Yankee, but he was beginning to change his mind. Being a little bit tipsy helped. If the hard-nosed Yankee wanted him he'd oblige, but not before she begged him. Perhaps, he thought, she was accustomed to having sex regularly and needed it badly enough to ask a Reb to service her. He grinned in anticipation of having her grovel before him.

Ashley jerked her eyes sharply upward, blushing furiously. The bastard, she thought. He enjoyed her discomfiture. She wouldn't give him the satisfaction of knowing that merely looking at him made her go all soft and wet inside. As for wanting him to make love to her, that was the last thing she needed. She couldn't wait until this journey was over so she could rid herself of the arrogant Reb.

"Well, Yank," Tanner said, "if you're done staring at me I'll turn in." He reeled slightly

50

but kept his balance.

Ashley gulped air as if she were starving. "I wasn't staring!"

He gave her a lopsided grin. "If you say so. Good night, Yank." He lay down on the blanket, pulling his saddlebag under his head for a pillow.

Ashley doused the light and turned her back on the blackhearted devil. It was pitch black inside the wagon, and briefly Ashley considered going to bed fully clothed as added protection against the Reb. She had given up wearing a corset in those first diffi-cult days on the trail and often wished she had the freedom to wear trousers. Yet wearing her mud-splattered clothing to bed did not appeal to her. Rummaging in the dark for her nightgown, she put it on over her clothes and undressed beneath it.

A brilliant display of lightning caught her kneeling beside her pallet, running a brush through her hair. The breath caught in Tan-ner's throat and he went still. Ashley gave a startled squeal and froze, her hand poised above her gleaming hair, her face a study of glowing beauty as the charged air vibrated around her. The mesmerizing sight reached out to him, stirred him, called forth feelings he hadn't felt in a long, long time. Feelings that made him feel alive for the first time in years. He wasn't sure he liked the emotional upheaval of his thoughts but he found himself

51

reacting in a manner totally out of character. Perhaps he was drunker than he thought.

"It's only lightning, Yank," he said softly. "It can't hurt you in here." He sat up, wanting her, ashamed of the need the Yankee schoolmarm had created in him but unable to help himself.

Ashley started violently. It didn't seem possible that the gentle voice belonged to the same bitter man who had married her for a price. "I . . . I'm not frightened. I find lightning fascinating."

"I find *you* fascinating, Mrs. MacTavish." She stiffened. "Does the name bother you? We are married, you know. All legal and binding." He reached for her hand, pulling her against him. She landed in his lap. He groaned. She felt his staff stab against her bottom and tried to rise. His arms came around her, imprisoning her in the solid cradle of his embrace.

"Let me go, Reb! This wasn't in our bargain."

"Neither was this," he whispered, grasping the back of her neck and bringing her lips to his. Sweet lord! Had he been sober he'd never attempt this.

She tasted sweet. Sweeter than anything he'd ever tasted before. He deepened the kiss, slanting his mouth over hers, prodding the seam of her lips with his tongue until he nudged them open. She fought his invasion, to no avail. Tanner would have his way, and right now he was intent upon devouring her, exploring her with his tongue, stealing her breath and robbing her of her senses.

His kisses grew frenzied as he bent her over his arm and plundered her mouth with ruthless abandon. He tasted of whiskey and smoke and a taste uniquely his. Ashley whimpered, knowing this was wrong, that the Reb was using her to appease his lust, not because he felt something for her. She didn't want him to feel anything for her. They despised one another. The heat she was feeling was the result of the storm. Tanner was drunk, and . . . and . . . Lord, had she unwittingly invited his kisses?

Ashley felt a breeze cool her heated flesh and was stunned when she realized that her nightgown had been shoved down past her shoulders and that Tanner's callused hand rested on her bare breast, and he was stimulating her nipple with his thumb and forefinger. Excitement thrummed through her. The feeling was exquisite torture.

She didn't want this.

She made a gurgling sound deep in her throat and exerted every ounce of her considerable will to break contact. Leaping from his lap, she retreated to the farthest corner of the wagon.

"How dare you! You have no right to handle me in such a disgusting manner. This

53

isn't a real marriage. Whatever made you think you could . . . could use me?"

"Isn't a Reb good enough for you? Perhaps you'd rather have Pratt Slater in your bed."

"Perhaps I would," Ashley shot back. The moment the words were out she wished she could call them back. She despised Slater, more than she hated Tanner MacTavish.

"Don't worry, Mrs. MacTavish; I'll not trouble you again, unless you keep looking at me like you did tonight. I prefer we remain antagonists. Someday I'll tell you how Yankees tore my life apart, but I'll have to be a hell of a lot drunker than I am now."

A flash of lightning revealed the stark planes of his face, raw with anguish against the backdrop of white canvas. Never had she seen an expression so devoid of hope, so utterly lacking in compassion, so filled with dark secrets.

Something stirred inside Ashley. She closed her eyes and willed it away.

Chapter Three

The plains on either side of the Platte were covered with short grass but bare of trees. At a distance of about three miles on both sides of the river, the land rose in sandstone cliffs higher, closer and more broken as the trail moved west. Sometimes Tanner was lucky enough to bag a deer or an antelope, which Ashley did her best to cook into something palatable.

More and more they had to depend on buffalo chips for fuel, which when dried burned hotter and with surprisingly less odor than a wood fire. Each night at their campsite Captain Cramer ordered the wagons into a circle, or corral, with the animals in the center to protect them from marauding Indians.

On those nights when the weather was fine the children organized games and the adults held impromptu dances. Harmonicas and fiddles were brought out, a place cleared and the communal fire kept burning brightly. Then the dancing began. Ashley did not lack for partners but Tanner never joined in, choosing instead to remain in the background, watching, always watching.

"Your husband ain't much for dancing, Mrs. MacTavish," Slater said as he whirled

Ashley around to the twang of fiddles. Ashley hadn't wanted to dance with Slater but saw no way to politely refuse.

Ashley's gaze sought out Tanner, finding him leaning against their wagon, his face without expression. "Tanner is a very private man," she said lamely.

"It beats me how you can let a damn Reb paw you. He has the stink of slaves on him. I sure as hell wish I could have gotten to you before you married the bastard. I know you were hard up for a man 'cause Captain Cramer told me. Once I saw you I wanted you. But that damn Reb got to you first. I'm a better man in bed than he is; I guarantee it."

Ashley stopped dancing. "You're disgusting." She started to walk away but Slater gripped her arm, swinging her around to face him.

"We ain't through dancing."

"I am."

Slater's grip tightened as he dragged her against him. Everyone was having such a good time no one appeared to notice the little drama taking place between Ashley and Slater.

"Take your hands off my wife."

Since Tanner hadn't taken his eyes off Ashley all evening, the heated exchange hadn't escaped his notice. He could not account for the anger that built inside him, nor could he stop himself from interfering.

Slater snorted derisively. "If you're not man enough to keep your wife happy in bed you can't blame someone else for horning in on your property."

Tanner gave Ashley a hard look. "Is Slater annoying you?"

Ashley was in a quandary. If she said yes a fight was inevitable. If she said no Tanner would think she had been deliberately inviting Slater's attention. After careful thought she decided it was better that Tanner think her a wanton and a flirt than for them to be dropped from the wagon train.

"N-no, Mr. Slater wasn't annoying me. I'm tired; I decided I had enough dancing. Mr. Slater merely wished for me to finish the reel."

Slater gave Tanner a triumphant grin. "What do you say to that, Reb?"

Tanner's lips flattened. He didn't know why he bothered. Obviously the Yank didn't want him interfering in her affairs. He could have sworn Ashley was angry and trying to avoid the Yankee reptile. "Go to bed, Ashley," he advised, ignoring Slater. "It's getting late."

Ashley moved her gaze from Slater to Tanner, afraid of what would occur if she left. They looked ready to fly at each other's throats. Then she became aware that the music had stopped and they were the center of attention. Even the children had become curious and crowded around them. Ashley's face grew hot as she turned her gaze to Tanner's stoic features.

"Let the little lady enjoy herself," Slater said, deliberately goading Tanner.

"Go to bed, Ashley," Tanner repeated without looking at her. "Now. I'll join you in a few minutes."

Ashley turned and walked away. Never had she been so humiliated.

The confrontation seemed to bring a pall to the festivities, and people began gathering their children and drifting away. A few minutes later Tanner and Slater were alone.

"Let this be a warning to you, Slater," Tanner said. "Keep away from my wife. You've been sniffing after her ever since we joined the train."

"Your 'wife' bought you, MacTavish," Slater said insultingly, "and now you can't please her. She could have done better than a Reb had she bothered to look around."

"Are you referring to yourself?"

"Who else? I wanted her the minute Cramer told me about her. Unfortunately I was too late. But there is still time. Accidents happen; things change. A pretty woman like Mrs. MacTavish won't have to look far for a new husband."

"I'm not prone to accidents, Slater. Keep that in mind."

Tanner's hand hovered near his gun. He

wanted to hurt Slater so damn bad he could taste it. Men like him had burned his home, killed his father, been responsible for the death of his mother and . . . Ellen. It didn't take much imagination to picture Slater in a blue uniform, killing and raping his way across the South. Tanner itched to bring the gun into his hand and . . .

Ashley didn't go back to the wagon as Tanner directed. She retreated into the shadows and lingered, fearing the worst but hoping for the best. She couldn't hear the heated exchange between Tanner and Slater but she knew Tanner was teetering on the edge of disaster. When she saw his hand resting on the hilt of his gun she reacted instinctively. The damn Reb firebrand would get them both into trouble if he didn't learn to control his temper.

She gripped Tanner's arm with surprising strength. "Tanner, no! Don't let him goad you. Please come back to the wagon with me."

Tanner shook his arm free and gave her a dark look. He knew she feared they would be asked to leave the train if he made trouble but the bastard had gone too far.

Ashley realized she was losing out to his anger, and the consequences frightened her. Tossing caution to the wind, Ashley threw herself at Tanner, winding her arms around his neck and pressing herself against him from breastbone to hipbone. Then she pulled down his head and kissed him. At first Tanner was too stunned to do more than stand there and let her kiss him. Then his body caught fire.

Clasping her tightly against the solid wall of his chest, he pressed his mouth to hers in surprise and pleasure. He made a sound deep in his throat — a groan or a curse, she could not be certain — and his lips sucked greedily at hers, his response so savage, so possessive, the shock of it sent her senses reeling. His fierce reaction had been unexpected and Ashley could not suppress the trembling, pulsing heat that gathered in her belly and pooled between her thighs. Dear Lord, what was the Reb doing to her?

Time and place receded as Tanner plundered Ashley's mouth. Her breath froze in her chest when his tongue slipped past her teeth to explore the sweetness within. It didn't seem to matter to him that they were standing in the open where they were the center of attention, or that Slater was watching them with his mouth agape. She heard titters and laughter and someone whisper the word *newlywed* but hadn't the will or strength to care. When Tanner picked her up and carried her toward their wagon, she knew she had defused a dangerous situation . . . but at what cost?

In an agony of need, Tanner couldn't get to

the wagon fast enough. His loins were heavy and he was hard with a kind of excitement he hadn't felt in years. He would know in a very short time if his *wife* was as experienced as she claimed. He broke off the kiss long enough to lift her into the wagon and follow her inside. The canvas flap came down with a flick of his wrist. Seconds later he was pulling off his vest and shirt.

"Take off your clothes," he rasped harshly.

Ashley barely had time to breathe, let alone think. When it finally dawned on her what Tanner wanted, she froze. How had things gotten out of hand so quickly? She had merely used her feminine wiles to distract the hotheaded Reb from his anger. She swallowed convulsively and tried to tame her racing heart.

"I don't want this, Reb."

Tanner laughed, a hard grating sound. "You could have fooled me, Yank."

She scooted to her feet. "I was merely trying to get you out of a difficult situation. Your temper is going to get us in hot water."

Tanner stared at her. Diffused light from a lantern illuminated her features. Her face was flushed and he knew the reason why. She wanted a man. Fortunately he was available. He wanted a woman — he wanted this woman. He reached for her, pulling her against his bare chest. His hands skimmed her arms and came to rest on her hips, molding her against his swelling loins.

"No. I want —"

"What do you want? This?" He kissed her, hard, with brutal thoroughness. "Or this?" His hands slid around to her buttocks, caressing the taut mounds through her clothing as he nuzzled her neck with his lips. "Or maybe this." One of his hands came between them and he cupped her between the legs.

Ashley gasped, frightened at the feelings he aroused in her. She had been engaged once, when she was eighteen, but her fiancé had never kissed her the way Tanner did, nor touched her in places that made her tingle and burn for things she could only guess at.

"I want you to let go of me," Ashley demanded. "You have no right to paw me. I'm paying you to be my husband in name only and that's the way it has to be."

"You little tease," Tanner snarled. "What in the hell am I supposed to think when you throw yourself at me? I should have left you to Slater; you appeared to enjoy his mauling. But I forgot: he's a Yankee and I'm a dirty Reb."

"That's not why. . . ." She bit her lip, afraid of what she'd blurt out. She was confused. Tanner's kisses made her yearn for more. How could a man kiss a woman as if he meant it and still hold her in contempt? The answer was obvious. She was a Yankee and Tanner hated Yankees. Men! They were conceited, overbearing and unpredictable. She'd learned that long ago, after her engagement had gone awry. Men could expend their lust with anyone, even someone they hated, the act nothing more to them than sexual gratification.

"Damn you," Tanner said from between lips gone taut with rage. "I have half a notion to leave you to your own devices since you're so almighty independent. I don't need your money. I don't need you. The only woman I ever needed or wanted . . . Damn!" He grabbed his shirt and vest, lifted the back flap and peered into the black night.

Ashley went still. Had Tanner been about to reveal some little piece of the puzzle he called his life? "You can't leave. We're married, remember?"

His bitter laughter sent chills down her spine. "If I hadn't given my word that I'd see you safely to your destination I'd light out of here so fast your head would spin. Go to bed before I forget I have some honor left and do what my body demands."

He left abruptly, jumping lightly to the ground. A few minutes later Ashley heard him bedding down beneath the wagon. She was still too stunned to move. Her mouth felt swollen from his kisses; her body thrummed with a strange kind of heat that set fire to her loins. What in the world was the matter with her?

The damn Reb was making her crazy. She was twenty-five years old, not some fresh-faced girl with stars in her eyes.

Disaster struck the next day. While crossing a swollen stream one of the wagons overturned, spilling out the occupants. A child drowned. They held the funeral on the banks of the stream, leaving a crude wooden cross to mark the small grave. Two days later a child broke out with chicken pox. Before it was over three children had perished.

Ashley rarely saw Tanner, which suited her just fine. She cooked their meals but that was the extent of their communication during the following hectic weeks.

After a particularly trying day of heavy rains and intermittent storms, the wagon train stopped early. Unable to light a fire, most families ate a cold meal of leftovers and retired early to the relative comfort of their wagons. When the rain slowed to a drizzle, Tanner left the wagon and climbed the hills surrounding their campsite, settling down against a rock. He had volunteered for guard duty again rather than sleep in the same vicinity as his wife in name only.

The feisty Yankee witch was going to be the death of him yet, he thought sourly. Had he known how difficult this was going to be he'd have told her to go to hell and taken his chances in an army stockade. Who would have thought he'd feel overwhelming desire for a damn Yankee who hated what he stood for as much as he hated what she represented? Yet want her he did. He walked around with an erection nearly all the time. Just thinking about the flame-haired Yank made him hard as stone.

The hell with her, he thought as he hunkered down inside his slicker and stared into the black night. Ashley wasn't Ellen and he didn't deserve another chance at happiness.

Ashley donned her nightgown and crawled into her cot, pulling the blanket up to her chin. She thought briefly of Tanner, sitting in the rain, and something stirred inside her. That she thought of him at all bothered her excessively. Punching down her pillow, she tried to sleep. An hour later the rain stopped and the moon rose high in the sky.

The noise was so slight Ashley hardly noticed it. What she did notice was the sliver of moonlight that came through the back flap when it parted to allow someone to slip through the opening. The flap fell back into place and the sliver of light vanished. Ashley knew she wasn't alone; heavy breathing gave the intruder away. She rose up onto her elbow, peering into the threatening blackness surrounding her.

"Tanner, is that you?"

His laugh was low and menacing, and

definitely not Tanner's.

"Who is it?"

"It ain't your husband, Mrs. MacTavish. I'm gonna show you what a real man feels like." His words were slurred.

"Mr. Slater! You're drunk. Get out of here! Tanner will kill you."

"I don't think so. Who's gonna tell him?"

"I will."

"No, you won't. You've risked a lot to get on this wagon train and you won't say or do anything to get thrown off. Captain Cramer won't think twice about abandoning you and your husband if the Reb bastard makes any more trouble. It's my word against yours."

He loomed above her, leering, his grin truly evil. "Go ahead and fight. I enjoy it more when women resist." Before she could react, he dropped on top of her, shoving the blanket down and her nightgown up.

"Don't touch me! I'll scream."

"Go ahead. I'll tell everyone you invited me here tonight. No one will dispute me."

His hands traveled the length of her bare thighs as he nudged the neckline of her nightgown down with his chin so he could reach her breasts with his mouth. Ashley opened her mouth to scream; he realized her intent and quickly placed a restraining hand over her lips. With his other hand he fumbled with the buttons on his pants.

Ashley knew she had to act quickly or

suffer the wretched consequences. She recalled her feisty aunt's instructions on how to defend herself against men like Slater and smiled grimly beneath Slater's hand. With a flick of his wrist he released his straining manhood, pausing as he struggled to subdue her. Ashley marshaled her strength, drew back her knee and slammed it into Slater's groin. He howled with pain, fell off the cot and rolled onto the floor, holding his privates.

Pulling the blanket from the cot, Ashley grabbed her boots and climbed through the front of the wagon, pausing only long enough to slip on her boots. Dropping to the ground, she ran toward the hills as fast as she could run, hugging the blanket around her. She had only one thought in mind, one goal.

Tanner.

Tanner was damn glad it had stopped raining. The night was still now. Nothing stirred but the sound of the rushing river and insects performing their nightly serenade. For no apparent reason he felt tense and uneasy. It reminded him of the war, and how he'd always known when an attack was coming. He could feel it in his bones. That was how he felt now; a bone-deep premonition.

Suddenly Tanner heard something or someone crashing through the tall buffalo grass and he leaped to his feet, his gun coming into his hand with lightning speed.

"Who is it?"

Until Ashley heard Tanner's voice she'd had no idea where to look for him. Now she headed in the direction of his voice; her only thought was reaching the safety of his large, comforting presence.

"Tanner! Where are you?"

Tanner holstered his weapon, his shock enormous. What was Ashley doing out at this time of night? His heart began pounding. Something was wrong; he knew it.

"I'm here, Yank; you're heading right for me." Then he saw her pounding through the tall grass, her white nightgown billowing out behind her, her flaming hair flowing down her back like a bloodred banner. Somewhere along the way she had lost the blanket. He held out his arms and she ran into them.

Ashley felt Tanner's arms close around her, felt his heart pumping against her breast and realized how much she had come to depend on him during these arduous weeks. He was always there when she needed him, ever ready to defend her, and suddenly she wished she understood him better. She sensed the darkness inside him, his anguish, the secrets he harbored, and ached for his pain.

Tanner held her away from him, searching her white face. "What happened? Why are you here?"

Ashley bit her lip to keep from blurting out the truth. She shouldn't have come here. She should have gone to the wagon of one of her friends instead. There was already too much bad blood between Slater and Tanner; she hated to add to it. She knew Tanner would react in his usual hotheaded manner if he learned that Slater had attacked her tonight. There would be a fight, and one of them might not survive. Tanner was a man with a short fuse. His anger might make him careless and Slater would use that weakness against Tanner.

"I had a bad dream," Ashley lied, hugging herself in an effort to stop her uncontrollable shaking. "I'm sorry. I shouldn't have come."

"Don't lie, Yank. A bad dream wouldn't send you fleeing in the dead of night in your nightgown. You're shaking like a leaf." A muscle worked in Tanner's jaw. "Did someone hurt you?"

Ashley bowed her head. If Tanner looked into her eyes he'd know she was lying. Tanner stared at her bent head, blinded by the radiance of her hair set aflame by moonlight, and lost his train of thought.

"No one hurt me," Ashley denied. "I couldn't sleep after that dream. I had to get out of the wagon. Can I stay here for a while?"

Tanner gave her a hard look but did not deny her request. He spread his slicker down on the ground and lowered both himself and her onto it. His arm went around her and she snuggled against him. The silence between them deepened, became almost companionable as Ashley's head dropped against his chest. Tanner's arms tightened as he maintained watch over the sleeping wagon train. Ashley dozed and the hours sped by.

Ashley awoke and stretched. Dawn was just breaking and she could hear sounds of movement in the camp. She opened her eyes and saw Tanner standing over her. Then all else fled beneath the keen onslaught of memory. Slater had tried to rape her last night and she had run straight into Tanner's arms. The last thing she recalled was being held tightly in his embrace. She sat up abruptly. Good Lord! She must have fallen asleep. How did she get back to the wagon?

"I carried you back at the end of my watch," Tanner said, answering her unasked question. "Do you want to tell me what happened last night?"

Ashley shook her head. "I already told you. The call will come to pull out soon. I have to get up and start breakfast."

He stared at her, his gaze dark and brilliant. "Very well, but I *will* find out." She stared at his hard-muscled back as he left the wagon, and swallowed hard. What was happening to her? She couldn't get to Fort

Bridger soon enough to suit her. Once she reached her brother and directed her energies toward clearing his name she'd have no time to think about a hard-eyed, hard-bodied Reb who tempted her beyond reason.

Two days later they camped for the night at Fort Laramie, where Ashley restocked her dwindling supplies of spices and staples and managed to buy some fresh fruit and dried apples. Mary Dench showed her how to bake a pie, and that night they had apple pie for dessert.

"You've come a long way, Yank," Tanner said with grudging respect as he devoured the last piece of pie. "One day you'll make some man a good wife."

Realizing what he'd said, he paused with the fork halfway to his mouth. "Some *other* man," he clarified. "One who will appreciate a Yankee wife."

"I'm not interested in a permanent husband," Ashley declared. "Catering to a man isn't my idea of independence, and I value my independence above all."

Tanner laughed. "We're alike in many ways, Yank. Neither of us wants to be tied down. I'm curious, though. Did none of the men you bedded please you?"

Ashley was grateful for the darkness. She felt as if her face were on fire. She supposed she had earned his low opinion. When she'd told him she was experienced he probably thought she meant sexually as well as worldly.

"My personal life isn't your concern," she replied with bravado.

"You're right, Yank, it isn't. And neither is my personal life your concern."

They left Fort Laramie early the next morning. To Ashley's relief she had only seen Slater from a distance since the night he had attacked her in her wagon. Occasionally she spotted him watching Tanner, his brow furrowed, as if trying to remember something. But more often than not he glared at her from afar, his dark gaze promising retribution for the injury done to him.

The train wended upward into the foothills of the Rocky Mountains without serious mishap. Many families had to jettison valuable heirlooms in order to negotiate steep passes. The trail was littered with furniture of all descriptions and, sadly, graves of people from previous wagon trains who never reached the promised land. The guard was doubled now because they were deep into Indian territory.

One morning, shortly after Tanner returned from night guard duty, Slater swaggered up to them. Ashley could tell by the look on Slater's face that he was up to no good. Ignoring Ashley, Slater stopped scant inches from Tanner.

"You know, MacTavish, I've been puzzling over your name for weeks. I know I heard it before. I thought on it a long time and it finally came to me. Back in sixty-four I was fighting around Atlanta. Captain ordered us to burn everything in our path." Tanner's eyes widened, then narrowed, and a muscle jumped in his jaw. It should have warned Slater.

"There was this plantation; people by the name of MacTavish owned it," Slater continued. "Of course the menfolk were gone" — he gave Tanner a leering smile — "but the women were still there. Some sick old hag, if I recall, and a pretty young woman. Sweet little thing, she was, with the tightest little —"

Tanner became incandescent with rage, and his face twisted into the visage of a demon from hell. His gun came out so fast Ashley did not see his hand move. "You're the one! Rapacious bastard! You're a dead man, Slater."

As if in slow motion Ashley saw Tanner aim his gun and cock the hammer back, saw his finger tighten on the trigger and realized he was about to shoot a man in cold blood. She reacted without thought. A cry left her throat as she launched herself at Tanner. She hit his arm just as the gun discharged. The bullet plowed a furrow between Slater's legs.

"Damn you!" Tanner cried, roughly

73

shoving Ashley away. She clung tenaciously to his arm, preventing him from getting a bead on Slater. "You don't know what the bastard has done!"

"I know you'll hang if you shoot Slater in cold blood!" Ashley shot back. "Are you crazy? Have you no concern for your own life?"

"My life is worthless," Tanner said bitterly. By now people were coming out to see what was causing the commotion. Captain Cramer made his way though the crowd, shoving people aside.

"What in the hell is going on here? This isn't the first time I warned you about your temper, MacTavish."

"It was an accident, Captain Cramer," Ashley said, sending a silent warning to Tanner.

Cramer's head swung around to Slater. "Is that true, Slater?"

Slater sent Ashley a cunning smile. If he agreed with her explanation of the situation she might be grateful enough to give him what he wanted. The slut he'd been banging had turned virtuous on him and refused to accommodate him any longer. He told her he'd kill her if she told her parents what he'd done, so he wasn't worried on that score.

Belatedly Slater realized he shouldn't have bragged about the plantation or the women to MacTavish. Who'd have ever thought he'd meet up with the man whose plantation he'd destroyed? He wondered about the relationship between MacTavish and the women he'd found at the plantation. Damn! There was no help for it. Tanner had to die. Otherwise, his own life wouldn't be worth a wooden nickel. Yes, he would have to kill Tanner MacTavish. Then he'd comfort the little widow.

"It was an accident, Captain," Slater agreed. "MacTavish was showing me his fancy piece when it accidentally fired."

Cramer grunted. "If you say so. Everyone get back to their chores. I want the wagons moving in an hour." The crowd dispersed and Slater slunk away.

"Why?" Tanner asked as he shrugged Ashley aside. "Why didn't you let me kill the rotten snake?"

"It would be cold-blooded murder. They'd hang you."

"What if I told you Slater was responsible for two deaths, both more horrendous than cold-blooded murder?"

She searched his face. "I'd want to know what he'd done."

Tanner turned away. His words had taken on a hard edge. "I can't talk about it. Not now, maybe not ever. Slater won't get away with it; that's one promise I'm going to keep. I won't be satisfied until I see him in his grave."

75

Ashley shivered as she watched him walk away, wondering what Slater had done to earn Tanner's hatred. She prayed he wouldn't do anything foolish.

That night one of the men walked a short distance from the wagons to relieve himself and he found Slater lying in a pool of congealing blood. He had been stabbed, but by some miracle he still lived. Unfortunately he couldn't identify his assailant.

Chapter Four

"I heard them arguing, Captain Cramer," a man said, pointing a finger at Tanner. "There was bad blood between them." Captain Cramer had waited until the morning after the attempted murder to tell the homesteaders that there was a potential murderer among them.

"What have you got to say for yourself, MacTavish?" Cramer demanded to know.

Tanner realized he was being hemmed in by angry homesteaders and figured he was as good as convicted. "I didn't try to kill Slater. If I had, I would have succeeded."

Ashley's heart sank. Nearly everyone on the wagon train had heard Tanner and Slater arguing on more than one occasion. Had Tanner tried to kill Slater? she wondered not for the first time since learning of the attack. Tanner had appeared eager to end Slater's life a few short hours ago.

"If you didn't attack Slater, who did?" Cramer challenged.

"I'm sure I'm not the only one with reason to want the bastard dead."

Tanner stared at the homesteaders. Some hung their heads and others shuffled their feet, leading Tanner to suspect that Slater

77

had made more than one enemy on this wagon train.

Though he hadn't attacked Slater, Tanner regretted the fact that Slater still lived. The bastard deserved to die for his acts of depravity.

"Anyone could have attacked Slater," Lyle Dench spoke up. "You can't place guilt where there is no proof."

"Everyone knows all you Rebs stick together," a grizzled settler spat disgustedly. "I say we hang MacTavish here and now. Or at least keep him confined until we find a tree sturdy enough to hold his weight."

"I say we turn him in to the soldiers at Fort Bridger," someone suggested. "Ain't right to hang a man without a proper hearing."

Ashley listened with growing horror. It didn't look good for Tanner. She was aware that his hatred for Yankees went deeper than mere geography or a difference of opinion; turning him over to the soldiers at the fort would be the worst thing that could possibly happen. Soldiers wearing blue coats made Tanner go crazy. No matter what she thought of the hotheaded Reb, she truly didn't believe him capable of cold-blooded murder. Sneaking up on a man and knifing him wasn't his style.

"My husband couldn't have attacked Mr. Slater," Ashley heard herself saying. "He hasn't left my side since early this evening."

78

Tanner sent her an indecipherable look. Why was Ashley defending him when she obviously couldn't stand him? They had traveled too far now to worry about being abandoned by the wagon master. Fort Bridger lay but a few days away.

"Are you sure about that, Mrs. Mac-Tavish?" Captain Cramer asked, sending her a hard look. "You're not lying to spare your husband's neck, are you?"

"Certainly not!" Ashley said indignantly. "Look elsewhere for your potential killer, Captain."

Ashley could summon no guilt for telling a lie. She had no idea where Tanner had gone after they parted last night. Thank God no one had seen him to challenge her claim. For all she knew Tanner *could* have attacked Slater. He certainly had been on the verge of doing Slater bodily harm on more than one occasion. Yet something deep inside her refused to accept Tanner as a killer.

"Did anyone see MacTavish around the area yesterday evening after his argument with Slater?" Cramer asked, searching the crowd for someone to come forth with a reply. There was much grumbling and muttering but no one stepped forward.

Ashley breathed a sigh of relief, even though Tanner's innocence was still in doubt. No one had seen him after his confrontation with Slater, and he sure as hell

79

hadn't been with her all that time.

"We can't hang a man if he's not guilty," Cramer declared after some thought. "I'll report this to the commander at Fort Bridger and let him decide if there's a case against MacTavish. Maybe by that time Slater will recall something, if he lives," he added ominously. He turned to Tanner. "Meanwhile, we'll be keeping an eye on you, MacTavish."

"I'm not going anywhere, Captain," Tanner drawled lazily. "But I'm warning you right now that I'm not going to end up in the stockade, even if I have to find the man responsible myself."

"You do that, MacTavish. All right, everyone back to the wagons. We've got a hard day ahead of us."

Tanner tied his horse behind the wagon and indicated to Ashley that he would drive the team. She offered no argument as she settled beside him on the seat, and for a while Tanner was too busy pulling the wagon in line behind the others to speak. Finally he turned to her, his eyes dark and intense as he searched her face.

"Why did you lie? Were you thinking of your own neck as well as mine?"

Ashley flushed. "Did you try to kill Slater?"

"No."

"Where were you?"

He gave her a cheeky grin. "With you. Isn't that what you told Cramer?"

"The truth, Reb. Did you attack Slater?"

"I told you I didn't."

Somehow Ashley believed him.

"After confronting Slater earlier I needed to be alone. Slater told me some things that I hadn't known before, things that were so upsetting I didn't want to see or speak to anyone until I had come to grips with this new knowledge and what I intended to do about it. Seems like I'm not the only one to hold a grudge against Slater. After what he told me I realized he must have made countless enemies during his lifetime. I didn't return to the wagons until just before dawn this morning."

"Do you want to tell me what Slater said to upset you?"

"No. I don't want to talk about it."

Ashley fell silent, trying to recall everything that Slater had said to Tanner last evening. Something about his name and burning a plantation near Atlanta. And something else. What was it?

Had the plantation been Tanner's home? Who were the women Slater had mentioned and what had happened to them? There were so many unanswered questions floating around in her head she became more confused than ever. When she turned to ask Tanner for the answers the words froze in her throat. A mask had settled over his features. His expression was grim, his eyes cold and empty. She felt his pain as if it were her own and knew that the only way she could help him right now was by maintaining silence.

That night they made camp later than usual to make up for the delay that morning. Tanner had shot a rabbit earlier and Ashley spitted it on a stick and roasted it over the fire. She was mixing up a batch of biscuits when a young woman approached her. She had seen the girl before but had not met her. She was traveling with her parents and brother.

"Mrs. MacTavish, I'm Susan Jones. May I speak with you a moment?"

Glad for the company, Ashley invited Susan to take a seat on one of the two chairs Tanner had brought out from the wagon. Idly she wondered what Susan wanted. One look at Susan's expression told her it was serious. She pulled her chair up beside the girl and sat down.

"Please call me Ashley. How can I help you, Susan?"

Susan was shaking visibly. She buried her trembling hands in her skirt and fixed Ashley with such a beseeching look Ashley knew she wasn't going to like anything the girl had to say.

"I don't know where to begin."

"Is this about my husband and what happened last night?"

Susan nodded. "Mr. MacTavish didn't attack Mr. Slater."

"I never thought he did."

Tanner chose that moment to walk into the circle of firelight. Susan jumped from her chair, her face pale. "Perhaps I'd better come back some other time."

"No, please don't go," Ashley pleaded. "If this is about Tanner he has a right to hear it."

Tanner's gaze flew to Susan. "Go ahead and speak, miss," Tanner said gently. "I'd like to hear what you have to say."

Susan's tongue darted out to lick moisture onto her dry lips. "Only if you promise to keep it between the three of us. No one else is to know."

Ashley had reservations about making such a promise but Tanner gave it freely. "We promise."

Susan appeared on the verge of collapse. Exerting tremendous effort, she pulled herself together. "I know who attacked Pratt Slater. When I heard you tell Captain Cramer that you'd find the murderer, I knew I had to try to talk you out of prying too deeply into the attack."

Ashley was stunned. "Why? Don't you want to see justice done?"

Susan gave her a rueful smile. "Justice would have been done if Pratt Slater had been killed."

Ashley went still. "I don't understand."

83

Tanner understood only too well. "Slater hurt you, didn't he, Susan? It's unfortunate he's still alive to hurt another woman."

Susan collapsed into tears. "He caught me away from the wagons one night and forced himself on me. I cried and threatened to tell my parents but he was so sweet afterward. He promised to marry me when we reached Oregon and I believed him. He seemed so apologetic, so contrite. He even t-talked me into m-meeting him two or three nights a week behind the wagons." She was sobbing so hard now she could hardly speak.

"The bastard," Tanner said venomously.

Ashley put her arms around the girl, trying to instill confidence in her to continue. "What happened? Who tried to kill him?"

"Two weeks ago I told him I thought I was" — she hung her head in shame — "in the family way. I wanted us to be married at Fort Bridger. He laughed at me. Said he never intended to marry me at all. That he was only using me until someone better came along. I wanted to die."

Ashley's heart went out to the girl. She could tell Tanner was affected too.

"I didn't know what to do," Susan continued tearfully. "I couldn't tell Ma and Pa; they'd be so hurt. So I told my brother. Oh, Ashley, it's all my fault. Seth is young and hotheaded. He told me he'd take care of it. He arranged to meet Pratt behind the wagons

84

late last night. Seth was so grim when he returned, I knew something terrible had happened. I think Seth was the one who tried to kill Pratt Slater."

Tanner spat out a curse. "Why are you telling us this?"

"I feared you'd find out the truth somehow and tell Captain Cramer. My brother is young; he has his whole life ahead of him. He isn't an animal who kills in cold blood. Pratt must have said something to enrage him."

Tanner could well imagine Slater goading young Seth. "Were you going to say nothing and let them hang me?"

Susan hung her head. "I hoped it wouldn't come to that. I don't know what I would have done if it had. I don't even know what Seth would have done."

"Go back to your wagon, Susan. I need to think on this."

"You promised!" Susan cried out in distress.

"I know. Did Seth actually tell you he tried to kill Slater?"

"No. I just assumed. . . ."

"Thank you for telling us, Susan. I know it must have been difficult."

Susan left a few minutes later. "What are you going to do?" Ashley asked when she saw the determined look on Tanner's face.

"I know young Seth," Tanner said. "I don't

think he's capable of committing murder."

"If not Seth, then who?"

"I don't know but I intend to find out. I'm going back to the scene of the attack tomorrow and look around . . . after I talk to Seth."

"Will you be gone long?"

He gave her a cheeky grin. "Will you miss me, Yank?"

"Like a toothache, Reb," she shot back.

He laughed. She liked the sound. Tanner rarely laughed, and when he did it usually wasn't a pleasant laugh.

"I'll probably be gone a couple of days. If you need help ask young Todd Lind, Nancy and Jake's son."

Ashley nodded. "When are you leaving?"

"Before daylight. Fix a packet of food tonight and leave it on the tailgate for me. I'll be leaving before daylight. I'm going now to talk to Seth Jones."

That night Ashley waited for Tanner to return until she couldn't keep her eyes open any longer. She undressed and climbed into bed, wondering what Seth and Tanner were talking about so long. She was nearly asleep when she heard him climb into the wagon.

"Yank, are you awake?"

Ashley rubbed the sleep from her eyes and sat up. "I am. Did you talk to Seth?"

"He's left the wagon train. I've been out scouring the hills for him."

"Left?" Ashley said in dismay. "Did you find him?"

"No. The young fool. Doesn't he realize how dangerous it is to roam alone in Indian country? I've seen signs of Indian activity for the past several days."

Ashley gasped aloud. "You have? Why haven't you said anything?"

"I did. To Captain Cramer. He's as aware of the fact that we're being watched as I am. We're both in agreement that if Indians were going to attack they would have done so long before now. Cramer has been this route before. He says they're Sioux, and that when they're good and ready they'll demand a toll for crossing their land."

Ashley shuddered. "Indians. We could all be scalped in our sleep. You can't leave now."

"I have to. We'll reach Fort Bridger soon, and if Slater's attacker isn't found I'll be turned over to the army for questioning. Slater could recover enough to name me as his assailant. I'm a Reb, Ashley; he hates me. I'll be judged guilty even though I'm inno-cent. I have to find out who did this. If I don't I could end up in a Federal prison. Attempted murder is no light matter."

"What do you expect to find?"

"Maybe nothing. If Seth hadn't lit out it would have made my job a whole lot easier. If I don't catch up to you before, I'll meet you at

Fort Bridger. Tell Cramer where I've gone."

Frightened by the thought that Tanner could be killed by Indians, Ashley made a small noise that sounded suspiciously like a sob. "Be careful, Reb."

Ashley had no idea how it happened but she found herself in Tanner's arms, clinging to him, offering her mouth to his with innocent fervor. His response was anything but innocent. His mouth crushed down over hers, so fierce, so possessive, the shock of it left her breathless and drowning in her own heat. She felt his swelling body press urgently against hers as his lips sucked and licked and his tongue stroked. She felt herself drowning in the sensations of taste, touch and sexual excitement.

His breath raged hot and fast, beckoning her to join in the dance of flame. His tongue stabbed inside her mouth while below his pounding loins kept pace with the rhythmic thrust and withdrawal. She let her tongue meet his with unaccustomed boldness, ignoring the warning bells ringing inside her head. She wanted this. She'd waited for this all her life. They were wed. Who had more right than a wife to the kind of pleasure Tanner was offering?

"Tanner," she gasped. "Tanner . . ."

If Tanner responded with words, the pounding in her head prevented her from hearing them. He was lowering her to the cot,

88

following her down, covering her with his body. His hands caressed her through the soft linen of her nightgown; then impatiently he tore the garment down the middle. Her hands cradled the heat of his mouth to her aching flesh as he buried his head between her breasts. Ashley arched her head back, her neck and throat laid bare for his nipping kisses.

He happily obliged, then added another dimension to his torment as his fingers delved into the moist, scorching heat of her torrid center. Ashley cried out, lost in a world she never knew existed. Tanner had kissed her before, and touched her body, but it had been nothing like this. Those kisses and caresses had been but a tepid prelude to what she was feeling now.

"Ashley, are you sure?" Tanner's voice was raw with a kind of excitement he hadn't experienced in longer than he cared to admit.

Ashley tried to focus on Tanner's words but she couldn't think, only feel.

"Ashley, answer me, dammit! What about the annulment? I'm willing to continue, but if we do, annulment of our marriage is out of the question. What we do here tonight could result in a child."

Suddenly his words began to make sense. She didn't want to remain married to the Reb, did she? There were too many dark secrets in his past. He hated Yanks. Hated her. Her desire to make love was lust-driven, just as his was. And what was it he just said about a child?

Oh, God, of course! She was no naive miss; she knew the facts of life. Her sole purpose in coming west was to help her brother; she didn't need the distraction of a husband or child. She went still beneath him.

"I must be mad," Ashley whispered raggedly. "This can't be happening. I won't let it happen. I don't want your baby."

Tanner lifted himself from Ashley and stared at her. His eyes were glazed, his heart pounding wildly against his rib cage. Her cruel words effectively quelled his passion but it took several minutes of deep breathing to bring a semblance of control to his surging, raging temper. As soon as he was able, he rose to his feet.

"I wouldn't give you anything you don't want, Yank. A child by you would be a living reminder of everything the Yankees deprived me of. You'll have to forgive me. I've been without a woman too damn long. I'll take care of it as soon as we reach Fort Bridger."

She couldn't see his face clearly in the dark but she knew from his chilling words that she had hurt him. She hadn't meant to be so brutally frank, but having a baby was out of the question. Even if giving in to Tanner this one time didn't result in a child, she couldn't guarantee that once she surrendered to him it

90

wouldn't happen again . . . and again. . . . She knew instinctively that being loved by Tanner could be addictive and she'd be better off not indulging.

"I'll see you in a day or two," Tanner said, breaking into her reverie. "Don't forget, you still owe me five hundred dollars."

"Tanner . . ." His name fell from her lips and wafted away on the night breeze. What could she say? She touched her lips, still swollen from Tanner's kisses, and wished things might have been different. If he wasn't so bitter. If she hadn't been required to buy his services. If he could love her just a little . . .

Todd Lind arrived shortly after dawn to help Ashley hitch the oxen. He offered to drive the wagon and Ashley accepted. Some days, after handling the oxen for hours on end, her arms felt as if they were being pulled out of their sockets. They had strengthened to a degree she would never have thought possible, but it still felt good to sit back and let someone else handle the reins.

The morning was cloudy and very warm. A bank of thin clouds lined in gold hung overhead. Ashley could see a glimmer of sunshine through the breaks and expected that the sun would prevail before too long. Sweat trickled down between her breasts and she plucked at her bodice, pulling it away from her damp skin. Her bonnet lay on the seat beside her. She had pulled it off to let the breeze ruffle through her thick hair.

Ashley's thoughts ran the gamut of her despair. She wondered if Tanner would find Seth, and if he'd learn anything about the attack upon Slater. She worried about Indians. A man traveling alone would be easy prey for a war party bent on mayhem.

Suddenly Ashley heard a cry of panic, then another, and another, until the entire wagon train reverberated with sounds of fear and distress. She glanced down the long line of wagons, her expression reflecting her fear. The word *Indians* finally got through to her frozen brain.

Indians.

Then she saw them. To the left of the train, a dozen or more red-skinned savages were riding down from the hills. They looked fierce even at a distance. There was no time to draw the wagons into a circle. All they could do was sit and wait. Captain Cramer rode out to meet them. Men bearing weapons gathered outside their wagons, prepared to defend their womenfolk and children. Cramer called for caution, explaining that the Indians were only here to collect a toll. Standing up, Ashley craned her neck, trying to see what was going on as the Indians wheeled their ponies to a stop a short distance from the train. When it appeared the men meant no harm, the women and children gradually crept from their wagons to stare openly at the red-skinned savages. Most had never seen Indians in their own environment before.

Curious, Ashley climbed down from the wagon and joined a group of women. Squeezing through to the front of the crowd, Ashley stood very still and listened, surprised to hear the chief speak broken but recognizable English.

"You trespass on our land, white eyes," the chief said.

"We're merely traveling through," Cramer said. "No one in this wagon train intends to settle here on your land. We go west, to where the land meets the great water."

"If you wish safe passage you must pay a toll. Chief Running Elk has spoken."

"Name your price, Running Elk," Cramer said, already resigned to losing a few head of cattle. It was a small price to pay for human lives.

Running Elk held up the fingers of both hands. "This many cows from your herd. They will feed our band through the winter when game is scarce."

Cramer nodded in agreement. "Take the cows. We will not stop you."

Suddenly the sun broke through the clouds, sending fingers of gold cascading from the sky. A ray of sunshine settled on

Ashley's head. One of the Indian braves happened to look in her direction and his mouth fell open in shock and disbelief. He pointed wildly, crying out words in his own language that caused the other braves to turn as one to gape at Ashley. Even the settlers turned to look at her, wondering what the fuss was about.

The sun, now a dazzling ball high in the sky, seemed to have singled Ashley out. Her hair, unrestrained by a bonnet, fell in a flaming mass down her back. Tendrils of pure fire framed her face with fingers of living flame. Murmuring among themselves, the Indians seemed mesmerized, and more than a little frightened.

Speaking with his companions in his own tongue, Running Elk seemed as thunderstruck as the others. The settlers shifted uncomfortably, staring curiously at Ashley. Abruptly the chief raised his hand and pointed directly at Ashley.

"Keep your cows, white eyes. Give us woman with hair like flame."

Ashley started violently as Cramer sent her a silent warning. Had she the power she would have evaporated into a wisp of smoke and become invisible.

"That's not possible, Running Elk," Cramer said. "Take double the number of cows you asked for."

"Keep cows. The woman with hair like

94

flame comes with us. Long ago the shaman predicted that such a woman would touch our lives. He saw it in a vision. He interpreted it to mean that the flame-haired woman would bring us good fortune, peaceful times and enough food to feed our bellies and the bellies of our children. So it has come to pass. Give us the woman."

"No!" Ashley cried, more frightened than she had ever been in her life. "I am not that woman. I won't go with you." She turned to Cramer, her eyes wild with fear. "Don't let them take me, Captain Cramer!"

"You can't take one of our women," Cramer insisted. He felt that he was losing control of the situation and didn't know what to do to remedy it.

"The woman will be called Flame and she will not be harmed. She will occupy a place of honor among the People."

Cramer decided it was time to become more forceful. "You are only a small group; we have four times your number. We have many guns."

Running Elk was not impressed. He lifted his arm and turned toward the hills surrounding them. As if on cue at least fifty mounted warriors crested the hill, waiting for Running Elk's signal.

"My God, look at them painted devils," one of the settlers gasped. "They'll kill us all."

"Is one woman worth the deaths of so many?" Running Elk asked, his voice taut with menace. "Give us Flame and no harm will come to you. You and your people may cross our lands in peace. Resist and you will all be killed, down to the last woman and child."

Those who heard cried out in protest. "Give them the woman!" a young man with a wife and two children shouted. "They said they won't hurt her. When we get to the fort we can send the soldiers to rescue her."

"I don't know," Cramer said, mulling over a decision that had only one conclusion. "Her husband isn't here; it isn't right to hand a woman over to Indians."

"They'll kill and scalp us all, even our children," sobbed a woman cradling a babe in her arms.

"We can fight them, Captain," Jake Lind said, stepping forward, ready to protect Ashley with his life. Young Todd Lind lined up beside him.

Though frightened nearly out of her wits, Ashley knew that a battle involving so many Indians would prove disastrous for the settlers. She couldn't allow that to happen. The thought of seeing her friends lying dead amidst the rubble of their belongings was too painful to bear.

While Cramer was still considering his options, which were damn few and hardly encouraging, Ashley stepped forward. "I'll go with them, Captain Cramer. If I don't, there's likely to be wholesale slaughter. I couldn't live with myself if that happened, not while it is in my power to prevent it."

Cramer's relief was enormous. He had come to the same conclusion. Ashley MacTavish would have to be sacrificed. Protecting one woman wasn't worth the lives of an entire wagon train of innocent victims. When Tanner MacTavish returned Cramer could say with honesty that his wife had made the decision of her own free will.

Running Elk's face remained impassive as Ashley expressed her willingness to be carried off. He rode to where Ashley stood, shaking in her boots.

"Flame is wise as well as brave," he said as he swooped down and lifted her from her feet. With a display of rippling muscles beneath golden brown skin, he set her on his pony behind him. Then he raised his lance high in the air, gave a bloodcurdling war whoop and rode off.

Ashley hung on for dear life, winding her arms around the Indian's supple waist, her hair flying behind her like a flaming banner. The other braves wheeled their ponies, raised their voices in yipping howls and pounded after them. The Indians cresting the hill disappeared as if by magic.

Standing beneath the blazing sun on the

windswept prairie, the settlers appeared rooted to the spot. Some felt relief, others pity for Ashley, and some were too frightened to feel anything.

"Back to the wagons, folks," Cramer ordered. "We've earned our safe passage; let's get the hell out of here."

Jake Lind reached for Cramer, spinning him around. "I can't believe you let them take her. I don't envy you when MacTavish comes back and learns what happened."

"It was Mrs. MacTavish's choice to leave with them," Cramer contended. "She wanted bloodshed no more than I did. She saved all our skins. On your way, Lind. We've got a lot of miles to cover before nightfall."

Tanner caught up with the wagons two days later. They were just pulling into a circle for the night. Seth was with him. He had tracked the youth to his crude campsite and confronted him about the attack upon Slater. Seth had broken down and confessed everything, including the fact that he had run away because he was frightened, not because he was guilty. After his sister had told him that she had confided her suspicions about him to Tanner and Ashley, he had panicked.

Together they had gone to the place where Slater had been found and discovered an important clue that had been previously overlooked. Unfortunately the clue was painful for both Seth and Tanner to accept. They rode into camp now, intending to ask Captain Cramer's discretion in the matter.

"Why is everyone staring at us?" Seth asked worriedly.

"Damned if I know," Tanner said. The back of his neck tingled, and his spine prickled with apprehension. Something was desperately wrong.

"Seth!" Susan ran up to greet her brother as they dismounted. But when she lifted her eyes to Tanner they were filled with pity. "Thank God you're both back."

Tanner didn't like the sound of that. "What happened, Susan?" He glanced around, seeing everyone but the one woman he wanted to see. And they were all staring at him.

"It's Ashley. Indians came. They took her."

The earth fell from beneath Tanner's feet. "What are you saying? How could Indians take Ashley and leave everyone else untouched?"

Cramer came up to join them. "Chief Running Elk wanted her, MacTavish. We couldn't have prevented it even if we tried. They all admired her red hair. They acted like she was some kind of goddess. They would have killed us all if we hadn't let them take her."

With a howl of outrage, Tanner threw himself at Cramer.

Chapter Five

Howling like a banshee, Tanner went wild. It took five men to pull him off of Captain Cramer. He couldn't accept the fact that the Indians meant no harm to Ashley. Even now she could be suffering all kinds of abuse, if not physical then mental.

"Dammit, MacTavish," Cramer said, moving a safe distance away from Tanner, "control yourself. Let the soldiers at Fort Bridger handle it. That's their job. They'll have your wife back in no time."

"You bastard!" Tanner spat. "She could already be dead. Why did you let them take her?"

"We had no choice. The Sioux outnumbered us and we were in no position to resist. Your wife knew it; that's why she went willingly with the savages. We would have all been slaughtered had we refused to let them take her."

The logic of Cramer's words didn't make them any easier to accept. Tanner sagged against the hands restraining him, trying to come to grips with the terrible anguish raging inside him. He knew he couldn't wait until the slow-moving wagon train reached Fort Bridger to find help; he had to go himself. As much as he detested the idea of asking help from Yankees, he had to swallow his pride for Ashley's sake. Going into an Indian camp alone was tantamount to suicide. He was desperate but he wasn't stupid.

"Let go of me!" Tanner shouted, shaking off five pairs of hands. "I'm not going to attack your leader. I've more important things to do than waste my time on a coward."

"Let go of him," Cramer ordered. "I don't know what you're going to do, MacTavish, but first I want to hear what, if anything, you learned about the attack on Slater. He's still alive, but barely, and you're still not off the hook."

"I don't have time now, Cramer." He started to walk away, but once again found himself seized and restrained.

"Wait, there's no need to detain Mr. MacTavish." Henry Jones, accompanied by Seth, stepped forward. "May I have a word in private with you, Captain Cramer?"

Cramer glanced curiously from father to son. "Very well, come to my wagon. You too, MacTavish. You're not free to leave until this matter is settled to my satisfaction, though I think you're crazy to single-handedly take on a band of savages."

They followed Cramer to the rear of his wagon, where they couldn't be overheard. "Go ahead, Henry; what is this all about? Do

101

you know something about the attack upon Slater?"

Henry Jones, a slight, mild-mannered man in his midforties, dropped his eyes. "I did it, Captain, and the only thing I regret is that he's still alive. I meant to kill him. He deserved it."

"You? What in the hell are you talking about?"

"You would have found out sooner or later anyway. Seth told me Mr. MacTavish found the knife I used on Slater. I was careless. Anyone who saw it could have identified it as mine. But I probably would have confessed anyway, if it came down to blaming an innocent man for something I did." He turned to Tanner. "I'm sorry, Mr. MacTavish, for not coming forward sooner. Seth told me you know about my Susan."

"I do, Mr. Jones, and I'm sorry as hell," Tanner said. "I probably would have done the same were I in your shoes."

"Will someone please tell me what's going on?" Cramer roared. "Where does Susan fit into all this?"

Henry looked squarely at Cramer, his face suffused with fury. "Pratt Slater raped my daughter, then continued to use her, promising marriage to keep her quiet. Then" — his voice faltered and he swallowed painfully — "she thought she was in the family way and demanded that Slater marry her at Fort

Bridger instead of waiting until the wagon train reached Oregon. He laughed at her, called her a gullible little slut, said he never intended to marry her."

"How did you find out about this, Pa?" Seth asked. "Susan confided in me because she didn't want to hurt you. I told her I'd take care of it but when I confronted Slater he grew belligerent and refused to honor his promise to Susan. I left Slater alive but intended to find a way to force him to do the right thing by my sister."

"I followed you to that meeting with Slater," Henry said. "I saw you and Susan whispering together and became suspicious when she started crying and you became angry. I listened to everything you and Slater said. Rage blinded me to all but the need to avenge my little girl. Susan was so innocent, so trusting, and that bastard ruined her. She believed he would marry her. When you left him, I sneaked up behind him and stuck my knife into him. He deserved to die."

Cramer stared at Henry, unable to believe the timid, peace-abiding man was capable of attempting murder. Yet the longer he considered it, the more he became convinced that Henry had a right to defend his daughter's honor. It was the code of the West — a man defended his family and his honor himself; he didn't wait for the law to get involved.

"Go back to your wagon, Henry. I'm satisfied that you acted in your daughter's best interest. I would have preferred that you let me handle it, but it's too late now for regrets."

"I'd prefer to keep my reasons for attacking Slater private. I don't want to shame my daughter. All I wanted was to avenge her and protect her from men like Slater. I'm sorry, Captain, for letting another man take the blame. I hope Mr. MacTavish will forgive me. Good night, Captain, Mr. MacTavish. Come along, Seth."

"You're free to come and go as you please, MacTavish. I've always known Slater had a mean streak, but I knew nothing about his rape of Susan Jones." He shook his head. "I don't understand it. I suspected he wanted your wife but I never thought he'd take an innocent young girl. If he lives, I'll do what I can to see that he does the right thing by Susan."

"Susan is better off without the bastard. There are many things you don't know about Slater," Tanner replied. "Things that happened during the war. Things that marked him as a cold-blooded murderer and rapist. But I can't dwell on those things now. I'm going after Ashley. Todd Lind can drive my wagon to Fort Bridger and leave it at the livery for me."

"Are you mad? You can't go after her alone."

"I don't intend to. I'll ride to the fort and

104

report the abduction. I'm hoping the army will send a patrol to accompany me on a rescue mission. They can't refuse; it's their job."

Cramer had reservations but did not voice them. There was no mistaking MacTavish for a Reb. Feelings still ran high against slaveholding Southerners, and if the commander didn't take a shine to Tanner, he was unlikely to lend support to his cause. He wasn't partial to Rebs himself but MacTavish had earned his reluctant respect. He wished him luck but held little hope that he'd prevail. His wife was as good as lost to him.

Tanner didn't even wait until morning to leave. After Todd Lind agreed to drive the wagon to the fort, Tanner removed money and valuables from Ashley's trunk, packed his saddlebag with clothing and food and rode off into the dark night.

Riding behind Running Elk that first day had been a nightmare, one Ashley didn't wish to repeat. His stamina and that of his companions was amazing. They had the ability to ride all day without stopping to rest, eat or relieve themselves. Only when she begged for respite did they allow a short rest beside a creek. Ashley sank down to the ground, so sore and stiff she could scarcely move. Once she recovered sufficiently her full bladder drove her into the woods. Running Elk watched her closely and Ashley was certain that had she not returned in a reasonable length of time he would have come after her.

That night they stopped long enough to rest the horses before resuming their journey at dawn. She was given pemmican and parched corn to eat and water from a stream to drink. When she lay down to sleep, Running Elk lay down beside her. She lay stiff and tense, ready to defend herself should Running Elk try to molest her, but she relaxed somewhat when he told her she would not be harmed, that he slept beside her to share his warmth. The intimacy of a male body beside her unnerved her. Not even her own husband had slept beside her all night.

Tanner. His name was a sweet ache inside her. Would she ever see Tanner again? Did he miss her? Or was he happy to be rid of her? Silent tears coursed down her cheeks when she thought of living the rest of her life with savages. And what about her brother? Her whole purpose in coming west had been to help Cole prove his innocence.

Eventually she fell asleep, wondering if anyone would come to her rescue, or if one insignificant woman was worth the trouble. The following day was much like the previous one. They rode through valleys, over hills and across streams. Had she been in an appreciative mood she would have enjoyed the spectacular scenery. Unfortunately her mind was

106

not receptive to anything but thoughts of an uncertain future with a band of Indians who thought her some kind of goddess because of a silly vision and her red hair.

And her thoughts always returned to her husband, the man whose loyalty she had purchased. The man who hated all Yankees with a passion that surpassed anything she'd ever seen or known. She was a Yankee. Yet his kisses had been so sweetly rendered, his caresses so boundlessly arousing. She wished . . . oh, how she wished she had permitted him to make love to her. If she had it to do over again she would happily give her virginity to him.

She would carry his child with pride.

Too late.

She would never experience Tanner's loving, or tell him she wasn't as immune to him as she pretended. If she didn't know better she'd think she . . .

Loved him.

They reached the Indian village late the next afternoon. Thirty or so tipis filled a small clearing between two hills, nestled on the bank of a meandering stream. Surrounded by trees, the village was situated to provide protection from human predators. Ashley's heart sank. Even if anyone were to look for her they'd never find her.

People came out to greet the returning

warriors. Ashley slid down the horse's rump, unsure of what would happen next, standing quietly as Running Elk dismounted. Ashley's presence created a stir, and a hush fell over the entire village. Suddenly a path cleared, and an old man made his painful way to where Ashley stood. Leaning heavily on a staff, the Indian wore an unusual necklace of bones and teeth around his neck and an elaborate headdress of eagle feathers upon his head. His body was bent with age and his hands gnarled and misshapen. Yet there was no mistaking the power he wielded within the tribe, or the esteem in which he was held.

When the old man bowed before Ashley she had no idea how to respond. Instinct made up for her lack of knowledge as she bowed back, which seemed to please the old man. Then he spoke to her in his own tongue and waited for Running Elk to interpret.

"Dream Spinner welcomes Flame to our village," Running Elk said. "Dream Spinner says he learned of your coming in a vision many, many moons ago, when he was young and vigorous." The shaman spoke again at length. "Dream Spinner says he is ready to walk the spirit path now that he has looked upon your face. He says you have powerful medicine."

"How can that be?" Ashley contended. "I am not one of your people."

Running Elk gave her a scathing glance.

"We do not question Dream Spinner's visions. He predicted your coming and we have been waiting a long time. A man's vision is sacred, not only to him but to the entire tribe. The People believe in portents and signs."

"What's going to happen to me?" Ashley wanted to know. "Am I a captive?"

"You will be honored and revered by the People. Your medicine is strong, powerful. Dream Spinner says sons from your loins will become strong leaders of men, with courage to match their wisdom."

"Sons? But I am childless. My husband and I are newly married."

For a moment Running Elk looked disconcerted. "The People do not recognize white man's laws. You have no husband."

A premonition of what was to come brought a protest to Ashley's lips. But before she could voice her fears an attractive maiden approached and addressed Running Elk.

"Welcome home, brother," she said in her own tongue. In halting English she greeted Ashley. "Welcome, Flame." Huge doelike eyes searched Ashley's face, then widened in awe at the sight of her fiery red hair.

Running Elk spoke at length to his sister. His words seemed to surprise her but she quickly recovered. Abruptly Running Elk turned to Ashley.

"You are to go with my sister. She is called

Morning Mist. She will give you clothing and food and teach you our tongue."

Ashley started to protest but changed her mind. She sensed no danger to her, and food and clean clothing sounded wonderful. Besides, she needed time to think, time to plan her escape. And escape she would. Spending the rest of her life with savages did not appeal to her.

Morning Mist was kind to her, bringing her a savory stew to eat and leading her to a section of the stream where only women bathed. After a refreshing dip in the cool water, she was given a pure white doeskin tunic, richly embroidered with colorful beads and embellished with feathers.

"You will be my sister," Morning Mist said shyly as she led Ashley back to the tipi she shared with her brother.

Startled, Ashley asked, "What do you mean?"

"When Dream Spinner decides the time is right you will join with Running Elk. He is divorcing his first wife for you."

Ashley's mouth fell open. "Join with . . . You mean marry?"

"You will be his woman."

"No, I will not! I am already married."

"It will be as the Great Spirit wills. Running Elk is a great chieftain. He is courageous and strong. When he joins with you he will become even more powerful."

"What about his wife? How can he abandon her?"

"A man may have more than one wife. Running Elk does you honor by divorcing Spring Rain and taking no other wife. He will find a good man for her."

Ashley thought the whole thing ludicrous but wisely remained silent. If she appeared to accept her fate perhaps they would not watch her closely and she could escape.

A short time later a woman entered the tipi. She was beautiful, with sleek black hair, luminous dark eyes and skin as golden as a summer day. Though her eyes remained downcast Ashley sensed her animosity. The woman lingered a long time as she gathered personal items from a parfleche hanging from a side pole. When she finished she spoke in sharp tones to Morning Mist. While she was speaking Running Elk ducked through the tent flap, filling the tipi with his commanding presence. He spoke harshly to the Indian woman. Holding her possessions to her chest, the woman slanted Ashley a venomous look and quickly departed.

"Who was that?" Ashley asked, fearing she had made an enemy and wondering why.

"That was Spring Rain. She returns to the lodge of her father."

"She must hate me a great deal."

"It is not her place to hate you. I will find a good man to provide for her. Dream Spinner said I must not take a woman to my mat until the day I join with you. Fast and abstinence will make my seed more potent. I want many sons from you, Flame. And daughters. Your blood will combine with that of the People and strengthen us."

"I am already married."

"You left your man's lodge; you no longer belong to him. It is the way of the People. Go to sleep, Flame. When the sun rises Dream Spinner will study the signs to find the best time for our joining."

Morning Mist took Ashley's hand and led her to a pallet at the rear of the tipi. Ashley lay down on the bed of buffalo robes and closed her eyes. She was bone weary and frightened. She wanted Tanner. She wanted the comfort of his big body, the protection of his arms. She wanted . . . Tanner. She wanted her husband.

She was nearly asleep when Running Elk lay down beside her. His body was warm, and so very hard. She sensed the leashed power of his sleek, athletic frame. He wasn't large or brawny like Tanner but all muscle, lithe and wiry as a cougar. Despite his dusky skin he was a handsome man. The stark planes of his face were cleanly defined, his cheekbones high, his eyes dark and penetrating. She knew instinctively that he could be harsh and ruthless, and prayed she would never become the object of his anger.

Tanner rode hell-for-leather to Fort Bridger, nearly running his poor horse into the ground before resting briefly and continuing. He begrudged every minute of rest he was forced to take. Each one of those minutes could be Ashley's last on earth. He blamed himself for not being with the wagon train when she was taken. Had he been there he would have fought tooth and nail to save her. What was she doing now? he wondered. Was she being abused, threatened, hurt? How had a Yankee come to mean so much to him? A marriage that had begun as an arrangement had become so much more in the short time he had been with Ashley. Feelings he had buried beneath a layer of bitterness stirred to life within him. Glimpses of a second chance at life stirred him each time he looked at Ashley.

Tanner reached the fort the following day, his horse foaming at the mouth and his own strength greatly strained. He staggered from his horse and asked directions to the post commander's office from the first person he saw. When he reached the commander's office, his agitation convinced the clerk to escort him into Captain Callahan's office immediately.

"A Mr. MacTavish to see you, sir," the clerk announced as he knocked on the door and peered inside. "He says it's urgent."

"Mr. MacTavish," Captain Callahan repeated distractedly. "Do I know you, sir?"

"No, sir," Tanner replied, struggling to overcome his aversion to blue uniforms. "I'm traveling with a wagon train. I reckon they'll roll into the fort in a day or two."

The captain's attention sharpened. "Did something happen to bring you here in such a state? You look as if you haven't been off your horse in days."

"Sioux braves stopped our train, demanding tolls for passing through their lands."

The captain sat back, clearly annoyed at being interrupted by so trivial a matter. "It happens all the time, Mr. MacTavish. It's nothing to get upset about."

Tanner's hands clenched at his sides. "It is to me. The red devils took my wife."

Callahan's head shot up. "Took your wife? Was the train attacked? Did your wagon master refuse to pay the tolls?"

"Nothing like that," Tanner explained. "My wife has flaming red hair. Chief Running Elk appeared enthralled with it. He demanded my wife in exchange for safe passage. He wanted her for a good-luck charm because their shaman had dreamed of a woman with red hair in a vision."

"Chief Running Elk, you say? He's a sly one. Refuses to return to the reservation. My men have had a devil of a time tracking him

114

down. I'm sorry about your wife, MacTavish, but there is nothing I can do. At the moment the fort's capacities are stretched to the limits. Only one company of troopers remains inside the fort and they're needed in case of an attack. Perhaps in a few weeks . . ."

Consumed by rage, Tanner lost all semblance of control. Living up to his reputation as a firebrand, he leaped across the desk and seized Callahan by the collar, bringing him up until they were nose to nose.

"Yankee bastard! If I wasn't a Reb I reckon you'd be eager to offer help."

"Take your hands off me, MacTavish. Your being a Reb has nothing to do with my decision. There's a serious Indian problem brewing and we're dangerously under-manned right now."

"I don't give a damn about that. My wife is missing and I demand you do something about it!"

Unable to free himself from Tanner's grip, Callahan called out loudly, "Private Stark, call out the guard!"

Nearly mad with frustration, Tanner shook Callahan like a rag doll. If words wouldn't sway him, perhaps sheer strength would. He hadn't counted on being bodily restrained by three soldiers and the sergeant of the guard, who had burst into the room.

"Get that madman off me," Callahan gasped as Tanner's fingers were pried off of him. "Relieve him of his weapons and take him to the stockade to cool off; then escort him from the fort in the morning. I'm not pressing charges because the man is mad with grief. His wife was taken by Running Elk."

"How can you live with yourself?" Tanner cried as he was dragged away. "Does a woman's life mean nothing to you?"

"Of course it does. But I haven't enough men available to launch a search for Running Elk's camp at the present time. You'll appreciate my position when you've rested and had time to reconsider. With any luck a night in the stockade will cool your hot head."

Howling in outrage, Tanner was wrested from the commander's office and out into the street. Realizing that resistance was useless, Tanner quit struggling. He had done all he could for now. There were too many here to fight. Tomorrow, after he was released from the stockade, he would search for Ashley on his own. He should have known better than to expect help from a damn Yankee, but he had hoped. . . .

The moment the cell door closed behind him Tanner banged his fist against the wall, cursing violently. Never had he felt so frustrated, so helpless. That wasn't exactly true, he reflected. One other time in his life he had suffered this same kind of anguish. The day Ellen . . . No, he couldn't think about Ellen now. He had to keep a cool head if he

116

wanted to save Ashley.

"Welcome to hell, mister."

Tanner started violently. He'd been so steeped in misery he hadn't noticed the man leaning against the wall in a dark corner.

"How long you in for?"

"They're letting me go tomorrow. How long have you been here?"

The man gave a bitter laugh. "Too long. Weeks, months, who knows exactly?" He walked into a beam of sunlight that had entered through the single window high up on the outside wall.

The first thing Tanner noticed was the man's red hair. The next was his eyes. He had only seen eyes that particular shade of brilliant green once before. The man's features were a masculine version of Ashley's. Twins? Tanner took in a great shuddering breath, recalling that Ashley's brother was being held in the stockade at Fort Bridger.

"Does your last name happen to be Webster? Are you Cole Webster?"

The man seemed only mildly surprised. "So you've heard of me. For your information, I didn't kill Lieutenant Kimball."

"I have it on good authority that you didn't."

Cole's brows shot upward. His gaze slid down Tanner's body, coming to rest on his gray army pants. "You're a Reb."

"So what?"

Cole shrugged. "The war is over. I hold no grudges."

"I wish I could say the same," Tanner muttered.

"Who are you? Should I know you?"

"You don't know me but I've heard plenty about you. The name's Tanner MacTavish. I'm your sister's husband."

Tanner waited for Cole to exhibit surprise and he wasn't disappointed. A look of utter disbelief crossed Cole's features. "Ashley is married? I never thought . . . That is, she is twenty-five and never expressed interest in marriage after being jilted by that bastard back in Chicago." Suddenly his face lit up. "Is she here?"

A frown creased Tanner's brow. He hadn't gotten past the part where Cole said that Ashley had been jilted. The man who jilted her couldn't have been in his right mind. Ashley was a prize worthy of any man.

"Tanner, did you hear me? Where is Ashley? And what are you doing in the stockade?"

Tanner stared at his boots, trying to find the right words to tell Cole about his sister. After careful thought he decided there was no easy way. "Ashley and I joined the last wagon train to leave St. Joe this year. She received your letter, the one stating that you were in the stockade, charged with murder. Your aunt passed away and Ashley was determined

118

to come to Fort Bridger and help clear your name. She sold everything she owned to outfit a wagon and buy oxen."

Cole gave him a narrow-eyed look. "Where do you fit in? Ashley never mentioned you in her letters. Where did she have the occasion to meet a Reb?"

"I'll let Ashley explain when . . ." His sentence trailed off. "If . . ."

Cole sensed Tanner's distress and felt a frisson of fear. Something was wrong, desperately wrong. He grasped Tanner's shoulders. "Where is my sister? What happened to her?"

"Dammit, Webster, I'm trying to tell you," Tanner said, shaking himself free. "Indians took her."

"What Indians?"

"Sioux. The wagon master said the chief's name was Running Elk."

Cole groaned in dismay. "Oh, God. How many captives did Running Elk take?"

"Just Ashley. I immediately rode to the fort to ask for help. Captain Callahan said he had no men available to send on patrol." He paused, his eyes dark and merciless. "I didn't like his answer."

Cole stared at him, aghast. "You attacked the captain?"

"Yeah," Tanner said, not at all contrite.

"Start from the beginning and don't leave anything out."

119

Tanner told Cole everything he knew about Ashley's abduction, which was damn little. He even explained his reason for being away from the wagon train when Running Elk showed up demanding a toll for crossing his land.

"The war is still fresh in men's minds," Cole said. "I can well imagine the prejudice you experienced during your trek west. What I can't understand, or even explain, is Ashley's reason for marrying a Reb. My sister is a staunch abolitionist. But that's not the important thing right now. Our primary concern is Ashley. We have to find Running Elk's camp and free her."

Tanner's dark brows shot upward. "We?"

"Running Elk is a wily devil. The army hasn't been able to find him and stop his shenanigans. I'm a good tracker, Tanner. I've got to get out of here to help you find Ashley. There's talk of transferring me soon to a Federal prison, and if that happens there's no way I can help my sister."

Tanner's attention sharpened. "What do you have in mind?" Never in a million years did Tanner think he'd be cooperating with a Yankee and glad for the help.

"Help me escape. I'm not a murderer. I was framed by a man who wanted me out of the way. Lieutenant Kimball and I stumbled onto a plot to sell army guns to the Sioux. We narrowed our suspects to two men. One was

Sergeant Harger. Harger killed Kimball in cold blood and fixed it so the blame fell on me. He even testified that he heard me threaten Kimball before the shooting. One day I'll find Harger and wring a confession out of him. I can't do it if I'm in prison."

"Where is this Harger now?"

"Mustered out of the army. For all I know he's still trading illegally with the Sioux." His eyes narrowed on Tanner. "They're letting you go tomorrow, aren't they?"

"Yeah, do you have a plan?"

Cole's voice lowered to a desperate whisper. "Listen carefully, Tanner, Ashley's life depends on my escaping. I know the area. There are only a few places Running Elk can maintain a campsite and I know them all. He's too wily for the army, moving from place to place one step ahead of a patrol, but two men alone can find him."

For the first time in days Tanner felt hope. He listened to Cole, his eyes opaque against the tension that drew his features taut. By the time Cole stopped talking, Tanner's eyes had lost their glazed emptiness. They glowed hot and dark and determined.

"What do you say, Tanner? Are you with me?"

"I'd cooperate with the devil to save Ashley," Tanner replied, meaning every word.

121

Chapter Six

"Move your ass, MacTavish; the captain said it was time to let you out. You can pick up your guns at his office."

The cell door clanged open and the guard motioned Tanner out. "It's about time," Tanner grumbled. "It's nearly noon."

"Yeah, he wanted to give you plenty of time to cool off."

Tanner said nothing as he walked down the corridor and stepped out into the brilliant sunshine.

"Follow me. The captain's waiting."

Tanner walked across the parade ground, his mind on Cole and the plan they had finalized during the night. It had to work. Cole was the only one who could help him find Ashley. Cole was convinced he could locate Running Elk's camp, and Tanner had no recourse but to trust the Yankee. Of course, this Yankee was Ashley's twin brother, which made him feel a whole helluva lot better.

"Come in, MacTavish," Captain Callahan said when his clerk announced Tanner's arrival. "I hope your overnight stay in our stockade served to cool your temper." He searched Tanner's face. "If not I can always arrange for a longer stay."

"I've seen enough of your fort, Captain. I'll replenish my supplies and move on. My wife is still missing and I'm going after her with or without your help."

"Good luck, though I don't hold out much hope. If you haven't found her in a few weeks, come back. We might be in a better position to offer help." He opened his drawer and removed Tanner's guns. "Here's your weapons. You can pick up your horse at the livery. I hope you've the coin to pay for boarding the animal."

"I'll take care of it," Tanner said as he strapped his gun belt around his narrow hips. He had felt naked without his weapons and was glad to have them back.

To Tanner's relief all his belongings were intact in his saddlebag, including the money he had taken from Ashley's trunk. He hadn't bothered to count it but it appeared to be a substantial sum. He bargained for a spirited bay gelding, paid the stable keeper the amount agreed upon and led both animals down the street to the mercantile. The clerk exhibited mild curiosity when Tanner purchased a saddle, saddlebag, two complete sets of buckskin clothing, a hat, a pair of Colt .45 six-shooters, a rifle, ammunition and supplies for a long trip.

"Going on a trip, mister?"

"You could say that," Tanner replied tersely. He paid for the lot and left. But he didn't leave the fort. Not yet. There was still the matter of Cole's escape, and that couldn't be accomplished until after dark.

Tanner spent most of the day in one of the saloons inside the fort. He drank a beer or two but remained stone-cold sober. He ordered a good meal and waited for darkness to descend. It was a long afternoon, made even longer by the stream of soldiers in blue uniforms parading in and out of the saloon. It took considerable effort on Tanner's part to stop himself from drawing on every Yankee devil he saw.

Late in the afternoon Tanner joined a poker game, surprising himself by winning. The game broke up at midnight and Tanner left the saloon as inconspicuously as he had entered hours earlier. The parade ground was deserted, the offices and homes dark. A sentry patrolled back and forth before the open gates while another kept watch in a tower above the palisade.

Leading the two horses, Tanner moved stealthily around to the rear of the stockade until he came to the small barred window set too high for him to reach.

"Cole," Tanner hissed, then waited for Cole to acknowledge his signal. It came almost immediately.

"Is that you, Tanner? Hand up the clothes and guns to me," Cole said in a loud whisper.

Leading his horse close to the outer wall,

Tanner removed several articles of clothing and the guns he had purchased earlier for Cole. Then he carefully stood up in the saddle until he could reach the window, passing the clothing and guns to Cole through the narrow opening between the bars.

"Wait for me by the gate," Cole called out. "Did you get me a horse?"

"Ready and waiting," Tanner whispered back.

Tanner had been leery of Cole's plan from the beginning. He thought it would be much simpler to break into the stockade with his guns drawn and demand Cole's release. But Cole was a cautious man. He didn't want Tanner seen or identified as his accomplice, thus linking him with an escaped prisoner. It was enough that he'd be a hunted man; he didn't want to drag his family down with him.

Tanner led the two horses around the perimeter of the parade grounds, keeping well to the shadows. When he reached an alley close to the main gate, he led the horses into the narrow passage, where he had been instructed to wait for Cole.

Cole hid the clothing and all but one six-shooter under the bare mattress of the bunk. Tucking the gun in his belt beneath his jacket, he stretched out on the floor. When all was in readiness he called out to the guard with just the right amount of desperation in

125

his voice. It took several minutes of calling and begging for help before the disgruntled guard appeared.

"What the hell is all the racket about?"

Cole rolled around on the floor as if in pain. He clutched at his chest and made desperate, gurgling noises deep in his throat. "Help me. I think I'm dying."

The guard merely stared at him until Cole was driven nearly mad with suspense. He couldn't fail, not now. Ashley needed him. Suddenly he stiffened, then went limp. Finally convinced that Cole wasn't pretending, the guard opened the cell door and knelt beside Cole's still form. Before the poor man knew what hit him, Cole withdrew the six-shooter and bashed the guard alongside the head. The man folded like an accordion and lay still. Cole scooted from beneath him, gagged him with his kerchief and bound his hands with his belt. Then he quickly changed into clean buckskins Tanner had provided, strapped on his guns and let himself out of the cell, locking it behind him. He threw the key into an alley and made his way to where Tanner waited.

Tanner felt a welcome rush of relief when he saw Cole slip into the alley. "Did everything go as planned?"

Cole gave him a cocky grin. "Exactly as planned. Distract the sentry; I'll do the rest."

Tanner grasped the reins of Cole's horse,

mounted his own and left the alley. When he approached the gate, the guard called out a challenge: "Halt, who goes there?"

"I'm leaving the fort, soldier, not trying to sneak inside," Tanner explained. "Is there a law against that?"

Clearly confused, the sentry peered at Tanner through the darkness, trying to make out his features. With his hat pulled low, nothing was visible except Tanner's well-shaped mouth.

"I reckon not, mister. Just so you know it's dangerous to travel at night. The Injuns are restless these days."

Tanner shrugged. "It's dangerous to travel anytime."

"That's a mighty fine packhorse, mister," the sentry said, eyeing the gelding curiously.

"I'm partial to good horseflesh. Am I free to go?"

"Suit yourself, though it beats me why anyone would want to leave the protection of a fort in the middle of the night. Good luck."

Tanner rode through the gate, grateful that the guard wasn't of a suspicious nature. He went but a short distance, then reined in close to the wall, where the sentry in the tower would have difficulty seeing him.

The sentry walked to the gate to peer into the darkness, thinking a man would have to be loco to venture out of the fort in the dead of night. He did not see Cole creep up behind

127

him. He never knew what hit him as Cole struck him from behind.

Moving stealthily along the wall, Cole easily found Tanner. They walked the horses away from the palisade and down a trench that had been dug around the fort for protection before mounting and riding hell-for-leather into the night.

As the days and nights turned into weeks, Ashley gave up all hope of rescue and began planning her escape. Unfortunately she was never left alone. Morning Mist became her shadow. Everyone in Running Elk's band seemed in awe of her, even the shaman. They treated her with deference and great respect, which seemed in direct opposition to everything she'd heard or read about Indian captives. Ashley was grateful that Dream Spinner had yet to predict a propitious day for her joining with Running Elk, and hoped the old man would never find one.

Ashley was beginning to pick up a few words of Sioux from Morning Mist, though her heart wasn't in learning the language. The longer she remained with the Indians the more determined Running Elk was to have her. The hard, hungry looks he gave her frightened her. He wanted her — she could see that — and his patience was growing thin. When he lay down beside her at night she could feel the coiled tension within him and the restraint he forced upon himself. She wondered how much longer she could expect him to practice control.

One day Running Elk asked Ashley to use her power to make their hunting foray successful. The band was in desperate need of fresh meat and they hadn't seen game after many days of hunting.

Ashley hesitated. "I can promise you nothing. I am a mortal woman with no supernatural powers."

"Your medicine is strong. Give us your blessing, Flame. The People want to believe in your power but my warriors are becoming disgruntled. They have experienced no good fortune."

"For all the good it will do, you have my blessing," Ashley said.

Running Elk's handsome face broke into a white-toothed smile. "I am grateful, Flame. Once we are joined I will show you how grateful. I am young and vigorous, and when I take you to my mat I will make you sigh with pleasure."

He gave her a heated look, then strode away.

The next day the hunters returned to camp jubilant. They had found game and killed enough elk and deer to last many weeks. That night a great celebration was held to honor the kill. Faith in Ashley's power had been restored. According to Dream Spinner,

Ashley's powerful medicine had been responsible for the bounty provided them by the Great Spirit. After that incident Ashley greatly feared she'd never be allowed to return to her own kind. The next day she tried to escape.

She had planned it carefully. When she went to bathe in the stream the following day, she sent Morning Mist back to their lodge for something she had deliberately left behind. The moment Morning Mist was out of sight, Ashley crossed the shallow stream and took off into the woods. She walked for hours, confused and lost. She was certain she had passed the same landmarks more than once, and indeed she had, for she had been traveling in circles. She had just decided to go back to the stream and follow it to the fort when she saw Running Elk come crashing through the forest astride his pony.

She turned and fled as fast as her legs could carry her but it wasn't fast enough. Swooping down on her like an avenging angel, Running Elk lifted her from her feet and seated her across his lap. Then giving a cry of victory, he wheeled his mount and headed back to camp. Ashley was surprised to find how close they were to the village and how short a distance she had traveled during the long hours she'd been walking. He released her outside their lodge and shoved her inside, following close behind.

"Why did you run, Flame? Have the People harmed you? Are you overworked, mistreated?"

Ashley shook her head. "No. You have treated me well but I wish to return to my husband."

"I will be your husband, Flame. Your powers belong to the People. Because of you our hunt was successful. I will press Dream Spinner to name a day for our joining."

He was angry, Ashley could tell. If she didn't have this cursed red hair Running Elk would have never noticed her that day he stopped the wagon train asking for tolls. He would have taken cattle and been satisfied. She'd always hated her red hair and tried to cover it whenever possible. For years she'd hidden it under bonnets, skinned it back into a severe bun and even tried darkening it with oil. Nothing seemed to work.

"You should not provoke Running Elk," Morning Mist admonished once her brother was gone. "He is determined to join with you."

"Your brother is a fine man," Ashley said carefully, "but I am already married. It is against the law to take more than one husband."

"It is not our way," Morning Mist declared. "You will forget all about your husband once you join with Running Elk. Spring Rain says he pleases her greatly beneath the blankets."

Ashley blushed and looked away. "Then let Spring Rain have him."

"Spring Rain is not a medicine woman. It is you Running Elk wants. Do not be foolish and try to run away again. The forest can be a very dangerous place."

"My power will save me," Ashley said with a hint of sarcasm as she turned away from the gentle Indian maiden.

Morning Mist smiled. "I understand your wish to return to your people, but we are your people now. If the Great Spirit did not wish for you to become one with us he would have sent someone to find you."

Ashley did not have to be told that no one cared enough about her to come after her; she already knew it. But she could hope, couldn't she? She could dream that Tanner wanted her, even if she knew it to be false.

"Dammit, Cole, I swear we've ridden up and down every hill within a hundred miles without encountering a single Indian. Where in the hell are those red devils?"

"I told you, Tanner, they're wily. We haven't looked everywhere. There are still one or two places they could be."

"The Sioux have had Ashley over two weeks. How do you know she's still alive?"

"I don't." Cole didn't want to give Tanner hope where none existed. "But she's my twin. I'd know if she was dead."

Tanner winced, not even wanting to think about Ashley no longer walking the earth. Everything he'd ever loved had been taken from him. If he allowed himself to love Ashley she'd be taken from him too. He'd loved Ellen and look what happened. He'd loved his mother, his father, and they were all victims of a war the Yankees forced on them.

"You must love my sister a great deal," Cole said, aware of Tanner's anguish.

"It's not what you think, Cole. Our marriage, it wasn't . . . That is . . . Oh, hell, I'll let Ashley explain."

Cole didn't need an explanation. No matter what Tanner said, he knew his sister was loved. "You don't like Yankees, do you?"

A coldness settled over Tanner's features. "Yankees are in league with the devil. They've made my life a living hell."

"The war is over, Tanner. I'd done my share of fighting back east before being transferred to Fort Bridger and I hold no grudges."

"Your mother didn't die in your arms in a slave cabin, deprived of food and adequate shelter, her body wasted away to mere skin and bones. Your wife didn't . . . Ah, hell, I don't want to talk about it. Since the war I've made a career of hating Yankees, and doing other things I'm not proud of. I've knocked around from town to town one step ahead of the law, trying to find a place where a blue

133

uniform wouldn't haunt me."

"You and Ashley must have found some common ground. I'd like to think it was love."

"Think all you like, Cole. Our marriage had nothing to do with love. If you must know, Ashley paid me to marry her. Captain Cramer wouldn't let her join his wagon train unless she was married, or accompanied by her parents. She was desperate to reach Fort Bridger and help you clear your name. She found me in jail in St. Joe."

Cole reined his horse to a halt, staring at Tanner in horror. "Ashley had to pay you to marry her?" That was more astounding to Cole than the fact that Ashley had found Tanner in jail.

"In name only," Tanner was quick to add. "And that's the way it's remained. I was to escort her safely to Fort Bridger, and then I'd be free to obtain an annulment. I'm not the marrying kind, Cole. Ashley needs a man who can be a real husband to her."

"How can you be sure you can't give her what she needs? If you were a complete bastard you wouldn't be risking your life for her. Deny it all you want, Tanner, but there's more between you and Ashley than you're willing to admit."

"When I met Ashley I had little to live for. She offered me a helluva lot of money to marry her and I took her up on her offer

134

because I had nothing better to do at the time. And I faced the prospect of going to Federal prison if I didn't. Let's leave it at that."

"If you say so," Cole said, deciding to drop it for the time being. Ashley was twenty-five years old, certainly old enough to know what she wanted and how to go about getting it. If she really wanted the Reb the poor sucker wouldn't have a chance.

Tanner dropped behind Cole, the trail too narrow now to accommodate two horses traveling abreast, and conversation came to a halt. At the edge of a bubbling creek they dismounted to drink and water their horses. Suddenly the horses shied and snorted in fear. Cole lifted his head from the water and tilted his head to listen.

Tanner felt a tingling along his spine as he grasped the dangling reins and tried to bring his mount under control. "What is it?"

"I'm not sure. Let's get the hell out of here." But before they could mount, a half dozen Indians smeared in war paint bounded out of the woods and surrounded them. "Ah, hell," Cole said as his horse's reins were snatched from his hand and he was seized from behind. He glanced over at Tanner and saw that he was in the same dire straits.

"I reckon we were closer to the Indians than we thought," Tanner drawled dryly.

"Let me talk to them," Cole advised. "If

they don't understand English, I know some sign language."

"You'd best talk fast," Tanner warned. "These savages don't seem too friendly."

The Indians started screaming at them and striking them with their weapons as they bound their hands with rawhide thongs. "Running Elk!" Cole cried, hoping to gain their attention. "Take us to Running Elk!"

One of the Indians gave him a hard look but said nothing that made sense. Trying to shake his hands free from the bindings so he could use them to sign with, Cole somehow managed to dislodge his hat. His red hair was like a bright flag amid the dark greenery of the surrounding forest and hills. The Indians drew back in alarm, speaking and gesturing wildly among themselves.

"What in the hell is that all about?" Tanner asked.

"Damned if I know. I hope they're not arguing over who gets my scalp."

Suddenly one of the Indians picked up Cole's hat and jammed it back on his head. "Running Elk," Cole repeated. "Take us to Running Elk."

Grasping the ends of the ropes that dangled from their bound hands, the Indians led Tanner and Cole through the woods to where their mounts were tethered. Leaping upon their horses' bare backs, the warriors jerked the bound men forward, forcing them to trot alongside or be dragged in the dirt behind the animals.

Gasping for breath, Tanner feared he wouldn't live long enough to help Ashley. He had no way of knowing if these savages were from Running Elk's band or belonged to some other fierce tribe. And from the look on Cole's face, he didn't either. If he didn't survive this ordeal, he'd die cursing Yankees. If the army had sent out a patrol as he'd asked, Ashley might now be safe.

Tanner was surprised at how close he and Cole had been to the village. If they hadn't been captured they would have come upon it very shortly on their own. By the time his captors halted, Tanner had fallen several times and been dragged through the dirt. His clothes lay in tatters around his bruised body, his chest was heaving and his face was flushed. Cole appeared to be in the same pitiful condition. Tanner rose clumsily to his feet and saw that he and Cole were surrounded by a ferocious group of dusky-skinned men, women and children.

A murmur went through the crowd, and Tanner looked up to see a sleek, long-muscled Indian striding toward him on lithe, limber legs, naked but for moccasins and a breechclout. One of the braves who had captured them started speaking and gesturing excitedly in a thick, guttural language. A brave nearest Cole pulled his hat off. Suddenly Tanner knew. Cole's red hair. Had they finally found Running Elk? Or more to the point, had Running Elk found them?

Tanner's attention sharpened as he searched the crowd for a face, a face that had become dear to him.

Then he saw her and forgot to breathe.

Curiosity had drawn Ashley from the tipi, where Morning Mist had been instructing her in the Sioux tongue. She had heard the commotion and despite Morning Mist's warning followed the crowd to the center of the camp.

Then she saw him. She felt a stillness form around her as Tanner raised his eyes and met her gaze. He had come. But to what avail? He was as much a prisoner as she. And judging from his swollen flesh and the condition of his clothing, he had not been treated gently.

Her gaze slid to the man beside Tanner, and she cried out in disbelief when she saw the sun reflecting off red hair just a shade darker than her own fiery tresses. Cole! Here! She didn't know how. She didn't know why. What she did know was that Tanner was here and her beloved brother was with him. She wanted to run, to kick up her heels and fly across the dirt, but her legs seemed disinclined to obey. The best she could manage was a sedate walk that led her straight to Tanner and Cole.

Tanner felt his heart quicken when his gaze

met Ashley's. A slow perusal of her face and body assured him that she hadn't been harmed. Her eyes widened slightly when she saw him and for a tense moment their gazes held and clung. Then he saw her look at Cole and Tanner couldn't help smiling at the rapt expression on her face. He'd sell his soul if Ashley felt half as much joy at seeing him as she displayed on catching sight of her brother.

Pushing her way through the crowd, Ashley went first to Cole, crying and hugging him at the same time. Then she went to Tanner, her face wet with tears. Because of the way Running Elk was staring at her, she refrained from touching Tanner. "You came."

He gave her a tender smile. "Did you think I wouldn't?"

"I . . . didn't know. You could have taken my money and disappeared forever."

Tanner frowned. "I could have."

"Who are these men, Flame?" Running Elk's stern voice cut into their tender reunion.

"The one with red hair is my brother. My twin brother. I haven't seen him in many moons. The other man" — she gave Tanner an uncertain smile — "is my husband. He has come with my brother to take me home." Not exactly true; she no longer had a home, but Running Elk didn't need to know that.

Running Elk sent Tanner a venomous glare

that should have warned him. "Flame has no husband. She lives in my lodge and sleeps on my mat. When the moon is full she will join with me."

Slowly Running Elk turned to stare into Cole's face, so like Ashley's it was uncanny. He frowned. "Twins are not regarded with favor by the People. You and your friend must die." He nodded his head and Cole and Tanner were seized and dragged away.

"Wait! You cannot kill them," Ashley cried, clinging to Running Elk's arm. She was desperate; she had to say something, anything, to save Cole and Tanner. "You said my medicine is powerful. I will turn my power against the tribe if you kill my brother and husband. You cannot expect me to stand by and watch my brother and husband die and do nothing. If I am unhappy, your people will suffer."

Running Elk gave Ashley a look that was half fear and half skepticism. Superstition was a large and important part of his culture. If there was any truth to Flame's words he must act with caution. He would ask Dream Spinner's advice on how to proceed.

"I will think on what you have said, Flame. Neither man will be put to death until I have reached a decision." Ashley nearly collapsed with relief. Her relief was short-lived when Tanner and Cole were dragged away and bound to stakes that had in all likelihood held

140

more than one hapless captive.

Once the captives were restrained to his satisfaction, Running Elk hurried off to Dream Spinner's lodge. As soon as he was gone, Ashley rushed to Cole and Tanner, dropping to her knees before them. Morning Mist followed, remaining slightly behind but peeping shyly through lowered lids at Cole.

"Are you all right?" Ashley asked, looking from Cole to Tanner. "I can't believe you're here together. Have the murder charges against you been dropped, Cole? Where is the army? You brought them, didn't you? Are they following behind you? There are people here I have grown fond of; I wouldn't want them harmed."

"People like Running Elk?" Tanner asked harshly. "I didn't know you were partial to savages. Well, don't worry. There is no army behind us. My death will leave you free to marry him. I should have known you'd land on your feet, Yank." Lord, what was wrong with him? He had risked his life to find Ashley and now he was acting like a jealous fool. Ashley thought so too.

"You're a fool, Reb," she bit out. "I have no intention of marrying Running Elk. I already have a husband. A husband crazy enough to come for me without an army at his back. I don't understand everything, but many years ago the shaman had a vision. He saw a red-haired, white-faced woman who would live among them and bring them good fortune. They think I'm that woman. I've been treated well, despite my trying to escape once, and Running Elk's sister has become my friend."

"I hate to break up this friendly chitchat, Ashley, but what are our chances of getting out of here alive?" Though Cole's question was directed at Ashley, he seemed to have eyes only for the lovely Indian maiden standing nearby. "Who is your friend?"

Dragging Morning Mist forward, Ashley said, "Her name is Morning Mist. She is sister to Running Elk. She also speaks tolerable English. Morning Mist, this is my brother, Cole, and the other man is my husband." Morning Mist nodded shyly. "As for getting out of here alive, somehow we will find a way. I will bring you food and water. Running Elk has gone to consult with the shaman about your future."

"Yank." Ashley looked at Tanner, shocked by the anguish visible in his dark eyes. "Are you truly well? Has Running Elk or anyone else harmed you in any way?" She saw the tension in his body, sensed the rage he was feeling and was relieved that she could truthfully tell him she was well.

"I haven't been hurt in any way, Reb. Running Elk's people think I possess some kind of power."

"Thank God."

She turned to Cole. "Are you out of the army now? Have you been completely exonerated?"

"I hate to disappoint you, sis, but I escaped from the stockade. Your husband helped me. When he told me about your abduction, and that the army wouldn't help him find you, I knew I couldn't just sit there and do nothing. I'm an escaped convict and a deserter."

"Oh, Cole, I'm so sorry the way things turned out," Ashley wailed. "I was so desperate to help you clear your name. I knew you weren't guilty."

"I heard how desperate you were," Cole said, sending Tanner an oblique look. "So desperate you went out and bought a husband."

Ashley flushed and looked away. "Let's not get into that now. We've more important things to worry about."

"Running Elk returns," Morning Mist said, touching Ashley's shoulder to alert her. "He does not look happy."

Ashley rose to her feet and waited for Running Elk to approach. She could tell little from his expression, except that he did indeed seem angry.

"Come away," Running Elk said, grasping Ashley's arm and pulling her none too gently away from the men.

"Take your hands off her!" Tanner cried, straining against the rawhide ropes binding him.

"Flame is no longer your woman, white eyes. I am the man who shares her mat each night. She has strong medicine and I have taken it for my own."

Tanner lost the ability to speak. Had the handsome savage taken Ashley against her will? Had he hurt her? "Damn savage bastard!" he shouted, seething with frustration.

Running Elk laughed as he dragged Ashley toward his lodge. When he shoved her through the flap, Tanner howled in outrage.

"Do not fear; he will not harm her," Morning Mist whispered as she scooted away.

"Don't let him goad you," Cole said. "We need our wits about us if we're to survive."

Inside the lodge, Ashley turned on Running Elk, green eyes blazing with fury. "What are you going to do to them?"

"Dream Spinner says your wishes must be honored if we are to receive your good medicine." His sour expression made it clear he wasn't pleased with the shaman's advice. "The white eyes will live, for the present. It has been decided that your brother will join with Morning Mist. He is your twin. He walks in your shadow. Dream Spinner does not believe Shadow Walker possesses your power but he has advised me to keep him within our family. The man with eyes the color of rain clouds before a storm, the one you call husband, will be given to Spring Rain as a slave. Perhaps Thunder Cloud will please her and earn her goodwill."

Ashley went limp with relief. Tanner would live. But at what cost? He would be Spring Rain's slave. Would she want him in her bed?

Chapter Seven

"What in the hell do you think they're doing inside that tipi?" Tanner asked, his eyes wild with jealousy and rage.

"Nothing, I hope," Cole replied in an effort to placate Tanner. "What do you suppose they're going to do with us?"

"We're still alive; that's something."

"But for how long?"

Tanner slumped against the stake, mulling over Cole's words. He'd known it was madness for two men to attempt a rescue, but desperation did strange things to men. Now here he was, as much a prisoner as Ashley, and in danger of losing his life. But what else could he have done after the army refused to help him? Abandon Ashley? He could not.

"Look who's coming," Cole whispered. Tanner lifted his gaze, not at all surprised at the note of admiration in Cole's voice. "It's Morning Mist." Tanner had seen Cole staring at the Indian maiden earlier and it appeared as if his regard was reciprocated.

"I bring food and water," Morning Mist said, kneeling before the men. Though she spoke to both men, her shy smile was for Cole alone.

"Thank you," Cole said, "but our hands

. . ." He shrugged, sending her an apologetic smile. "It seems we cannot feed ourselves."

"I will help you." Morning Mist held the bowl of water first to Cole's lips, then to Tanner's, allowing them to drink their fill. Then she offered chunks of meat from another bowl, picking the pieces up delicately and holding them to their lips so they could grasp them between their teeth.

"Where is Ashley?" Tanner asked between bites.

"Running Elk will not let her come to you. He fears the hold you have over her. If not for Dream Spinner's words of caution he would have ordered you tortured and killed."

"Remind me to thank your shaman when I see him," Tanner said dryly. "You are Ashley's friend; can you not help her escape?"

"I am her friend," Morning Mist admitted, "but I am loyal to my brother. Running Elk is a good man. He will not harm Flame."

"You said Dream Spinner will not allow Running Elk to kill us. What will become of us?" Cole wanted to know. "Somehow I don't think your brother will allow us to go in peace."

Morning Mist's dark, expressive eyes lingered on Cole's face. "I cannot say. It is for Running Elk to tell you. I must go now."

"Thank you for the food, Morning Mist; we are grateful," Cole said, wishing the lovely maiden would stay and talk to him. Her smooth golden face was perfection, her lilting voice excessively pleasing. Her doeskin tunic clung becomingly to her lithe curves, and he could visualize a body as tempting as her face.

Morning Mist rose gracefully. "Wait!" Tanner cried as she turned away. "Is it true that Running Elk shares my wife's bed?"

"For God's sake, Tanner, why torture yourself like this?" Cole admonished. "There's not a damn thing you can do about it."

A cold, altogether too calm expression settled on his face. "Tell me, Morning Mist. I want to know. Does your brother share my wife's bed?"

Morning Mist opened her mouth to speak, thought better of it and merely nodded. Then she turned and scooted away.

"I hope you're satisfied," Cole argued. "You know damn well if Running Elk shares Ashley's bed it's because he's forced her. You're in no position to protest. Besides, you told me yours was an arranged marriage. Why should you care?"

"I'm going to kill him."

Cole shuddered. Tanner spoke with such lethal determination that for a brief moment Cole felt pity for the Indian chief. "You'll have to beat me to it. Twins have a special bond. I will avenge her."

Ashley lay down on her mat but sleep wouldn't come. She knew Morning Mist had brought food and water to Cole and Tanner but she couldn't help worrying about them. Yet she didn't dare go to them for fear of angering Running Elk. It was obvious he was just waiting for an excuse to kill the two men.

Ashley had been stunned earlier when she had recognized the captives as Tanner and Cole. Just the thought that Tanner cared enough for her to risk his life on her behalf sent warmth flooding her veins. She recalled in vivid detail each moment she'd spent with him, wanting yet fearing to take what he offered. She remembered his kisses, the feel of his arms around her, the smell of him. His scent was totally male and utterly intoxicating. He was big and warm, his body hard; his mouth could be soft or demanding, depending upon his mood. She swallowed with difficulty, wishing she could bring back those days on the trail.

Were she given a second chance she would give herself to Tanner, gladly, freely, with great joy, even knowing that they would separate at the end of the trail. If she had learned anything from her association with Tanner it was that she was not a cold, passionless woman. Her fiancé had been wrong. She could still recall Chet Bainter's hurtful words, telling her she was a prude who

149

should remain a spinster. She knew now she wasn't like that. It had just taken the right man to release her passion. Not that the Reb was the right man, she tried to tell herself. He just knew where and how to touch her to wring a response from her.

Suddenly Running Elk ducked through the entrance, filling the lodge with his commanding presence. With trepidation Ashley watched as he came to loom over her, staring at her with those dark, penetrating eyes of his. She feigned sleep but he nudged her with his toe until she responded.

"Morning Mist will join with Shadow Walker. When the sun rises I will take him to the purification lodge so he may prepare himself. My sister is pleased with the match."

"And Tanner?" Ashley's voice shook but she tried not to show her fear. She couldn't bear it if anything happened to the Reb.

"I told you. Spring Rain will have him as her slave."

The thought was ludicrous. Tanner would never stand for such a thing.

Running Elk crouched down beside Ashley, his face etched with longing. "Forget Thunder Cloud. You belong to me. When the sun rises seven times I will take your body. My seed will grow within you and the People will rejoice. Your medicine will flow into me and I will become more powerful than I am."

"No, Running Elk, it is not so," Ashley tried to explain. "I have no power. Dream Spinner was mistaken. It is dangerous to believe in special powers."

Running Elk touched her face with poignant tenderness. "You are the woman of my heart. You will become my strength." He stretched out beside her. "Soon we will become one in body. I can feel my seed building inside me. When I release it inside you, the son we make will have your power."

He lay down beside her but Ashley felt no fear. She was amazed that she could actually admire an Indian. He appeared to be an honorable man who lived according to the code of his people. If he had killed, it was because he had been driven to it by those who invaded his home and decimated his race. She loved Morning Mist like a sister, and the others she'd met weren't the bloodthirsty savages she'd been led to believe. If they were left to hunt and raise their children in harmony with nature, she suspected they would be a peaceful people. But she would not choose to live with them of her own free will. And she didn't want to become Running Elk's wife.

Tanner, his eyes burning with murderous intent, watched as Running Elk emerged from the lodge the next morning, walked a short distance away and urinated against the base of a tree.

"Bastard," he spat from between clenched teeth. He had been too consumed by the thought of Running Elk possessing Ashley's body to sleep last night. He could see the Chief's tipi from his position, and the activities taking place inside Running Elk's lodge ran the gamut of his imagination.

Tanner's outburst wakened Cole. Cole hadn't had any problems sleeping. In fact, his dreams were amazingly peaceful and pleasing. He thought Morning Mist a singular woman, beautiful, graceful, shy; he could go on forever singing her praises. Her golden skin reminded him of warm sunshine and her sleek, black hair and dark eyes held him in thrall. When Tanner cursed again, he asked, "What's going on?"

"I wish to hell I knew. Running Elk just left the tipi. Ashley and Morning Mist are still inside."

"I wish Running Elk would tell us what he's going to do with us and get it over with. Uh, oh, brace yourself," Cole warned. "Here he comes."

Running Elk approached the two men, loathing in his eyes. "You owe your lives to Flame," he said at length. "Dream Spinner says we must appease her lest we turn her medicine against us."

"Are we free to go?" Tanner asked. If Running Elk said yes Tanner vowed to take Ashley with him or die trying.

"You cannot go free. The soldiers at the fort are combing the hills for our village. If I free you, you will lead them to us."

"They will find you eventually," Tanner warned.

"By that time we will have moved our village to another place equally hard to find."

"You won't release us, and you aren't going to kill us, so what are your intentions?" Cole asked.

Suddenly Morning Mist appeared through the opening of the lodge and walked over to them. She stood quietly at her brother's side. Cole couldn't help but smile at her; just looking at her gave him pleasure. She returned his smile, then quickly dropped her gaze.

"Shadow Walker pleases my sister," Running Elk began in a sonorous voice, directing his gaze to Cole. "I have spoken with Dream Spinner. He has suggested a match between you and my sister. When the sun drops below the horizon you will join with her. According to our custom, you will stay seven suns in a honeymoon lodge placed a substantial distance from the village. Upon your return you will be considered husband and wife."

Cole stared at Running Elk as if the chief had just lost his mind. "You want me to marry Morning Mist?" Excitement raced through him. Cole knew the marriage

153

wouldn't be considered legal by white society, but just the thought of having Morning Mist for a short time pleased him immensely.

Running Elk removed a knife from a sheath at his waist and slashed away Cole's bonds. "Come, Shadow Walker, I will take you to the purification lodge. There you will fast and sweat in preparation for the joining."

Cole rose shakily to his feet. He wanted to say something to Morning Mist but it was too late. Running Elk had already sent her away. He watched the graceful sway of her hips until the chief prodded him forward.

"Come, the purification lodge awaits you."

Cole balked. "What about Tanner? You can't keep him tied to a stake like an animal; it's inhuman."

Running Elk's upper lip curled in derision. "I have not forgotten Thunder Cloud. I have given him to Spring Rain. He is to be her slave."

"Who in the hell is Spring Rain?" Tanner roared, living up to the name Running Elk had given him.

Running Elk did not answer as he led Cole to the purification lodge and disappeared inside. Tanner's brow furrowed as he recalled the chief's words. "Who in the hell is Spring Rain?" he repeated, unaware that he had spoken the words aloud.

"She's the wife Running Elk divorced. He

154

says he does me honor by taking me as his only wife."

"Ashley." His head swiveled around to stare into her troubled green eyes. She must have arrived while he was puzzling over Running Elk's words.

Ashley sank to her haunches beside him. "You're to be Spring Rain's slave."

"Like hell! Release me, Yank; no one is watching. We'll leave this cursed place together."

Ashley shook her head. "It won't work. I tried it. They'll catch us. Running Elk will become angry and order your death. We must wait for a better time to escape. Meanwhile, do what you must to stay alive, and when the time comes you must go. Don't worry about me; just go."

Tanner pulled against the ropes binding him, cursing violently. "You sound as if you want to stay with that savage. Is he better than your other lovers? Dammit, Yank, you have no idea the anguish I suffered when I learned you had been abducted by Indians. I've heard some of the things Indians do to female captives and nearly lost my mind imagining them."

"I experienced nothing like that. Running Elk won't harm me."

"Do you enjoy having him rut over you?" Tanner spat irrationally. "You can't marry him; you already have a husband."

"You haven't learned anything, have you, Reb? You're still hotheaded, still stubborn. Nothing has happened between me and Running Elk," she said earnestly. "He hasn't forced me. Dream Spinner has warned him against it. But he doesn't recognize the fact that you and I are married."

"He told me he shares your bed."

"He lies beside me, nothing more."

Tanner gave a snort of laughter. "That's more than I ever did. You've allowed him privileges you denied me."

She swallowed with difficulty. "Ours was a marriage in name only; you knew that."

"Get the hell away from me, lady," Tanner barked. "I knew you were trouble the moment I set eyes on you. I hope you and Running Elk will be very happy together."

Ashley paled. Why couldn't Tanner understand that none of this was her choice? The hotheaded firebrand. Running Elk wasn't entirely convinced that keeping Tanner alive was a good idea. It would take little provocation for him to order Tanner's death.

"Think what you want, Reb, but if you wish to live I suggest you do whatever Spring Rain asks. I still have seven days to think of a way to keep from becoming Running Elk's wife."

"Flame, you must come away," Morning Mist said, rushing forward to pull Ashley away from Tanner. "If Running Elk sees you he will become angry. Come with me; you

156

can help erect the lodge where your brother and I will spend the first seven suns of our life together."

Ashley rose hastily to her feet. "I must go. Don't give up hope. I beg you to do whatever Spring Rain asks."

"Hurry, Flame," Morning Mist urged. "The lodge must be completed by sundown. The others are waiting for us."

After a lingering look at Tanner, Ashley followed Morning Mist away from the village. "Where is your lodge to be erected?"

"Far from the village, where we may be alone."

"Why so far away?"

Morning Mist laughed merrily. "It is the custom for the husband and wife to isolate themselves for the first seven suns after their joining. Your brother and I will be left alone so that we might get to know one another. Our meals will be left for us and we will leave the lodge only to bathe and relieve pressing needs. The women help the bride erect the lodge and take it down after the couple returns to the village. It will be the same for you and Running Elk."

Not if I can help it, Ashley thought but did not say.

Ashley was surprised at the distance they traveled before reaching the site where the lodge was to be erected. They followed the stream for nearly a mile before they arrived. It

157

was a beautiful place, tranquil and totally isolated. She had seen the way Cole looked at Morning Mist and she him, and envied them. But she also worried excessively. It bothered her that Morning Mist would end up losing her heart and being hurt by Cole. Knowing Cole, he wouldn't be satisfied remaining with Morning Mist, away from the white world and his own kind. Cole had had many women. She feared Morning Mist would become but another woman on his list of conquests. And she knew Cole would want to return to civilization and clear his name.

She thought of Tanner and their own marriage. It had been a hurried affair, a desperate attempt to reach Cole when all else had failed. They hadn't liked one another, but both had agreed it was sensible to cast their lot together. When had things changed between them? The first time he'd kissed her, she imagined. The shock of it had left her breathless and wanting more. Tanner wanted more too, but something deep and dark and disturbing kept interfering. Something had made him a bitter man, one who hated with all his heart and soul. If she could but break down the barriers around Tanner's heart she had the feeling she would solve the mystery that kept them apart.

Spring Rain claimed Tanner shortly after Ashley left with Morning Mist. Though she was exotically lovely, Tanner did not want her. Spring Rain slashed his bonds and motioned him to his feet. She uttered a guttural command and prodded him with a stick toward the stream. Several woman followed in their wake, tittering behind their hands. When they reached the bank, Spring Rain motioned for Tanner to enter the water.

Realizing that she wanted him to bathe, Tanner strode into the water in his tattered clothing, more than happy to wash away the dirt and blood encrusted upon his skin. He washed hurriedly and at her command he left the stream. Then Spring Rain began pulling at the remnants of his wet clothes, indicating that he should remove them. Tanner balked. Spring Rain began beating him with her stick. Tanner took the abuse only a few minutes before turning on her. She recognized his rage and cried out for help.

Suddenly a dozen women fell on him, beating him with sticks and fists and rawhide thongs. As strong as he was, Tanner fell beneath their blows. They held him down while Spring Rain tore off his breeches and shirt. Tanner howled in outrage. Then the hands fell away and Tanner jumped to his feet, madder than hell and ready to fight. Unfortunately it wasn't his nature to strike women. Not even rude savages who stared at his male appendage, tittering behind their hands and pointing to different parts of his anatomy.

Clenching his hands at his sides, Tanner appeared as if carved in stone. Not a muscle on his body twitched. Let them look their fill, he thought, gritting his teeth in frustration. After what seemed like hours, Spring Rain moistened her lips with the pink tip of her tongue and sent him a smile he had no difficulty interpreting. Spring Rain wanted him, but he'd be damned if he'd oblige her. Then Spring Rain dug in the parfleche she had carried down to the stream and thrust a breechclout at Tanner. Tanner donned it without hesitation.

The festivities began long before Cole and Morning Mist arrived at the ceremony honoring their joining. Tanner found himself alone with Cole and took advantage of the privacy to whisper a few words of advice. Spring Rain had kept him fetching and carrying all day, beating him with that damnable stick when he didn't move fast enough. If not for Ashley he'd break the stick over Spring Rain's head and take off for the woods.

"Don't worry, Cole; this is no real marriage. It's not legal in our world."

Cole looked strikingly handsome dressed in a soft doeskin shirt and leggings that were richly embroidered in colored thread and extravagantly beaded.

"She's beautiful, isn't she, Tanner?" Cole said, hearing little of what Tanner said. Morning Mist was dressed from head to toe in pure white doeskin. Her black hair hung down her back like an ebony curtain, and her eyes were soft and dreamy.

"Dammit, Cole, listen to me! I know you can't get out of this but don't get romantically involved with Morning Mist. She seems like a sweet girl but she's an Indian. You don't belong in her world and she doesn't belong in yours. Try to remember that somewhere out there is the man who framed you for murder. Ashley came all the way out here to help you clear your name. Keep that in mind when you're bedding Morning Mist, or it will be difficult to extricate yourself when the time comes."

"You don't have to remind me of a damn thing," Cole spat. "Don't you think I know I have no future with Morning Mist? When the time comes to leave, I'll be ready."

Cole walked away, wishing his brother-in-law to hell. Until Tanner reminded him of the bastard who had framed him, he'd felt like any other happy bridegroom anticipating his wedding night.

Tanner watched Running Elk closely during the feasting and dancing. When whiskey was produced, Tanner wondered who had supplied the Indians with the illegal liquor. Probably the same man who sold them guns, he thought with disgust. Tanner wanted to attack Running Elk when he saw the handsome Indian lean toward Ashley and whisper into her ear. Tanner could tell that the Indian was besotted with her. Running Elk couldn't take his eyes or his hands off of her, repeatedly touching her flaming hair with a possessiveness that Tanner found irritating.

The men drank and danced, sometimes joined by the women. When Running Elk leaned over and spoke to Morning Mist, she rose gracefully and held out her hand to Cole. Cole clasped her hand, uncoiled his long frame and followed her away from the village. Tanner looked at Ashley with longing and almost envied Cole his bride. His thoughts scattered when Spring Rain jerked on his arm, urging him toward the lodge they were to share.

Ashley watched Tanner and Spring Rain leave the festivities and tried not to think of the things Spring Rain might demand of Tanner. Did Spring Rain want him in her bed? Did she think him strong and virile? Dear God, imagining Spring Rain and Tanner together intimately turned her stomach. She arose abruptly and fled to her lodge, aware that she and Running Elk would be sharing it alone tonight. The thought was not comforting.

Cole studied Morning Mist in the pale

moonlight and found her more beautiful than any woman he'd ever seen. She stood with him before the tipi they were to share during the next seven days, smiling shyly at him.

"Would you like to bathe?" she asked. Her voice was fragile and uncertain.

He took her hand and led her to the edge of the stream. He was shaking so badly he was afraid to touch her lest she break beneath his large hands. Morning Mist smiled at him and undid the lacing at her shoulders. When the soft cloth fell away, Cole pushed the tunic down her body. It pooled at her feet and she stepped out of it. Cole's swift intake of breath broke the silence of the forest. She was golden all over. Her breasts were small but firm and round, her waist tiny enough for him to span with both hands. Her legs were long, lithe and athletic. The black triangle of hair at the juncture of her thighs was thick and luxurious. Cole looked his fill, unable to speak, too choked to express his appreciation properly.

When Morning Mist began tugging at his shirt with her small hands he made quick work of his own clothing, tossing it aside to join hers. She touched the curling red hair on his chest and giggled. When she nuzzled it with her face, Cole grew instantly hard. She felt his manhood stir against her stomach and stepped back to look at him. Her eyes widened as she visually measured him, wondering if she could take all of him.

"Come," Cole said, taking her hand. "Let's bathe. The cold water will do me good. I fear I'll ravish you if I don't cool down and I don't want to hurt you. Are you a maiden?"

"I have lain with no man," Morning Mist admitted shyly. "It is not forbidden but I felt no desire for a man until I looked upon Shadow Walker."

"I prefer that you call me Cole." He urged her into the stream. She shivered as the elongated tips of her breasts puckered into tight little nubs. Cole noticed and groaned, finding scant relief in the cold water. His erection was still strong and pulsing, his need for the Indian maiden enormous.

They bathed each other. Cole let his hands wander at will over Morning Mist's body, marveling at such perfection. He saw no blemish to mar her loveliness; she saw nothing but strength and power in his muscular frame. With a groan of surrender he pulled her into his arms, taking her mouth with his in a demanding kiss. She trembled in his arms, like a leaf in the wind, accepting the movement of his lips on hers though touching mouths was new to her. When he thrust his tongue into her mouth she moaned and melted further into his embrace.

"So sweet . . . so damn sweet," Cole groaned against her lips. "Do you want me,

Morning Mist? I can't promise that I'll always be here. I want to be honest with you. There are things I must do and one day I will leave. I've been charged with a terrible crime, one I did not commit. My pride demands that I clear my name."

"I want you, Cole," Morning Mist murmured. "I understand pride. I will take you for as long as the Great Spirit allows. But I do not think Running Elk will permit you to leave."

Cole felt the magic of the moment and wished he could stay forever with his lovely Indian maiden, but it could not be. Restoring his good name was too great a need to deny. "We will face my leaving when the time comes. The next seven days belong to us." Lifting her high in his arms, Cole carried her from the stream into their honeymoon lodge. He laid her down on a pallet of buffalo robes, adoring her with his eyes without touching her.

Morning Mist held out her arms and Cole dropped to his knees beside her. Then he worshiped her with his hands and mouth. He loved her gently, tenderly, using great restraint, for passion raged hot and quick within him. When he entered her she stiffened but did not cry out. With a patience that belied his driving need, Cole waited until she grew accustomed to his size and could accept all of him before beginning the slow, tantalizing in-and-out movement that would take them both to that place where rapture reigned. With tender care he brought her to pleasure. When his seed burst forth from his body, he cried out her name.

Tanner entered Spring Rain's lodge and flung himself into the farthest corner. His brooding expression reflected his horror at the way things had turned out. Unless he thought of something fast, Ashley would remain Running Elk's property and he'd belong to Spring Rain. As for Cole, his damn Yankee brother-in-law seemed besotted with Morning Mist, and the longer he remained with the Sioux the more entrenched she'd become in his life. Yes, he definitely had to do something about their situation . . . but what?

Suddenly Spring Rain nudged Tanner with her toe. Tanner glared up at her, surprised to see that she was nude. Her shapely body glistened like warm honey, licked by light from the flames of the dying fire. Tanner looked his fill, surprised that he was so little affected by the inspiring sight. When Tanner failed to respond as Spring Rain wished, she nudged him again and pulled on his arm, pointing to her pallet. It finally dawned on Tanner what she wanted. She wanted him in her bed.

Tanner shook his head. "No!" He knew she understood, for she scowled fiercely. She pulled on him again, and again Tanner denied her. Spring Rain grew livid, screaming at him in her own tongue. Seizing a stick propped against a pole, she began beating him. Tanner's temper snapped. He shoved her hard and plucked the stick from her hand, flinging it aside.

Scrambling to her feet, Spring Rain grabbed her tunic and ran out into the night. Tanner had no idea what she intended to do about his disobedience, but he knew he wouldn't like it. Moments later Running Elk burst through the entrance, followed by Spring Rain and two braves Tanner had seen in the village. Tanner rose to his feet to face his irate captors.

Running Elk scowled at Tanner. "You are Spring Rain's slave. You must do as she asks."

"Like hell!" Tanner roared. "No one can make me bed a woman if I don't want to."

Running Elk translated for Spring Rain. She immediately flew into a rage, speaking rapidly to Running Elk. "Spring Rain wants to know why you do not find her desirable. Is she not beautiful enough? Is her body not to your liking?"

"Spring Rain is very beautiful," Tanner said cautiously. "I'm sure men find her desirable. But as you know, I have a wife, and in my culture married men do not bed other women."

"Pah, you are a slave! You have no rights. You will do as Spring Rain asks."

"No! I will not."

"We have ways to make rebellious slaves docile," Running Elk threatened.

Tanner appeared unmoved. Running Elk spoke at length with Spring Rain. When she nodded in answer to his question, he ordered Tanner seized and dragged outside. Once again Tanner found himself bound to the stake in the center of the village. Only this time he wasn't left alone. People began gathering in a circle around him, casting about for sticks and sharp instruments. Running Elk gave a harsh command and the people fell upon Tanner, beating him and poking him unmercifully.

Suddenly Tanner caught a movement from the corner of his eye. He watched in horror as Ashley pushed and shoved her way through the crowd, taking some of the blows meant for him.

"Stop!" she commanded. Her voice was shaking but loud and clear as she stood protectively in front of Tanner. "If you hurt him I will turn my medicine against you."

Chapter Eight

Running Elk glared menacingly at Ashley. "Out of the way, woman."

Her eyes turned as darkly threatening as the storm clouds rolling in from the west. "No, your people will kill Tanner if you don't make them stop."

"Perhaps it is well that he should die at their hands. Once he has walked the spirit path you will not pine for him, and you will accept me as your husband."

"I will use my medicine against you," Ashley warned.

"Don't interfere, Yank," Tanner cautioned. "Don't make them turn against you."

Ashley glared at him. "Don't tell me what to do, Reb." She turned back to Running Elk, her firm little chin raised in challenge. "Well, which will it be? Harm Tanner further and suffer my wrath or let him go in peace and receive my goodwill?" Being some sort of lucky charm should have its advantages, she thought as she delivered her ultimatum.

Running Elk's eyes narrowed. He didn't like being dictated to. What if Dream Spinner was wrong about Flame? What if she was merely a white captive with no powers? What if she was making a fool of him and his generosity?

Abruptly the approaching storm burst across the night skies in a daunting crash of booming thunder. Bolts of jagged light pierced the sky, emerging from bloated dark clouds and streaking earthward in a brilliant display. The People shifted restlessly and looked with longing toward their lodges. When a jagged bolt of lightning struck a nearby tree an outrageous idea occurred to Ashley.

"Your God is angry because you doubt my powers," she cried, gesturing toward the heavens. "You will all perish if you do not heed me. My medicine is strong. You must free my husband, Running Elk, or suffer the consequences."

As if to reinforce her words another lightning bolt struck so close the earth around them shook. Then the sky opened and a deluge of rain poured down upon them. The People cried out in fear and scattered to the safety of their lodges. All except Dream Spinner, Spring Rain and Running Elk, who stared at Ashley with a mixture of fear and anger.

"Why did you not heed my warning, Running Elk?" the shaman asked of his chief. "You have angered Flame and now the Great Spirit must be appeased. What did she say to you?"

"Flame says the Great Spirit is angry and we must release Thunder Cloud if we wish to keep her goodwill," Running Elk explained. "She says that if I force her to join with me she will use her power against the People."

Dream Spinner stared uncertainly at Ashley. In all his years he had never encountered such awesome power. "We must not anger Flame. Indulge her until Grandfather tells you what to do. You must go on a vision quest. You will rend your flesh and offer tobacco to the four directions. Grandfather will reveal his wishes to you."

Ashley didn't know what Dream Spinner said but she could tell Running Elk wasn't pleased.

"What about Thunder Cloud? Does he live or die?"

"He must live."

"What did Dream Spinner say?" Ashley demanded to know.

Running Elk turned on her, his eyes dark pools of rage. "He says Thunder Cloud will live until Grandfather reveals his wishes to me. He says the Great Spirit is angry and must be appeased. I go now on a vision quest. I will not return until the Great Spirit gives me an answer through a vision."

Ashley nearly collapsed with relief. She had just been granted a reprieve. "Did I not tell you so? Are we to be freed?" she asked hopefully.

"You will remain here. Do not use my absence as an opportunity to escape. You will be watched and guarded. Nothing will happen to you, Flame. If the Great Spirit wills, you will still be mine."

"Tanner is my husband. I will not accept you in his place."

Tanner gasped, amazed at Ashley's courage. Did the fool woman have no sense? Most women forced into captivity would have been driven to obedience long ago. But not his Yankee wife. She had persevered and triumphed, wielding authority as if she truly possessed a mysterious power.

"Is it not enough that Thunder Cloud will live?" Running Elk shouted.

"Thunder Cloud is mine," Spring Rain said to Running Elk. "You gave him to me."

Ashley sent her a look of utter disdain and then ignored her. "I am taking my husband to my lodge. If you stop me, Running Elk, I will use my power to bring disaster down upon your people." It was an empty threat but Running Elk did not know it.

The look of raw hostility Running Elk bestowed upon her gave her pause for thought. Had she gone too far? For a moment she could see loathing in the fathomless depths of his dark eyes. She realized it must be difficult for a man with Running Elk's fierce pride to accept that a mere woman possessed such awesome power.

"For God's sake, don't provoke him!" Tanner warned. "You've got more courage than brains. He said he wouldn't kill me; let it go at that."

Tanner strained furiously against the rawhide strips binding him. Dampened by rain, they had tightened painfully, biting into his flesh until blood ran down his wrists.

Ashley's chin rose to a defiant angle. She had gone this far; she wouldn't back down now. "If you do not do as I say I will beckon the lightning down from the sky." Oh, God, what had made her tell such an outrageous lie?

A hissing sound came from Tanner's throat. "Dammit, Ashley, you're asking for trouble."

"I'm not going to leave you out here, Tanner, or let Spring Rain have you. And I'll be damned if I'm going to become Running Elk's wife, so please be quiet. I've had about all I can take of submissiveness."

Running Elk directed a scornful gaze at the lowering sky, not at all convinced that Ashley held the power to call down lightning. "I do not fear you, Flame. Soon I will plant my seed in you, and you will become submissive to me."

"Over my dead body," Tanner growled beneath his breath.

Then something so incredible happened that if Tanner hadn't seen it, he wouldn't have believed it. A roar of thunder shook the ground. Lightning illuminated the sky and earth below it. Ashley raised her arm and a jagged bolt of raw fire snaked earthward from a menacing black cloud. Almost immediately a tipi burst into flame, sending its occupants spilling out into the rain. Both Running Elk and Dream Spinner stared at Ashley in sudden fear. Spring Rain was so frightened she threw up her hands and ran to her lodge.

"No more, Flame!" Running Elk cried. He pulled his knife from its sheath and slashed downward at Tanner. Ashley cried out, certain he meant to kill Tanner. Then Tanner pulled free of his bonds and she realized that Running Elk had merely cut away the ropes. "He is yours; take him. I no longer wish to join with you. When I go into the hills, Grandfather will tell me through a vision what course to take where you are concerned. Perhaps your medicine is so powerful you should be destroyed. You will be guarded day and night. If you are foolish enough to try to leave the village, my people will risk Grandfather's wrath and bring you back."

Ashley held her breath as Running Elk turned and strode through the pounding rain toward the hills, taking nothing with him but the medicine bag he wore around his neck and his knife.

"We must leave now, while the People still fear your power," Tanner hissed into her ear.

He grasped Ashley's hand, dragging her toward the line of trees surrounding the village.

He hadn't taken a dozen steps when several armed warriors appeared from nowhere and surrounded them. They used their rifles to force them back to the village. When they reached Ashley's lodge, she grasped Tanner's arm and pulled him inside. His expression rivaled the storm raging around them.

"Dammit, Yank, you shouldn't have angered Running Elk. If you're so important to these savages, why can't you persuade them to let us go?"

"They think I bring them good fortune," Ashley said between bouts of shivering. "But I think you're right about Running Elk. He doesn't know whether to fear me or treat me as he would any other captive."

"Little fool," he muttered. Suddenly he became painfully aware of the way her wet doeskin tunic clung to her body, revealing every lush curve and indentation. "You're going to catch your death if you don't get out of those wet clothes. I'll build up the fire."

He knelt before the small fire burning in the center of the tipi and added a handful of sticks. The smoke hole had been closed to keep out the rain, and soon a fragrant blue haze wrapped them in a cozy cocoon of intimacy. Already aroused by her nearness, Tanner stared at Ashley and was pleased to find her gaze resting on him.

Ashley's eyes drifted over Tanner's body. His upper torso glistened with moisture. A diffused golden glow licked over his muscular chest and shoulders. His breechclout clung damply to the impressive contours of his loins, and Ashley watched in awe as the corded tendons of his masculine thighs and legs tensed reflexively. Ashley's mouth went dry and she tried to look away but couldn't.

"I'll get us a couple of blankets." She unrolled the pallets, removed two blankets and handed one to Tanner. When she tried to untie the rawhide laces of her tunic, her fingers were suddenly too numb to undo the knots.

"Here, let me," Tanner said, dropping the blanket and brushing away her hands.

His hands were nearly as clumsy as hers and it took a long time before the knots were freed. His sudden intake of breath was nearly as loud as hers when his hands rested on the bare flesh of her shoulders. She felt blasted by the heat of his palms resting on her skin and made no effort to escape as Tanner brought her against him. One of his large hands wound firmly around her slender waist and his other tangled in her hair. His mouth came down on hers. He tasted rain and an essence uniquely hers, headier than the most potent whiskey. He licked along the seam of her lips, sucking her pouty lower lip, then probing for the entrance with the hard tip of his tongue. Ashley went rigid; then she sighed in pleasure and opened her lips beneath his, drawing his tongue into her mouth.

Tanner groaned and slid his hands down her hips to cup her buttocks, wanting, needing to feel every inch of her against every inch of him. His kiss deepened; his mouth slanted over hers as his tongue probed intimately. Fire erupted inside Ashley and she kissed him back, stunned by the yearning pleasure he was giving her.

"You scared the hell out of me tonight," Tanner said as his hands slid over her buttocks and lower, his long fingers curving into the apex of her thighs. She was so hot there he could feel the moist heat of her through her tunic. Suddenly he cursed impatiently and grasped the hem of her tunic.

"I want you naked. Dammit, Yank, no savage is going to have you. I might die for this but no one is going to stop me from making you mine."

Ashley clutched his head between her hands, wanting him as much as he wanted her. The rake of his stubbled cheeks against her palms aroused her. The smell of rain mixed with his sweat. She felt the thrust of his sex against his breechclout. She might never be with him like this again. When the Indians released them, Tanner would go his own way, harboring his deep, dark secrets, leaving her with only this one night to remember him by.

Emboldened, she drew his head down and kissed him, using her tongue to explore his mouth, moaning when he sucked her tongue deep into his mouth. The heat inside her grew hotter, brighter, until she ached with it. She smiled at him and raised her arms so that he could lift the tunic over her head.

"I want you, Tanner. Make me yours."

With shaking hands Tanner lifted her tunic over her head and tossed it aside. He closed his eyes, afraid to look at her, afraid if he did he wouldn't be able to curb the fire raging inside him. He'd wanted the little Yank for so long that if he wasn't inside her soon he'd explode. He pulled her hard against him, trailing hot kisses along the sensitive skin of her ear and neck, nipping, then licking the tiny love bites to soothe them.

Ashley turned to liquid fire in his arms, feeling a wildness she hadn't known she possessed. Tanner thrust his hips into the cradle of her thighs, letting her feel his hunger, his desperate need. Trusting him completely, Ashley felt no fear. He filled her with a heady sense of awe, purely tempting and utterly engrossing. She hovered on the verge of a great discovery and Tanner was the only man with whom she wanted to share that enlightened moment.

"Tanner . . ." She wanted to tell him how

wonderfully alive he made her feel but couldn't find the words.

"Don't tell me to stop, love; it's too late."

Much too late, Ashley silently agreed as she rubbed herself against him in shameful need. Her tender nipples scraping against the rough, hair-covered ridges of his chest sent intense pleasure licking along her spine, and the sensitive place between her thighs wept to feel the thick, thrusting length of him. Her legs buckled and he lowered her down to the pallet.

Kneeling beside her, his smoldering gaze raked her from head to toe, and when he stripped away the breechclout, Ashley felt a shattering sensation deep within her. She was oblivious to everything but the magnificent power of his aroused sex and the rushing of blood in her ears that followed. The world nearly stopped when Tanner covered her with his body, melding them together from breastbone to thigh. His sharp exhalation of breath exploded sweetly against her cheek.

"Forget your other lovers, Yank. I know you're a woman of experience but tonight you're mine."

Ashley went still. She recalled telling Tanner she was experienced, and of course he would assume that she meant sexual experience. In matters of love she was as innocent as a babe, unless one counted those passionless kisses she'd shared with Chet, and those rather heated moments in Tanner's arms on the trail. But having Tanner's magnificent body, so hard, so heavy, so needy, weighing her down was so marvelously arousing, she didn't care what he thought.

Then he was kissing her again, fevered, passionate, his hands sweeping over her breasts and teasing her nipples. His tongue parted her lips, savaged her mouth, tasted and hungered for more. His lips blazed a trail of fire down her neck to her breasts, where her erect nipples beckoned the heat of his mouth. He sucked and licked those ripe fruits until Ashley thought she'd go mad with wanting. When he slid his hands between their bodies and into the flaming triangle between her legs, she jerked convulsively.

One callused finger parted slick, silken folds and thrust inside. The scalding heat of her intensified his raging hunger. "You're so wet, love," he whispered huskily. "And tight, oh, God, so tight." His finger slid deeper. He dipped his thumb into her heat, then stroked the moisture over the sensitive hidden nub he found there as he continued thrusting his finger and withdrawing, thrusting and withdrawing.

When he lowered his head and nuzzled the lush triangle between her legs, Ashley cried out in protest. "What are you doing?"

"Have none of your lovers tasted you?"

Unable to speak, Ashley shook her head.

The world seemed to hold still as he removed his finger and replaced it with his mouth, laving the sensitive folds of skin with his tongue. His lips and tongue worked a devil's magic on her as they caressed some hidden spot she never knew existed, driving her toward some mysterious goal.

"Tanner . . . I want . . . I want . . ."

He raised his head and smiled at her. "I know. And you're going to have exactly what you want. What we both want. I can feel your body quivering. Those tiny bursts inside you drive me wild. Dear God, Ashley, I've never wanted a woman as badly as I want you. If I'm not inside you soon I'm going to embarrass myself. But I haven't had my fill of you yet."

She had no idea what he meant as his mouth returned to torture her. He parted her slick folds with his tongue and thrust into her heated depths. Scant moments later she went rigid. A ragged cry tore from her throat. The very first climax of her life convulsed her, frightening her with its scope and intensity. Tanner was in agony as she writhed and twisted beneath him, the musky scent of sex driving him wild.

"What happened?" she asked in a choked voice when reality returned.

"Hasn't anyone loved you like this before?" When she shook her head, Tanner laughed and said, "I'm surprised you didn't seek more inventive lovers."

"Tanner," Ashley began, "about those lovers. I . . ."

Tanner placed a finger against her lips. "No. I don't want to hear about them. Tonight I'm your only lover."

"But, Tanner . . ."

He shushed her with a long, lingering kiss. "No, love, just concentrate on me." He took her hand, bringing it to his loins. "Take me in your hand." She curled her fingers around him. He let out a long, drawn-out sigh and grew even harder. "I can't ever recall being this aroused. Only for you, love, only for you." He nudged her thighs apart and settled between them. "Open for me, Yank. No matter what tomorrow brings, tonight is ours. I intend for us both to enjoy it."

He pulsed against her palm and Ashley was awed by his size and strength. He was hard as steel, and big, so big. Surely too big for her. On the other hand she had never felt anything so soft to the touch. Velvet on steel. The combination was incredibly erotic. She stared up at him and their gazes locked. He smoothed a strand of hair back from her brow as his eyes searched her face.

Was that a hint of fear he detected in her expression? Surely not, he scoffed. For a woman of experience, Ashley seemed incredibly naive.

"Guide me inside you, love," Tanner urged raggedly.

A hand slid between her legs and his fingers opened her. His other hand sought hers and curled it around him, letting her guide him to the very portal of paradise. Her hand fell away as he slowly pushed inside her, stretching her, filling her, until she thought she would rip apart. She wanted to scream. She couldn't do this. He was too big. She was too small. Oh, God, she wanted him, even if it killed her!

Unaware of her distress, Tanner kissed her, his tongue delighting and distracting her, pushing into her mouth in the same way he was shoving himself deeper inside her from below. The pain of his entry worked its way through the haze of her pleasure and she stiffened, dragging her mouth from his. Her eyes registered panic and her mouth opened in a silent scream. She'd expected it to hurt but not like this. She struggled in an effort to escape the torture he was inflicting upon her.

Tanner went still, his eyes blank with disbelief. "Why didn't you tell me?"

"T-tell you what?"

"You've never had a man. You're as pure as the day you were born." He cursed long and fluently.

"It doesn't matter. It . . . it's not so bad." She nearly choked on the lie. It hurt like hell.

"It's going to get better, I promise."

His hand slid between their dew-damp bodies, touching and teasing that place that

183

was the font of her pleasure. She felt a rush of moisture to her loins and then the deep slide of his staff inside her as he broke through her barrier. She exhaled sharply. The pain was still there, but somewhat blunted, more like a burning and stretching sensation.

He cupped her face and kissed her, simply resting inside her as she adjusted to accommodate him. His control was tested to the limits as he forced his body to a stillness that was more agony than pleasure.

"Are you all right, Yank?"

Ashley gave him a wobbly smile. "I'll survive. What now? What happens next?"

"Oh, God, I thought you'd never ask."

He moved ever so gently, the merest shifting of his hips that brought him deeper inside her. Ashley's eyes flew open in unexpected pleasure and she pressed upward against him and held her breath, waiting for the pain. There was none.

"How does that feel, Yank?"

"It feels . . . very . . ."

"Good?" He flexed his hips and she tightened around him. Her tight passage was doing incredible, erotic things to him.

Ashley sighed. "Yes, very good. No, better than good."

She lost the ability to breathe when he thrust, withdrew and thrust again.

"Oh, Tanner . . ."

"Should I move faster? Slower? Tell me,

love. Tell me what you want."

"I want . . . I want . . . both. Oh, please, Tanner, don't torture me." His sensual assault was driving her insane. She reached for him, tracing the hard muscle and bone beneath his hair-roughened skin. She felt him shudder and grew bolder, sliding her hands around to grasp his buttocks.

Tanner groaned as if in pain. "What I'm doing to you is nothing compared to what you're doing to me, Yank."

At once his thrusts grew harder, faster, violent pleasure feeding his need to bring them both to throbbing culmination. He suckled her breasts and she responded, touching him in places that excited him unbearably. His thrusts grew frenzied. Wilder. Higher. Sinking into her again and again, his breath exploding from his chest, Tanner felt his seed rising and knew there was no stopping it now. He had waited for Ashley beyond the point of human endurance.

A buzzing began in Ashley's head as sweet, hot pleasure spiraled through her, sweeter than any she'd ever known. Her loins were on fire as Tanner stroked her into a frenzy of chaotic splendor. Vaguely she wondered how he could sustain such intense concentration.

"Oh, God, Ashley, I can't wait! Hurry; I don't want to leave you."

He plunged wildly, his whole body vibrating. Ashley feared she couldn't reach the goal she strove for, but incredibly she did. Her climax burst upon her in a tumultuous clash of flesh on flesh, of pounding loins and violent tremors. A series of swift contractions against his sex triggered Tanner's release. Their hearts thundered in unison. He thrust one last time, called out her name and filled her with his seed. Sapped of energy, he collapsed atop her and lay there panting. Incredibly, in the center of his tumultuous climax was peace. After a few minutes he slid down beside her.

Ashley wanted to hold him close, to keep him fast in her arms and never let him go, but she knew he would never stand for that. Something dark and dangerous drove him, and until he came to grips with his demons, he'd never accept her love.

"Why did you save my life out there?" Tanner asked. "Running Elk is dangerous; you could have turned him against you. I've never known a woman like you, Yank. You have more courage than sense."

"I can't explain it. I just knew I couldn't let you die. Or permit Spring Rain to have you. You are my husband, even if our marriage was for all the wrong reasons and likely to be of short duration."

"Are you sorry we made love?" Tanner asked at length. "You should have saved your virginity for the man who will eventually be your life partner. I thought you were experienced, otherwise I wouldn't have taken you." That wasn't exactly the truth. Nothing could have stopped Tanner from making Ashley his. Wanting Ashley so desperately had shot his resistance all to hell. Not that he had much where she was concerned.

Instantly defensive, Ashley thought he was reminding her that their marriage was one of convenience, and that he'd soon be gone from her life. "Don't worry, Reb. My word is good. Once we get out of this mess you're free to go your own way. We'll get an annulment and you can forget this part of your life. What happened just now happened because I wanted it to. No regrets, no recriminations."

For some unexplained reason her words offered Tanner little comfort. Of course he wanted an annulment, didn't he? That was their agreement, wasn't it? He had no right to happiness. Loving hurt. Loving was dangerous. There was nothing in this world he hated worse than Yankees.

And Ashley was a Yankee.

Tanner forced a grin. "No regrets, no recriminations. I'm glad you feel that way. Will you go back to Chicago when we leave here?" It didn't cross Tanner's mind that they might not leave Running Elk's village alive.

Ashley shook her head. "There's no reason to return to Chicago. Cole and I haven't had the opportunity to discuss the future. I'd like for us to settle in Oregon."

"Cole seems entranced with Morning Mist. What if he doesn't want to leave her?"

Ashley sent him a startled look. "I don't know. It never occurred to me that he wouldn't."

"It's a possibility you might want to consider. If you return to Chicago I'll see that you reach there safely. It's the least I can do."

"I can manage on my own, thank you." Her curt reply made Tanner realize how callous he'd sounded. But she'd known the kind of man he was before she asked him to marry her. He was a hotheaded Reb. He was bound to bring her heartache if they didn't part as they had planned.

"Have you noticed that whenever we attempt civilized conversation we seem to hurt one another?"

"I've noticed." She turned on her side to look at him. "What do you suppose we should do about it?"

"I think," Tanner said, his voice low and seductive, "that we should forget conversation and do something we both enjoy."

Ashley swallowed convulsively. "What is that?"

"Why don't you let me show you?"

Chapter Nine

Ashley blinked up at Tanner; she felt her throat go hot and hollow. His sharply chiseled features held a hungry yearning that she knew was reflected in her own eyes. What had happened between them moments ago had been beautiful beyond words. They were mismatched in everything except the pleasure they gave one another. She'd had no idea making love could be such an earth-shattering experience. Tasting his kisses and feeling his hardness inside her made her tremble with desire. If this was all she would have of Tanner she would live it intensely, so that she could look back on the memory when he was gone.

Tanner's stomach clenched when he saw his own hunger reflected in Ashley's eyes. He groaned and swept her up in a kiss that scalded, plundered and stormed her senses. Her mouth opened beneath his, inviting the rough stroking of his tongue.

He took her slowly, caressing, teasing, kissing every part of her body, his hands, mouth and tongue moving restlessly over her lush curves. With a boldness she would have never imagined with any other man, Ashley returned his caresses with avid and breathless anticipation.

"Touch me, Yank," Tanner rasped against her mouth when she deliberately avoided that part of him that had grown hard as marble.

Without hesitation she reached for him, holding him in her hands, testing his hardness and length and reveling in his strength. She gasped in pleasure when he flipped suddenly, lowered her slowly onto him and slid full and deep inside her. Tiny hidden muscles contracted around him and Tanner knew an almost painful kind of pleasure.

"Ride me, love. Ride me to glory and back."

Glory didn't adequately describe that place Tanner took her. Arching her back, she rode him furiously, tossing her glorious mane of flaming hair from side to side as her body moved wantonly upon his. She came in a rush of sweet liquid fire that brought sensations, one tumbling upon another, until her entire body convulsed with them. Bathed in the sweet essence of her passion and embraced tightly by her pulsing sheath, Tanner exploded, the violence of his climax lifting him off the pallet.

Collapsing atop him, Ashley could not speak for several minutes. She saw that Tanner suffered from the same affliction. His chest rose and fell sharply as he fought for each shallow breath. When she tried to lift herself away from him he held her fast, wanting to hold himself within her as long as possible. Not until he softened and slipped from her body did he lift her and lay her down beside him on the pallet.

"That was . . . I didn't know." Ashley sighed dreamily.

"I'm glad I was the first to show you." He pulled her into the curve of his body and curled himself around her.

"It stopped raining," Ashley observed sleepily. She started to rise.

"Where are you going?"

"To open the smoke hole."

"Lie still. I'll do it."

After adjusting the smoke flap with a long pole used for that purpose, Tanner poured water from a water bag into an earthen bowl, found a soft deerskin cloth and returned to Ashley's side. Her eyes widened as he spread her legs.

Her thighs clenched reflexively. "What are you going to do?"

"Just relax and let me wash you. We've made love twice; you're sticky with virgin blood and my seed."

Ashley's face flamed. "I can do it."

Ignoring her, Tanner spread her knees wider and gently cleansed away all traces of their joining. Then he used the cloth on himself. "You'll probably be sore tomorrow," he said as he felt her eyes on him. "I would have been gentler the first time had I known you were a virgin. You were foolish not to tell me."

Ashley grew thoughtful as she watched moonlight dance through the smoke hole and listened to crickets hum their song. At length she asked, "Would it have made any difference?"

Tanner hesitated for the space of a heartbeat. "Probably not. Frankly, I don't think any man ever wanted a woman as much as I wanted you."

Ashley's mouth went dry. "Lust is a powerful emotion," she responded lightly.

For some reason her words seemed to upset Tanner. There was more than lust involved here; he just wasn't sure what to call it. "Go to sleep, Yank. It's going to take all our ingenuity to get us out of this mess."

Ashley tried to settle down, truly she did, but too many questions about Tanner demanded answers. Something in his past had embittered him to the point where he didn't give a damn about life or himself. She understood war and the terrible trauma men suffered because of it, but Tanner was too strong a man to brood over something he could not change. No, there was more to it than that; there was something too disturbing for him to forget or forgive. Had he been a prisoner? He'd mentioned that his home had been destroyed but offered little else.

Since her mind refused to accept sleep,

192

Ashley decided to assuage her curiosity. "Tanner?"

"Hmmm?"

"Are you sleeping?"

"Not anymore. Is something wrong?"

"Not really. Tell me about yourself. I know so little about you."

A long silence ensued. "I'm a Reb. What more do you need to know?"

"I know you hate Northerners because of the war, but there's more to it than that, isn't there?"

"I don't want to talk about it. Don't ruin a perfect experience by opening old wounds."

"What kind of wounds? Were you hurt in the war?"

"Those wounds healed long ago. Go to sleep, Ashley."

"Why do you hate Pratt Slater so much? What did he say to you to make you want to kill him?"

"You won't let it rest, will you? Very well, I'll tell you. Slater led the patrol that burned my home to the ground. My mother was forced to live through the winter in an abandoned slave hut with little food and no heat. She died in my arms the day I arrived home to recuperate from a wound suffered in battle."

"No wonder you hate Yankees."

He laughed harshly. "There's more to it than that, Ashley, but I won't bore you with the gory details."

Ashley blinked. "More? What could be worse than that?"

"Go to sleep, Yank."

Ashley realized she wasn't going to get any more information from Tanner tonight. The deep, dark secret he harbored was going to remain his alone. Closing her eyes tightly, she drifted off to sleep. Sometime later — it could have been minutes, it could have been hours — Tanner began thrashing and muttering in his sleep. Awakened by the sound of his voice, Ashley turned toward him, wondering whether or not to nudge him awake. Suddenly his words began to make sense and she paused to listen.

"No! Put the gun down, Ellen. For God's sake don't do it! I swear it doesn't make any difference to me. I love you."

He thrashed wildly and cried out the woman's name over and over. Dimly Ashley wondered if his mother's name was Ellen, but something told her it wasn't his mother he called for so desperately. And the gun. What did it mean? It could only mean one thing, Ashley decided. Tanner loved another woman. Loved her so much she haunted his dreams. Suddenly Tanner jerked violently and the thrashing stopped as abruptly as it had begun. He made a noise that sounded suspiciously like a sob before settling into a deep sleep.

Ashley was not so lucky. She wanted to

comfort Tanner, to tell him she would help him with whatever troubled him. She wanted to assure him that he would have his annulment after they reached civilization so he could return to his Ellen. What they had just done here tonight had no bearing on their separate futures. Making love was something they had both wanted. Unfortunately it had meant more to her than to him. It hurt to think that Tanner was thinking of a woman named Ellen after making love to her.

Despite her confused thoughts her eyes grew heavy and she fell asleep.

Ribbons of sunlight streamed through the smoke hole and stabbed against Tanner's eyelids. He blinked and opened his eyes. He was somewhat surprised, pleasantly so, to find his hand filled with a firm, warm breast. Ashley. He turned his head and stared at her. He could find no words to describe her beauty. And to think he had once thought her plain. Her flaming hair rivaled the most glorious sunset; it was no wonder the Indians considered her a goddess.

They had come together last night in mutual need, but he knew better than to read more into it than that. Ashley didn't want a Reb husband any more than he wanted a Yankee wife. Or any wife, for that matter. He had loved Ellen, always would, and he was still haunted by the unspeakable event that

195

had robbed him of a future with her.

Damn all Yankees to hell, most especially Pratt Slater!

Tanner hoped Slater had succumbed to his injuries and that he now rested in hell, where he most definitely belonged.

"Tanner, what is it? Is that fierce expression for me?"

Tanner started violently. He hadn't realized that Ashley had woken. She was staring at him with a mixture of curiosity and fear. He eased his features into a semblance of a smile. "Why would I be angry at you?"

She flushed. "When we're not making love you're always angry with me."

"I'm not angry now. Would you like to bathe? Running Elk's people shouldn't object to our going down to the stream. Then we'll see what's available to eat. My appetite is enormous this morning."

Two braves trailed them down to the stream. When they separated, Tanner going to the men's bathing place and Ashley to the women's, both braves followed Tanner, leaving Ashley free to bathe in private. She returned to the lodge before Tanner. He arrived sometime later, carrying a rabbit one of the braves had bagged with an arrow. Ashley gathered the ingredients for stew and set the pot over the cooking fire. Then she mixed cakes of ground corn and set them on hot stones to bake.

"Do you think Running Elk's vision will help us or hurt us?" Ashley asked when Tanner joined her later for their meal.

"Damned if I know. We should be prepared for any eventuality. It might be best if we weren't here when he returns."

"Do we have a choice?"

"There are always choices. We should make plans just in case."

"What about Cole?"

"He's a big boy; he can take care of himself."

They ate in silence. Tanner studied the layout of the village while he chewed, casting about for the best route of escape. He couldn't swear he'd find the way back to Fort Bridger without Cole but he sure as hell would try. Late night would be the best time, he decided, to slip past the guards. They had to sleep sometime.

Ashley was clearing away the remnants of the meal when a commotion at the edge of the village caught her attention. At first she thought Running Elk had returned already, and then she saw a white man riding into the village on a big bay horse, leading two packhorses.

Tanner was already on his feet, striding toward the knot of people gathering around the man and his horses. Ashley was close on his heels. The man was signing with his hands when they arrived, more than a little upset upon learning that Running Elk was not there.

"Can't anyone here speak English?" he asked, exasperated when his signing proved inadequate for his needs. Then he spied Tanner, but his gaze lingered on him only a few seconds before settling appreciatively on Ashley. His eyes widened as he stared at her hair, then his gaze slid down her body with almost insulting intensity.

"Well, well, who are you, missy?"

Tanner moved protectively in front of Ashley. "Who are you?"

"Harger's the name. Jake Harger. Been trading with Running Elk for a couple of years now."

"Trading what?" Tanner asked harshly. "Contraband?" The bundles on Harger's packhorses looked suspiciously like rifles, a strictly forbidden trading commodity.

Harger's eyes narrowed. "Who in the hell are you to question me? Where is Running Elk? My business is with the chief."

"Running Elk has gone on a vision quest. We're . . . guests here."

It was obvious Harger didn't believe him. "Guests?" He scratched his thatch of limp brown hair. It was dirty and looked as if it hadn't been combed or washed in weeks. Of medium height, his age somewhere between thirty and forty, Harger still wore the filthy remnants of a blue army uniform. "That's a

198

new one on me. I've never known Running Elk to invite white guests to his village." He stared hard at Ashley. "Course I could see why he'd want you, missy. As for your friend, he don't strike me as an Injun lover."

Dream Spinner hobbled up to them, tugged on Harger's sleeve and pointed to his lodge. "I gotta go powwow with the shaman. When I'm finished maybe you and me can . . . talk," Harger said to Ashley.

"My *wife* isn't interested in talking with you," Tanner retorted in a voice that sent Harger's eyebrows shooting upward.

"Wife? This whole situation don't smell right to me. Think I'll wait around for Running Elk to return." After giving Ashley a lingering glance that made her cringe in revulsion, he joined the shaman.

Cole's gaze lingered on Morning Mist. He wished he didn't have to leave his bride, but he knew that one day he must. The first day of their honeymoon had come and gone and they lay in each other's arms now, sated after a heated bout of lovemaking. "Where did you learn English?" he asked her.

"My mother was white."

Cole looked at her with surprise. "White? That's something you never mentioned. Was she a captive?"

"My father, Crazy Wolf, captured her during a raid and took her as his wife."

"So Running Elk is only your half brother."

"True. But my mother taught us both the white man's tongue; that is why we speak it so well."

"Where is your mother now?"

"Both Mother and Father died of fever during an epidemic."

"Have you ever thought of living in the white world?"

"No, never. I know nothing of white society. Pony soldiers kill our people and take our land. I hate whites. Look at me. Do I look white? I belong with the People."

"You know I cannot stay with you forever. One day I must leave. I've been charged with a crime I did not commit. I must find the man responsible and bring him to justice."

Morning Mist felt as if she'd been kicked in the stomach. "When will you return?"

"I don't know." Cole felt a kind of sadness he'd seldom felt before.

"Then we must not waste a moment, husband."

"You're right as usual, wife." He took her into his arms and kissed her, finding little comfort in the fact that they still had five days left of their honeymoon.

"Shall we bathe in the stream?" Morning Mist asked shyly.

"No, not yet. Let me love you first. I hunger for the taste of you. I need you, little love."

He loved her fiercely, savagely, knowing in his heart the happiness he'd found with Morning Mist could not last. Living in an Indian village was hardly the life he had envisioned for himself. Soon he must find a way to leave Running Elk's village. He didn't want to spend the rest of his life on the run from the law. He would scour the West for Harger, and when he found him he'd force the bastard to own up to his crime. Only then would he feel vindicated.

"Where have I heard Harger's name before?" Tanner asked Ashley. His expression grew thoughtful as he searched his memory.

"I don't know. The name is new to me."

"I'm sure I've heard it before. Maybe from Cole."

A few minutes later Harger came out of Dream Spinner's lodge and stopped before them, a pleased look on his face. "Looks like I'll be staying until Running Elk returns. Dream Spinner has offered me a woman to make my stay more enjoyable." He leered at Ashley. "You wouldn't be available, would you?"

Tanner shoved Ashley protectively behind him as he glared at Harger. "My wife sleeps in my lodge. Find another woman to satisfy your lust."

"What in the hell are you doing in Running

Elk's village anyway? Are you trying to horn in on my territory?"

"What you're doing is illegal," Tanner said.

"I'm a trader. Traders sell all kinds of merchandise."

"Guns?"

"None of your damn business, mister. Say," Harger said suspiciously, "you're not a government man, are you?"

"Far from it. But I still know it's illegal to sell guns to Indians. I suppose you have whiskey too."

"You're damn nosy, mister. I could tell you were a Reb the minute you opened your mouth. My business is with Running Elk." He turned and walked away.

Grasping Ashley's arm, Tanner literally pulled her into their lodge. "Stay away from that man while he's in the village, Yank. I don't like him."

"I don't need you to tell me what to do, Reb. Besides, the man repulses me."

Tanner gave her a cheeky grin. "Still prickly, aren't you? After last night I thought . . ."

Ashley flushed and looked away. "Last night was wonderful but it changes nothing. You still hate Yankees; that will never change. You'll have your freedom, just like I promised. It's what you want, isn't it?"

"Of course," Tanner agreed somewhat uncertainly. "Neither of us wants to stay in this marriage. We want each other physically, that's all. We're two healthy people with normal appetites and what happened between us was inevitable."

Ashley did not contradict Tanner. Before she met him she knew nothing about lust or *normal appetites*. The times Chet had accused her of being passionless during their engagement had been too numerous to count, and he had probably been right. But with Tanner the passion was spontaneous. He had but to look at her for her body to respond positively. That warm feeling that pooled in the pit of her stomach and lower when Tanner kissed and caressed her had been curiously lacking in her relationship with Chet. Unfortunately Tanner loved another woman. Loved her so much he called out her name in his sleep.

Tanner felt a hollowness he was hard-pressed to understand. He told himself that he didn't want a wife. His greatest fear was becoming too close to another woman. He couldn't bear to lose Ashley in the same violent manner he'd lost Ellen. Everything and everyone he loved had been taken from him, and he was partly at fault, especially where Ellen was concerned. He didn't deserve happiness. He should have seen it coming, should have known Ellen couldn't live with her shame.

Damn Yankees!

Damn war!

Damn his miserable, useless life. The only way he could ever relate to Ashley was sexually, and she deserved better than that.

Despite his bout of guilt and retrospection earlier, they made love that night with almost desperate fervor. They came together in a frenzy of need and desire that nearly overwhelmed them. Ashley had no idea the human body was capable of reaching such highs or maintaining them for such long periods. In her heart she knew what they had together was too hot, too potent to last.

Afterward, Tanner ran his fingers gently over Ashley's face, as if to memorize its shape and texture. He kissed the sweet curve of her cheek and nuzzled the hollow of her throat, lapping the single tear that slid from the corner of her eye.

"Are you crying? Did I hurt you?"

"N-no, it's just that it was so . . . so beautiful," she said on a sigh. It wasn't entirely the truth but would suffice. Her tears were for all those lonely nights she would spend without Tanner once they parted.

Jake Harger remained in the village, tormenting Ashley with his sly scrutiny and bold words, making certain Tanner wasn't nearby when he accosted her. Harger was too smart to tangle head-on with the big, dangerous Reb. If he played his cards right he might work a trade with Running Elk when he

204

returned. Guns for the girl.

Thus far Harger had been unable to learn where the girl and the Reb fit into the tribe. He'd never known Running Elk to cozy up to whites. Hell, the chief even held him, Harger, in contempt, despite the fact that Running Elk needed the illegal guns and whiskey he provided.

Ashley tried her best to keep out of Jake Harger's way. Though he had moved into the tipi of an obliging widow, his hungry gaze devoured Ashley whenever they chanced to meet, which was too often for Ashley's liking. She feared Tanner would take note and confront Harger, or instigate a fight. His position in the village was too precarious for him to cause trouble.

Later that day Tanner went off with two braves to hunt, leaving Ashley on her own for the rest of the day. Ever watchful, Harger took note of Tanner's absence and decided to follow when Ashley wandered into the woods to look for wild onions for the stew she was planning to make for supper. Trailing a discreet distance, Harger grinned his satisfaction when Ashley plunged deeper into the woods than she'd intended, until she finally found the onions growing on the banks of the stream a mile or so distant from the village. Dropping to her knees, she began digging in the dirt, too pleased with her find to hear Harger's soft footfall behind her.

"So, missy, we're finally alone."

Dropping the onions she had gathered, Ashley turned sharply, more annoyed than surprised to find Harger leering down at her. She wasn't frightened yet, but she was astute enough to know the man was up to no good. "What are you doing here? Did you follow me?"

Harger laughed nastily. "Reckon I did. Since you won't give me the time of day with that big Reb around, I wondered what you'd do when it was just you and me, with no one to bother us."

Rising abruptly, Ashley spun on her heel and started to walk away. "Now you know," she threw over her shoulder. "Tanner and I are married. I want nothing to do with you or any other man."

Grasping her arm, Harger stopped her in midstride. "You ain't going nowhere, missy. It's been a helluva long time since I had me a white woman. Squaws are all right but they don't satisfy me like sweet white flesh." He yanked her against him.

Ashley struggled fiercely. "Let me go! Tanner will kill you if you touch me. And if he doesn't, Running Elk will."

Her words gave Harger pause for thought. His grip on her arm tightened. "Are you pleasuring both the Reb and Running Elk?" He scratched his head. "What in the hell is going on? You ain't a captive; that much is certain. But you ain't exactly guests, either. Anyone with eyes can see that your man doesn't go anywhere without guards following him." He eyed her greedily and rubbed his crotch. "You must be something special in bed, missy. I aim to find out real soon."

Ashley struggled against his bruising grip, but he was relentless. "Let me go! I'll scream."

He laughed nastily. "Go ahead. There ain't no one around to hear you. Running Elk is off chasing a vision and the Reb is hunting for his meal. No one followed you into the woods; I made sure of that."

Finding strength she didn't know she possessed, Ashley twisted out of Harger's grasp and began running. But she was no match for Harger's long-legged stride and he caught her easily, throwing her to the ground with a force that knocked the breath from her lungs. Placing a foot on either side of her writhing body, he leered down at her and began unfastening his filthy buckskin breeches. Finding her breath, Ashley let out a bloodcurdling scream.

While Ashley fought off Harger, Cole and Morning Mist wandered hand in hand along the bank of the stream. Soon they must leave their honeymoon lodge and return to the village. Neither of them wanted their time of solitude to end, for neither knew how long they would have together. They had stopped now to kiss and cuddle and Cole was thinking how nice it would be to lower Morning Mist down on the soft bed of pine needles and make love to her. Then he heard the scream.

Morning Mist started violently. "What is it?" she asked fearfully, thinking some wild animal was about to attack them.

Cole knew the scream came from no animal. "Wait here," he ordered, pushing Morning Mist away as he pulled his hunting knife from his belt and headed in the direction of the scream.

Meanwhile, Harger had removed his gun belt and dropped his pants down around his ankles. "Now you'll feel what it's like to have a real man inside you." Grasping the obscene appendage between his legs and pumping it vigorously, he took perverse pleasure in what he perceived as Ashley's fear.

But Ashley wasn't as fear-stricken as Harger supposed. When abruptly he fell across her and tried to push inside her, she gathered her strength and rolled aside, letting out another ear-piercing scream. Harger hit the ground with a grunt, enraged to find his engorged flesh embedded in dirt instead of soft flesh.

"Bitch!" he ground out, reaching for her before she could scramble to her feet and pulling her beneath him. Roughly he lifted her tunic to her waist and raised his fist.

Cole heard the second scream and knew whoever was doing the screaming was in desperate trouble. He burst upon Harger and Ashley just as Harger lifted his fist to pummel Ashley into compliance. Cole recognized Harger instantly. It had been over a year since he'd seen the man but he'd never forget his face — or his lies, which had helped convict him of a murder he didn't commit. When he looked down and saw Ashley, rage exploded inside him.

"Take your filthy hands off my sister!"

Harger's fist halted in midair as he stared at Cole, his surprise evident in the widening of his eyes. "Cole Webster! I thought you were in prison."

"Move off my sister," Cole said, brandishing his knife in a threatening manner. "Make no sudden moves. I've become quite proficient with a knife. It would be easy to cut off that obscenity you seem so proud of."

"Cole." His name left Ashley's lips in a shaky sigh. "Thank God."

Harger moved off Ashley, his gaze glued to the knife. When he reached for his pants, Cole allowed him to pull them up. Then he picked up Harger's guns and thrust them into his own waistband. He used Harger's belt to bind his wrists together. Not until Harger was securely bound did Cole move to Ashley's side and help her to her feet.

"Did he hurt you, Ash?" he asked with concern. "Just say the word and I'll kill the bastard."

"He didn't hurt me, Cole, not like you mean."

"Where in the hell is Tanner? And what is Harger doing here in Running Elk's village?"

Dragging in a shaky breath, Ashley said, "Tanner went hunting and I wandered into the woods looking for wild onions. I don't understand. Do you know Mr. Harger? Tanner and I think he's supplying rifles to Running Elk."

Cole's green eyes blazed with pure hatred. "You're damn right I know the bastard. He killed my friend. His lies sent me to jail."

Chapter Ten

"Harger is the man who lied on the witness stand?" Ashley asked, sending Harger a virulent look. "Why? What did he hope to gain by sending an innocent man to prison?"

"I can answer that," Harger said with a snarl. "Your brother and his cohort were closing in on me. I had a good operation going, stealing guns from the quartermaster and trading them to Injuns for prime pelts and buffalo skins. Made me a tidy little sum selling my goods to Easterners. Sergeants don't make much money in today's army. Then Lieutenant Webster and Captain Kimball got wind of my little operation and started an investigation. I knew I had to do something to take the pressure off me."

"So you killed Kimball," Cole charged hotly. "And set about framing me for the murder."

"It was a brilliant plan," Harger said with a sneer. "Especially since you and Kimball were heard arguing in front of the barracks."

"What you called arguing was simply a discussion. We were trying to decide whether or not to bring charges against you. I wanted to do it immediately but Kimball said we didn't have an ironclad case against you yet. He wanted to catch you in the act of stealing."

"Looked like arguing to a lot of men who saw you. Course, my subtle hints that you were jealous of Kimball's recent promotion didn't harm my cause any."

"Nor did hiding stolen weapons in my quarters."

"How could army officials believe a lying thief like Harger instead of a respected officer?" Ashley wanted to know.

"Brent Kimball was dead and they needed a scapegoat," Cole explained. "They had already begun to suspect that weapons were being smuggled off the fort, and Harger's charges made sense. Especially when a search uncovered contraband weapons in my quarters."

"Didn't you tell them you were being framed?" Ashley asked.

"Even I knew that was a weak defense. Kimball and I hadn't taken our suspicions to the proper officials yet and then it was too late. Washington was clamoring for a quick conviction and, flimsy as the evidence was, I was handy. The rest is history."

"How did you get out of the stockade, Webster?" Harger asked. "I mustered out of the army shortly after the trial. Things were getting too hot for me to operate out of the fort. I've got a better setup now. I have regular suppliers from back east who ship guns to me. Some of the rifles are old and not much good, but these dumb Injuns are a gullible lot."

"Cole, are you all right?" Morning Mist burst through the underbrush, stopping abruptly when she saw Cole and Ashley. She stared from them to Harger, whose hands were still bound.

"Morning Mist, I thought I told you to stay where it was safe."

"I was worried about you," Morning Mist said. "You've been gone so long."

"Well, well, if it ain't Running Elk's little sister."

Morning Mist stared hard at Harger. "It's the trader. Why are his hands bound? What did he do?" Her eyes widened in understanding when she saw Ashley's disheveled condition. Ashley's tunic was ripped over the right shoulder, and the hemline was torn clear up to her thigh. It took only a moment for Morning Mist to realize that something bad had happened in this place. "Did the trader do this to you, Flame?"

"Ashley said the trader arrived while we were gone from the village," Cole told her. "The bastard followed my sister from camp and assaulted her. I arrived just in time."

Morning Mist cried out in commiseration and immediately went to her new sister-in-law. "Are you hurt, sister?"

"The trader didn't harm me, Morning Mist."

213

"I will see that Running Elk is told of the trader's insult to you."

Harger laughed harshly. "Your brother needs what I bring him. Don't count on him doing anything to harm our business dealings."

"Forget Running Elk," Cole barked. "This is the man who is responsible for sending me to prison, Morning Mist. I intend to take him back to Fort Bridger and force him to confess to the crime of which I was accused. He murdered a man in cold blood."

"I ain't going anywhere with you, Webster. I admit finding you in Running Elk's village came as quite a shock, but I know from experience the chief will do what is best for his people."

"Shadow Walker is my husband," Morning Mist said with a hint of pride.

"Well, well, you never know where a bad penny will turn up, or with whom. I gotta hand it to ya, Webster, ya sure do get around for a condemned man. How did ya escape from the stockade?"

"I don't owe you an explanation, Harger. I'm taking you back to Running Elk's village and then to Fort Bridger. Turn around and walk," Cole ordered.

Seemingly unperturbed by his change of fortune, Harger trudged through the forest toward the village. Cole followed close behind, his knife pricking Harger's back.

Ashley and Morning Mist closed in behind them. When they reached the village Cole tethered Harger to the post in the center of the camp while Morning Mist explained to Dream Spinner and the council what the trader had done to deserve such treatment.

During the rather lengthy explanation Tanner returned to the village with the hunting party. He spied the knot of people gathered in the center of the camp and fear raced through him. Had Running Elk returned? Had something happened to Ashley? Then he saw Cole and his fears eased somewhat. He quickly pushed his way through the throng of people to Ashley's side. He sent Ashley a searching look when he saw Harger tied to the stake and Morning Mist engaged in a rather heated discussion with Dream Spinner.

"What happened? What did Harger do? I don't like the man but I thought he was pretty secure in Running Elk's esteem. Has Running Elk returned from his vision quest?"

Before Ashley could answer, Cole rounded on Tanner. "Where were you when your wife needed you, MacTavish? If I hadn't arrived when I did, Harger would have raped my sister. For God's sake, Tanner, didn't you remember me telling you that the man who framed me was named Harger? You should have realized who the man was when he rode into camp and identified himself."

215

Tanner was stunned. He turned to Ashley, noting for the first time the condition of her clothing. His hands clenched at his sides and it was all he could do to keep from launching himself at Harger. But first he had to find out how badly the bastard had hurt Ashley. "What did he do to you, Yank?" His voice was coldly threatening.

"Fortunately, nothing," Ashley replied with a shudder. But it had been a close thing. Too close.

Tanner could tell by Ashley's reaction that she was still shaken, and it did nothing to ease his conscience. He should have been here for her, especially in light of Harger's obvious fascination with Ashley. "I'm sorry."

"You couldn't have known. If it's anyone's fault, it's mine. I shouldn't have gone off in search of wild onions by myself. Harger followed. Thank God I wandered in the direction of Cole and Morning Mist's honeymoon lodge. They heard me scream and Cole came to my rescue."

Tanner took a menacing step in Harger's direction. "I ought to kill you. But I know Cole wants to take you back to Fort Bridger so I'll harness my temper for the time being. Lord knows you deserve to die for what you did to Cole and Ashley."

"Running Elk will have a say in this," Harger warned. "He needs me. He ain't gonna let no white man take me to prison."

216

"Dream Spinner and the council have agreed that the trader should remain a prisoner until Running Elk returns," Morning Mist said when she returned to Cole's side. What she didn't say was that the general feeling was that Running Elk valued the trader for the guns and ammunition he sold them and wouldn't agree to give him over to Cole.

"Do you think he'll let me take Harger back to the fort when I tell him what the lying bastard did to me?"

"We don't have to wait for Running Elk's decision," Tanner said quietly. "Escape has been on my mind for some time. It's probably best we do so before Running Elk returns. Indians don't hold to white man's laws."

Cole sent Morning Mist a look that spoke more eloquently than mere words. His whole heart was in his gaze. His brilliant green eyes expressed his reluctance to leave. They said that he loved her, that he had to go away in order to clear his name. Though it nearly broke her heart, Morning Mist understood his silent plea and nodded. She had known she would lose Cole one day, but not this soon. She wondered what she had done to anger the gods. Why had they taken Cole away from her so soon after she'd found him?

That night Cole and Morning Mist shared Tanner and Ashley's meal. They sat inside

217

the tipi eating and whispering, away from prying ears of the guards stationed outside.

"When do we leave?" Cole asked, eager now to follow Tanner's plan for a nighttime escape. "What plans have you made?"

"Will Morning Mist accompany us?" Ashley wanted to know.

Morning Mist shook her head sadly. "I belong here. My heart goes with Cole but I must remain with the People. I will not betray you but you must go soon, before my brother returns."

"Tomorrow night," Tanner said without hesitation. "Dragging Harger out of camp won't be easy. He'll have to be bound and gagged and taken by force. I'll leave that to you, Cole. I'll take care of our two guards. We'll meet at the corral shortly after midnight, when the camp is most likely to be sleeping. Morning Mist and Ashley can cull some horses out of the corral for our use. If Morning Mist decides to join us," he continued, "we'll be more than happy to take her with us."

Morning Mist gave Cole a tearful smile. "I cannot." She rose solemnly and grasped Cole's hand. "Come, husband; we still have tonight."

"I feel sad for Cole and Morning Mist," Ashley said after the newlyweds left for their own lodge. "I think Cole truly loves Morning Mist, and it's obvious she loves him. It isn't fair, Tanner. They should be free to love where they want."

Free to love where you want, Tanner thought as Ashley's words died away. If only that were true. He'd never be free to love. What had happened to Ellen had rendered him incapable of bestowing love again. The things he believed in, what he had fought for, had ultimately destroyed those he loved most. If only he had realized it in time he might have taken measures to protect Ellen from herself, but he had no idea her mind had been so unstable.

"Tanner, is something wrong? You're so quiet."

Tanner started violently at the sound of Ashley's voice. "Just thinking."

"About tomorrow night?"

"Among other things. If we succeed in escaping, what do you intend to do? I'm beginning to suspect that Cole will return to Morning Mist after his name is cleared. Where will that leave you?"

"With or without Cole, I'm going to Oregon City," Ashley said without hesitation. "I'm a schoolteacher. My profession will provide me with an adequate income. Meanwhile, I have some money left from the sale of my aunt's house and my inheritance to live on for a time." She sent him a searching look. "You can obtain an annulment in the nearest town. Perhaps Denver. I'll not contest it."

"Did you ever consider that legally we no longer have grounds for an annulment? We've already slept together, on more than one occasion. Or have you forgotten?"

Ashley flushed and looked away. How could she forget something that gave her so much pleasure? "I haven't forgotten. If that bothers you, a divorce will suffice. It's what you want, isn't it?" She held her breath and let it out slowly when his answer wasn't forthcoming.

Tanner stared glumly into the dying embers of the fire, mulling over Ashley's words as an unbidden thought came to him, and it terrified him. "What if we've made a child? I never meant for that to happen, but we simply can't ignore the possibility."

"There's no need to worry on that score," Ashley said brightly. "I can take care of myself."

A groan issued forth from Tanner's throat. Damn, he thought despondently. He wasn't the kind of man who would leave a woman carrying his child. On the other hand, he had nothing to commend him but empty pockets and a healthy hatred for Yankees. Ashley deserved better than that. If not for his hatred of Yankees his life would be empty and without direction. Men like Slater and Harger didn't deserve to walk the face of the earth, and Tanner had set himself up as judge and jury, though admittedly his association with Ashley and Cole had tempered his perception of Yankees somewhat.

"Your opinion of me must be pretty low if you think I'd leave you pregnant with my child," Tanner said tightly. "I realize I'm not what you'd want in a husband but until I learn you're not carrying my child I'm not going to leave you."

Ashley swallowed audibly. "I thought we had both agreed on an annulment. Our marriage was one of necessity." What she didn't say and hoped he'd understand was that she'd be freeing him to return to Ellen once their marriage ended. She'd make no demands on him. Somehow she had to convince him she wouldn't hold him responsible.

"I thought I made myself clear, Reb. Your concern is admirable but unnecessary. I can take care of both myself and a child should our loving produce one. Perhaps I can't even have children," she said as an afterthought.

Tanner stared at her. "You really do want to get out of this marriage, don't you?"

Ashley gave a careless shrug. "That was our agreement."

Oh, God, she was dying inside. If Tanner had said he loved her, or even cared for her just a tiny bit, she would have admitted that she had no stomach for either a divorce or an annulment. But it was Ellen he loved, Ellen he wanted. The best thing she could do for Tanner was free him to return to the woman whose name he cried out in the night.

"What kind of bastard would abandon a woman carrying his child?" Tanner demanded. His features had hardened into a dark scowl. "I'm not leaving you until I know for sure."

As far as Ashley knew she was as capable of having children as any other woman. What she'd never realized was that she was capable of the kind of passion Tanner inspired in her. After Chet had broken off their engagement, he had accused her of being cold-blooded and unresponsive. Soon after, he'd married Barbara Harrison, the banker's daughter. It had hurt at first, and for years Ashley thought she was somehow lacking. Afterward she had immersed herself in her work and kept to herself. No other man had arrived to pique her interest, and as the years passed she had settled comfortably into spinsterhood.

Meeting Tanner had shown her that she wasn't a passionless spinster. Tanner made her blood sing and her body burn hot. He made her *feel*. Who would have thought that a slaveholding Reb would have such a devastating effect on her? She had always been such a staunch abolitionist, working for freedom and equality in any capacity demanded of her, so why in God's name had she fallen helplessly under the spell of a man who hated her for her beliefs?

"Some men wouldn't care about the possibility of pregnancy."

Tanner sent her a disgruntled look. "I would."

Ashley flushed. "Shouldn't we be making plans for our escape tomorrow night?" she asked, abruptly changing the subject.

"It's a simple plan. Cole will take charge of Harger and I'll take care of the guards. You and Morning Mist have only to go to where the horses are kept and wait for us. If Morning Mist decides not to come with us she can return to her lodge."

"Poor Cole. Life has been so difficult for him . . . for us."

"How so?" Tanner asked softly.

She searched his face. "I'm sorry I interfered in your life."

Tanner gave a bark of laughter. "My life left much to be desired. You found me in jail, remember? Go to sleep, Yank. Tonight's likely to be the last full night of sleep we'll have for a while. At least until we reach Fort Bridger. Is my saddlebag accessible?"

"It's stowed in the back of the tent."

"Your money and valuables are in it. I didn't want to leave your valuables behind when I left the wagon train so I packed them in my saddlebag and brought them with me. The wagon should be waiting for us at the fort. I paid to have the horses boarded and the wagon stored at the livery." He babbled on, trying to overcome his yearning for her.

223

Deliberately he turned away, thinking it would be easier to part if they didn't make love again.

"Thank you." She watched in silence as Tanner laid out their pallets facing each other across the fire. When he lay down upon the mat and turned away from her, somehow Ashley found the courage to speak his name. "Tanner."

He turned toward her, the stark planes and hollows of his cheekbones highlighted by golden fireglow. She thought him the handsomest man she'd ever seen. "What is it, Yank?"

Mesmerized, Tanner watched as she dragged the wet tip of her tongue over her dry lips. "This might be the last time we'll be together like this."

Tanner bit back a groan. Did she mean what he thought she meant? "Don't you think I'm aware of that?"

"We may not agree on many things but I've learned we're compatible in one or two areas." Lord, why was he making this so hard on her?

A ghost of a smile played at the corners of Tanner's mouth. "What is it you're trying to say, Yank?"

"Dammit, Reb, are you just dense or don't you want me?"

He raised up on his elbow and stared at her across the firepit. "I don't know if it's such a good idea. Making love to you could become habit-forming. If you aren't pregnant now you sure as hell might be after tonight. And we might find ourselves missing this intimacy once we go our own ways."

"All the more reason to . . ." — her voice trembled in her fear that he would reject her — "make this last night one to remember. If you want me, that is."

Heat pounded in his blood and in his manhood as he scrambled to his feet and knelt beside her. "Want you? How could you even ask such a thing? I thought it would be easier for you if I left you alone tonight." With his hands he swept aside her tunic and drew it over her head, flinging it into a dark corner. The look he gave her was almost tortured. "We'll always have this, Yank."

Ashley closed her eyes and swallowed hard. "No matter how fleeting or turbulent our association, making love with you is something I'll always remember."

"Keep that in mind when you take another lover, or a husband," Tanner said lightly.

I'll never take another lover or husband, Ashley thought frantically. *You're the only man I'll ever want.* That forlorn thought was swept away by Tanner's kisses. Her hand brushed his hair, then fell away to skim his face.

Her fingers felt cool against his heated forehead and cheek, and Tanner groaned as her hand slid downward, gliding over the thick wall of his chest to his hip and downward, her palm curving around, then clasping, the hard ridge straining against his breeches.

He stiffened as raw fire pounded through his veins.

With trembling fingers he shoved his breeches down his hips. Moments later they lay beside her discarded tunic and he was touching her, trailing shaking fingers through the soft curling hair of her mound to the sweet female flesh below. The silken, pliant folds felt feverish to his touch and swollen with moisture.

Ashley gave a long, abandoned sigh and arched up against his questing fingers. His eyes glittered as they feasted upon her breasts, thrust up to him in sweet invitation. He lowered his mouth and suckled her, teasing her tender nipples with his teeth and tongue. With gentle insistence his fingers parted soft pink flesh, continuing his onslaught from below as his mouth worked havoc upon her breasts. Circling and stroking in a tormenting foray, he aroused and explored with mouth, tongue and fingers until her passion dampened his hand.

Desirous of giving him the same kind of pleasure he was giving her, Ashley reached for his shaft. It rose huge and pulsing against her thigh, and a half-strangled cry left her lips as her hand curled around him. She felt the muscles of his belly tighten and his hand clamp around hers, wordlessly showing her the motion he desired.

It was torment. Sheer, sweet torment. Yet Tanner couldn't have stopped her even if it meant his death. He threw his head back, his powerful neck bowed, his eyes slitted narrowly. He gritted his teeth, driven half mad by her caress. He bore it until his body began to vibrate and he could stand it no more, fearing he would spill himself in her hand.

"No more!" he cried, flinging her hand aside. It was going too fast, much too fast. Grasping her hands, he pinned them on either side of her head, then reared back to look at her.

He thought her exquisite. Her breasts were sized perfectly for his hands, tipped with delicate nipples the color of roses. He dropped his head and wet her nipples with the tip of his tongue, watching in fascination as they curled into taut little buds and stiffened against his tongue. Her breath came quick and ragged, inflaming him almost past bearing.

"Tanner, no more!"

His heart was pounding. He was panting, scarcely able to breathe. His manhood was throbbing, ready to burst, but he was not yet ready to make her his. His mouth slid downward from her breasts across the flat plane of her stomach to the sweet pink folds of slick flesh. Her entire body jerked convulsively as he brushed the tiny bud of sensation that lay hidden within sleek, swollen petals. She cried out in helpless surrender when with one strong finger he delved within the hot cleft of her womanhood, taunting her, teasing her, the pressure of his finger inside her blatantly erotic, unbearably pleasing.

"Tanner, please!" Wanton sounds of pleasure worked their way up from her throat through lips damp and parted.

Only then did Tanner take pity on her. With one burning thrust he buried himself deeply, oh, so deeply within her. Again and again the swollen round head of his rigid flesh pierced her, touching her very soul. He filled her until there was no more of him to give, thrusting hot and wild into her clinging heat.

Ashley responded by arching up against him, taking everything he had to give as flames of excitement shot through her. Burying her face in his neck, she clung to him blindly, caught in the wild frenzy of his passion. Surrounded by the musky scent of sex, hips grinding, breaths mingling, violent pleasure overtook them. A series of chaotic contractions swept through Ashley as shudders convulsed her. She moaned, the erotic cries she uttered triggering Tanner's climax. He thrust into her hard, once, twice, then again, before he cried out hoarsely and spilled himself inside her.

Gasping, he pressed his forehead against hers. "Lord, Yank, that's as close to heaven as I'll ever get."

His arms were shaking when he levered himself up and off of her. He was breathing hard, every part of his body still throbbing when he flopped down beside her and gathered her into his arms.

"That was . . . extraordinary, Reb." Ashley sighed, still consumed by mind-drugging rapture. She doubted anything in this lifetime could top what she and Tanner had just shared.

"I agree. Sexually we're unbeatable."

The breath left Ashley's lungs. Sexually. Did nothing except gratification matter to Tanner? Didn't he know that her response wasn't possible with any other man? Suddenly Ashley was curious about the other woman with whom Tanner had shared passion. The need to know about the woman named Ellen emboldened Ashley to ask a startling question.

"Tanner, who is Ellen?"

Tanner went still. "Where did you hear that name?" His voice rose on a note of anger.

"You spoke it in your sleep once. You must love her very much. What happened? Why aren't you with Ellen now?"

His lips thinned and flattened. "Don't inquire into things that don't concern you."

"Do you love her?" Ashley probed.

"Drop it, will you? I can't talk about Ellen. Not now, not ever, and especially not with you."

"I understand." Actually, Ashley understood only one thing. Tanner loved Ellen so much there was room in his heart for no other woman. Ashley wasn't stupid. She knew he had married her for the money. Whatever had happened between Tanner and Ellen had been so devastating that he couldn't talk about it. Ashley knew that his home had been destroyed by Yankees, and that his mother had died, but what about Ellen?

Tanner's hatred for Yankees was so virulent Ashley realized he could never care for her. As pleasurable as sex with Tanner was, she wanted more than a response from his body. And obviously his love was held in reserve for a woman named Ellen.

"You don't understand a damn thing," Tanner muttered beneath his breath.

He didn't want to talk about Ellen. Not with Ashley curved sweetly against him, her naked flesh next to his. He knew she couldn't wait to be rid of him as a husband, but she couldn't deny the way her body responded to him. When he was with Ashley the pain associated with Ellen receded to the distant past. He was the first to admit that Ashley had made his life more bearable. But once they parted he knew he would return to that dark

230

world that had led to self-destruction. And he didn't even care.

"Make me understand, Tanner. What has Ellen got to do with your hatred of Yanks? Did she leave you for a Yankee?"

"Suffice it to say she is gone," Tanner said tightly. "That's all you need to know."

"I can feel the hurt deep inside you. It was there when I first met you and it's there now. It's like a raw wound that refuses to heal. Perhaps if you talked about it . . ."

Tanner forced a laugh. The sound had a ragged edge to it. "You're being fanciful, Yank. I really don't want to talk about this. I want to love you again. If anything can help me, it's the feel of myself embedded in your sweet flesh. God, Yank, I never thought I'd feel this way about a woman again. Wanting you is the one bright spot in my life. Don't spoil that now."

The note of desperation in his voice made Ashley silently vow to help Tanner, even if it meant sending him away to regain his lost love. As she opened her legs and took him into her body, she realized she loved him enough to give him up to another woman.

Chapter Eleven

Plans had a way of going awry. Running Elk returned the next morning before Tanner's escape plan could be implemented. Both Tanner and Ashley were outside when the chief emerged from the hills. Gaunt and hollow eyed, Running Elk appeared on the verge of collapse. His flesh was rent in numerous places, where he had slashed himself with his own knife, and he looked as if he hadn't slept or eaten in days. He looked neither right nor left but went directly to Dream Spinner's lodge.

Ashley watched in trepidation as Running Elk ducked into the shaman's lodge, dismayed that their escape had been placed in jeopardy by the chief's return. As if reading her mind, Tanner's arm made a protective circle about her shoulders.

Inside Dream Spinner's lodge, Running Elk collapsed onto a mat beside the holy man. He closed his eyes, trying to recall his vision so he could repeat it exactly for Dream Spinner.

Dream Spinner waited patiently as Running Elk gathered his strength for the recital. He offered his chief water and Running Elk drank thirstily.

"I feared the Great Spirit had abandoned me when no vision came," Running Elk said weakly. "I offered tobacco, prayed, fasted, sprinkled sage upon the fire to chase away evil spirits and rent my flesh, but still no vision was forthcoming. Last night I truly believed I might die on the mountain. I closed my eyes, preparing to accept the Great Spirit's will, when my mind suddenly awakened to the vision."

Dream Spinner nodded sagely. "What did Grandfather reveal to you? Were you shown what path to follow?"

"I came directly to your lodge so you can interpret my vision," Running Elk said. His voice raw with emotion, he relaxed against the backrest, closed his eyes and began speaking. "My vision was very confusing. Before my eyes the prairie erupted into flames. A path cleared and the enemy rode through the flames unscathed. Then suddenly I was there, mounted upon my pony and surrounded by our warriors. Our faces and our horses were painted for war as we rode out to meet the bluecoats. Time after time flames and heat drove us back. To our dismay, the flames and heat didn't seem to affect the enemy in the same way.

"Suddenly Flame appeared at my side. She told me she would call down rain to douse the fires if I granted her freedom. With the enemy nearly upon us I had no choice but to agree.

Before we rode to meet the enemy she cut off a hank of her hair and gave it to me. I wove it among my own tresses and felt great strength flowing into me. The enemy fled before us and the day was ours. When I returned from battle Flame demanded that I release her. I appeared to be reluctant and Flame became angry, visiting her wrath upon me. Then there was thunder, and great slashes of lightning rent the sky. If I didn't agree to Flame's wishes our people would perish. I saw it clearly."

Abruptly his recitation ended. He shuddered and opened his eyes, weary and drained. "What does it mean, Dream Spinner?"

Dream Spinner was silent a long time. At length he began interpreting the vision.

"Your vision is a warning. Flame's medicine is even more powerful than we first thought. She is unhappy with us. She wants to leave. Your vision shows how easily she can turn her medicine against us if she wishes. It is clear that Grandfather wishes us to let her go."

"But what of your own vision?" Running Elk asked. "Did you not see a flame-haired white woman in your vision? One whose strong medicine would benefit our tribe?"

"Your vision reveals that her power can remain with us after she departs. In your vision, when you wove her hair amid your

234

own locks you became strong and invincible."

Running Elk nodded. "That is true."

"The flames you saw ravaging the prairie represented bloodshed. Flame's intervention brought about victory for our people. Your vision was quite clear. We cannot afford to anger Flame."

"When I mate with her, her power will become mine," Running Elk boasted.

Dream Spinner shook his head. "Flame already has a mate."

"Pah, a white man. He is not a fitting mate for Flame."

"You cannot mate with her. Grandfather has forbidden it. Go to your lodge and rest, Running Elk. When you are refreshed, you must fulfill your vision according to Grandfather's wishes."

There was nothing left to be said. Weary in body and mind, Running Elk rose and walked unsteadily from Dream Spinner's lodge. He strode toward his own lodge and stopped abruptly when he saw Jake Harger tied to a stake in the center of the village.

"About time you got back," Harger grumbled. "I thought we were friends. I came with a shipment of . . . trading goods and was treated like an outlaw."

Morning Mist hurried to her brother's side, prepared to defend her husband. "The trader is not an honorable man," she told

Running Elk. "He followed Flame into the woods and tried to rape her. My husband prevented him from doing so."

Running Elk scowled. "Why didn't Flame's man protect her?"

"He was hunting. Flame went into the forest to gather wild onions. But that isn't the trader's only transgression. Shadow Walker was sent to prison for a crime the trader committed."

Running Elk turned his scowl on Harger. He had left orders that Flame was not to be harmed and the idea of Harger touching her did nothing to endear the trader to him.

"Jake Harger is trading in contraband," Cole explained as he, Ashley and Tanner walked up to join Morning Mist. "It is illegal to sell guns to Indians," Cole explained. "Do not forget that he tried to hurt my sister."

"Trading is no crime. Sioux law does not forbid it," Running Elk said. "We need to arm ourselves to fight the enemy."

"You cannot win that fight," Cole said sadly. "There are more white men than blades of grass upon the prairie. They cross the mountains from the east in ever increasing numbers. We must learn to coexist. You must let me take Harger to Fort Bridger and turn him over to the authorities."

Harger disagreed violently. "Don't listen to him, Running Elk! Free me now and I'll continue to supply you with trading goods.

236

You can't afford to lose what I provide your people."

"Shadow Walker is my husband, Running Elk. If you care for me you'll let him take Harger to Fort Bridger. Harger is the only man who can clear Shadow Walker of a murder charge. My husband isn't capable of killing in cold blood."

"I care for you, little sister, but what you ask is not possible. We need guns if we are to defeat the enemy."

"You can go into the mountains and live in peace," Ashley suggested. "If you let us go, I will leave my power with you." She had no idea how she would accomplish that, but she felt obliged to say something.

Running Elk sent her an inscrutable look. "How can your medicine help us if you are not here?" His vision had already told him how but he wanted to hear it from Flame.

For a moment Ashley looked puzzled. Then she brightened. "I will leave something with you, something that will give you power."

She had no idea what she'd leave, but the idea seemed to please Running Elk.

"Don't listen to the bitch," Harger snarled. "She's a fraud."

"I will think on it," Running Elk said as he turned in the direction of his lodge. "I must rest and refresh myself before I am capable of thinking clearly."

"What of your vision, brother?" Morning

Mist called after him. "Can you tell us nothing about it?"

"I cannot share my vision. Only Flame can make it become reality. She will be free to go only if she leaves her medicine with me."

"What in the hell does that mean?" Tanner wanted to know. He didn't like the sound of that one damn bit.

Ashley worried the soft underside of her lip, puzzling over Running Elk's words. "I wish I knew."

"You'll never take me back to Fort Bridger," Harger warned. "Running Elk will not allow it. He won't let the woman leave, either. A fool can tell he wants her in his bed. As soon as he comes to his senses he'll free me. Mark my words, I ain't gonna spend the rest of my life behind bars."

"You talk too much, Harger," Cole said, turning away. "I'll kill you before I let Running Elk set you free to continue your life of crime."

"Don't waste your breath on the bastard," Tanner said. "Let's wait for Running Elk's decision before doing anything rash. Meanwhile, we've all got to think of a way for Ashley to leave her medicine with Running Elk."

"I don't have any special powers," Ashley reminded him. "How can I leave it with Running Elk when it's not there in the first place?"

"Running Elk thinks otherwise. It's dangerous to disabuse him of that notion right now. The reason we're still alive is because of the strong power he thinks you possess. That lightning display a few days ago cinched it. So let's all think of something that will persuade Running Elk to free us. You know your brother best, Morning Mist; what do you think he means?"

"It is clear that Running Elk's vision concerned Flame. He expects something from her. We must wait until he reveals what it is he wants. Perhaps Flame will have an idea when the time comes."

Running Elk emerged from his lodge when the sun was at its highest. He looked refreshed and relaxed. A few hours' rest had returned him to his former vigor. Immediately Spring Rain hurried over to him with a bowl of food. He smiled at her, and Spring Rain beamed back with a smile that bespoke her eagerness to regain the affection of the man who had once been her husband.

After Running Elk had eaten and drunk his fill he sent Spring Rain to summon Ashley, Tanner and Cole. Morning Mist accompanied Cole, though she hadn't been summoned. Running Elk waited patiently until they were settled in a circle around him before speaking.

"The Great Spirit granted me a vision," he

began without preamble. "I cannot reveal it to you in its entirety. I can only tell you that I saw the prairie aflame and the People in grave danger of being annihilated. Then Flame appeared at my side. In my vision, Flame summoned rain from the heavens to douse the fires, and she gave me the power to defeat the enemy. In return, she demanded freedom."

Ashley grew excited. "If I give my power to you, will I truly be free to leave? Can Tanner and Cole leave too? Will you allow us to take Jake Harger with us?"

Tanner squeezed her hand, trying to convey a need for caution. Running Elk was sly. Tanner didn't trust him. "Just how did Flame transfer her power to you, Running Elk?"

Running Elk stared at Ashley's red hair, thinking the color rivaled the sunset. No, it surpassed it, he thought as he reached out and let a lock of the shining mass slip through his fingers.

With sudden insight Ashley knew exactly what she must do in order to gain her freedom and that of Tanner and Cole. Running Elk's vision had provided the clue. Acting spontaneously, and without a thought for her reckless behavior, she plucked Running Elk's knife from its sheath at his waist.

"Ashley!" Tanner blanched, appalled at Ashley's audacity. Didn't she realize they were at the mercy of Running Elk?

Running Elk made no move to stop Ashley. He stared at her, apparently aware of her intent, though the others were not. He stopped Tanner from taking the knife from Ashley with a slash of his hand, watching, waiting.

Ashley wound her left hand in her hair, raised her right hand and slashed downward. Morning Mist cried out in dismay when she saw a generous length of Ashley's shining hair lying limply in her hand. Ashley stared at it with regret, then offered it to Running Elk.

Tanner's heart thumped wildly against his chest and didn't stop until he noted Running Elk's pleased expression as his fingers curled around the severed tresses.

"Now you have a part of me, Running Elk," Ashley said solemnly. "I am giving my medicine to you. You no longer need me to bring good fortune to your people. Let us go. If you continue to keep me against my will, my power will be of no use to you."

Running Elk stared at the bright hank of hair curled within his palm and felt power seeping into every part of his body. Deeply superstitious, he imagined he could feel his body swell and strengthen. He felt invincible, indestructible. Grasping a hank of his own hair, he deftly plaited Ashley's hair into his. A moment later a sunbeam pierced through the smoke hole and settled on the bright red strands intermingled amid the black, and incongruous as it looked, it actually seemed to give Running Elk added vigor.

"You are free to leave, Flame. My vision revealed that keeping you against your will would bring your wrath down upon us." He touched his braid. "Your medicine is now mine."

"May we all leave? I won't let you harm Tanner or Cole."

"You are all free to go. You may take horses and supplies for your journey back to the fort. Do not even think of leading the soldiers to us," he warned, "for we will not be here when they arrive."

Morning Mist drew in a shuddering breath. She loved Cole beyond reason. The thought of parting with him gave her unspeakable pain.

The look on Morning Mist's lovely face told Cole exactly what she was thinking. Regardless of his feelings for his Indian bride, taking Harger back to the fort to stand trial for murder was something he had to do for his own peace of mind. "I'm taking Jake Harger with me, Running Elk. He is a murderer, among other things, and must be punished for his crimes."

Running Elk frowned. "You are my sister's husband, Shadow Walker. She does not wish you to leave her."

Ashley sent Morning Mist a sympathetic

look. She knew exactly how the Indian girl felt, for she was experiencing the same despair. Once they left Running Elk's village she'd have no hold on Tanner. She'd only paid him to see her safely to Fort Bridger. Now that she had a brother to see to her welfare, Tanner would undoubtedly feel no need to stick around.

Cole gave Morning Mist a tender smile before answering Running Elk. "I am indeed your sister's husband. I'm not abandoning her. My absence is not meant to be permanent."

Morning Mist gave a cry of gladness.

"I will remain away only as long as it takes to bring Harger to trial and clear my name," Cole promised.

"Cole, are you saying you intend to live out your life here in Running Elk's village?" Ashley asked, stunned.

"I cannot abandon the woman I love, Ash. Please understand. I'll do all in my power to convince Morning Mist to live in my world, but whether or not we remain with her people is up to her. Besides, you have Tanner now; you don't need me."

Ashley waited for Tanner to dispute Cole's words, and when he did not she briefly considered informing her brother that her marriage to Tanner was not a true marriage, that Tanner had married her to escape prison, and for the money. Except for their lovemaking, which they both truly enjoyed, their marriage had been a false one and undertaken for all the wrong reasons. Then the time for confidences passed as Cole once again addressed Running Elk.

"What is your answer, Running Elk? If I am to prove my innocence, Harger must return with me to the fort."

"Please, brother," Morning Mist said on Cole's behalf, "do as my husband asks. The trader is a vile man. He tried to hurt Flame. For that alone he must be punished."

Running Elk sat in silent contemplation, his eyes resting on Morning Mist. He was more than fond of her. Yet releasing Harger would certainly terminate the flow of guns the trader provided. Without guns his people could not defend themselves against the white eyes who violated their lands and killed their buffalo. Were his people truly fighting a losing battle, just as Shadow Walker said? he wondered. Were guns and ammunition only a temporary solution?

Running Elk was astute enough to realize that one day his people would be driven from their lands to live in inhospitable places that lacked the means to sustain them. Sioux chiefs greater than he had been forced to concede to the pony soldiers' demands and move their people to reservations. How long before he would join their ranks?

"Well, Running Elk? What is your

answer?" Cole prodded. "I vow I will kill Harger before I'll see him set free."

"And my medicine, which you seem to respect, will no longer protect you if you do not heed my brother," Ashley added for good measure.

Running Elk spread his arms in surrender. "Go, all of you. Take Jake Harger with you. I do this for my sister, and because I hold Flame and her power in high regard. If the trader meant her harm he deserves punishment. If he were of the People he would be driven from the village in disgrace, forever to live as an outcast."

"You have my sincere gratitude," Cole said, rising. He extended his hand to Morning Mist. "Come, wife, let us say our good-byes in private. The sooner I leave, the faster I can return to you."

Tanner stood at the same time, his face inscrutable. Ashley wondered if he was already making plans for a life without her. She couldn't blame him for wanting to get on with his own life. But, oh, how she would miss him. He had risked his life for her, following her into Running Elk's village when he could have taken her money and belongings and fled. Would Tanner go back to Ellen? she wondered.

"We have plans to make," Tanner said as he searched Ashley's face for a hint of her thoughts.

He tried to keep his own expression devoid of emotion. If Ashley had her way their association would soon end. But he wouldn't leave her at Fort Bridger. Oh, no. He'd not leave her until he knew for sure whether or not she was carrying his child. And the only way he could do that was to keep his hands off of her for the next month or so.

That thought tugged his lips into a smile. The lust he and the little Yank shared was so volatile he couldn't conceive of remaining with her and not touching her. And if he didn't keep his hands off her . . . That intriguing thought deserved further consideration.

"Yes," Ashley said, swallowing past the lump in her throat. "We have plans to make."

As they walked toward their own lodge, Tanner almost wished . . . No, he didn't deserve happiness, didn't merit a woman like Ashley. She was a Yankee and he still hated Yankees, although he had to admit Cole and Ashley were two of the better ones. Because of Yankees his entire family had been wiped out.

After the tragedy that had taken his mother and Ellen, his restless urge to kill all Yankees had driven him from his beloved South. But he could not run far enough or fast enough to escape the inevitable truth: he should have been able to prevent Ellen's death. His own failure had turned him into a vindictive, rage-driven seeker of revenge. He wasn't a fit mate for Ashley. She deserved someone with a heart. Someone who could love her without ghosts haunting him.

Some hours later, after a passionate and tearful good-bye from Morning Mist, Cole stood before Jake Harger, waiting for Ashley and Tanner to join him.

"Are you here to release me, Lieutenant?" Harger taunted. "I told you Running Elk needed me too much to keep me prisoner at the whim of a white man." His smile was pure evil.

"Think again, Harger. You're mine. Running Elk isn't going to let you go free."

Harger's smile wobbled then disappeared altogether. "You're lying!"

"I'm telling the truth. And here come Tanner and Ashley to confirm it."

Narrow eyed with disbelief, Harger watched as Tanner and Ashley strode up to join Cole. Tanner's saddlebag was slung over his shoulder and Ashley carried a parfleche filled with food for their journey.

"Are you ready, Cole?" Tanner asked, anxious to leave now that he knew they wouldn't be stopped. The only reason he had delayed this long was to allow Cole and Morning Mist to have a proper good-bye.

Cole sent Harger a look of pure loathing. "I

will be as soon as I get this scum up and moving."

"I ain't going anywhere with you, Webster. And furthermore, you can't get me to confess to murder no matter what."

"We'll see about that, Harger," Cole retorted.

Five days later they rode into Fort Bridger. As troublesome as Harger was, Cole and Tanner were more than a match for him. During their journey Cole had found a letter on Harger's person that implicated him in illegal trading in guns and whiskey. It was from his supplier in the East, advising him when and where to pick up the next shipment of guns. He also had Harger's packhorses, still loaded with contraband rifles and whiskey. Together it was more than enough evidence to incriminate Jake Harger and send investigators after the supplier.

"What now?" Tanner asked as they rode through the gates of the fort. Thus far no one had recognized Cole, but Tanner knew it was just a matter of time. It wasn't all that long ago that he had helped Cole bust out of the stockade.

"I'm taking Harger to Captain Callahan's office," Cole said. "He's ready to confess to the murder of Lieutenant Kimball. I'll take care of this, Tanner. I know you and Ashley have business of your own at the fort. If you need a place to stay, try Widow Talmadge's boardinghouse."

"Are you sure, Cole?" Ashley asked. "Tanner and I are willing to accompany you and testify on your behalf."

"I can do this on my own, sis." He sent Harger a look that made the man cringe. "Harger knows what will happen to him if he doesn't tell the truth. Besides, I have the letter. I intend to wait around for Harger's trial and make sure he gets all that's coming to him."

"Then what?" Ashley asked.

Cole sent her a smile that came straight from his heart. "Then I'm going back to Morning Mist. I love her, sis. One day I hope to convince her to leave her people and live with me in the white world. Until then, I'll stay with her. I'm glad you have Tanner. It makes it easier for me to pursue my own happiness knowing you are taken care of. Reb or no, I can see the love you and Tanner share. I'm happy you found someone. Chet Bainter doesn't know what he gave up when he broke his engagement to you. Where will you and Tanner go from here?"

Ashley spoke up before Tanner had a chance to reply. "I'm going on to Oregon City. There is nothing left for me in Chicago. The idea of new land, new opportunities, intrigues me."

"I might try farming," Tanner added, startling Ashley, "or logging. They say the Pacific coast is fertile and thickly forested. My family owned a plantation before the war. Farming isn't new to me. It's my heritage."

They parted then. Cole continued on to headquarters with Harger after arranging to meet them for supper at a local eatery. After Cole left them, Ashley stared at Tanner, her expression one of total disbelief.

"You're going to settle in Oregon City? I thought . . . That is . . . You're no farmer, Reb. But I thank you for the lie. I don't want Cole worrying over me. He doesn't need to know our marriage was one of convenience, or that it will soon end."

Tanner sent her an inscrutable look. "Cole does know about the conditions of our marriage but he doesn't seem concerned. Don't worry, Yank; I wouldn't think of interfering in your life. Once I see you safely to your destination I'll get out of your life. I can see how uncomfortable the idea of a permanent marriage makes you."

"As it does you," Ashley shot back. "Neither of us wants a permanent relationship. There is no need to escort me to Oregon City. I can hire someone to take me the rest of the way. Our arrangement was only to Fort Bridger. You've done your part."

"Dammit, Yank, your thinking is flawed. I told you I'm sticking with you until I'm certain you're not carrying my child. Besides, it

250

would be difficult to find a trustworthy man willing to take you to Oregon City. I'm certain there are lawyers in Oregon who can handle our divorce. It's settled. Let's get on over to the livery and see if your wagon and animals are still there. Perhaps we can even find out what happened to the Cramer party. I hope Pratt Slater had the good sense to die of his wounds."

Their wagon was still at the livery. Nothing was missing. Ashley's clothes were folded neatly inside her trunk and all the bedding was still in place. The only thing missing was Ashley's money and valuables, which Tanner had removed and still carried in his saddlebag.

The hostler supplied the information that Pratt Slater was indeed alive. It seemed that he had rallied after being treated by a doctor at the fort and continued on with the wagon train.

"The bastard is too ornery to die," Tanner said from between clenched teeth. "Next time we meet I won't walk away. A man like Slater doesn't deserve to live."

"Why? Because he led the patrol that set fire to your plantation?" Ashley asked. "Not that I like the man any better than you do, but he was probably following orders."

A grimness settled around Tanner's lips. "My grievance against Slater goes far deeper than that. You can't begin to understand what he's done."

251

"I would if you told me. Does it have something to do with Ellen?"

"For God's sake, Yank, let it rest! I can't talk about Ellen. Suffice it to say I have plenty of reason to hate Slater."

"Will you go back to her after our divorce? You'll have money after I pay you. You could go back and pick up where you left off. I don't know what made you leave, Tanner, but it's nothing that can't be fixed. If Ellen loves you . . ."

Tanner sent her a look of such pure rage that Ashley stepped backward in fear. Never had she seen him so angry. "Get us a couple of rooms at the rooming house," he bit out. "I'll finish up business here." Sensing his anger, Ashley merely nodded and turned to leave. "And Yank," he warned as she walked away, "if I hear another word about Ellen I won't be responsible for my actions. The subject is not up for discussion. Now or ever."

The widow Talmadge had only one room to let. Since she and Tanner were still husband and wife, Ashley felt no guilt in registering as Mr. and Mrs. MacTavish and sharing the room with Tanner. When Tanner arrived at the rooming house later, Mrs. Talmadge directed him to his room. He was surprised and somewhat disgruntled to find Ashley soaking in a large wooden tub. How in the hell was he supposed to keep his hands off her if they shared a room? Didn't she know he was trying to be noble? He wasn't made of steel! Except for one part of him. That part that rose stiff and undaunted between his legs.

"I thought I told you to get two rooms."

Ashley gave him a beguiling smile, making no effort to hide herself from him. "Only one was available."

Tanner's gaze was drawn to her like a moth to flame. Her skin looked like pale silk, and from experience he knew it felt as soft and smooth as it looked. Her face was raised to his, her vivid green eyes warm and inviting. A riot of red hair tumbled down around her shoulders and the upper portion of her breasts, framing the perfect oval of her face. He approached the tub and reached out to touch a shining lock of her hair. He could see the thin spot where she had shorn off a large hank to give to Running Elk, and it saddened him.

"Your hair is beautiful. Like living fire. Just like you. You have so much life, so much fire inside you. I envy the man who will be your lifelong mate."

Hurt by his words, Ashley blinked back her tears. "Be careful, Reb. If you wish for something enough, you just might end up with it."

Chapter Twelve

Abruptly Tanner turned away, afraid to trust himself with a naked, gloriously tempting Ashley. Her last words had stunned him. He had no idea how to respond, so he changed the subject.

"I made arrangements for the wagon to be harnessed and ready to roll first thing tomorrow morning. As soon as you're ready I'll take you to buy supplies for our trip. We need to cross the mountains before bad weather shuts the passes. We're cutting it close as it is."

"Give me a few minutes to dress," Ashley said.

Tanner heard water splash as Ashley rose from the tub. His mouth went dry and he swallowed convulsively.

"I'm anxious to meet Cole and learn what happened," Ashley continued blithely as she dried herself. "Do you suppose he convinced Captain Callahan that he was innocent of murder and gun-smuggling?"

"I'll place my money on Cole," Tanner said, forcing the words past his parched throat. He had to get out of there fast, before he threw caution to the wind and made love to Ashley, good intentions be damned. He hadn't touched her during the five days it took to reach the fort and was quite proud of his ability to resist temptation. But seeing Ashley like this pushed his control to the limit. Didn't she know how she tantalized him? He strode to the door, eager to escape the temptation of his seductive wife. "I'll wait outside. Come down when you're ready."

"Why are you leaving?" Ashley knew she was baiting him but couldn't help it.

Tanner paused in midstride. "Dammit, Yank, I'm leaving for your sake. If I stay, I'll make love to you. I thought you wanted to get rid of me, not lengthen the time I have to stay with you. I told you I'd never abandon a woman carrying my child. If we tempt fate we might be stuck with one another longer than you anticipated. Abstinence is the only way to prevent you from conceiving, and that means I have to keep my hands off you. And you sure as hell aren't helping, lady."

"Tanner . . ." The door slammed behind him and whatever Ashley was going to say died in her throat.

Thirty minutes later Ashley joined Tanner on the porch. He was frowning fiercely, staring at nothing in particular. "I'm ready. Let's go."

Tanner took her elbow and guided her across the dusty parade ground toward the general store. They followed the clerk's rec- ommendation concerning supplies and

255

learned that the journey to Oregon City would take almost two months, barring mishaps. Upon hearing those words Tanner rolled his eyes and groaned aloud. Two whole months in Ashley's company without touching her was going to be pure hell. He almost hoped there would be a child. That thought startled him. Only a fool would wish for things that could never be.

The sun had moved behind the surrounding hills, bathing the sky in scarlet when Tanner and Ashley entered the eatery where they were supposed to meet Cole. Cole hadn't arrived yet, so they found a table and sat down to study the menu. Cole found them fifteen minutes later.

Ashley was so anxious to learn what had happened in Captain Callahan's office she didn't wait for Cole to seat himself before blurting out, "What happened, Cole? Is Harger in the stockade? Did the captain believe you? Did Harger confess?"

"One question at a time, sis," Cole said, laughing. "Yes, Harger is in the stockade. Yes, Harger confessed to both murder and selling guns to the Indians, but not without a little prodding. The letter I found on him and the illegal weapons he took to Running Elk's village helped. Harger will face trial soon for murder. Meanwhile, there will be a hearing to clear my name. I fear it will be longer than I anticipated before I can return to Morning

Mist. What are your plans?"

"We're leaving tomorrow," Tanner said. "We need to get through the passes before the first significant snowfall."

"You're definitely settling in Oregon City, then," Cole remarked. "Why not wait a bit? Perhaps you can join other travelers going to Oregon."

"Ours was the last wagon train to leave Missouri this year," Ashley said. "There will be no others traveling through."

"There are always men on horseback traveling west," Cole told her.

"I think we'll fare better on our own," Tanner said, aware that most of those men were riffraff and fortune-hunters posing as decent men.

"Perhaps you're right," Cole agreed. He turned to Ashley. "God, sis, I'm going to hate to see you go. I'm grateful you have Tanner to take care of you."

Ashley bristled indignantly. "I don't need anyone to take care of me. I got along well enough on my own after our aunt died."

Cole and Tanner exchanged looks that suggested they thought otherwise.

"I just wish you and Morning Mist could join us," Ashley added wistfully. "Will you promise to keep in touch?"

"Perhaps in time we'll join you and Tanner," Cole said. "I'm going to try damn hard to convince Morning Mist to give white society a try. I'll write you in care of general delivery in Oregon City. I know I won't have to worry about you, Ash. For a Reb" — he grinned at Tanner — "Tanner has a lot of sense and seems capable of taking care of you."

"Thanks, Yank," Tanner returned. "For a Yankee you are amazingly perceptive."

Dinner ended on a note of forced gaiety. Ashley kept her tears at bay through sheer determination. She would miss Cole fiercely. She felt as if a part of her were being ripped away. Before they parted, Cole hugged her tightly and shook hands with Tanner.

"I'll be on hand to see you off tomorrow," Cole said, speaking past the lump forming in his throat. "Captain Callahan offered me a bunk in the barracks and I've accepted."

"It isn't right to let your brother think we're going to remain married," Tanner chided once Cole left. "I told him how we came to be married but it didn't seem to phase him. He acted like ours was a love match."

"Let him think what he wants," Ashley advised. "Cole has enough to worry about. He'd feel responsible for me if he thought our marriage was a sham and about to end. Cole's future is with Morning Mist. I told you before, I can take care of myself. I don't need you. I don't need anyone."

Tanner went rigid. Ashley's vehement

words more than convinced him that she didn't want this marriage to continue. "I'll be damn happy to let you take care of yourself, if that's your want, Mrs. MacTavish, just as soon as you give me proof that you're not carrying my child." He turned abruptly. "Good night, Yank. I'll see you in the morning."

"Where are you going?"

"To find my bed. I don't trust myself in the same room with you, lust-driven creature that I am, and God forbid that we make love again. You want your freedom and I want to give it to you."

Ashley watched Tanner disappear into the dark before turning in the direction of the boardinghouse. Damn stubborn Reb, she thought, disgruntled. How did that old adage go? Marry in haste, repent at leisure? She should have found someone less attractive, less tempting to marry. Had she done so she wouldn't be having second thoughts about divorcing the handsome rogue.

She didn't need a man beset by devils, Ashley rationalized. Not only did Tanner refuse to confide in her, but he became angry whenever she mentioned Ellen's name. If he loved Ellen so much why had he left her? What dark secret was he hiding? It was a puzzle she intended to solve before reaching Oregon City. Ashley wasn't exactly looking forward to the next few weeks. Since she couldn't have Tanner the way she wanted

259

him, it was going to be excessively painful pretending she didn't want him at all.

Tanner stretched out on his bedroll inside the wagon and tried to sleep. He thought of Ashley alone in her bed at the boardinghouse and it took considerable fortitude to keep from joining her. If he thought tonight was difficult, he had only to imagine what the next two months would be like. If he'd had any idea how tempting the hotheaded little Yank would be to him he'd have never agreed to this temporary marriage. Temporary torture was a better word. Remaining in jail would have been less of a danger to his heart and mind. Hell, he was even beginning to feel charitable toward certain Yanks!

The day dawned bright and clear, with a promise of stifling heat to come. Ashley arose early, washed, dressed and went down to breakfast. She was more than a little surprised to see Tanner already seated at the table with their fellow boarders.

"I told Mrs. Talmadge you'd be a bit late," Tanner said as Ashley sat down in the vacant seat next to him. "Eat hearty, love; you won't have another meal like this until we reach Oregon City."

Ashley stared at him. Obviously he felt it necessary to make everyone believe they had shared the same room last night. Since she

260

had nothing to add to his comment, she concentrated on the excellent breakfast Mrs. Talmadge set before them. All too soon the meal ended. Tanner finished first and stood up.

"Finish your meal, Ashley. I'll get our belongings from the room and pay for our lodging."

By the time Tanner returned to the dining room with his saddlebag and her small suitcase, Ashley was ready to leave. They bid their hostess good-bye and walked to the livery. Cole was standing beside the wagon waiting for them. While Ashley was inside the wagon bed organizing the supplies they had purchased the day before, Cole pulled Tanner aside.

"I'm depending on you to take care of my sister," he told Tanner. "Ashley can be headstrong but I'm convinced she loves you. And I know you love her. I don't care what your reasons were for marrying Ashley; I feel comfortable with your marriage."

Tanner didn't trust himself to speak. He didn't want to disabuse Cole of the notion that Ashley loved him, but he feared his brother-in-law suffered from delusions. Ashley needed him but she sure as hell didn't love him. His own emotions were still muddled. He freely admitted he lusted after the Yank, but his feelings went deeper. Thus far he'd been able to keep from delving too deeply into those feelings.

"I knew Chet Bainter wasn't right for Ash, but at the time she was set on marrying him."

"What happened?"

"I'm not sure. I think Ashley realized he wasn't the man for her. It didn't take the bastard long to find a rich woman to marry. He wed the banker's daughter shortly after he and Ashley broke their engagement. It hurt Ashley more than she cared to admit and later she told me she'd decided never to marry. As the years passed I began to believe her. I was surprised when you introduced yourself as her husband, but I can see you're exactly what she needs, despite the fact that you're a Reb. Make her happy, Tanner; she deserves it."

Tanner remained mum, knowing he'd be unable to keep that promise if he gave it.

The conversation came to a halt when Ashley joined them. After a poignant parting, Tanner tied his horse to the back of the wagon, climbed onto the seat beside Ashley and took up the reins. When Ashley turned back to look, Cole was still standing where they had left him, waving good-bye.

They traveled north toward Soda Springs. The first day was slow going as they settled into a routine. Tanner drove the oxen for the first few hours, then rode ahead to scout while Ashley took over the reins. They didn't stop for nooning but ate a cold meal from their supplies. The sun was setting behind the hills when Tanner finally called a halt beside a small mountain stream.

Few words were exchanged while Ashley prepared a fire and Tanner went off to hunt for small game. He returned a short time later with two fat rabbits, which he had already skinned and cleaned. Ashley threaded them on sticks to cook, then took a towel and soap from her trunk and headed toward the stream.

"Don't go too far," Tanner warned. "We haven't seen any Indians but there might be some lurking about."

"I'll be careful," Ashley called back.

She returned to find Tanner sitting in front of the fire, staring moodily into the flames. She sat down across from him, self-conscious beneath his hungry look. When he continued to stare at her she turned away and busied herself with their food. She couldn't think straight when he looked at her as if she were part of the meal.

They ate in silence. Tanner dreaded the next hours, and all the nights to come until they arrived in Oregon City. They finished their meal in awkward silence and Tanner went to the stream to bathe. When he returned Ashley was inside the wagon preparing for bed. Muted lamplight projected her image against the canvas and Tanner stared at her shamelessly. She had stripped down to her shift, a diaphanous garment that caressed the high points of her breasts like a lover's hands.

Tanner stifled a groan, entranced by the totally captivating sight. Tanner had no difficulty recalling the last time they were together intimately at Running Elk's village, and he hardened instantly. Her skin beneath his hands had been as smooth as silk, her breasts swelling with desire for him. She had been wild beneath him, wanting him as desperately as he had wanted her. When she opened to him and he slid inside her, she had been hot and wet and, oh, so tight.

A groan slipped past his lips. If he didn't stop this fantasizing he'd storm into the wagon and give her what they both wanted. God, he must be insane to torture himself in such a manner. He shook his head to clear it of such dangerous thoughts, then called out, "Toss out my bedroll. I'll make my bed beneath the wagon."

Ashley poked her head out the end of the wagon. "That won't be necessary, Tanner. There is plenty of room for two to sleep inside."

"There might be room but I don't think you'll be happy with the arrangement. Just do as I say and toss out my bedroll. It's a pleasant night. I don't mind sleeping outside."

"Oomph!" The bedroll came out of the wagon with such force it nearly bowled him over.

"I hope a snake crawls into your bed, Reb," she called out crossly as she let down the end flap. It hit the tailgate with a resounding bang.

"And a pleasant good night to you too, Yank," Tanner replied, unamused.

Ashley gave an inelegant snort. What would it take to get the stubborn Reb to share her bed? She'd beg him if she thought it would do any good. To her chagrin, she knew exactly why Tanner would refuse if she begged him. Neither she nor Tanner had the ability to resist one another, and he feared he'd get her with child. The only reason he'd stayed with her now was because his moral code demanded that he not abandon a woman carrying his child. Dear God, didn't he know she'd welcome his child? Didn't he realize that she didn't want him if the only reason he remained with her was because there might be a child?

Two weeks later they crossed the Wasatch Range without mishap and reached Soda Springs. They spent two nights at the site so Ashley could wash all their dirty clothing. Then they pushed on to Fort Hall, encountering their first snowfall high on a mountain pass. When they came down from the pass

265

into a fertile valley, a fierce thunderstorm was in progress, forcing them to seek shelter beneath a large, overhanging rock. When the storm continued unabated they ate a cold repast of leftovers inside the wagon and prepared to settle down for the night.

"You'll have to sleep inside the wagon tonight," Ashley remarked offhandedly as she put away the supper leavings.

"Not damn likely," Tanner replied gruffly as he gathered up his blankets and prepared to leave. He stuck his head outside the wagon and was met with a violent display of lightning. All hell broke loose as thunder rolled across the sky and a nearby tree burst into flames.

Tanner turned to stare at Ashley, one eyebrow raised. "Have you called down God's wrath upon me, Flame? Were the Indians right in claiming you had special powers?"

Ashley snorted derisively. "You know I have no special powers."

"You have more power than you give yourself credit for," Tanner muttered beneath his breath. "No one knows that better than I."

"What did you say?"

"That I'd be a fool to sleep outside on a night like this."

Pleased with his explanation, Ashley placed his bedroll beside her cot and extinguished the light. She could feel Tanner's eyes on her as she undressed in the dark.

Chills ran down her spine even though she knew he couldn't see her. Her skin felt scorched where she imagined his gaze touching her. She folded her clothes neatly and slid beneath the blankets. If only he wasn't so attractive, she thought glumly. If only she didn't want him.

Tanner lay down fully clothed, unable to relax with his body rigid with need. The light from a lightning bolt had revealed Ashley stripped down to her shift just moments before she slid into bed. He'd tried not to look but he wasn't strong enough to turn away. So he lay stiff and hurting, wanting to reach out across the narrow space and sweep her into his arms. If only she wasn't so damn tempting. If only he didn't want her.

The same old nightmare visited Tanner that night. This time the dream was even more vivid. He thrashed about wildly, mumbling and crying out in his sleep. Ashley awakened instantly, recalling the last time she'd caught Tanner in the midst of a nightmare and learned about Ellen.

"My God, Ellen, don't do it! It doesn't matter to me. Please, put down the gun."

Tanner's voice held a note of desperation. Rising from her bed, she knelt over Tanner, shaking him gently so as not to startle him.

"Tanner, wake up. You're dreaming."

Tanner came out of his nightmare slowly. "Ellen?"

Ashley gulped down her disappointment. Hearing another woman's name on Tanner's lips was like a punch in the gut. "No, it's Ashley. You were dreaming."

He groaned and his arms came around her. He was shaking; she could feel his heart pounding against his rib cage. "Oh, God, Yank, you don't know how good it is to wake up and find you in my arms. That nightmare becomes more unbearable each time I have it."

"Do you have it often?"

"Often enough. It's wonderful to wake up and find you in my arms. Lie with me tonight, Yank. I'll not do anything to keep you from the divorce you want. I'll be careful, I promise." With shaking hands he lifted her shift.

I don't want you to be careful, Ashley almost screamed out. She wanted him to love her, without restraint, without recriminations, without thinking of Ellen while he loved her. And she wanted it to last forever.

His touch was incredibly gentle on her sensitive breasts, turning the sweet ache into quivering hunger. He rubbed his knuckles against one nipple, then lifted it up to his greedy mouth. Sucking it between his teeth, he bit and teased it, then laved it with his tongue. Ashley whimpered from pleasure that was nearly painful, wanting him to go on doing it forever.

He released that nipple and went to the other, drawing it deeply into his mouth, and Ashley groaned from the delightful shock of it. When he left her breasts to go on to other places aching for his touch, her nipples, left wet from his mouth, puckered up tightly in the cool night air.

His hands began to stroke the length of her as his mouth took hers in slow, drugging kisses, his tongue delving in deeply, drinking her sweet essence. He was mad for her. He hadn't known a woman could affect him the way Ashley did. He had loved Ellen, but it was a gentle love, not this deep, gut-wrenching hunger he felt for the red-haired Yankee who had turned his life upside down.

He groaned against her mouth. "Ashley . . . Ah, God, Ashley . . ." Shifting slightly, he dragged her shift over her head and tossed it aside. Impatient to feel the warmth of his skin against hers, Ashley tugged on his shirt. Eager to oblige, Tanner shed his clothing.

"Say you want me," Tanner whispered against her mouth.

"I want —"

"Me inside you," he said before she had time to finish her sentence.

"You inside me."

His hand slid down between her legs, tracing the outer edges of the fiery triangle nestled below her belly. Instinctively her legs fell open, inviting further intimacy. As if in answer to her silent plea, his fingers thrust into her tight sheath. Her hips rose up and she cried out in mindless pleasure. He slid his fingers in and out of her, again and again, feeling her heat, her wetness, reveling in her response. If nothing else, they would always have this.

"You've got me, love; all I have is yours," he said.

He straddled her, rubbing his swelling arousal against the softness between her legs. Then he bent to her, sliding his mouth down her body, tracing a burning path over her breasts, belly and lower. Ashley gasped and arched upward, seeking the heat of his mouth, welcoming the sweet aching need he was creating inside her. When he slid his hands under her bottom and lifted her to his hungry mouth, Ashley jerked violently in response. He moved his lips along her hot, sweet cleft and felt her taut muscles clench against the bold thrusting of his tongue. She whimpered as her control shattered.

"Tanner! Oh, God, Tanner!"

Her head flailed back and forth; her hands clenched into fists at her sides. She wanted to scream at the top of her lungs but couldn't summon the strength. Her guttural moans spurred him on, making him feel powerfully male that he could affect her in such a way. When he scraped her swollen bud of pleasure with his teeth she came in a rush against the heated center of his open mouth.

It was all Tanner could do to keep from yelling out he loved her as her last tremors faded away. He knew it was the last thing in the world she wanted to hear. Knew, too, that he didn't deserve to find love after failing Ellen.

He rose over her and came down on top of her, pressing his mouth over hers as he drove into her. She raised her hips to meet his piercing thrust, needing to feel him inside her as her swollen flesh tightened around him. She sighed wordlessly as his hips began grinding against her, driving her into a frenzy of incredible splendor. Her soft moans were almost enough to bring him to blinding culmination.

A ragged cry left Ashley's lips, followed by a convulsive shudder. Then she buried her head against Tanner's shoulder, violent pleasure suffusing her as she found fulfillment for a second time. She could tell that Tanner was nearing his own climax and her muscles tightened around him. She gasped in dismay when he suddenly pulled out of her and spilled his seed against her stomach.

Panting, he pressed his forehead to hers, struggling for breath and composure. When his strength returned he rolled over to lie beside her.

Ashley stared at him, appalled at what he had done. "Why did you do that?"

"It's for your own good. You've made it clear that you don't want to remain married, and a child would only complicate matters. Our arrangement was to be temporary, remember?"

"Temporary," Ashley repeated beneath her breath. "God forbid that I should saddle you with unwanted responsibilities."

"What did you say?"

"Nothing important."

"Lie still. I'll clean you up. I told you what would happen if we shared the wagon. Now maybe you'll believe me. No matter what we might feel for one another we'll always have this ability to give each other pleasure. Together we're like tinder and flame. You ignite the fire and I kindle the flame."

Ashley didn't argue Tanner's logic. They were indeed like tinder and flame. But they were much more. Unfortunately Tanner was too beset by dark secrets and obsessed with Ellen to know it. Until he resolved his past there was no future for them. Whether or not she was carrying his child made little difference. Tanner had to shed his smoldering hatred for Yankees and convince her that he no longer cared for Ellen before she could give her love freely.

In her heart Ashley felt that Tanner cared for her, that he was suppressing the truth because of something that had happened a long time ago. Intuition told her it involved more than the vagaries of war. And that Pratt Slater was somehow to blame. She just hadn't been able to put the puzzle together yet.

After cleaning his seed from Ashley, Tanner lay down beside her. Rain still pounded against the canvas but the worst of the storm had abated. Not so the storm raging inside Tanner. Ashley made him forget the war and the unspeakable horror of what had happened to his family, and that was something he couldn't allow until Slater was dead. He'd never dreamed he'd find the man responsible for making his life unbearable, and he wouldn't rest until Pratt Slater was punished for his depravities.

Slater should have died from his wounds, Tanner reasoned. If he had, Tanner could have put the past behind him and told Ashley that he cared for her. Life was so damn unpredictable. Somehow the feisty Yank had burrowed her way into his heart when he was least prepared for it. But before he'd bring his own misery into her life, he'd let her go.

Chapter Thirteen

The rain continued all night and didn't stop until noon the following day. When they took to the trail again after nooning they slogged along at a snail's pace. The rutted roadbed was awash in thick, gluey mud and they bogged down often. The rigors of the trail had prevented them from mentioning the rapturous hours they had spent in each other's arms the previous night, giving and receiving pleasure. But when night arrived and they prepared to bed down, there was no question of Tanner sleeping beneath the wagon in the mud.

When they finally sought their beds, Tanner held the covers aside so she could join him. "I hope you want this as much as I do, Yank," Tanner said as she snuggled into the curve of his body. "Does this mean you're having second thoughts about ending our marriage?"

"What do you want, Tanner? Thus far all we've talked about is being free of one another."

"You made it clear when we struck our deal that you didn't want a permanent husband."

"I found you in jail. I thought you were some kind of a criminal. And a Reb, besides. I had only the sheriff's word that you wouldn't murder me in my sleep. If you recall, you wanted a wife no more than I wanted a husband."

"Have you changed your mind?"

"Have you?"

"Dammit, Yank, must you throw my question back in my face? Can't you give an honest answer?"

Ashley heaved a sigh that was full of anguish. "Very well, Reb, you want an honest answer, I'll give you one. Perhaps I do have second thoughts about ending our marriage but I know it's not what you want."

"Are you sure about that?"

Ashley went so still she could hear her heart pounding. "Are you saying . . . ? No, it won't work. I don't want a husband with dark secrets in his past. Are you willing to tell me about Ellen? Do you still love her? Where is she and why did you leave her? I don't want a man who loves another woman."

"Ellen is my past. I don't want to talk about her; it's too painful. I'm hoping to put an end to that part of my life when I track down and kill Pratt Slater."

"What did Slater do?"

"Something too unspeakable to talk about."

"Do you love Ellen?"

"I did. Can't you let well enough alone?"

"Dammit, Reb, you can't just make statements like that and not explain them. Why do you want to kill Slater?"

"The bastard deserves it."

"No, Tanner, you can't! Killing is against the law. You could go to prison. I know you hate Yankees but if you want us to try to make this marriage work you can't go gunning for Slater. I can't live with your past, Tanner."

"You don't understand. Now that I've met the man who tore my life apart I can't just ignore it. I couldn't live with myself knowing what he did and not doing anything about it."

"What has Slater done? How can I understand if you won't talk about it?"

Tanner's face convulsed with pain. "You won't let up until I dredge up memories that have haunted me for more than three years, will you? Very well, Yank, I'll tell you," he choked out. "When I've finished my tale you'll know exactly the kind of man I am and run as far away from me as you can get."

Ashley was no longer certain she wanted to know the dark secrets Tanner harbored. What could bring a strong man like Tanner to the verge of tears?

Tanner's arms tightened involuntarily around her. Ashley was shocked to discover he was shaking, and her heart went out to him. No matter what he told her she'd try to understand.

"You wanted to know about Ellen,"

Tanner began. "Ellen was my wife."

"*Was* your wife?"

"Ellen is dead."

"Oh, Tanner, I'm so sorry. You must have loved her a great deal."

"I did love Ellen. We were childhood sweethearts. We married young and lived a carefree, idyllic life until the war came along. Naturally I considered it my patriotic duty to enlist. Everyone thought the war would last no more than a few months, and that the South would be victorious.

"It didn't take long to disabuse me of that notion. War is hell. I learned that after the first battle. I rose quickly in the ranks and soon had command of a company of green men more suited to farming than fighting. Even those who went into the war with high expectations soon grew disenchanted with the deprivations. That first winter made men of most of the boys in my company."

"How horrible for you," Ashley sympathized.

Tanner gave a snort of disgust. "I survived. Your sympathy should be with all those unfortunate men and boys lying in unmarked graves. When I heard that Yankees were marching through the South burning and pillaging an already downtrodden people, I worried constantly about my mother and Ellen. When I received word that my father had been reported

277

killed in action, I wanted to go home and comfort them, but I couldn't leave my post."

"How senseless it was to die over the question of slavery, when enslaving humans is so wrong," Ashley contended.

"If you think the war was about slavery, you're wrong, Yank. The war was about cultures and politics. Slavery was only one of the issues."

Ashley had no idea what he was talking about. As far as she was concerned the war had started because slave owners refused to free their human chattel. "You said you were wounded."

"I was, toward the end of the war. I was sent home to recuperate from a stubborn wound that refused to heal. It's a miracle I still have my leg."

"You said you found your home burnt to the ground," Ashley said, wishing he'd get around to Ellen. But she knew she couldn't hurry him. In his own time, in his own way, Tanner would tell her what she so desperately wanted to know.

"My home was gone. Only one or two charred slave cabins had been left standing. The condition of the remains indicated that the torching hadn't been recent. I hadn't heard from my family throughout the long winter, and when I saw the ruins I feared both Mother and Ellen were dead. Perhaps it would have been merciful if they had perished in the fire."

Ashley thought that was a terrible thing to say but did not remark on it.

"I found my mother in one of the slave cabins, sleeping on the dirt floor. She was sick, ill nourished and close to death. At first Ellen appeared well, but I soon learned she wasn't the same woman I had married, the woman whose image I had carried in my heart throughout the war. She was a hollow-eyed imitation of a woman whose soul had been destroyed. She refused to let me touch her. She cringed when I tried to take her into my arms to comfort her, and she refused to talk to me about what had happened to change her."

Ashley murmured in commiseration.

"Have you heard enough?" Tanner asked. "I warned you it wasn't a pretty tale."

Ashley shook her head. No matter what, she had to hear the story to the bitter end.

"Mother told me everything before she died. She said the only reason she'd fought off death this long was to see me one last time and tell me what had happened so I'd understand. She recounted how Yankee soldiers had burned the fields, stolen the livestock and food and then ridden up to the house. A sergeant was in charge of the detail. He'd been ordered to burn homes and plantations belonging to men who fought in the South's defense. He'd barely given Mother and Ellen time to leave the house before setting it ablaze.

"Then —" His voice broke and it was several minutes before he could continue. "Then Mother told me how the sergeant had seen Ellen and chased her down. How he had viciously raped her before passing her on to his men. Two of the Yankees, unable to wait their turn, used my mother in the same manner."

"Oh, God!" Ashley cried out. "It was Slater, wasn't it? Slater was the man who torched your house and raped your wife."

"It was. I didn't know he was the one until I met him on the wagon train and heard him bragging about torching the MacTavish plantation. He didn't come right out and confess to hurting Ellen and Mother, but what he'd hinted at was enough to convince me that he was the man responsible. If Henry Jones hadn't gotten to him first, I truly meant to kill him."

Ashley seemed surprised. "I never thought to ask if you'd discovered who had attacked Slater. I never considered Susan's father. He's such a mild-mannered man."

"He learned about Susan and Slater by accident and wanted to punish Slater for ruining his daughter's life."

"What will happen to Mr. Jones?"

"Cramer isn't going to charge Jones with

the crime. He said Jones had a right to protect his daughter's honor."

"I'm glad. Now, tell me how Ellen died. I can't even begin to imagine the horror of living with the terrible thing that was done to her."

"You're strong, Ashley; you would have survived. But Ellen was weak. She had been pampered and protected all her life. She couldn't live with her shame. I did my damnedest to convince her that it didn't matter to me, that I still loved her, but she deliberately blocked out my words. Then Mother died and I was so grief-stricken I failed to recognize Ellen's state of mind. The warning signs were there. I should have been more vigilant.

"After Mother's death something snapped inside Ellen. Apparently caring for Mother during her illness was all that had kept her from taking that final step. I should have seen it coming. I blame myself for what happened. I should have helped her. I should have been more responsive to her needs. But, dammit, I'd lost both my parents in a very short time, both violently, I still wasn't recovered from my wound, and I had to deal with the knowledge that my wife had been raped repeatedly by Yankees."

"You don't have to explain yourself to me, Tanner."

"I do, dammit, don't you see? I should

281

have recognized Ellen's frame of mind and known she would attempt something desperate. While still on convalescent leave I learned that the war had ended, that the South had been beaten into the ground. I knew it was inevitable but it was still a shock. I had no idea what Ellen and I would do, where we would go. I expressed my fears to Ellen and she told me not to worry about her. The next day she took my service revolver, put the muzzle to her head and blew out her brains."

By now Ashley was crying openly.

"Don't you see? I failed her. If I'd been more observant, or more sympathetic, she wouldn't have died so violently. I couldn't help her, Ashley; I couldn't give her what she needed. I buried her the next day and left everything I'd known and loved behind. I became a saddle tramp, stealing when I needed money and picking a fight with any Yankee soldier unlucky enough to cross my path.

"Drunk or sober, I was consumed by self-loathing every waking moment and I cursed my dreams. I was my own worst enemy and a damn nuisance to the army. If Sheriff Beardsley hadn't insisted that I accept your offer I'd probably be sitting in the stockade right now. If there is a God, Pratt Slater will be waiting for me at the end of the trail. I won't be able to live with myself until Ellen's death is avenged." He paused for effect.

"Now you know the kind of man I am. I was insensitive to the needs of my wife. I don't deserve a second chance at happiness. Maybe after I take care of Slater . . ."

"You can't kill in cold blood, Tanner. It's not in you."

Tanner's face hardened and his eyes turned glacial. "You don't know me if you think that. Ellen killed herself with my gun, for God's sake! You can't imagine the abject horror of knowing that my wife used my gun to end her life."

"It was a long time ago, Tanner. Let the past go."

"No! Have you ever seen the brains of someone you love splattered against the wall? I know that's not a pretty picture but I want you to understand the agony I went through. I swore that if ever I found the man responsible I'd take his miserable life."

"Does punishing Slater mean more to you than I do?" Ashley wanted to know. "I-I care for you, Tanner."

Tanner gave a harsh laugh. "I don't deserve you, Ashley. I lost the right to happiness. I care for you, I reckon you know that by now, but you'd be better off finding someone worthy of your love."

"I have," she choked out. "But he's too obsessed with revenge to notice. I understand now why you don't want a wife. You can't love and hate at the same time. I won't stand in your way. Once we reach Oregon City I'll release you from our arrangement. In time you'll have the divorce you want so badly. Without a wife to hinder you, you can continue your headlong rush toward disaster."

A plaintive sigh hissed from between Tanner's lips. "You don't really understand, Ashley. I knew you wouldn't."

"I'm not stupid. If you go after Slater, at the very least you could spend your life behind bars. At the most you could lose your life to Slater's gun. I'm glad you told me, Tanner. At least now I know there is no hope for us."

"Ashley, I —"

"No, there is nothing more to say. Go to sleep, Reb. I'm suddenly incredibly weary."

"Ashley, you will tell me if you're carrying my child, won't you? I'll fight the divorce if you're pregnant. The last time I spilled my seed inside you was at Running Elk's village. You should know soon."

"Don't worry, Reb. I'd know if I was pregnant and I don't feel at all like I am."

"Time will tell. I wouldn't mind. Ellen and I were married five years and we never had any children. Perhaps I'm lacking in some way. In my situation it wouldn't be a bad thing."

"Would a child change your mind about killing Slater?"

Tanner went still. He couldn't lie to Ashley.

"No difference at all. My child would have a name no matter what happened to me."

His answer strengthened Ashley's determination not to tell Tanner if she found herself in the family way.

Two days later they reached Fort Hall. After a brief stop to purchase supplies, they continued along Snake River to Boise. Tanner had returned to his previous sleeping arrangement of bedding down beneath the wagon. He'd revealed nothing more about his past and Ashley didn't inquire. During this time Ashley learned that there was no possibility of a child.

After traversing a particularly harrowing mountain pass they arrived in Boise. Tanner told her they would rest the oxen a day or two before continuing on to Fort Walla Walla. Ashley took the opportunity to replenish their food supplies at a local store while Tanner saw to the animals and wagon. She was browsing the shelves when she heard her name called.

"Ashley! Thank God you're safe!"

Ashley whirled, surprised that someone in Boise would know her. She was delighted to see Mary Dench standing a few feet away.

"Mary! What are you doing here? I would have thought by now you'd be in Oregon City."

"After you were abducted by Indians we suffered one tragedy after another," Mary explained. "The worst was a virulent fever that swept through the wagon train. There wasn't a family unaffected. We think it was spread by people from another train we encountered on the trail. It was bad, Ashley, very bad."

"Oh, Mary, tell me. Is your family well? What about Nancy and Sarah? And the Jones family?"

"My husband and I had the fever and recovered, thank God, but Nancy lost a son and Sarah lost her husband. Henry Jones died but his family survived. Captain Cramer succumbed also. Before it was over more than half the people on the wagon train were buried on the prairie. We traveled on to Boise but our hearts weren't in the journey anymore. Those who survived decided to settle here in Boise. It's beautiful country, and I've come to love it here."

"Mrs. Dench, I'm surprised to see you in Boise."

"Oh, Tanner, a terrible tragedy has occurred," Ashley said as Tanner approached the two women. "Mary was just telling me that soon after we left the wagon train fever took the lives of half the settlers. The survivors chose to settle in Boise rather than to continue on to Oregon City."

Tanner's eyes narrowed. "What happened to Pratt Slater? Did he recover from his wounds? Did the fever get him in the end?"

"Mr. Slater survived his wounds," Mary said. "He was one of the lucky ones who recovered quickly from the fever."

"Is he in Boise?"

"Tanner, let it go."

"Keep out of this, Ashley." He repeated his question to Mary. "Is Slater in Boise?"

Something in Tanner's tone frightened Mary. She took an involuntary step backward. "Mr. Slater went on to Oregon City. I have to get on home now but I'd be pleased if you and Ashley could come to supper tonight. We built a cabin on the north edge of town. It sits on about twenty acres of tall trees. You can't miss it. I'd like to hear how you rescued Ashley from the Indians."

"There is nothing to tell, really. I was more of a hindrance to Ashley than a help. She managed her rescue all on her own. As for supper, I'm sorry we have to decline. I thought we might rest a day or two in Boise but I've decided to go on immediately. There are still the Blue Mountains and the Cascades to cross before snow flies. We can't afford to waste a minute."

Mary expressed disappointment but insisted she understood. Ashley knew the real reason Tanner was so anxious to continue. Pratt Slater. Tanner was closing in on his prey and even a moment's delay was too long for him.

"Oh, did I tell you about Susan Jones?" Mary said in parting.

Ashley shook her head.

"She married the McCall boy. They both seem real happy."

"That is indeed good news," Ashley said. "Give them our best wishes when next you see them."

One day out of Fort Walla Walla they encountered five men traveling to Oregon City. Tanner didn't like the looks of them and refused their offer to travel together. They were a rough lot and Tanner didn't like the way they stared at Ashley. He rode with his rifle at his feet the rest of the afternoon and when they camped that night in a small clearing he wouldn't allow Ashley to leave the campsite without him. When it came time to bed down for the night, Tanner built up the fire and fixed two bedrolls, one inside the wagon and the other beneath it.

"Good night, Tanner," Ashley said as she turned toward the wagon.

Tanner grasped her arm with one hand and his rifle with the other and literally pulled her into the thick forest surrounding the clearing.

"Tanner, what are you doing?"

"Be quiet. We're going to have company in a little while and I don't intend for them to find us sleeping like sacrificial lambs."

"Company? What are you talking about?" They were well into the woods now and Tanner shoved her behind a thick trunk and pushed her down.

"Those men we encountered today. They've been trailing us all day. Didn't you see the way they looked at you? Those men are starved for a woman. They plan to kill me in order to get to you. They're holding off until dark to launch a surprise attack because they're cowards. They're afraid I might get off a lucky shot and kill one of them. They don't know I've been aware of them all day. Surprise will be on our side. We won't be sleeping, that's for damn sure. No matter what happens, Yank, stay hidden."

"Let me help. Give me one of your guns."

"Can you shoot?"

Ashley nodded jerkily. "I can hit what I aim at."

"The best thing you can do is stay out of sight and keep quiet."

"What are you going to do?"

"Kill the bastards. They wanted a surprise and they're going to get one."

"K-k-kill them?" The taut planes of Tanner's face and his flattened mouth told Ashley that he did indeed intend to kill the intruders if they had the bad judgment to attack in the dark of night. This was a Tanner she didn't recognize, a Tanner she hardly

289

knew. One entirely capable of killing five men in cold blood.

Another hour passed before Ashley saw something disturb the bushes at the edge of the clearing. A few minutes later five dark figures emerged from the forest.

"Here they come," Ashley hissed.

"I see them. Remember what I said; stay put no matter what. Take my rifle in case one of them comes your way." He patted his holster containing twin .41-caliber double-action Colt Lightning pistols. "These are all I need."

Before Ashley could form a reply, all five gunmen fired into the bedroll beneath the wagon. Had Tanner been sleeping in it he wouldn't have had a chance.

"Get the woman!" one of the men called out. "I'm hard as a rock. Ain't had a white woman in a coon's age."

Two men leaped into the wagon bed while the others gathered around the fire. One man produced a bottle and passed it around. Tanner chose that moment to step out of the bushes. He gave no warning as he leaped forward, both his pistols blazing. Two men fell immediately. The third was shot drawing his gun. Of the two men inside the wagon, one was picked off as he leaped from the tailgate but the other had been given enough warning to squeeze off a shot at Tanner.

Ashley stifled a cry of terror when she saw

Tanner fall to the ground. She was on the verge of rushing out of her hiding place to help Tanner when he rolled over, aimed and fired. The last gunman dropped to the ground with a resounding thud. Ashley was unable to think, unable to move. Tanner had killed all five men within seconds, as if taking human lives came naturally.

The shock of it remained with her even though she knew it was self-defense. It was either kill or be killed, but it was the way he had done it — methodically, with cold-blooded accuracy. He was a soldier. Nothing about him now reminded her of the tender lover whose gentle hands had given her incredible pleasure. Tanner staggered to his feet and all thought ceased as Ashley ran to his aid.

"Where are you hurt?" She helped him rise, searching his face and body for blood. She found a dark, wet patch on his forehead and touched it. Her hand came away sticky. Tanner brushed her hand aside.

"It's nothing; he just grazed me. Move aside, Ashley. I need to make sure none of these bastards are still capable of doing us harm."

Tanner bent to examine each gunman in turn. "Two are dead and three just wounded. They aren't going anywhere anytime soon. I'm going to tie them up and leave them in the woods. I'll notify the soldiers at Fort

Walla Walla and they can come out and get them. I'll take care of things here. You try to get some sleep."

Ashley didn't think she could sleep after the excitement, but she didn't argue with Tanner as she headed for the wagon. The danger they had been in finally hit her as she undressed and lay down on her cot. Five men against one. If Tanner hadn't been aware of the men's intentions he would have been killed and terrible things could have happened to her.

She began shaking and couldn't stop. The Indians hadn't frightened her as much as these five white men bent on mayhem. Coldness swept over her and she shook even harder.

Having disposed of the five intruders, Tanner poked his head inside the wagon to check on Ashley. Moonlight lit a path to her bed. He saw her shaking beneath the blankets and concern colored his words.

"Ashley, are you all right?"

"T-T-T-Tanner, please hold me."

"Yank, I don't think —"

She sat up, holding her arms out to him. "Please, Tanner, it's just hitting me that we could have been killed. I don't ever recall feeling so helpless or frightened. Not even in Running Elk's village."

Tanner couldn't deny Ashley's innocent request. In truth, he needed to hold her as

292

much as she needed to be held. Fortune had been with him tonight — fortune and the good sense to make damn certain the odds were on his side. The intruders were so sure of themselves it was almost laughable. Tanner had always been a good shot, even as a lad when his father had taken him hunting. His army years had taught him to recognize danger, and his instincts had served him well.

Tanner climbed into the wagon and pulled the bedding from the cot to the floor. Then he eased Ashley onto it and took her into his arms. She wasn't the only one shaking. He had never enjoyed killing and his body was belatedly reacting to the danger he had faced single-handedly.

"Oh, God, Tanner, you could have been killed." Ashley sobbed into his shirtfront.

"I wasn't killed. Those men won't bother us again. Try to get some sleep, love."

"I don't want to sleep. Love me, Reb. I don't want to think about what might have happened if you hadn't been such a good shot. I don't want to think about anything except being loved by you."

"Sweet Lord, Ashley, I want to love you so desperately it's a constant pain that never goes away. I'm not going to lie. You know where I stand where Pratt Slater is concerned, and I won't change my mind. Do you still want me?"

"I know how you feel and you know my

view on the subject. I also know that making love now isn't going to change a thing between us. I need you, Reb. What I'm asking isn't a forever thing. Can you accept that?"

His answer was a low, rumbling growl. Cupping her face between his hands, he brought her mouth to his.

Chapter Fourteen

Ashley opened her mouth to the sweet warmth of his tongue. She lifted her hand and brushed back his hair, then lowered it to skim his face. His forehead felt hot to her cool fingers. As he ravaged her mouth with fervid kisses, her hands lowered to his chest, then slid downward over his hips. When they reached the belt of his trousers, her palm curved over the hard ridge beneath the taut fabric.

Tanner sucked his breath in sharply, jolted by raw fire coursing through his veins. "Dear God, Yank, do you know what you're doing?"

"I know exactly what I'm doing, Reb." Her fingers went to the buckle of his holster. "Take this off." Tanner complied with alacrity. "And this," she said, pulling on the waistband of his trousers.

He undressed swiftly, then pulled Ashley's shift over her head and tossed it aside. He stared at her in wonder. Moonlight bathed her in pure shimmering silver. "You're so beautiful." Lowering his head, he tasted the delicate arch of her throat. His lips trailed downward, following the cleft between her breasts. Pillowing his face on the satiny swells, he inhaled her intoxicating womanly scent. With consummate tenderness he kissed and licked her breasts and nipples.

Ashley moaned with pleasure. "I want to touch and love you." She reached for him, rolling him to his back and stretching out atop him.

His breath ragged with effort, he grasped at control. A hard, thrumming pulse beat in his temples and in his loins. He could feel her damp female heat scorching him as she pressed herself against him. She gave an abandoned sigh that nearly unmanned him and he went rigid when he felt her mouth slide downward, across the hard ridges of his stomach. He sucked in a hard breath and let it hiss out between his teeth when she knelt between his legs and took his rigid length in her hand. She stared at it a moment and then placed a kiss on the moist tip.

Tanner arched violently. "Oh, God!"

"I like your taste, Reb," she said, pausing to smile up at him. "I like your body too. You're so big, so strong. I always feel safe with you."

"A taste is all you're going to get if you don't stop," Tanner growled. His voice held a note of desperation. "You're torturing me, Yank."

"Now you know how I feel when you do this to me," Ashley teased as she lowered her lips to continue her sweet torment.

Tanner stood it for several more minutes

before shouting out an oath, rolling over and trapping Ashley beneath him. Then he buried himself inside her with one fierce thrust. Just being inside her was almost enough to bring him to climax. The musky scent of sex sent a tempest raging through his blood. He feared he couldn't hold out long enough for Ashley to find her pleasure, and then there was no longer a need for constraint. Her hips began grinding against him and he felt her shudder and convulse around him. Her contractions triggered his own release and he thrust one last time before pulling out of her and spilling himself into the bedding.

Before he left her Tanner loved her one more time. After Ashley drifted off to sleep he returned to his bed beneath the wagon. He realized it wouldn't do to become accustomed to holding Ashley in his arms throughout the night, for once they reached Oregon City their marriage would end.

They reached Fort Walla Walla the next day and reported their confrontation with the five gunmen to the authorities. After signing a deposition they were allowed to go on their way. Their stop at the fort was necessarily brief. Snow had been reported in the higher elevations of the Cascades, and Tanner thought it wise not to linger. His prudence paid off. Two weeks later, when they traversed the pass through the Cascades, it was slippery and dangerous but still negotiable. But the dark, swirling clouds overhead promised more foul weather in the coming days.

The days and nights had turned cold and blustery. They had left Missouri in May, nearly six months ago. If not for their sojourn in Running Elk's village they would have already been in Oregon City. Fort Bridger had been Ashley's original destination, but Cole's marriage to Morning Mist had changed everything. Cole was free now but he had chosen to return to his Indian bride. And that had left Ashley adrift.

Harsh weather had sent Ashley digging into her trunk for heavy clothing and extra blankets. When she offered to share the wagon with Tanner on those cold nights, he had politely declined. If he and Ashley were going to part, he thought it best to make the separation as painless as possible. And that meant keeping out of her bed. He could only take so much torment.

After traveling two thousand miles, crossing the Rocky Mountains, the Blue Mountains and the Cascades, following the Platte River and crossing Snake River twice, as well as several other dangerously swollen rivers, they entered the Willamette Valley.

Six months to the day after they left St. Joe, Tanner drove the wagon down the muddy main street of Oregon City. It was already a bustling city inhabited by homesteaders, farmers and businessmen, so the sight of another wagon did not elicit much excitement. Tanner asked directions to the livery and within minutes they found the building at the north end of town.

"You folks looking to sell your wagon and oxen?" the hostler asked as he helped Tanner unhitch the animals.

Tanner deferred to Ashley, since the wagon and team belonged to her. "Why, yes, do you know of a buyer?" Ashley said.

The hostler nodded. "There's a party fixing to start back east come spring. They're looking for good wagons. 'Pears as if yours came through in good shape. Surprised to see you traveling alone, though. Most immigrants prefer to travel with wagon trains."

"We were with the Cramer party but had to leave," Tanner said, declining to offer details. "Can you recommend a good hotel?"

"The Willamette is the best in town. Nothing fancy by Eastern standards, but clean. The food is good too. You folks plan on homesteading?"

Ashley took a deep breath and said, "I'm hoping for a teaching position. I was a teacher in Chicago and would like to continue my profession. As for Mr. MacTavish, I can't answer for him."

"You folks ain't married?" The hostler seemed surprised.

Ashley sent Tanner a speaking look. "No. Mr. MacTavish and I aren't married. The wagon train we were traveling with encountered difficulty. Half the settlers succumbed to fever and those who survived settled in Boise. I decided to continue on to Oregon City. Mr. MacTavish is a close family friend. More like a brother. He promised my twin brother he'd see me safely to Oregon."

Tanner felt inexplicable rage when Ashley boldly announced that she considered him a brother. After everything they'd been through, everything they'd shared, hearing her deny their true relationship sent incredible pain surging through him. He knew he shouldn't feel hurt; their agreement was that they would part once she was safely delivered to her destination. If Ashley wasn't so damn obstinate about Pratt Slater it wouldn't have to end this way. Ashley couldn't understand his need for revenge and he refused to agree to compromise. Had Ashley lived through the horror of Ellen's tragic death she would feel differently.

"Did you say your brother will be joining you?" the hostler asked.

"Eventually," Ashley hedged. "As soon as he's able."

"I'll return later for our belongings," Tanner announced tersely as he hoisted his saddlebag over his shoulder. "I'm sure Miss Webster will be grateful if you can sell the

300

wagon and oxen for her. You can reach her at the Willamette Hotel." He paused, then asked, "You don't happen to know a man named Pratt Slater, do you? He should have arrived in Oregon City a couple of months ago."

The hostler scratched his unshaven chin, then broke out in a grin. "Now that you mention it, I do recall a man by that name. He works for Sam Stark and rents a room at the Red Garter, a gambling emporium and saloon, among other things," he added with a sly wink at Tanner. "Don't know much about him, though; he kinda keeps to himself. He boards his horse here when he's in town. Is he a friend of yours, mister?"

Tanner went rigid. "He's no friend of mine. If you see him, tell him Tanner MacTavish is looking for him."

"He ain't here. Left just yesterday on a mission for Sam. Didn't say when he'd return."

The hostler seemed so well informed, Ashley inquired, "Do you know if there is a teaching job open? I'd like to find work as soon as I can."

The hostler gave a whoop of laughter. "A pretty lady like you don't need to worry about finding a job. Why, every bachelor in town will be knocking at your door as soon as they get a good look at you."

"I'm a spinster, Mr. . . ."

301

"Most folks just call me Pops."

"I'm a spinster, Mr. — Pops. Marriage isn't a priority with me. About that job . . ."

"I did hear tell that the schoolmarm is getting married real soon and that the council is having the devil's own time finding a replacement. The young, pretty ones don't last long; they usually marry soon after they arrive."

"They ought to hire a man," Tanner said grumpily. All this talk about Ashley finding a husband grated on him.

"Well, now, the town fathers tried that but the men didn't last any longer than the women. They got the wanderlust and moved on. If you're interested in that teaching position, miss, the man to see is the mayor."

"Thank you, Pops. You've been most helpful."

They had no sooner left the livery than Tanner rounded on her. "It didn't take long to rid yourself of a husband. You couldn't even wait for the divorce, could you?"

"If people knew I was married I'd never have a chance at that teaching position. They only hire unmarried women. I have to support myself, Tanner. Divorced women are no more acceptable as teachers than married women. Even out here in the wilderness the stigma of divorce can ruin a woman's reputation."

Tanner gave her an amused grin. "We've been traveling companions for several

302

months. You've let out that we're not married. What does that say for your precious reputation?"

"I told Pops you were a close family friend. People can assume but they won't know," Ashley responded. "I can assure you my teaching credentials are very impressive. If they need a teacher as badly as Pops said, the town fathers won't look too closely into my past."

Her words made Tanner search for anger, but instead he found sadness. He stared at her. "It doesn't have to end like this, Yank."

Ashley stared back. "No, Reb, it doesn't."

They both recognized the impasse they had arrived at.

"Give up on your vendetta against Slater. Let the law deal with him."

Tanner gave a bark of laughter. "The law doesn't give a tinker's damn about what happened during the war. I do. When Slater returns to town, I'll be waiting for him."

"Then there is nothing more to say, is there? After I reimburse you for your services, we're quits. My money is still in your saddlebag, isn't it?"

"It is. But I don't want your money."

"It's what we agreed upon," Ashley persisted. "I insist that you take it. Few men would have done what you did for me. You've more than earned your fee."

Tanner's face flushed with anger. "If

you're paying me for *all* my services, it's not enough. My fees come much higher. My name and my protection is trivial compared to my . . . shall we say . . . intimate duties."

Ashley gasped in outrage. How dare he insinuate that she had hired him for anything other than his escort and protection. She had been desperate to reach Fort Bridger. Their marriage had been necessary; he knew that. He had agreed to it; she hadn't twisted his arm or held a gun on him. His need had been as urgent as hers.

She scowled at him, hating his crude insinuation. Once again he was the hateful Reb she had first met. "That was a cruel thing to say."

"So is the way you refuse to consider my feelings. I have good reason to want Slater dead. I know I'm a penniless Reb, that I have no right to place a claim on you. I can offer you nothing but my name, and you've already refused that. We've had this argument before and neither of us is ready to compromise. Let's part now before we hurt one another even more than we already have."

Ashley felt as if a giant hand had reached inside her chest and squeezed her heart. "Very well, if that's the way it has to be."

"You have our marriage papers. You can handle this any way you want. I'll go along with anything you tell the lawyer. If you want to say we never shared a bed, that's fine with me. As you've just said, the circumstances of our marriage were a bit unusual."

"Tanner . . . I . . ." Damn, how could the man be so obtuse? Didn't he know she loved him? Didn't he realize she didn't give a hoot about money? "If that's your last word on the subject, then please take your fee from the money you're keeping for me and bring what's left to my hotel room."

"I'll see that you get your money and that your belongings are delivered to the Willamette."

"What about Slater? Pops said he isn't in town."

"I'll wait." Turning abruptly, he left her standing in the middle of the street.

Ashley watched him walk away, trying valiantly to stave off the tears that hovered so close to the surface. When she'd asked Tanner to marry her it was supposed to have been a temporary arrangement. Who would have known the big Reb would find the way to her heart? Or that she could love a man who carried hatred on his sleeve like a flag? Few people saw the tender, sensitive side of Tanner, but she had. Unfortunately the uncompromising hatred bubbling inside of him made loving him a formidable task.

Tanner stopped at the end of the street and watched Ashley enter the Willamette Hotel. The promise he'd made himself after Ellen's death was all that kept him from following his heart's desire. Running Elk had named Ashley well. Flame. It was appropriate, Tanner thought, and not just because of her glorious red hair. Indeed not. He had kindled her passion into a white-hot flame and she had burned for him. He was the only man alive who had experienced her ardor, had released the hunger within her.

If he had been a man without a conscience he would forget his promise and seize the happiness that awaited him with Ashley. But as long as Slater lived he had to deny his own heart.

The room Ashley rented at the hotel was adequate for her needs. She ordered a bath and supper and went directly to bed after she had eaten. She hoped that things would look brighter tomorrow. Tonight she had a lot to think about. Tanner expected her to end their marriage one way or another, but in truth that was the last thing she wanted. She knew now that she wasn't carrying Tanner's child, so there was no impediment to a permanent separation, but the thought of severing all ties nearly broke her heart.

Bright and early the next morning Tanner arrived with her belongings. Ashley thought he looked wretched. He hadn't shaved or changed his clothes and his eyes were blood-

306

shot, as if he hadn't slept all night. Or else he had spent the night drinking.

"I arranged to have your belongings delivered," he said without preamble. "I'll carry them into the room for you."

Ashley stood aside while he dragged two trunks and three carpetbags into the room.

"You look like hell, Reb. Didn't you get any sleep last night?"

"Good morning to you too, Yank. Don't worry about my sleeping arrangements; I managed just fine." Managing meant stretching out in the wagon and tossing all night. He'd have to find lodgings today, Tanner thought. He had no idea when Slater would return to Oregon City, or even where he'd gone. All he could do was sit tight and wait until he returned.

"I have your money." He dug into his saddlebag and pulled out a cloth sack into which she had stuffed all the money she had in the world.

"Did you take out your share?"

"I already told you I don't want it."

Ashley opened the bag and counted out five hundred dollars. "Here, take it. You earned it. It was what we agreed upon."

"Dammit, Yank . . . Very well," he capitulated, too weary to argue. He'd spent half the night at the Red Garter asking questions about Slater, but had learned little more than he already knew. He took the bills and stuffed

307

them into his vest pocket. Somehow he'd see that the money was returned to Ashley. "Have you decided on your next move? Will you get a divorce or an annulment?"

Ashley turned away and walked to the window. She stared absently at passersby on the street below. Tanner watched the tantalizing sway of her hips and wanted to reach out and pull her into his arms. He was startled when she suddenly whirled about to confront him.

"I've thought a lot about this, Reb. I'm not going to get a divorce. Or an annulment, either. Since I have no intention of ever remarrying, there is no need." She walked to her trunk, opened it and took out a folded sheet of paper. She shoved it under Tanner's nose. "Our marriage certificate. You take it. If you want to get out of this marriage you can damn well do it yourself."

Tanner stared at the paper as if it were a serpent about to strike him. "I don't want it. I know damn well I'll never remarry. You keep it. You're young and beautiful. One day some man will come along and sweep you off your feet. When that happens you'll want your freedom, and you'll need the marriage license to show to the lawyer."

Ashley wished she could pound some sense into Tanner's hard head. Didn't he know he was the man she wanted, the only man? Why couldn't he see past his need for revenge?

Fortunately, during the long sleepless night she had thought of a clever way to delay the dissolution of their marriage. She feared that once they were no longer husband and wife she would lose Tanner forever. Postponing their permanent separation was a last-ditch effort to force Tanner into realizing he needed her more than he wanted to kill Slater.

"There won't be another man, Tanner," Ashley insisted. "I was a spinster before I met you and I learned to live with my unmarried state. It won't be difficult to remain a spinster."

"What about that teaching position you want? What are you going to tell the town council about me? We were seen entering the city together. And what about Slater? He knows the truth about us. When he returns he's bound to let out that we're married."

Ashley grew thoughtful. She hadn't considered that. Actually, that might not be as disastrous as it sounded. By that time Tanner might have decided to give up on Slater.

"We'll just have to handle that when the time comes. Meanwhile, I'll simply tell the town council that you're my brother's best friend, and that I'm waiting for my brother and his wife to join me here. Are you sure you don't want our marriage license?" She held it out to him and he shoved her hand away.

"You keep it. I'll inform you where I'm

staying in town in case you need me for anything. Let me know if you change your mind about . . . anything."

"Let me know when you're ready to devote yourself to our marriage," Ashley returned. "We could be happy if you weren't so damn stubborn and riddled with hatred."

"I don't hate you." He reached for her.

Ashley wanted to resist but couldn't find it in her heart to do so. Since the night he had killed the intruders he hadn't so much as kissed her. She ached for him. But she wanted all of him: his heart, his body, his soul. She wouldn't settle for the small part of him he allowed her.

His mouth slammed down on hers and he hauled her abruptly against his loins. She felt clearly the hard thrust of his arousal against her stomach. She let her hands climb up his shoulders and clung to his neck, trying to show him by action how much she cared for him.

"Tanner," she moaned, pressing herself against him.

He answered with a short oath. He pushed her away, suddenly aware of what he was doing. Seducing her would only make parting more difficult. "I'm sorry. I shouldn't be here." He turned to leave. "I hope you get that teaching job."

"Tanner, wait. . . ." He was gone before she finished her sentence.

★ ★ ★

After Tanner's visit Ashley felt better about her decision not to visit a lawyer just yet. She was sure Tanner loved her; she just had to try harder to find a way to make him admit his life would be empty without her.

After a leisurely breakfast in the hotel dining room, Ashley returned to her room to prepare for her visit to the mayor. First she donned a plain, high-necked brown dress, one that did little to enhance her beauty. Then she skinned her hair back into a severe bun, topping it with an unattractive hat that almost completely covered her flaming hair. Satisfied except for one last touch, which she intended to remedy shortly, she left her room.

Ashley's first stop was the mercantile, where she purchased a pair of wire-rim glasses. Since she was slightly farsighted anyway, the magnifying lenses did more good than harm. She perched them on her nose, delighted with her image reflected in the mirror. She looked like a mature woman with little to commend her except startling green eyes somewhat disguised by her spectacles. She was convinced that no one would doubt her claim of being a spinster schoolmarm.

Before calling on the mayor, Ashley visited the bank, where she opened an account in the name of Ashley Webster and deposited all but a few dollars of her money. Even if she didn't get the teaching position she would have money enough to live frugally until something came along, thanks to the modest inheritance from her aunt. Besides, she hadn't yet given up on Tanner.

From the bank Ashley proceeded on to the town hall, where the mayor kept an office. She was obliged to wait an hour before Mayor Thornton was free to see her. The stout, gray-haired man sitting behind the desk gave her a distracted smile. The smile scrunched up his eyes until they all but disappeared in his plump face.

"What can I do for you, miss? I was told you wanted to see me. I'm rather busy, so if you could state your business . . ."

"I'm here to apply for the schoolmarm position, sir," Ashley said in a prim little voice. "I heard there was an opening."

The mayor sat back and studied Ashley objectively. Perhaps, he thought, if the council hired this mouse of a woman she wouldn't be inclined to marry and leave like the others. The good-looking ones were the first to find husbands. And the not-so-good-looking ones found husbands soon after, more was the pity. Women were at a premium on the far Western frontier.

"We do have an opening, Miss . . . ?"

"Webster. My name is Ashley Webster."

"Well, Miss Webster, our schoolmarm is getting married Saturday next. We tried to get her to wait until the end of the school year but she declined. As you know we don't hire married ladies.

"Have you credentials, Miss Webster?"

"I taught in Chicago before I left to meet my brother at Fort Bridger. He'll be joining me here soon," she lied. "I have both teaching credentials and letters of recommendation. You'll find my record is without blemish." She dug in her reticule and handed a sheaf of papers to the mayor for his perusal.

Thornton studied them carefully. "Well, now, this is certainly impressive. Unfortunately I can't hire you without the approval of the town council. We meet day after tomorrow at two o'clock sharp. In my office. You can present your credentials then and answer any pertinent questions."

"I'll certainly be there, Mayor Thornton. May I ask what the job pays?"

Thornton cleared his throat and mentioned a number. "I wish it could be more but the position does include a small house as part of the salary. If you work out you'll receive an increase next school year."

Ashley nodded. "It will be sufficient." She rose to leave. "Thank you, Mayor Thornton. I'll see you day after tomorrow."

Ashley was pleased with the interview. The way she'd dressed and worn her hair was exactly the way she had looked nearly every single day that she taught school in Chicago.

313

Since her broken engagement five years before she'd had no desire to attract another man, until she met Tanner.

Speak of the devil, Ashley thought as she glanced across the street and saw Tanner coming out of the Red Garter. He stared at her a full minute before recognizing her. A moment later he was striding in her direction.

He eyed her critically and with obvious distaste. "What in the hell are you doing dressed like that?"

"It's how schoolmarms are supposed to look," Ashley shot back. "I want that job, Tanner."

"You look like you did the first time I saw you. Plain as dirt. I thought you were a prim and proper spinster until you boldly announced that you needed a husband. Then I didn't know what to think."

Ashley smiled at the memory.

"Then you took off your hat," Tanner recalled, "and all that glorious red hair tumbled down around your shoulders. It was then I knew there was more to you than met the eye."

He stared at her and Ashley felt herself go liquid inside. Why did she let him do this to her? "I have to go, Tanner. If I'm going to be the new schoolmarm I can't afford to be involved in gossip."

Tanner scowled at Ashley. Hearing her speaking about a future without him did not

314

sit well. He knew his inflexible position on Slater had forced her to take a stand, but it still rankled that she was as inflexible as he. "I just wanted to tell you that I've taken a room at the Red Garter. The rooms there are cheaper than any of the hotels in town."

"How convenient for you." Ashley sniffed, aware of what went on upstairs at places like the Red Garter.

"It's just a room, Ashley. I wanted you to know where I was staying in case you needed me." He paused, then said as if it made a difference, "Slater rents a room at the Red Garter when he's in town."

"I'm sure I won't need you for anything, Reb. Now if you'll excuse me . . ."

Stepping carefully around him, Ashley continued down the street. Had she eyes behind her back she'd have seen Tanner staring after her with inexplicable sadness. She had no idea that no matter how unattractive she tried to make herself look, to Tanner she was still beautiful, still desirable.

Tanner remained thoughtful long after Ashley had disappeared inside her hotel. It seemed incredible that for a time she had been all his. For the first time since vowing to kill Slater, Tanner began to have second thoughts.

Chapter Fifteen

Ashley adjusted her spectacles on the bridge of her nose and dragged in a calming breath as she entered the mayor's office. She had been kept cooling her heels in the outer office fifteen minutes while waiting to be called before the town council.

Her sweeping glance took in five men seated around a scarred table, engaged in earnest conversation. Cigar smoke wreathed their heads. Talk ceased the moment Ashley walked into the room. Five pairs of eyes swung around in her direction.

"Gentlemen, this is the young lady I've been telling you about. As you all know, we are in desperate need of a teacher to finish out the school year. I've studied Miss Webster's credentials and was duly impressed." He motioned Ashley forward. "Miss Webster, would you be so kind as to show the other board members your credentials and letters of recommendation?"

Ashley smiled as she handed a folder containing her credentials to the mayor, who in turn passed it around the table.

"Allow me to introduce the other board members," the mayor said. "The gentleman at the head of the table is Mr. Hannibal

Newley, the town banker. Next to him is Mr. Chris George. He's the best barber in town. Continuing around the table, the gentleman smoking the dollar cigar is Mr. Samuel Stark, the owner of several local establishments, and next to him is Mr. Fester Langley, who owns the sawmill."

All the men, except for Samuel Stark, were beyond middle age. Two were too fat, two were too thin, and all four showed signs of considerable hair loss. They represented the leaders of Oregon City society and looked as if they were made from the same mold. Samuel Stark was the exception. He was younger than the rest, handsome in a suave, polished way, and much too sure of himself. He boldly stared at Ashley, all the while fingering his blond mustache in a way that made Ashley shudder.

The men acknowledged Ashley in turn. She inclined her head and tried to quell her nervousness. She wished Tanner were here.

Newley spoke up first. "Since you've taught school before, you are aware that we expect unwavering dedication to our children. Placing them in your hands gives you great power over them. We must make certain you take that responsibility seriously."

"I understand," Ashley assured them. "I am dedicated to the teaching of children."

"We expect you to maintain a high standard of morals," Chris George instructed.

317

Ashley nodded, not trusting herself to speak. She had no idea that several strands of hair had worked loose from beneath her hat, providing a glimpse of gleaming red tresses. Her mind had been too occupied with the pompous men judging her to think about her appearance. She seriously doubted that these men were models of propriety themselves, and deplored their high-handed manner.

"You understand why these questions are necessary, don't you?" Samuel Stark said in an effort to soften his colleagues' pompous words. His blue eyes held a predatory gleam, as if to convey that her prim and proper manner didn't fool him. "I am not a married man myself, but I know how concerned the board members are about their children's welfare."

Ashley acknowledged his words with a taut smile. "I understand perfectly. I am a mature and responsible adult. The town's children will be safe with me."

"Well, I'm convinced," the mayor said. "I'm all for hiring Miss Webster as our new schoolmarm."

"Wait a minute," Fester Langley interrupted. "My wife, upstanding citizen that she is, heard through the grapevine that Miss Webster arrived in town in the company of a man who is not her husband, brother or father. Since Miss Webster's morals are of grave concern, I feel she owes us an explanation."

Ashley could tell by Langley's scowl that he was a mean-tempered individual. "I'd be more than happy to explain," Ashley offered. "I left Missouri in the company of Mr. Tanner MacTavish, a close and trusted family friend. Since he was traveling west anyway, my brother asked him to act as my escort to Fort Bridger, where Cole was stationed with the army. Cole's enlistment was up soon and he planned to settle in Oregon City. Cole is the only family I have left. He's my twin.

"When we arrived at Fort Bridger I learned that Cole had gone to Denver to collect his new bride. I wired Cole and he wired back, asking Mr. MacTavish to escort me to Oregon City. Cole and his wife will join me as soon as possible. There is nothing irregular in the situation, gentlemen. Mr. MacTavish is like a brother to me."

Ashley had a feeling that the board wasn't completely satisfied with her explanation, but she hoped they were desperate enough to overlook the impropriety of her sojourn across the prairie with Tanner.

"I for one think Miss Webster will make an admirable teacher," Sam Stark opined. "Her explanation satisfies me."

"If any of you gentlemen aren't convinced, I suggest that Miss Webster be placed on probation for the remainder of the school year, and if she works out her position can become

319

permanent next year," Mayor Thornton said.

"I agree," Stark said. "Shall we vote, gentlemen? A show of hands will do." Four hands raised in the air, with only Langley abstaining.

Thornton banged the gavel down. "Close enough. You're hired, Miss Webster."

Ashley allowed herself to breathe again.

"You can start Monday next, Miss Webster. The house you'll occupy is situated on the same street as the schoolhouse. Number fifteen Cascade Street. Miss Palmer has already moved out, so you're free to move in this weekend. Oregon City is one of the few towns today that offers lodging for its teachers," the mayor explained. "The town fathers decided early on that we'd be better able to keep teachers if lodging was provided. Unfortunately it hasn't worked out as we'd hoped. Be that as it may, you are free to occupy the house for as long as you're employed as schoolmarm."

"Which I hope will be a good long time," Stark added with an inflection that made Ashley mistrust his friendliness.

"Thank you," Ashley said. "You won't be sorry, gentlemen." She turned to leave.

"Wait, Miss Webster," Stark said, rising with easy grace. "Our meeting is over. Let me escort you to your hotel and acquaint you with our town."

"That's kind of you, but . . ."

Stark wouldn't take no for an answer. Grasping Ashley's elbow, he guided her from the room. He said nothing until they were standing outside in the misty air. Snow seldom fell in Oregon along the coastal regions, but rain was a common occurrence. Ashley would welcome the lack of snow, but decided that constant rain would take some getting used to.

"You're staying at the Willamette Hotel, aren't you, Miss Webster?"

"Yes, but I know the way, Mr. Stark."

He ignored her. "I'll be happy to arrange for your trunks to be taken to your house on Saturday," he told her. "I know how alone you must feel, with no one to turn to in a strange city and all."

"Oh, but I'm not alone," Ashley said before thinking how it would sound. "I have Tanner."

Stark's eyes narrowed. "Tanner?"

Realizing her mistake, Ashley flushed and gazed down at her folded hands. "Tanner MacTavish. He's as close as a brother to me."

"Of course," Stark said with a nasty chuckle. He didn't for a minute believe the prim little schoolmarm's explanation. If he looked beyond the shapeless, nondescript clothing and spectacles that hid the startling green of her eyes, he felt certain he'd find a hot-blooded woman. He'd almost laughed at

321

her effort to hide her red hair beneath her unbecoming bonnet. And he'd bet his considerable fortune that MacTavish was more than just a family friend. Mysteries had always intrigued him, and he intended to explore fully the mysterious woman who tried to hide her beauty and failed.

"Do you own a business in town, Mr. Stark?" Ashley asked in an effort to change the subject.

"Several. I won't bore you with my accomplishments." He stared at her. "Tell me, Miss Webster, do you really need those spectacles?"

"I beg your pardon?"

In a move totally unexpected, he pulled the glasses from her face. "I don't think you need them at all." He searched her face in slow perusal. "You're a raving beauty, Miss Webster. Why are you trying to hide it? I'm not exactly a stranger to women, and intuition tells me there's more to you than meets the eye."

"How dare you!" Ashley could feel her temper slowly rising. The man was insufferable. Other women might find him attractive, but she did not. He was too suave, too sure of himself, too damn pushy.

Stark laughed. "Don't worry; I won't tell anyone." He carefully placed the glasses back on her face. "You're a fraud, Miss Webster, and I wonder why. No matter," he said

322

cheerfully. "The board values my opinion. I think you'll do just fine as our new school-marm with me as your champion. And I predict you and I are going to become close friends. Mysterious women intrigue me."

"I think not," Ashley said in curt dismissal.

"I'll call at your hotel Saturday morning with a wagon and two men to help with your move to your new lodging." They were standing in front of the hotel now. Stark tipped his hat and strode off down the street before Ashley could reject his offer.

Samuel Stark was a man accustomed to getting his way, Ashley decided, but this time he was going to be disappointed. It had never occurred to her that she would attract a man like Sam Stark looking as she did. Ashley couldn't possibly know that men like Stark constantly craved new conquests.

"What was that all about?"

Ashley started violently. "Where did you come from? Must you sneak up on me, Reb?"

"Stay away from Sam Stark," Tanner warned.

"Why? He's one of the city's leading citizens."

"Ha! He owns the Red Garter, a saloon with an unsavory reputation."

Ashley frowned with annoyance. "He sits on the town council."

"I'm told he also owns some respectable businesses. His money gives him enough clout to assure him a seat on the town council."

"How do you know all this?"

"I room at the Red Garter, remember? One hears things in saloons. Besides, I've seen him come and go often enough. He keeps an office behind the bar. Pratt Slater works for him."

Astonished, Ashley clucked her tongue. "You have been busy, haven't you?"

"Just keep away from Stark. He's notorious where women are concerned. And I needn't tell you why."

Ashley's heart jumped with joy. Tanner was jealous! He had to care for her or he wouldn't be jealous. She decided to test him. "Mr. Stark has kindly offered to help move me into my new quarters."

"You didn't need to ask Stark for help. I'm still your husband, remember?"

"How could I forget? I didn't ask for Mr. Stark's help; he offered." She sent him a guileless smile. "It was nice of him, wasn't it?"

Tanner spit out an oath that singed her ears. "I can see you're going to be stubborn about this. Very well, I realize I've lost the right to interfere in your life. I'm sorry."

"We're still married," Ashley reminded him.

"That was your choice. Personally, I can't see the sense of it if we're not going to live as husband and wife. And we've gone over that often enough to know it won't work as long as neither of us can agree on . . . a certain matter."

"Has that 'certain matter' returned to town yet?"

Tanner's jaw clenched. "No, but when he does, I'll be waiting."

"Then you won't care if I avail myself of Mr. Stark's kindness."

"Just as long as you don't 'avail' yourself of anything else Sam Stark offers," Tanner gritted out harshly.

Ashley gave him a heart-stopping smile. "I'll remember that. Good-bye, Reb." With a toss of her head, she turned and entered the hotel, leaving Tanner fuming in impotent rage.

"Damn stubborn Yank," he muttered as he watched the enticing sway of her hips. Didn't she know she was flirting with danger? He'd learned enough about Stark from Nell, the woman who ran the Red Garter, to know that one didn't trifle with him. Stark wasn't as young as he looked, either. He was over forty if he was a day. Nell said he was from New York City and had arrived in Oregon City ten years ago with a pocket full of ready cash. He started buying up property and businesses soon after he arrived.

Still muttering to himself, Tanner went back to the Red Garter and ordered a beer.

He carried it to a table and stared moodily into the foaming brew.

"Can you use some company, handsome?"

Tanner recognized Nell's voice and smiled up at her. She was still a stunning woman despite her being over thirty years old, Tanner thought. She looked almost exotic with her coal black hair, dark eyes and milk-white complexion. Only a few tiny crow's feet gave hint of her true age.

Though Nell ran the saloon, everyone knew Stark owned it. At one time Nell had been Stark's mistress. During recent years their relationship had changed. It was a well-known fact that Stark had courted several different women in the past few years. Tanner had learned all this through his conversations with Nell, and from some of the girls working at the saloon.

"You can sit if you want, Nell, but I'm not good company right now."

"Still waiting for Pratt Slater?" Nell asked. "He's on some kind of errand for Sam. What do you want with him?"

In the course of their conversations, it hadn't been difficult for Nell to learn Tanner's reason for being in Oregon City, and that he hated Slater. Hell, she wasn't surprised. She couldn't stand Slater herself.

"It's a long story, Nell. And far too personal to matter to anyone but me."

Nell shrugged. "Suit yourself, Tanner."

Her dark eyes slid down the length of him, liking what she saw. So far she'd been unsuccessful in luring him into her bed. Men like Tanner didn't come along every day. She never took customers upstairs anymore, not since Sam had dumped her, but when someone like Tanner came along, she was sorely tempted.

Not since Sam Stark had literally pulled her up from the gutter and made her his mistress had she felt such compelling interest in a man. She and Sam were history now, though she wished it were otherwise. She hadn't been seriously involved with anyone since Sam. The saloon she managed for Sam was her only passion. It would do her good, she thought, to take a lover. She hoped Tanner would be that man.

"I noticed you haven't expressed much interest in any of my girls. If you're looking for something different, I'd be more than happy to oblige."

Tanner eyed her with wry amusement. She couldn't have been more direct than that. Unfortunately her considerable charms were wasted on him. "I appreciate your offer, Nell, but this damned mood of mine would spoil the pleasure for both of us. How about I take a rain check?"

Nell stood. She wanted Tanner but obviously his mind was on someone or something else. She wasn't a woman to beg for a man's attention. She sent him a look filled with regret yet ripe with promise.

"It's your loss, handsome. But if you change your mind you know where to find me." To Tanner's surprise, she bent and brushed a kiss across his lips.

"Consider that a sample of what I can offer you. We'd be good together, handsome." Then she walked away, sending Tanner a sultry look over her shoulder.

Strangely, Tanner wasn't thinking of Nell when she'd kissed him. He was so consumed with his Yankee wife that other women held little appeal. Not that Nell wasn't desirable. She was damned appealing, but not to him. His eyes narrowed in silent contemplation. Maybe, he thought, another woman was what he needed to cleanse Ashley from his blood. The little Yank had the power to make him forget he ever knew a man named Pratt Slater, and he couldn't allow that to happen. Killing Pratt Slater was something he had to do for Ellen.

Sam Stark turned up at Ashley's door bright and early Saturday morning. His wagon was parked at the curb, and two of his brawniest men waited in the hallway to carry her trunks down. Ashley had packed the day before and paid her hotel bill, so everything was in readiness for her move. She stood aside while the two men shouldered her

328

trunks and carried them down the stairs.

"You and I will ride in my buggy, Miss Webster," Stark said as he waited for her to descend the stairs. "The schoolhouse is only two streets over."

Once they reached the street, Stark grasped her around the waist and lifted her into the buggy. A short time later they arrived at a small clapboard house that sat adjacent to the one-room schoolhouse. It was painted white just like the school, and both showed signs of weathering. Stark lifted Ashley down from the buggy and produced the door key.

"I took the liberty of obtaining the key from the mayor," he said as he inserted the key into the lock and pushed open the door.

Ashley saw at a glance that the previous schoolmarm had left the tiny house sparkling clean. The house was like a dollhouse, consisting of two rooms and a kitchen, each room sparsely furnished with bare necessities. A potbellied stove sat in one corner of the parlor, and a wood-burning cookstove all but filled the tiny kitchen. Ashley assumed that the bedroom lay just beyond the parlor. The rear exit was through the kitchen.

"It's very nice," Ashley commented. "Thank you for your help, Mr. Stark."

"My pleasure, Miss Webster."

Ashley assumed Stark would leave and was disconcerted when he stood there smiling at her, making no effort to depart. So upsetting

329

was his gaze that she wondered if she had omitted some important article of clothing when she dressed. She was wearing the same drab, unappealing dress she had appeared in before the town council.

"Is something wrong, Mr. Stark?"

"My name is Sam."

"It wouldn't be proper to address you by your given name."

"It wouldn't hurt in private. And I'll call you Ashley; the name suits you. It's not all that common for a woman and adds to your mystique."

"I prefer to be called Miss Webster," Ashley said primly. What did this man want from her? She'd never had this problem in Chicago. Few men looked past her prim exterior and drab clothing. No one except Tanner had ever cared enough to learn what she was really like inside.

"I can't figure you out, Ashley," Stark continued as if she hadn't spoken. "But I assure you, I will. You're concealing something. Whatever could it be?"

His teasing tone did nothing to allay Ashley's fear that Stark wanted something from her, something she wasn't willing to give. Telling him she was married was out of the question if she wished to keep her job.

"I find you fascinating, Ashley. I'm taking it upon myself to see that you adjust to your new job and our fair city."

330

The men arrived with the trunks, and Ashley used that as an excuse to get rid of Stark. "I'd like to look around and settle in," she said, inviting Stark to leave as she held the door open. "There is much to be done before school convenes on Monday. Goodbye, Mr. Stark." She couldn't be more direct than that, Ashley thought smugly.

Stark took the hint and bid her good day. Ashley closed the door behind him and heaved a relieved sigh. She wished the man would quit pestering her. With an efficiency of motion, she pulled the pins from her hat and tossed it on the faded brown settee. Then she ran her hands through her hair until it tumbled freely down her back in a riot of gleaming red curls, and unbuttoned the high collar of her bodice. She had just removed her spectacles when the door burst open.

Sam Stark stood on the threshold. "I just wanted to warn you to lock . . ." A surprised breath caught in his throat as his gaze slid over her unbound hair, coming to rest on the patch of skin visible beneath the opening of her neckline. "My God, you're more beautiful than I imagined! It's a sin to hide such beauty."

Ashley bristled indignantly. "It's no one's business how I choose to dress. You shouldn't have come in without knocking. Was there something you wanted?"

He gave her a cocky grin. "I just wanted to

331

remind you to lock the door."

"I'll be sure to remember."

"Before I saw you like this I was intrigued by the prospect of discovering what you were really like. Now that I know, I predict we're going to become close friends, very close friends. Of course we'll have to be discreet. No one except for me will ever know what the new schoolmarm is really like. In fact, I prefer it that way. There really isn't a brother coming to join you, is there?"

"Of course there is a brother," Ashley said hotly. "He will join me . . . eventually," she added lamely.

"What about Mr. MacTavish? I've seen him in the Red Garter. He's more than a trusted family friend, isn't he?"

"My brother trusts him implicitly," she said with complete honesty.

Stark gave a hoot of laughter. "Keep your little secrets, Ashley, if they make you happy. I'm giving you fair warning. We're going to be intimate friends and I don't want another man horning in on my territory."

Ashley lifted her hand and slapped him hard across the face. "How dare you! Please leave, Mr. Stark."

Stark touched his cheek and sent her a look so dark and forbidding that Ashley stepped back in fear. "I'll warn you just this once; don't do that again. I always get what I want, and I want you. I've never had a prim and

332

proper schoolmarm before. I'll be calling on you again real soon," he promised. "I'll come at night, so no one will suspect a thing."

"Can't you get it through your head that I'm not interested in a tawdry affair? Don't come again, Mr. Stark. I won't let you in." With a strength born of anger, she pushed him out the door and slammed it in his face. This time she locked it. No job was important enough to put up with a nuisance like Sam Stark.

"The man isn't going to take no for an answer, Yank."

Ashley nearly expired from fright. Whirling, she spied Tanner standing in the doorway between the kitchen and the parlor, his arms crossed over his chest, a sardonic smile thinning his lips.

"How did you get in?"

"Through the back door. Stark was right; you should lock your doors."

"How much did you hear?"

He pushed himself away from the doorjamb and walked toward her. "Enough. I told you the man is dangerous. He's not a fool like the others sitting on the town council. He knows uncommon beauty when he sees it. The man isn't going to be satisfied until he has you."

"Does that bother you?" Ashley asked coyly. "It shouldn't. Ours isn't a real marriage."

He grasped her shoulders and gave her a hard shake. "Dammit, Yank, you're no strumpet! You know what Stark wants as well as I do. I won't have it!"

Ashley's heart soared. Whether Tanner knew it or not, he was acting like a jealous husband. "I didn't encourage him, Tanner. Most men wouldn't look twice at a drab little mouse like me."

Tanner shook her again, harder this time. "You're not drab, Ashley. Or a mouse. You couldn't be however much you wanted to. You're a vibrant woman, gloriously female and sexy as hell. I can't look at you without wanting you." He dragged her hand to his groin. "See what you do to me? I'm hard as stone. If I had an ounce of sense I'd let Nell or one of her girls work the frustrations out of me."

The breath caught in Ashley's throat. "You mean you haven't bedded another woman since you and I . . . ?"

Tanner gave a snort of disgust. "Yeah, that's right. Dammit, Yank, you've spoiled me for other women."

Ashley's breath came in ragged little spurts. "We're still married, Tanner." She wound her arms around his neck, tugging his head down to meet her lips. For the space of a heartbeat, Tanner's mouth settled over hers. When she swept her tongue over his lips, he groaned and flung her away, but just as quickly he pulled her back into his arms.

"Dammit, Yank, you drive me crazy! When are you going to come to your senses? Neither of us is happy this way."

Ashley smiled, secretly pleased. "It makes me happy to hear you admit it. You can remedy that easily enough, Reb. Forget Slater. I can't live with the knowledge that I could lose you. You could pay with your life for killing Slater. Have you considered the possibility that Slater could kill you?"

Tanner nodded slowly. "I've considered that. My life has had little meaning since Ellen shot herself with my gun. What kind of man would allow such a travesty to go unavenged?"

"A good man," Ashley said softly. "A man big enough to forget the past and get on with his life instead of blaming himself for something that wasn't his fault."

"I'm not that man, Yank."

"Do you love me, Reb?" It was the first time Ashley had had the temerity to ask that question, and she was sorry she had when Tanner turned away from her.

"No, dammit, look at me," Ashley all but shouted. "I need to know how you feel about me. Because I love you, Tanner, you stubborn fool!"

"You want to know how I feel about you? Very well," Tanner said, his voice resigned as he turned back to face her. "I never thought

335

I'd feel again after Ellen took her life. I've made no secret of the fact that I didn't give a damn what happened to me. I was on the fast track to hell before you came along. To answer your question, I care a great deal for you. As for love, I'm not sure I'm capable of loving again."

Seething with frustration, Ashley said, "Do you want me to divorce you?"

"It would be in your best interest. You have no future with me. You're a beautiful, passionate woman; no one knows that better than I. At one time I thought we might have had a chance. But letting Slater escape punishment is beyond me. And if I succeed in killing him I'll either be on the run from the law or behind bars. I can't do that to you."

Ashley didn't want to think about that. Slater still hadn't returned to town and until he did she would do everything in her power to convince Tanner to give up his vendetta against the man. She wasn't above using feminine wiles, or exploiting Tanner's lust for her. With grim purpose, she moved into his arms. Tanner dragged her hard against him, his lips hovering mere inches above hers.

"You're a witch, Yank, but I've always known that. I'm warning you, I'm not playing your little game. Seducing me will get you nowhere."

336

"Make love to me, Reb. God, I've missed you. If I can never have you again, let this last time be our good-bye."

Chapter Sixteen

"Don't ask that of me, Ashley." His voice was raw, taut, fraught with more agony than a mortal soul should have to bear. He wanted to make love to Ashley more than anything, except killing Slater.

Ashley pushed herself against him until not even a breath separated them. She felt Tanner's body go rigid. "Why are you resisting, Reb? Are you afraid to bid me a proper goodbye?"

"Damn right, I am. You're dangerous, Yank. When I'm with you I can't even recall my own name, let alone Slater's."

"I don't care, Reb, as long as you remember mine," she whispered against his lips.

She tugged at his shirt. His jaw clenched. She watched, fascinated, as a tiny muscle began to tighten at the corner of his mouth. His eyes darkened as they met hers, then shifted to rest unwillingly upon the lush contours of her mouth. She swallowed visibly and licked her lips. His gaze upon her was like a physical caress, only more potent. Her lips parted involuntarily and her breath quickened.

"Do you want me, Tanner?"

"Do I need to breathe? Do I need food? Or water? Those things can't begin to describe how desperately I want you."

"I'm here, Tanner, and I want you just as much."

"I won't change my mind," he warned her. "If you want a proper good-bye, I'll give you one. But nothing you can do or say will change my mind about Slater."

Ashley's confidence in her ability to convince Tanner otherwise did not waver. She'd never give up, not as long as a breath remained in her, or a slim hope existed that she could turn Tanner from his foolish course. She and Tanner belonged together, but she wanted him on her terms, without the ghosts of his past haunting him.

"You talk too much, Reb. Help me take off your clothes." She pulled the shirttail from his pants. "I haven't seen the bedroom yet but there is bound to be a bed in it."

Tanner's hands shook as he unbuttoned his shirt. Ashley was already tugging at his gun belt. He shoved her hands aside and worked it loose. It fell to the floor. Ashley had managed to get the top buttons of his trousers undone before Tanner stopped her.

"No. Your clothes first."

She stared up at his bare torso. She thought him wonderfully arousing, all hard muscle and bronzed flesh. There was such strength in his hard body, such masculine beauty in his angular face. His hips were narrow, his stomach flat and ridged with muscles. Parts of him were enormous, especially that part of him still covered by his trousers.

Ashley's mouth went dry when Tanner reached for her. His hands were shaking as they fumbled with the tiny buttons on her bodice. He finally gave up, ripping the gown apart to the waist, sending buttons flying in every direction. By the time her dress lay in a puddle at her feet, he was shaking all over.

"It's been too damn long," he growled against her mouth.

His kiss was not gentle, nor were his hands as he tore away what remained of her clothing. When she was naked, he held her away from him and looked his fill. His heated gaze scorched her, rendered her senseless with need. "I'll always remember how you look right now, with your eyes glazed with passion and your body swelling with desire."

Ashley wanted to tell him that there would be no need to hold the memory in his mind, for they could be like this every day, if he'd but listen to reason. But she sensed he was in no mood now to listen to anything except the churning in his blood. "Now it's your turn," she said, tugging at the waistband of his trousers.

In moments he'd stepped out of them and stood facing her, as gloriously naked as she. Ashley's eyes grew enormous as they moved

340

over him. He was magnificent — huge and pulsing — and she rejoiced in his need for her. She licked her lips and reached for him.

Tanner groaned and shoved her hands aside. "No, not yet. If this is to be our last time I don't want it to end too soon."

Dropping to his knees before her, he spread hungry kisses on her breasts, suckling first one and then the other. When he had lavished them with sufficient attention, his mouth followed a downward path to the parting of her legs. When he thrust two fingers inside her tight sheath, Ashley sobbed with frustrated need. "You're torturing me, Reb!"

"You're weeping for me, Yank," he said when his hand came away wet with her dew. After easing her down onto the floor, he let his mouth follow his fingers on an erotic path across her glistening flesh, down to the vee between her legs. She cried out as his tongue delved deeply into the heated center of her.

She tried to pull him down to the floor with her but he would have none of it. His mouth and tongue continued to torment her until Ashley felt a great shattering inside her. But Tanner wouldn't allow it to happen. He pulled his mouth away and stood so abruptly Ashley's knees buckled. Grasping her, he raised her up and urged her legs around his waist. She complied eagerly, crying out in fury when Tanner still withheld what she so desperately wanted.

"Tell me how you want it, Yank. Hard and fast or slow and easy?"

"Both!" Ashley screamed at him. She wiggled her bottom in an effort to force his erection into her, but Tanner continued to deny her. "Damn you, what are you waiting for?"

"The right time," Tanner said cryptically. With her legs still wrapped around his waist, he carried her into the bedroom and fell backward onto the bed. She ended up on top of him.

When he tried to roll her beneath him, her legs grasped his middle and she refused to be dislodged. "Now it's your turn to suffer frustration," she whispered. Her teeth nibbled on his neck with an erotic hunger that made his body convulse.

Her lips moved lower, to his flat male nipples, and Tanner moaned with pleasure. His breath was choppy and uneven as she scooted lower still; he was fully aware of what she intended and wanted it desperately. The agony of waiting to feel himself inside her soft, wet mouth was almost unbearable. Abruptly the waiting ended when she touched her tongue to his pulsing tip and opened her mouth to him.

Splendor, sheer, glorious splendor rolled through him, within him, consuming him in an erotic whirlwind. Clenching his teeth, he bore it for several agonizing minutes before grasping her shoulders and dragging her upward, until she rested fully on top of him. "Witch," he growled against her mouth. He had never known this complete trust and giving that Ashley offered. He had loved sweet Ellen dearly, but never with the wild storm of intensity he felt for Ashley.

Sobbing with the need to have him inside her, Ashley raised herself in blatant invitation. With a groan of surrender, Tanner thrust into her. Lightning leaped from her body to his, jagged, violent, kindling a flame within him that would burn for the rest of his days. He penetrated deeper than he ever had before, and Ashley went wild, as wild and out of control as he was.

Flinging her head back and arching her neck, she cushioned her lower back against his thighs and rode him shamelessly. Ashley's last thought before she succumbed to shattering rapture was that he fit her as if God had fashioned him for her alone. His throbbing against her sensitive interior intensified the magnificent explosion, making her senseless to all but the bursts of wonder and thunderous waves of pleasure sweeping through her. She didn't make any sound; she wept from sheer joy.

Tanner gave a shout of capitulation and poured his seed into her, his release every bit as consuming, as shattering, as Ashley's. He gave only a passing thought to the niggling voice telling him to pull out of her and spend himself in the bedclothes. When he did remember, it was far too late. As he came down from that high place where he had found bliss, a single thought cut through his haze of passion and lust: he loved her. On the heels of that thought came another: he'd loved Ellen but had failed her. He didn't deserve a second chance.

Ashley came to her senses slowly, aware that Tanner was still buried deep within her. It had just begun to sink in that he hadn't taken his usual precaution of pulling out of her before spilling his seed. In the back of her mind lurked the tiny hope that his seed would produce a child.

A small sigh of regret hissed through Tanner's teeth. He seriously doubted that his one indiscretion would result in a child, yet a perverse devil inside him yearned for a baby by Ashley. He shoved that thought aside. A child would complicate both his life and Ashley's.

"I didn't mean for that to happen, Ashley. I can't recall when I've allowed myself to be carried away like that. I hope my seed won't find fertile ground."

"I hope it does."

"No! It would ruin your life. You're supposed to be a spinster, remember? Pregnancy

344

would mean the end of your teaching job and would ruin your chances of finding a husband."

"I have a husband. I don't want another man." She gave him a whimsical smile. "I've never felt more married to you than I do now." She ground her hips against him and her eyes widened when she felt him growing inside her. "This is how I want you, husband, hard and throbbing inside me. Not just today, but forever."

Tanner groaned with dismay. Her erotic words were a potent aphrodisiac. He was instantly hard and pulsing inside her. Rolling her on her back, he began thrusting powerfully. The fever that filled him became a tempest. He thrust and stroked until he felt Ashley convulse around him; then he erupted in a climax nearly as violent as his first one. When he started to withdraw scant moments before his seed spilled forth, Ashley grasped his buttocks and held him captive within her, thwarting his effort to withhold his seed from her.

Day turned into night, enclosing them in a cocoon of warm darkness and blissful surrender. Shortly before the gray, dismal dawn filtered through the bedroom window, Tanner loved her yet again. Then he rose silently and began to dress.

"Tanner, don't leave."

345

"This was supposed to be our good-bye, remember?"

Ashley felt a deep, abiding sadness as she stared into his determined countenance. "Did last night mean nothing to you?"

"You'll never know how much," Tanner said truthfully. "When I'm with you it's difficult to recall a man named Pratt Slater. But I couldn't live with my conscience if I let him go free."

"Dead men don't have to worry about their conscience," Ashley reminded him. "I'd rather you lived with your misplaced guilt than died following your conscience. You didn't pull the trigger on the gun that killed Ellen."

"Don't lecture me, Yank. I know what I'm doing. Ellen's finger might have been on the trigger, but Slater was the one who destroyed her will to live. And I failed to stop her. That makes me as fully responsible as Slater."

Ashley's temper exploded. "Go on, you damn stubborn Reb, get out of here! Kill Slater, get yourself killed, get sent to prison; I don't give a damn. I've done everything in my power to dissuade you from your foolish, ridiculous and dangerous course. There is nothing more I can do."

Tanner felt like a bastard. Being true to one's conscience was hell, he thought dismally.

"Promise me something, Yank."

"If it pleases me."

"No matter what happens to me, don't put your trust in men like Sam Stark."

A spark of hope kindled in Ashley's breast. If Tanner was that concerned about her there was still hope that she could change his mind.

"I won't promise you a damn thing, Reb. Sam Stark has money and position, and I'll need someone to take care of us if I have your child." She felt no guilt over goading him — it was for his own benefit. He was just too damn stubborn to know it.

His fists clenched at his sides. "If you have a child, I'll raise him myself."

Ashley rejoiced in his answer but tried not to show it. "How do you intend to accomplish that if you're dead or in prison?" she taunted. "Promise me you won't call out Slater until we know whether or not I conceived last night. If you feel that strongly about another man raising your child you'll grant me that concession."

She held her breath and prayed. She prayed she had become pregnant the night before. She prayed Tanner meant what he said about raising his own child should there be one. She wasn't proud of using a nonexistent child to bring Tanner to his senses, but what was pride compared to the life of the man she loved?

"Suppose there is a child," Tanner said quietly.

"If there is a child you'll be the first to

know. Do I have your promise?"

"For what it's worth, you have my promise. As long as there is the possibility of a child you'd better hold off on the divorce. And I don't want Sam Stark sniffing around your skirts. If you don't want me interfering, I suggest that you discourage him."

"I've never encouraged Mr. Stark," Ashley stated emphatically. "What do we do now?"

Tanner gave her an inscrutable look. "We wait. And make sure there are no more occasions to make a baby. We've been lucky thus far." He turned to leave.

"Tanner! Wait." He turned back to her. "Aren't you going to kiss me good-bye?" She shifted to her knees, holding the sheet to her naked breasts.

Tanner groaned. "Dammit, Yank, you're not making things easy for me."

She lifted her face. "I hope not."

The invitation was more than Tanner could resist. Grasping her face between his large hands, he brought her lips to his. The kiss was poignant and touching, reaching into her very soul, stirring her to tears. Willing them back, she waited until he left before allowing them to fall.

Later that afternoon Sam Stark called Nell into his office. "What do you know about Tanner MacTavish?" he asked Nell as he handed her a snifter of his private-stock brandy.

Nell shrugged and took a generous slug of the brandy. "Not much. The man is notoriously tight-lipped."

"Has he bedded any of your girls?"

"Not to my knowledge."

"Why not?"

"Damned if I know. He doesn't seem interested."

"Has he mentioned the new schoolmarm?"

"Not to me. Should he have? I've seen her. She ain't much to look at."

Stark chuckled. "That's how much you know. Did you know Miss Webster and MacTavish arrived in town together? She claims he's a trusted family friend, that he was escorting her at her brother's behest."

"Why are you so interested? The schoolmarm isn't your type."

"That's where you're wrong, Nell. That fiery redhead is exactly my type. And I want to know what she's hiding from me and the town council. I want her bad, Nell. I want something to hold over her head, something, anything, that I can use to get her into my bed."

"What am I supposed to do, Sam? This ain't exactly my line of work."

"It can be. Entice MacTavish into your bed. Men tend to get talkative when they're sated sexually. Pump him for information.

Find out everything you can about him and Miss Webster. I'll make it worth your while."

"I already know one thing. He's damn anxious to see Pratt Slater."

"Slater? What in the hell does he want with Slater?"

"I ain't sure, but he hates the man. I wouldn't give odds that Slater will survive their confrontation."

Stark stroked his mustache. "Interesting. That's all for now, Nell. I'm counting on you to bring me something I can use."

Later, with the revelry in the saloon in full swing, Nell knocked discreetly on Tanner's door. Tanner was still awake, having spent endless hours trying to come to grips with the promise he'd given Ashley. It was going to be damn difficult keeping his hands off Slater when he returned to town. Perhaps Slater would have the good sense to stay away until Tanner learned whether or not Ashley had conceived his child. He'd done an irresponsible thing last night and he wouldn't let Ashley suffer for it.

Tanner almost didn't hear the knock on his door, so disturbed were his thoughts. His attention was finally captured when Nell softly called out his name. Tanner leaped to his feet, staring at the door.

"Who is it?"

"Nell. Can I come in?"

"It's late; what do you want?"

"Please, Tanner, I need your help."

Cursing beneath his breath, Tanner unlocked the door and flung it open. "This had better be good, Nell."

Nell stumbled inside, shut the door behind her and flung herself into Tanner's arms. "I'm so frightened. One of the customers didn't like it because I refused him my favors tonight. He left, but I'm afraid he'll come back. He won't think to look for me here in your room."

Tanner carefully set her aside. "Where is Stark?"

"At some social function."

"What about your bouncers? They look fully capable of handling drunks."

"Jetters is out sick and Monty is doing what he can alone. Just let me stay here until closing. I won't be no bother, I promise. If you don't want to . . . you know," she hinted coyly, "we can just talk."

Tanner sighed in resignation. He couldn't very well throw Nell out of his room if she was in danger. And since he couldn't sleep anyway, he supposed it wouldn't hurt to talk. He crossed to the bed and sat down. "Take a chair, Nell. It's going to be a long night."

"It doesn't have to be, handsome," she said suggestively. "There are more pleasant ways to pass time than simply talking."

"I'm not interested, Nell."

"What's wrong with you? Don't you like women?"

"I like them just fine. If you must know, I'm married. And I don't cheat on my wife." Startled by his admission, Tanner had no idea why he'd said such a thing.

"Married! Funny, you don't look like a married man. Where are you keeping your wife?" Surely this was something Sam could use, Nell thought, warming to the subject.

"Appearances aren't always what they seem. Once I've settled with Pratt Slater I'll probably be leaving town."

"Didn't you and that little schoolmarm arrive in town together?" Her innocent question put Tanner on his guard.

"Yes, Miss Webster's brother asked me to escort his sister to Oregon City. Since I already had business here, it was no hardship for me to comply."

"Married, who would have believed it," Nell repeated, unable to get past the notion that Tanner had a wife he loved enough to be true to. Wait until Sam heard he'd have a clear field with prim Miss Webster, though she didn't for the life of her know what Sam saw in the unattractive schoolmarm.

"You seem surprised. Have you never encountered a man who loved his wife?"

"You're damn right I haven't. Something mighty important must be keeping you from returning to the little lady. What's your business with Pratt Slater?"

Tanner bared his teeth in a feral smile. "I told you before: my business is private. Have you heard anything that might indicate when he'll return?"

"I don't keep track of Sam's hirelings. Your business must be pressing."

Tanner stifled a yawn. "Do you think it's safe to leave now, Nell? I really would like to get some sleep."

Realizing she was unlikely to get any more information from Tanner, Nell agreed to leave. The next day she had several things of import to relate to Sam Stark. One was that Tanner was married, another that he was totally faithful to his absent wife, and yet another that he was gunning for Pratt Slater.

Ashley settled into her job with little difficulty. She had twenty students in all grades. The first thing she did was to enlist the help of some of the older students to teach the younger ones while she was preparing lessons for the older group. She was getting to know her students, which made the days fly by with amazing speed. To her chagrin, she hadn't seen Tanner since that extraordinary night two weeks before. They had loved one another with unrestrained joy and she missed him dreadfully.

Today, the students had already been dismissed and Ashley was grading test papers when an unwelcome visitor arrived at the school.

"You shouldn't work so hard, Ashley."

Ashley started violently. "Mr. Stark. What are you doing here?"

"I told you I intended for us to become good friends. I was waiting for you to settle into your new job before calling on you. How are things going? Is there anything you need to make your job easier?"

"Thank you for asking, but the previous schoolteacher left everything in order. Things are progressing to my expectations. Now if you will excuse me, I have papers to correct."

"Are you trying to get rid of me, Ashley?"

"I don't have time to socialize, Mr. Stark."

"Why didn't you tell me MacTavish was married? Nell tells me he's devoted to his wife." He laughed harshly. "Did you know I was actually jealous of him?"

Ashley stared at Stark as if he had two heads. "Tanner said he was married?"

"You seem surprised. Didn't you know he had a wife? I thought you said he was a trusted family friend."

"Of course I knew Tanner was married," Ashley said huffily, trying to imagine just how much Tanner had revealed. "His wife is very dear to me. I'm puzzled, though, at the reason for your jealousy. I've never given you the least encouragement."

"I've decided to pursue you, my dear. You're refreshing and original. And somewhat of a mystery. Pretend all you want; I can see through your innocent facade. I want you; it's as simple as that."

"I'm not available, not interested and certainly not in the market for a tawdry affair. This job is important to me."

Stark grinned at her. "See what I mean? Definitely refreshing. I'll derive great pleasure from peeling away the layers and discovering the real woman beneath those drab wrappings. I'll come to your house tonight around nine o'clock."

"Don't bother; I won't let you in."

Grasping her arms, he hauled her out of the chair and dragged her halfway across the desk, until they were nose to nose. "I won't take no for an answer." Then his lips slammed down on hers, forcing her teeth against her lips as he plundered her mouth. Whimpering beneath his unexpected onslaught, Ashley struggled to escape, more angry than frightened.

"I don't think Miss Webster welcomes your advances."

Abruptly Stark released Ashley, cursing beneath his breath as he turned to face Tanner. "Mr. MacTavish, I don't believe we've met formally." He stuck out his hand. "I'm Sam Stark."

Ignoring Stark's gesture, Tanner looked

past him to Ashley. She appeared pale but unharmed. Satisfied, he shifted his attention back to Stark. "I know who you are. It 'pears you're bothering my . . . Miss Webster. I strongly suggest that you leave."

"Are you Ashley's appointed guardian?"

Stark's use of Ashley's first name did not sit well with Tanner. He wanted to smash the silly smirk off the man's face. "I am if I'm needed in that capacity. Her brother placed her in my care. I'd be remiss in my duty to Cole if I allowed Ashley to be taken advantage of."

"What makes you think I'd take advantage of Ashley? How do you know my attentions aren't honorable?"

Ashley sent both Tanner and Stark a fulminating look. "I'm capable of making my own decisions, gentlemen. I've already told Mr. Stark that his attentions aren't welcome. Now if you'll both excuse me, I'm going home." Slamming shut the answer book she'd been using, Ashley left the schoolhouse with as much dignity as she could muster.

Ashley fumed in silent fury. She'd hated Stark's kiss, and was preparing to bash him across the face when Tanner had burst upon the scene. Did Tanner think she was a helpless innocent who didn't know what Sam Stark wanted from her? Damn that stubborn man, anyway, Ashley thought as she recalled the look on Tanner's face when he'd walked

356

in on Stark kissing her. If he didn't want her, why was he hanging around, acting like a jealous husband? When would he realize that opening his heart to love was more healing than revenge?

After Ashley flounced out of the schoolhouse, Stark and Tanner continued to stare at one another with unfeigned animosity. Finally Stark said, "Heard tell you're waiting for Pratt Slater to return to town."

"You heard right."

"Any special reason you want to see him?"

"It's personal."

"Well, then, I reckon you're going to have to wait a while longer. He's in Portland waiting for a ship to arrive. He's to meet my partner and bring him to Oregon City. The ship's been delayed by bad weather."

"I'll wait as long as I have to," Tanner said.

"All I've got to say is that your business must be important to keep you away from your wife all this time. By the way, where did you say you left the little lady?"

"I hope you paid Nell handsomely for that information," Tanner gritted out. "It's none of anyone's business where I've left my wife."

"Tight-lipped bastard," Stark muttered as he headed out the door.

Tanner stared at his departing back. Just because the man owned half the town didn't mean he could move in on Ashley. Ashley might think she was worldly and experienced, but in truth she was an innocent when it came to men. Any woman trusting enough to travel halfway across the country with a man she knew nothing about had to be too naive for her own well-being. The more he thought about Ashley struggling in Stark's arms the angrier he became — so angry that he strode out of the schoolhouse and went directly to Ashley's house.

"Yank, let me in," he called, pounding on the door to emphasize his words.

"Dammit, Reb, what's all the ruckus about?" Ashley exclaimed upon flinging open the door. "Are you trying to get me fired?"

"Are you all right? Stark didn't hurt you, did he?"

"I wouldn't have let him," Ashley said confidently. "What brought you to the schoolhouse, anyway?"

"I followed Stark," Tanner admitted, not at all ashamed of keeping an eye on Ashley. "I saw him heading in this direction and became curious. I'm glad I followed. Surely you know what he wants from you. I stopped him this time, and I also learned from listening to him that Slater is in Portland waiting for a ship to arrive."

"Slater." The name tasted bitter in her mouth. "Don't ever mention that man's name to me again. Just remember your promise to me."

"You haven't . . . You're not . . ."

"I don't know yet."

When Tanner would have said more, she slammed the door in his face.

Chapter Seventeen

Two weeks later Pratt Slater returned to Oregon City. He stood before Sam Stark, trying to explain why he had returned without Bernard Culp, Stark's partner, who had been scheduled to arrive aboard the *Sea Skipper*. The ship had arrived nearly a month late and, according to Slater, Culp had refused to debark, expressing his intention to remain aboard ship and continue on to Alaska.

"What do you mean Culp refused to debark?" Stark all but shouted. "He was to bring my share of the proceeds from the sale of the business we owned together in New York. Damn that cheating bastard! He took off with my money."

"I don't know anything about that," Slater muttered with a shrug. "I only talked a few minutes with the man."

Slater shifted his gaze about uneasily, refusing to meet Sam Stark's eyes. His mouth was dry and he licked moisture onto his lips.

Stark was too suspicious a man to believe Slater. "Are you certain that's all Culp said? Did he give any reason for continuing on to Alaska?"

"He mentioned something about prospecting," Slater offered. "You didn't tell me he had money that belonged to you."

With good reason, Stark thought. He didn't trust Slater enough to give him that kind of information. He was glad now that he hadn't and wondered if Slater could have found out some other way. It just wasn't like Culp to cheat his partner. They were long-time associates as well as partners in several business ventures, and it didn't sound like something Culp would do. Unfortunately Stark had nothing but Slater's word to attest to what had happened.

"I don't like any of this," Stark groused. "I'm not going to let this rest until I learn the truth."

Still refusing to look his employer in the eye, Slater said, "Can I go now? I haven't had a decent meal in days. I aim to buy the biggest steak in town and then hit the sack."

"There is one more thing. Do you know a man named Tanner MacTavish?"

Slater's head shot up. "Don't tell me that bastard turned up in Oregon City? I kinda hoped the Indians would do him in."

"He's here, all right. And he's made no secret of the fact that he's gunning for you."

"There ain't a Reb alive fast enough to outdraw me," Slater bragged. "Let him come. Is his pretty little bride with him? I sure wouldn't mind a piece of that. Sweetest little redhead I've ever seen. Indians must have thought so too. They kidnapped her off our

361

wagon train. MacTavish went after her. Wonder how they got free."

Stark's attention sharpened. "Did you say redhead? With green eyes?"

"Yeah, that's her. When did they arrive?"

"They arrived about a month ago, right after you left town. But the woman with him calls herself Miss Webster. I always suspected something wasn't right about that relationship. Trusted family friend, she said. Ha! I wonder why Miss Webster wants to conceal her relationship with MacTavish? Do me a favor and don't say anything to anyone until I decide how I want to use this information."

Slater gave a bark of laughter. "Well, I'll be damned. You want the little bitch."

"You're damn right, I do, and I'm going to have her. If her husband won't claim her, I will. I don't know what you ever did to MacTavish and I don't care, but take my advice and keep out of his way."

"Is that all?"

"For the time being. Check with me later."

His eyes narrowed thoughtfully, Stark watched his hireling leave. He should have known better than to send a man he'd just hired to meet Culp, but at the time no one else was available. He didn't like the way Slater kept avoiding his eyes, as if he had something to hide. Nor would he accept the flimsy explanation Slater offered for Culp's

362

failure to arrive with his money.

A short time later Stark called one of his most trusted henchmen into his office and dispatched him to Portland. He told his man not to return until he had the answers he sought. Meanwhile, Stark decided to keep an eye on Slater. If he made any attempt to leave town, Stark could only assume that the bastard knew more than he let on.

Slater collected his saddlebags from the livery and went directly to his room above the saloon, having no idea that Tanner had rented a room just down the hall from his.

Slater thought back to his meeting with Bernard Culp. When Culp had casually mentioned that he carried a substantial amount of money belonging to Sam Stark, Slater had immediately seen a way to line his own pockets. Slater had seen to it that Culp suffered an unfortunate "accident" a few miles from Portland, and then made up the story he had told Stark.

Slater slapped his saddlebags on the bed, chuckling at his sudden windfall as he pulled wads of crisp green bills and some gold coins from the pockets. Dimly he wondered if he had done the right thing by coming back to Oregon City instead of taking off for parts unknown. If he hadn't known Stark so well he wouldn't have returned. In their short association he had learned that Stark had connections all over the West, and the East, for that matter. Slater feared he would always be looking over his shoulder, wondering if the man following him was Stark's hired killer. So he'd hit upon a plan he thought would satisfy Stark and absolve him of guilt.

By claiming that Culp had simply taken off with Stark's money, Slater hoped he wouldn't be suspected of killing Culp and stealing the money for himself. Of course that meant he'd have to stick around Oregon City long enough to convince Stark that he was innocent of any wrongdoing. If he took off too soon, Stark was sure to think something was amiss.

The first order of business was hiding the money, Slater decided as he stuffed it beneath the lumpy mattress. Satisfied that not even the slovenly chambermaid would find it on her infrequent visits to his room to change the bed linens, Slater went out in search of a steak.

After dispatching his man to Portland, Stark mulled over everything Slater had told him about MacTavish and his red-haired wife. His wife! Stark had no earthly idea why the pair continued to deny their relationship. Perhaps they were desperate for money and the teaching position sounded too attractive to resist, he reflected. And since only unmarried teachers were hired, they had conveniently claimed not to be married. Whatever the reason, Stark had ideas of his own about using the information.

Misty twilight had settled over the town when Stark rapped lightly on Ashley's door. Ashley looked up from the lesson she was preparing for the next day and assumed her caller was Tanner. She hadn't seen him in several days and missed him desperately. Besides, she welcomed another opportunity to try to convince him that pursuing Slater was bound to destroy the fragile love that existed between them.

Her smile was warm and welcoming when she opened the door. "Tanner, I'm so glad —" Her smile slid away when she recognized Sam Stark. She started to close the door in his face but he pushed it open and stepped inside. "What are you doing here?"

"I told you I'd come calling one night," Stark said as he closed the door behind him and turned the key in the lock.

A frisson of fear snaked down Ashley's spine when she heard the key grate in the lock, but she tried not to show it. Men like Stark fed on other people's fear. "Please leave. Your presence places my job in jeopardy."

"Is that a fact?" Stark said with a grin. "You should have thought about your job when you lied to the town council."

"L-lied? I don't understand."

"Pratt Slater returned to town today. Did

365

you think he'd keep your secret?"

"S-secret?" She and Tanner had already discussed what was likely to happen when Slater returned and learned they weren't living as man and wife. But Tanner hadn't seemed worried about it. Could it be that Tanner was secretly hoping to have their marriage made public knowledge?

"Come on, honey, don't take me for a fool. I've known all along there was something between you and MacTavish. I admit I never suspected you were husband and wife. Lovers, maybe. What's the matter? Couldn't the bastard satisfy you? Is that why you left him?"

"It's a long story," Ashley said. "I'll turn in my resignation immediately."

Stark stepped closer, cornering Ashley against the sofa. "No need for that, honey. We can work out a deal. Slater won't tell anyone if I tell him not to. If you're real nice to me I'll see to it that you keep your job. But you have to keep MacTavish in line; he's dangerous. I don't understand what's going on between the two of you and I don't care, just as long as he doesn't suddenly turn into a jealous husband."

"Now that you know I'm married you can't possibly expect an intimate relationship to develop between us," Ashley contended. "Surely you don't believe I'd go along with such an outrageous arrangement. You'll have my resignation first thing Monday morning. Good night, Mr. Stark."

"Oh, but we are going to be intimate, Ashley. I'm looking forward to it." He leered at her. "Come on, honey, you're no timid young virgin. You've already had a man between your thighs. There's no need to pretend with me."

He seized her roughly and pulled her hard against him, making her physically aware of his erection. "I'll make it good for you, I promise. I'm a good lover."

Ashley struggled in his arms, managed to get one hand free and slapped his face. "I'm married! What makes you think I'd betray my husband with another man?"

Stark reared back in shock, lashing out reflexively with his right hand, catching her across the cheek. Her head slammed sideways and pain exploded in her brain. "You little bitch! I warned you once. Don't ever try that again." His lips peeled back from his teeth in a feral snarl and his expression turned from fierce to cunning. "I hear MacTavish is gunning for Pratt Slater. Sooner or later there's going to be a shootout. If you're not nice to me I can guarantee that your husband will end up in an early grave."

Stark's blow had stunned Ashley but his words penetrated the pain. "You wouldn't dare hurt Tanner. There are laws to handle men like you."

Stark gave a bark of laughter. "I own this town. If you want that big Reb to live, let's talk about what you can do for me in bed. You can begin by kissing me."

Ashley drew back in revulsion as Stark grasped her chin between his fingers and lifted her face to his. She opened her mouth to protest and nearly gagged when Stark's mouth slammed down on hers. His tongue became a sword, thrusting insistently between her open lips. Sickened by the taste and scent of him, Ashley prayed for strength as she struggled to escape. When Stark bore her down onto the sofa, she broke free of his mouth and screamed.

"Damn you, you're going to wake up the whole damn town."

"I hope so," Ashley retorted with an angry rush of words.

"Cooperate and I could make this real good for you. I don't know why you're being so damn stubborn. You leave me no choice. Since you refuse to be accommodating, I'm duty-bound to tell the town council that you're married. Today is Friday. I'll give you till Monday to change your mind. You know where to find me. Meanwhile, think about your man, and how badly you want him alive."

"You can't hurt Tanner."

He sent her a threatening look. "You think not? I hope you're not too fond of that big

Reb. Something tells me he's headed for trouble."

Ashley's legs were shaking as she walked to the door, unlocked it and held it open, praying that Stark would leave. He did, with great reluctance and even greater anger. He had assumed that Ashley would fall gratefully into his arms when he told her the condition for keeping her job. Who would have thought the little witch would be so belligerent? Women usually ran after him. He was handsome enough, and rich. Experience with the opposite sex had proven that all women were alike, willing to bed a man if he made it worth their while.

Stark refused to consider the possibility that Ashley actually loved her husband. They would be living together in wedded bliss if she did, instead of trying to convince the whole town they were simply friends. He gave Ashley a mocking grin and walked out into the night.

Ashley slammed and locked the door behind Stark. She was shaking all over. She'd be a fool not to take Sam Stark's threat to Tanner seriously. Tanner had to be warned and warned now about the danger he was facing.

Tanner rode into town at sundown. He had been gone three days. A steady rain was falling. He was tired, hungry and chilled to the bone. He hankered for a hot meal and his bed. Of course his bed would have been more inviting if Ashley were in it, but he tried to put that thought from his mind. He pulled his hat lower over his forehead and tugged at the collar of his slicker as he reined his horse toward the livery. The hostler came up to take the reins as Tanner dismounted. He flipped Pops a coin, instructing him to see to his horse, then walked the short distance to the Red Garter. As he walked through the rain he thought about the sights he'd encountered during his absence and the man he had spoken to. He'd seen rich, fertile land in the Willamette Valley, and thickly forested hills. The hills and mountains were abundantly endowed with game and wildlife, making it a hunter's dream. The man he'd spoken to was looking for a partner in a logging venture, and Tanner had been sorely tempted.

He was still mulling over the incredible possibilities of logging in this lumberman's paradise when he met Ashley halfway between the livery and the saloon. Or rather, they collided when Ashley came rushing around the corner and nearly bowled him over. He caught her against him and felt her body shaking.

"What is it, Yank? What are you doing out this time of day? Where is your wrap? You're soaking wet."

"Tanner! Thank God I've found you! I

have to talk to you. It's urgent."

He frowned, wondering what Ashley was doing out in the freezing rain without a coat. "Not here. You're not dressed properly and you'll catch your death."

"My house, then." She grasped his hand, pulling him along with her. "Hurry."

Sensing her urgency, Tanner withheld his questions until they reached the privacy of her small house and Ashley closed the door behind them. Tanner flung off his hat and slicker and turned to face her. "What is this all about, Ashley?"

Still shivering, Ashley moved close to the stove and held out her hands to the fire. It took a moment or two before she calmed down enough to answer. "You're in danger, Tanner. I had to warn you."

She turned abruptly and found him standing behind her, so close the heat of his big body penetrated through her chill. He wrapped his arms about her and curled his body around her.

"You're wet. Get out of those clothes and then we'll talk."

"Dammit, Reb, how can you —"

"If you won't undress yourself I'll do it for you. And that's likely to take a very long time."

Ashley stared at him. At any other time she would welcome the chance to lie in Tanner's arms, but not when his life was in danger.

371

Turning abruptly, she rushed into the bedroom. She returned a few minutes later wearing a warm dressing gown. Her damp hair hung in loose waves around her shoulders and the sight of her made it difficult for Tanner to swallow.

"Now can we talk?"

He took her hand and led her to the sofa. He sat down, tugging her down with him. "Very well, tell me what this is all about."

"Have you seen him?" Ashley asked in a rush. "Mr. Stark said he arrived in town just today."

Tanner stiffened; then his full lips curved into a slow smile. "Slater? Finally. He's kept me waiting long enough."

"There's more," Ashley said, wringing her hands. "It's Stark. He was here tonight and threatened your life."

Rage filled Tanner. "What in the hell was Stark doing here? Didn't I warn you about him?"

Ashley turned her face toward the lamp as she composed her thoughts. Muted light licked at her features, revealing the dark swelling on her left cheekbone. Tanner sucked in his breath and let it out slowly as anger built inside him. He touched her chin, turning her face toward him.

"Who did this to you?" His voice was hard and menacing.

Despite the numbness in her cheek, Ashley

had forgotten about the blow Stark had dealt her. She touched the darkening bruise with the tips of her fingers and flinched when she felt the swelling there. "I-I fell," she stammered lamely.

She couldn't tell Tanner the truth. If he found out Stark had struck her she feared he would do something rash and foolish.

"You're lying." His voice was gentle but determined. "The truth, Yank."

Ashley knew Tanner wouldn't be satisfied until she told him everything. "Sam Stark was here tonight. Slater told him we were married."

"We expected that might happen. If you weren't so damn stubborn we could have avoided all this."

"If you weren't so set on killing Slater there would be no need to pretend we're not married. It's obvious neither of us wants a divorce. Your vendetta against Pratt Slater is the only thing keeping us apart."

"Don't change the subject, Yank. I asked how you got that bruise. And don't tell me again that you fell. What happened with Stark tonight?"

Ashley looked away. "He said he wouldn't tell the town council we were married if I became intimate with him."

"The stinking bastard!" He smashed his fist against the arm of the sofa, shattering the fragile wood.

"I told him I wasn't interested and asked him to leave," Ashley added hurriedly. "He wouldn't take no for an answer." Her voice dropped to a whisper. "He . . . he kissed me and I slapped him. He slapped me back. After a struggle, I finally got him to leave."

"I'll kill him, right after I take care of Slater," Tanner bit out. He ran his thumb over the bruise, then gently kissed it.

"No, Tanner, don't say that! You can't ignore Stark's warning. He threatened you; that's what frightened me. He said he knew you were gunning for Slater, and if Slater didn't put you in an early grave, he would."

"And you believed him? You ought to know by now that I can take care of myself. I'm not afraid of Stark."

Panic raced through Ashley. "Don't you see? I don't want to be the cause of your death. If I had given in to Stark he wouldn't have threatened you."

Tanner went rigid. Grasping her shoulders, he pulled her against him until they were nose to nose. His voice held a thread of steel. "Stark is a dead man for even suggesting such a thing. You're mine, Ashley. I can't bear the thought of another man touching you." Suddenly he frowned as a thought came to him. "You didn't consider his proposal, did you? You don't want Stark, do you? He's rich and can give you everything I can't."

"Oh, God, Tanner, how can you even ask? The man repulses me. I've done nothing to warrant his attention. You're the only man I want, the only man I'll ever want. Forget the war; forget Slater. Why can't we just live our lives together and forget everything else?"

Tanner searched her face, visualizing the kind of future that could be his if he could forget his past. Ashley had no inkling of the torment he'd suffered since the day Ellen had killed herself with his gun. She had died in his arms, a tragic victim of a vicious rape. There was only one reason Tanner would even consider letting Slater live.

"Are you . . . Do you know yet if you're . . ."

"If you are referring to the possibility that I might be pregnant, no, I don't know yet. I've had no proof one way or another." That wasn't entirely true, but Ashley wasn't completely sure she was expecting a child. Her woman's time was a week late, but she needed more proof than that.

"I'd better leave," Tanner said, suddenly wishing Ashley actually was carrying his child. There was no longer a doubt in Tanner's mind that he loved the determined little Yankee, and he was beginning to understand why men went to such lengths in the name of love. "Don't worry about Stark. I owe him for hurting you." He rubbed his knuckles against his hand as he contemplated all the ways he'd make Stark suffer for touching Ashley.

Ashley objected vigorously. "No! I'll take care of it. Sam Stark is a powerful man in town. I don't want you doing something you'll be sorry for. I'll simply resign first thing Monday and find another job. Perhaps there are families in town whose children need private tutoring. I still have my inheritance. I'll move into a respectable boardinghouse after I resign my job. I'm confident my brother will convince Morning Mist to leave the tribe and join me in Oregon soon. You needn't worry about me, Tanner."

"I have a better idea," Tanner suggested. "I'm no longer comfortable living above the saloon. I've had lots of time on my hands to look around and there is a furnished house for rent at the edge of town. It isn't any more expensive than living at the hotel or a boardinghouse. I've spoken with the owner and he's agreeable to renting it to us . . . as a married couple."

The breath caught in Ashley's throat. "Are you saying you want us to live together like a real married couple? Are you ready to forget the past? Oh, Tanner, you can't begin to know what this means to me."

Hope churned within Ashley. This was the first time Tanner had even hinted that he was ready to forget about a divorce and acknowledge their marriage. Had he finally come to his senses concerning Slater? In the same breath she wondered if he could come to love her as much as he had loved Ellen.

Tanner would have given everything he possessed if he could have answered Ashley as she hoped. He loved the way her green eyes shone with happiness and wished he could keep that look there forever. He cursed himself for having to disappoint her.

"What I'm saying is that for the present, living together makes sense. Stark would be a fool to pursue a married woman with a husband to protect her."

Ashley's heart plummeted to her toes. Tanner wanted them to live together for all the wrong reasons. He'd made it sound as if there was no permanence to his proposal. But if she had her way, it would indeed be a permanent arrangement. She wasn't about to give up on Tanner MacTavish yet. As long as there was a breath left in her body she'd use it to make Tanner love her so much he wouldn't want to leave her.

"Your idea does have merit," Ashley said. "It would be a relief not to have to lie anymore, though I fear there will be a lot of speculation about why we tried to conceal our marriage."

She pretended to mull over Tanner's suggestion. Suddenly she brightened. "I know! We can find a preacher and get married again. No one will suspect we've been married all this time if we get married again. I'll just be another schoolteacher who found a husband. It happens all the time."

At first Tanner balked. But the more he thought about it the better he decided it sounded. There was no law he knew of forbidding a couple to renew their vows. He strongly suspected that his heart had already decided to let the past go and live his future with Ashley. Otherwise he wouldn't have suggested that they live together. Now he had to convince his mind that his heart knew best. His love for Ashley was a wild, devouring thing, so unlike what he had felt for gentle, delicate Ellen, who had neither the strength nor the will to live with disgrace. After the rape Ellen had retreated into a dark, silent void of dementia, whereas Ashley would have fought those dark devils back and emerged stronger for it at the end of the battle.

Yet he hadn't blamed Ellen for taking her life; he blamed himself for failing her. Perhaps, just perhaps, he wasn't to blame. If anyone was at fault it was Pratt Slater, a foul beast who had cruelly raped his innocent wife. Every time he thought about the bastard he wanted to kill him. Could he possibly let Slater live?

Ashley watched the play of emotion across Tanner's face and knew what he was thinking. Just when she thought she'd finally convinced him that their feelings for one another were stronger than his hatred for Slater, memories of his first wife's death intruded. Would she never have his entire heart?

"I'll contact the preacher and see to the rental of the house," he finally said.

Ashley's heart soared. She'd won! Tanner's words just proved he loved her.

"We'll be married tomorrow, and on Monday I'll be at your side when you resign your job. I don't want Sam Stark bothering you again."

"Don't go, Tanner," Ashley said when he made as if to leave. "We're married; there's no need for you to leave."

Tanner felt his blood rise, hot and thick, his body readying for her. "You know what will happen if we share the same bed."

Ashley smiled up at him through a fringe of rich red hair. "I'm counting on it. What can it matter?"

He grinned back. "What, indeed? I can't guarantee I'll be able to withdraw at the crucial moment. You know what happened the last time we made love. We don't even know yet if you're pregnant." Suddenly comprehension dawned. "I think you want to be pregnant. You made me vow to do nothing about Slater until we learn if you're increasing. You hatched that idea about remarrying. You really want us to be together, don't you?"

"I love you," Ashley whispered. "But I want you to want me because I'm more important to you than Pratt Slater."

He took her face between his large hands and tenderly brushed her lips with his. "You are. I'm just beginning to realize how much."

"Show me, Reb. Show me how important I am to you."

His arms went around her. He pulled her close. "Oh, God, Yank, I want you so damn much it hurts."

She felt the rapid beating of his heart and knew hers was pounding just as loudly. "I can't bear the thought of losing you. Kiss me, Tanner; kiss me until I'm too dizzy to think how close I came to losing you."

His gaze went to her throat, where a pulse beat furiously beneath her pale, fragile skin. He shoved his fingers into her hair and gently brought her face up to his. He kissed her with melting tenderness, exploring her mouth with his tongue until a breathy exhalation escaped from her throat and her body went limp against his. Then the pressure of his lips increased and his tongue became bolder as it searched out the moist sweetness of her mouth.

"I didn't have a life until a feisty Yank schoolmarm burst into my world," Tanner admitted hoarsely. "You're the flame that blazed into my life and scorched the fabric of my dismal existence. I was ready to give up on life until I met you. You gave me a reason to live, to heal, to love again."

Tanner's words were the closest he'd ever come to admitting he loved her and couldn't live without her. "I love you, Tanner. I don't know when exactly it happened but I suppose it began when I saw you riding alone into Running Elk's camp. I thought you either the bravest or the most foolish man I've ever known."

He kissed her hard and swept her off her feet. Her arms slid around his neck and she rested her head in the warm curve of his shoulder as he carried her into the bedroom. He undressed her slowly, almost reverently, adoring every inch of her sweet flesh with his eyes. Then she undressed him. When they were both naked, Ashley saw that he was ready for her. Dampness flowered between her legs as she touched him.

"You're trembling," she whispered.

"You're the only woman who has ever had that kind of power over me."

They came together in mutual need, their joining wild and uncontrolled. She turned to flame in his arms and he fed the fire raging inside her. When it was over they loved again, this time with such consuming tenderness it brought tears to Ashley's eyes.

She clung to him throughout the night, fearing to face the light of day lest she find that all this was a dream and Tanner was still intent upon sacrificing his life and their love to avenge his dead wife.

Chapter Eighteen

Ashley awakened to a dreary winter morning. Instead of the usual rain, sleet fell from an overcast sky. She turned to look at Tanner and found him smiling at her. She smiled back and snuggled up against him.

"I like waking up with you in my arms," he remarked.

"No more than I like being in your arms," Ashley returned, burrowing deeper into his embrace. The fire had gone out during the night and the air was freezing cold.

"Much as I'd like to lie here with you all day, I do have some matters to take care of."

"I'll fix breakfast," Ashley offered.

"Lie still. Let me build up the fire first."

Ashley watched him pad naked to the stove, admiring the long, masculine line of his torso and the taut mounds of his buttocks. By the time the fire took hold, goose bumps had risen on his flesh and he hurried into his clothes. Leaving the warm bed with marked reluctance, Ashley went into the kitchen to start breakfast, feeling that at last everything was right in the world. At long last Tanner was hers.

While Tanner enjoyed a home-cooked

breakfast, Pratt Slater entered Sam Stark's office, having been summoned there by one of Stark's henchmen. Slater had no idea why Stark wanted him and could only hope that Stark hadn't discovered something to link him to Bernard Culp's disappearance. "You sent for me, boss?"

Stark appeared to be in a foul mood as he glared up at Slater. "Sit down, Slater; I have a little job for you. Shouldn't be too hard, knowing how you feel about Rebs."

Slater dropped into the nearest chair, nearly shaking from relief. He'd do anything to keep Stark from suspecting him of murdering his partner and stealing his money. "Tell me what you want, boss. Who's the Reb you want me to blow away?"

"Have you seen MacTavish yet?"

A slow smile lifted the corners of Slater's mouth. "MacTavish, huh? I should have known that bastard would make enemies wherever he went." He fingered his gun. "I haven't run into him yet but I'm surely looking forward to it."

"I don't know what you ever did to him and I don't care. I just want you to take care of him for me. Once he's out of the way maybe his widow won't be so damn uppity about who she beds."

Slater made the mistake of laughing. "Turned you down, did she?"

Stark's face grew mottled with rage. He

leaped to his feet and glared at Slater. "I didn't invite your opinion. You'll be paid handsomely to rid the town of the Reb bastard; that's all you need to know."

Slater swallowed visibly. "Sorry, boss. I didn't mean no offense. Sure, consider it done. It will be my pleasure to take out MacTavish for you."

"Don't make it look too obvious," Stark warned. "You can outdraw and outshoot him, can't you?"

"You're damn right I can," Slater bragged. "What if he's too cowardly to call me out?"

"I don't think that's likely. Use your ingenuity . . . if you have any," he added disparagingly. "Jump him in a dark alley if you have to."

Slater left a short time later. Once out of Stark's intimidating presence, he began to doubt his ability to outdraw and outshoot MacTavish. One mistake and he was a goner. No amount of money in the world was worth his life. Besides, he already had enough greenbacks and gold hidden beneath his mattress to last him a long time. He'd have to think twice about calling out MacTavish and placing his life at risk. Perhaps he should consider leaving town.

Though Slater knew an encounter with Tanner was inevitable if he remained in town, he was nevertheless startled when he met Tanner in the hallway as he was returning to his room. Slater stopped dead in his tracks, his hand hovering inches from his gun.

"Well, if it ain't MacTavish. Fancy meeting you here in Oregon City. How's your pretty little bride? I'm looking forward to seeing her again."

"Bastard," Tanner hissed from between clenched teeth. "You keep away from Ashley. No woman is safe around a raping bastard like you."

Slater stiffened, his voice dangerously tight. "Them are strong words, Reb."

"True, nonetheless. What you did to my wife and mother was cruel and savage beyond belief."

Slater shrugged. "There was a war on."

"War is no excuse for hurting women who offer no resistance. After you finished with my wife, her mind couldn't deal with the shame. She killed herself, Slater. Do you hear me? Ellen killed herself because of what you did to her." The bitter accusation left Tanner's throat in an explosion of rage.

Slater gave him a leering grin deliberately intended to goad him. "So that little filly in Georgia was your wife. Tasty little morsel, but she couldn't hold a candle to the one you got now. I'm not surprised the woman in Georgia ended her life. Timid as a mouse, she was, but good nonetheless. Especially since it had been a long time

385

since I'd had any —"

His sentence exploded in a yelp of pain. Tanner knew Slater was deliberately baiting him, but the man had gone too far. Doubling his fist, he drew back his arm and smashed Stark in the face. Slater hadn't been expecting the move, so he did not attempt to brace or defend himself. He flew backward, hit the wall with a loud thud and slid to the floor, out like a light.

Tanner would have killed Slater on the spot if it weren't for Ashley. He had been so close, so damn close to drawing, but at the last minute he had remembered his promise to Ashley, and the love they shared. If he was dead or in jail, she would be all alone. He would be abandoning her to wolves like Stark and Slater, who fed upon the innocent. Yet the urge to kill Slater was so compelling he either had to put space between them or submit to his instincts.

Slater was still slumped against the wall when Tanner entered his own room and slammed the door behind him. Placing his saddlebag on the bed, he filled the pockets with his spare clothing and shaving gear and was ready to leave a scant fifteen minutes after entering.

Earlier that morning he had spoken to the preacher and completed arrangements to rent the house he and Ashley would share after their wedding on Sunday. Then he had returned to the Red Garter and knocked on Nell's door, informing her that he was moving out. Nell had expressed shock when Tanner had told her he and Ashley were going to marry the next day.

"I don't understand, Tanner. Why did you lie about being married if you really weren't?"

"It's a long story, Nell. Circumstances I can't go into forced me to lie. I've been married to Ashley for months. Rather than explain our deception to the townspeople, we decided to remarry and pretend it's the first time. It's the only way I can protect her."

"It's because of Sam, isn't it?"

"He's part of it. I've confided in you because I feel I owe you an explanation after telling you I was married but not that I was married to Ashley. I'd appreciate it if you'd not tell anyone."

"Mum's the word, handsome. Good luck to you and your wife. I don't think I've ever met a man before as crazy about his wife as you obviously are."

Tanner smiled to himself as he recalled Nell's words. She certainly had read him right. He *was* crazy about Ashley.

Having packed his saddlebag, Tanner left his room, deliberately skirting Slater, who was beginning to stir. Tanner was halfway down the stairs when from behind him came the metallic click of a revolver being cocked.

"No one does that to Pratt Slater and lives."

Tanner stopped and turned slowly, not really surprised to see Slater standing at the top of the staircase, braced against the wall, a gun swaying dangerously in his hand. Tanner couldn't help smiling. He knew he had a good right arm but didn't realize he packed such a powerful wallop. His mirth was short-lived as he suddenly realized he had backed himself into a tight spot. Slater had but to pull the trigger and Tanner would be a goner before he could reach for his gun. He tried to buy time.

"Shooting a man in cold blood is just what I'd expect from a yellow-bellied coward like you." It was with some surprise that Tanner realized shooting Slater in cold blood was exactly what he had planned before Ashley's love had changed his mind. Except he would have given Slater more of a chance than Slater was giving him. There would have been a face-off between two equally armed men.

"Say your prayers, MacTavish."

"Put the gun down, Slater."

"Wha—" Slater spun around, stunned to see Nell standing behind him. His gaze flew to the gun she held in her hands.

"You ain't murdering no one, Slater."

"I don't have time for you, Slater," Tanner said as he turned and continued down the stairs. "I'm getting married tomorrow. If you're so anxious to die, it will have to be on my time. I owe you, Nell," he said as he tipped his hat and ambled out the bat-wing doors.

"I'll get you for that, MacTavish," Slater growled as he shoved his gun in his holster and swung around to confront Nell. "Why in the hell didn't you let me shoot?"

Nell shrugged. In her opinion Slater was lower than dirt. The walls were thin; she had heard Slater and Tanner arguing in the hallway about the despicable thing Slater had done to Tanner's wife during the war. No woman deserved to be raped. Scum like Slater should be eradicated from the face of the earth. Tanner was twice, no, three times the man Slater was, and he didn't deserve to die at the hands of a vile rapist. She had armed herself with a gun when she heard Slater threaten to kill Tanner, and had come to Tanner's defense.

Slater turned around and slammed into his room. Nell continued on down the stairs. Stark met her at the bottom landing. He grasped her arm and dragged her into his office.

"What in the hell did you do that for? Slater had the draw on him."

"Slater is a despicable pig. Do you know why Tanner has it in for him?" No answer. "I didn't think so. During the war Slater raped

Tanner's wife. She killed herself because she couldn't live with the shame."

Stark shrugged. "It's no business of mine what happened during the war. I don't want you interfering again."

His remark stunned Nell. She could draw only one conclusion. "You want Tanner dead!"

"I didn't say that. Just don't interfere."

"Sure, Sam," Nell agreed. It was a good thing he didn't suspect she was lying through her teeth. She suddenly realized that Sam had a personal reason for wanting Tanner dead. And that reason had red hair. Since Stark was too smart to get personally involved in a killing, Nell suspected he had hired Slater to do the job for him. She hoped Tanner realized he was in grave danger. There was really little she could do to help Tanner except keep her eyes and ears open.

Tanner moved Ashley's personal belongings into the house he had rented on Saturday, and that night after making love she slept in his arms. It was heaven; she had never expected to be so happy.

Over breakfast Sunday morning, Tanner told Ashley about his confrontation with Slater. She was proud of him for his restraint and grateful to Nell, and she told him so.

"You know it won't end there, love," Tanner warned. "Both Slater and Stark want me dead. Slater because he fears me and Stark because he wants you."

"We can move away," Ashley suggested. "We don't have to stay in Oregon City. We can go to Seattle. Or even San Francisco. I still have a little money left."

"I'm not running away, love. One way or another I'll take care of Slater and Stark."

Tanner hoped Ashley didn't suspect he was feeding her empty words. He had no idea how to get both Slater and Stark off his back. He believed he could best Slater in a shootout, that would be the obvious solution, but that would still leave Stark.

"I want you to release me from my promise, Yank. I can't protect you against Stark with Slater breathing down my neck. I'll try to make it look like self-defense. It wouldn't be difficult. Nell would testify that Slater had already threatened me once."

Gorge rose in Ashley's throat. She swallowed bile and her stomach lurched with sick despair. The thought of Tanner facing death was more than she could bear. She jumped out of her chair so fast it crashed to the floor. In seconds she was in the bedroom, retching into the chamber pot. Tanner followed close on her heels. He offered her water and a wet cloth after she had heaved up her breakfast, then drew her to her feet and held her in his arms until she stopped trembling.

"I guess we don't have to wonder if you're

carrying my child," Tanner observed dryly. "How long has this been going on?"

"This is the first time," Ashley said. "And it doesn't prove a thing."

"Doesn't it? Time will tell, love. Are you sorry?"

"That I might be pregnant?" She gave him a wobbly smile. "I'm not sorry at all. We'll be a real family and I no longer have to worry about you gunning for Slater. You did promise me."

Tanner frowned. "What if he comes gunning for me? I'll need to defend myself."

"Oh God, Tanner, I can't stand it."

He kissed the top of her head. "It will be all right, I promise."

"Are you happy?"

"About the baby?"

"About the possibility," Ashley corrected.

He chuckled; Ashley loved the sound. He laughed far too seldom.

"It's going to take some getting used to but I can't deny I've often thought about having a child. I always wondered why Ellen . . ." His sentence ended abruptly. "I'm sorry. I didn't mean to bring Ellen into it."

Ashley swallowed hard. "It's all right, Tanner. Ellen was a part of your life for a long time. I don't expect you to forget her. I hope in time our love will heal the raw wound left by her violent death."

"Only Slater's death will do that," Tanner

muttered beneath his breath.

"What did you say?"

"Nothing important. Are you up to a wedding this afternoon?"

Ashley gave him a saucy grin. "More than ready. This time our marriage will be for the right reasons. I love you, Reb."

He pressed a tender kiss on her lips. "I love you to distraction, my sassy Yankee bride."

They were married by Reverend Doolittle in the Methodist church, with Mrs. Doolittle standing as witness.

Their wedding night was a far cry from their first marriage more than six months before. When at last they fell into an exhausted sleep, Ashley no longer doubted Tanner's love for her.

The following morning Ashley prepared for her visit to the mayor.

"I'll go with you," Tanner said as he watched her dress.

"There's no need," Ashley returned with a smile. Abruptly she thought of their future with no job in the offing for either of them, and a frown worried her brow. "Tanner, what are we going to do once my money is gone and we have another mouth to feed? My inheritance won't last forever. Have you thought about what you'd like to do to make a living?"

"I've thought a lot about that," Tanner said with a grin. "I met a man, Ashley. He's looking for a partner in the logging business he plans to establish. The area holds a wealth of opportunity. Immigrants arrive daily from the east. They come by water and overland across the prairie. The need for wood and its by-products is growing apace with the surge in population. Logs can be floated downriver to Portland and shipped abroad, or fed into the closest sawmill."

"You've thought a lot about this, haven't you?" For the first time since she'd met Tanner he sounded excited about the future. She felt like cheering.

"I have to support my family. I wasn't sure there was going to be a family but I wanted to be prepared just in case. Once I had the gumption to admit I loved you, I began thinking about our future."

A sigh slipped past Ashley's lips. A year ago she had been a spinster with no hope of marriage; now she had Tanner. It didn't matter that she'd had to almost hogtie Tanner to bring him to the altar, or that their marriage had been one of convenience; he was hers now. Together they'd find a way to surmount the problems facing them, notably Stark and Slater.

"I don't want to sound crass, Reb, but where are we going to get the money to go partners with this nameless man?"

"His name is Curtis Webber. He's a Yankee, but for some reason I trust him." He smiled. "I actually like him too. Do you suppose you and Cole have anything to do with that? As for money . . ." He grinned. "I still have most of the money I earned for marrying you."

Ashley swatted him and tried to look indignant. "I did not pay you to marry me! I paid you to get me safely to Fort Bridger."

He grinned in response. "Whatever. I'll give Webber the cash I have on hand and borrow the rest from the bank."

"You won't need to. I still have what's left of the inheritance from my aunt. It's in the bank. You can have all of it. It's yours anyway, since you're my husband."

"I don't deserve you, sweetheart. Are you sure?" Ashley nodded. "Then I'll be taking a trip to Portland next week to close the deal. Come on, sweetheart, I'll buy you a wedding breakfast at the hotel before we face the mayor."

Trouble struck as they walked hand in hand to the mayor's office after breakfast. Someone shot at Tanner. The bullet plowed through the crown of his hat. People scattered as Tanner shoved Ashley against a building, drew his weapon and shielded her with his body, but there were no more shots.

Tanner hurried Ashley down the street and people began peeping out from the stores to assess the safety of resuming their business.

When they reached the mayor's office, Tanner pushed Ashley inside so fast she nearly lost her balance.

"I'm afraid you're going to have to face the mayor on your own, sweetheart," Tanner said, his eyes scanning the buildings across the street. "I'm going to report the shooting to the sheriff. I'm afraid someone will take a shot at us when we leave here. Stay with the mayor until I return and tell you it's safe to go back out on the street."

"Tanner, be careful."

He sent her a cocky grin. "I have to now. I have a family to take care of." He ducked out the door before she could tell him she loved him.

"You can go on into the office, Miss Webster. The mayor isn't in right now but you can talk to one of the council members."

While she had been talking with Tanner, the mayor's secretary had announced her arrival and had been told to show her into the office.

"Thank you. But my name is Mrs. MacTavish now." Marshaling her nerve, she lifted her chin and walked into the mayor's office. The door closed behind her and for some reason the sound was strangely unsettling. She knew why the moment she saw that Sam Stark was the sole occupant of the room. He sat in the mayor's chair, his fingers steepled in front of him.

"When will the mayor return?" Ashley demanded to know.

"Soon. He's out on an errand. You ignored my warning. It wasn't wise of you. I hope MacTavish lives long enough for you to enjoy."

"Why do you hate Tanner? He's done nothing to you."

"He has you. When I decide I want something or someone, nothing stands in my way. You will be mine, Ashley, in my bed, in any way I want you. I always get what I want."

"Why me? I'm nothing special."

His blue eyes glowed with an inner fire that made Ashley shiver. "You're the first woman who's ever resisted me. That intrigues me. Why can't you be sensible and give me what I want? What can it hurt? Meet me tonight and maybe you can convince me to let your man live."

Ashley recoiled in horror. "Did you shoot at Tanner a little while ago?"

"Do I look stupid?"

"Don't lie. You issued the order; it makes no difference who did the actual shooting."

Stark twirled the ends of his mustache. "About that meeting. Come to my office tonight. Come around to the alley behind the saloon. Knock twice on the rear door."

Ashley shook her head. "I can't."

"You'd best think twice about it. You never know when your man will meet with an accident. He dealt Slater a blow to his pride. Slater is raving to get even. A word from me and he'll calm down."

Could she afford to take a chance with Tanner's life? Ashley wondered. "If I do meet you in private it will be to talk, nothing else. Understand?" She would do anything to save Tanner's life. Anything except . . . But, no, she wouldn't think about that now.

"Perfectly. We'll talk about how you can save your husband's life if you're willing. Can you come tonight?"

"No. I can't get away without Tanner suspecting something. Tanner is going to Portland next week on a business trip and he expects to be gone two nights."

Stark grinned. "Perfect. I'll come to your house so you won't have to venture out alone after dark. No need to tell me which nights your man will be gone; one of my men will be watching your house."

Ashley knew she was in dangerous water but she thought it worth the risk if she could save Tanner. She hoped that once she told Stark she was expecting a child it would put an end to his craving for her. But she wanted a promise from Stark before she would agree to anything.

"I'll only agree to see you if you promise me that nothing will happen to Tanner in the meantime. No one, not even Slater, is to threaten his life. Is that clear?"

"I won't be dictated to, my dear,"

His harsh words did not daunt Ashley's determination. "Those are my terms."

He was silent so long Ashley feared she had gone too far.

"Very well. I agree."

The mayor chose that moment to return to his office. He greeted both Ashley and Stark as if nothing were amiss. He nodded to Sam Stark before addressing Ashley.

"My secretary told me I had visitors. Had I known you were coming to see me, Miss Webster, I would have delayed my errand. I'm grateful that Sam was here to entertain you. Why aren't you in school teaching our children?"

"I dismissed school for the day," Ashley told him. "As soon as I explain, I'm sure you'll understand."

The mayor sat behind his desk and waited for Ashley to continue.

"First of all, I'm not Miss Webster. I'm Mrs. MacTavish."

After that rather startling remark, Ashley told the mayor that she and Tanner had been married the day before.

"I'm sorry I deceived you and the town council about my intentions but I had hoped to wait to marry until the school year ended. Tanner decided he didn't want to wait."

Both Stark and Mayor Thornton appeared stunned, but for different reasons.

"You just got married yesterday?" Stark questioned sharply. "I thought . . ."

"I don't care what you thought, Mr. Stark," Ashley said, heading off his remark. "Tanner and I were married yesterday by Reverend Doolittle. You have only to ask him to confirm it."

"I don't know what your game is, but this changes nothing."

"I'm resigning my position as of today," Ashley continued as if Stark hadn't spoken. "I sincerely hope you'll be able to find another teacher. I just want to add that I greatly enjoyed teaching the town's children. I've already vacated the house and moved to new lodgings."

The mayor looked more than a little bewildered. He couldn't make head or tail of the conversation between Ashley and Stark and decided to ignore it. "This puts us in a bind, yes, indeed. I'm glad you're here, Sam," he said, addressing Stark. "Perhaps together we can solve this dilemma."

Stark pretended to give the problem considerable thought. "There is only one solution that I can see. The town's children can't be let loose to roam the streets. I suggest we change our policy temporarily and keep Mrs. MacTavish on until the end of the school year. That will give us time to hire another teacher. We should get an influx of immigrants and homesteaders next summer.

Surely there will be a teacher among them."

"Hmmm. That does seem the most logical solution. What do you say, Miss . . . Mrs. MacTavish? If the town council agrees, and I'm sure they will when they learn it is the only way to keep their children from underfoot during the winter months, will you stay on?"

Ashley was stunned. She'd never expected this turn of events. Evidently the need for a teacher far surpassed any of the drawbacks of her married state. She would very much like to finish out the school year but feared Sam Stark would expect some kind of reward for suggesting it.

"I don't . . ."

"Of course you will, Mrs. MacTavish," Stark blustered. "You've already admitted you need the salary. The rest of the council will give you no problems, I promise. You and your husband may remain in the house, if you like."

"My husband has already rented a house for us. I moved in over the weekend. It's on Second Street, not far from the school."

"Ah, you're living in the Carmichael house. The Carmichaels moved into a larger home a couple of months ago, after their second child was born," Stark recounted.

"You haven't said one way or the other if you'll remain until the end of the school year," the mayor said.

Ashley wished Tanner were here to advise her. She truly wanted to retain the position until the end of the school year, but the knowledge that Stark was pushing for her to stay worried her. However, with Tanner to protect her what could he do to her? And she did have Stark's promise that no harm would come to Tanner for the time being. Ashley was no fool; she knew what Stark wanted, but she hoped to convince him how foolish it was to pursue a pregnant woman. If meeting Stark this once would save Tanner's life, she had no recourse. Once Stark lost interest in her he'd have no reason to want Tanner dead.

"Very well, I accept your offer," Ashley said. "And thank you."

Tanner chose that moment to sweep into the room. He had spoken with the sheriff, and the lawman had promised to look into the random shooting. Then he had hastened back to the mayor's office to give Ashley moral support. He wasn't pleased to see Sam Stark with the mayor.

"What offer are you referring to?" Tanner asked, moving to stand beside Ashley.

"I've been asked to remain as schoolmarm until the end of the school year," Ashley explained. "I've accepted."

"Are you sure that's wise, Ashley?"

"What can it hurt? And I love my job."

"Then it's settled," the mayor said, signaling the end of the meeting by rising from his chair. "Since you're no longer living in the house the town provides for its teacher, your salary will be adjusted to reflect the change. I'll inform the council members."

He held out his hand to Tanner. "I don't believe we've met, Mr. MacTavish. Welcome to Oregon City. I'm not pleased with this turn of events but I can certainly understand two young people wanting to get married. I'm sorry your wife saw the need to lie to us in the beginning about your relationship."

Tanner grasped the mayor's hand. "Thank you, Mr. Mayor. I appreciate your understanding."

Stark snorted in disgust and turned away.

"Let's go home," Tanner said as he guided Ashley from the office.

"Until we meet again, Mrs. MacTavish," Stark called after them.

Ashley faltered, frighteningly aware of what Stark was referring to. She felt a chill pass over her and moved closer to Tanner. She hoped to God he would never find out what she intended. If Tanner ever learned what she was going to do in order to protect him, he'd be furious. If he found out she was going to talk to Stark, alone and without his protection, she didn't know what he'd do . . . or what he'd think.

Chapter Nineteen

Nothing out of the ordinary occurred the following day. Tanner had spoken with the sheriff again, and the lawman told Tanner he thought the shot on Monday had been a stray bullet and not meant for him. Tanner wasn't at all convinced, knowing what he did about Slater and Stark, but since calmness seemed to prevail, Tanner decided to go to Portland on Wednesday. He had promised Curtis Webber that he'd give him his answer about the partnership before the week was out.

"Are you sure you'll be all right while I'm gone?" Tanner asked again. Ashley had lost count of the number of times Tanner had asked that same question in the past few hours.

"I'll be fine, truly." She couldn't look him in the eye for fear he'd recognize her anxiety and ask questions. She never was any good at lying to him, and she didn't want Tanner to find out she planned on confronting Stark in his absence.

"Keep your doors locked at night."

"Don't worry."

"I'll leave my spare gun in the bureau drawer. I'll be back Friday night at the latest."

Tanner gave her a hard, quick kiss, then left before he changed his mind.

Since Wednesday was a normal school day, Ashley's mind was sufficiently occupied with her students. It wasn't until she was home that the utter recklessness of what she was going to do struck her forcibly. She must have been desperate or crazy to agree to let Sam Stark come to her house while Tanner was gone. At the time, she'd thought her reasons sufficient to warrant the risk. It was imperative that she convince Stark to spare Tanner's life, to make Stark aware that she wasn't worth his effort. He might own half the town but he didn't own the law, did he?

Not only did Ashley lock her doors that night, but also her windows. She was taking no chances with a man as devious as Sam Stark. It was past midnight when she finally sought her bed. Before she slid between the covers, she checked the gun Tanner had left to make sure it was loaded. She didn't believe Stark would come this late, but if he did she wanted to be prepared. She lay awake until nearly dawn before sleep finally claimed her. Her last thought was one of relief: perhaps Stark had lost interest in her.

Ashley's belief that Stark had lost interest persisted throughout the following day. It was Thursday and Tanner would be home tomorrow, she thought as she closed the schoolhouse door and walked the short dis-

405

tance home. She tried to convince herself that Stark was no longer a problem.

Thursday night Ashley locked her doors and windows and prepared for bed early. Having lost sleep the previous night, she was exhausted. Ashley had no idea what awakened her shortly before the hour of midnight. The room was pitch black, yet she knew she wasn't alone. Her heart was thumping so loudly it sounded like thunder in her ears.

She sat up abruptly, peering into the darkness. "Tanner, is that you?"

"I'm afraid not, my dear. I assumed you'd be expecting me."

Ashley's fear fled before her anger when she recognized Stark's voice. "How did you get in here?"

"Actually, it was quite easy. At one time I'd considered renting this house. I recalled that I hadn't returned the key to Chad Carmichael after I looked at the house and decided not to rent it. Carmichael had several other keys, so he didn't miss it."

Ashley could hear his footsteps as he made his way to the bed and she looked longingly toward the bureau where the gun was hidden. Maybe she wouldn't need it, she hoped. Maybe Sam Stark would listen to reason. Suddenly a light flared and Stark's grinning countenance appeared above the flaming match. Then Stark spied the lamp and set the match to it. Ashley gasped and pulled the blanket up to her chin as light flooded the room.

"What a charming picture," Stark said, leering at her. He approached the bed, grasped the blanket and pulled it from her fingers. "I want to see what I'm getting."

Ashley's mouth went dry and she tried to summon sufficient moisture to speak. "You're getting nothing. I merely agreed to talk. I thought by now you'd realize how ridiculous this is. You could have any woman in town. Why do you want me?"

"That's exactly why. I could have any woman I want but you're the one woman who doesn't want me. You're not going to change your mind about giving me what I want, are you? If you have any thoughts along those lines, forget them. A word from me and your husband will be ambushed before he reaches Oregon City." He placed his hand on her shoulder and slowly drew it down her arm. She shivered violently. "Now, where were we? Ah, yes, take off that damn nightgown. I want to see all of you."

"I have no intention of doing any such thing," Ashley returned hotly. "You have no business coming into my house like a thief in the night. If you recall, I told you I wouldn't do anything to jeopardize my marriage."

His eyes turned cold and resolute. "You will if you want your man to live. I don't know whether you are newly married or have been married all along, and I don't care. Your games are your own business, as long as they don't interfere with what I want."

"I'll go to the sheriff."

He gave a bark of laughter. "The sheriff is my man. I got him elected. I told you I was a power in this town."

"This isn't Dodge City, or Tombstone. This is a law-abiding town. You can't just kill a man and expect to get away with it."

"You can if your name is Sam Stark. Are you going to take off that nightgown or am I going to do it for you?"

"You're going to listen to me," Ashley said, easing from bed. She felt safer facing him that way, and her voluminous flannel nightgown covered as much of her as her dress. "I'm going to tell you something I hope will change your mind about wanting me. Then there will be no need to hurt Tanner."

Stark searched her face, his gaze slowly traveling down the length of her body. Ashley shuddered and hugged herself with her arms, suddenly feeling alone and vulnerable.

"You're trying to buy time, Ashley, but it won't work. I doubt there is anything you could say that will change my mind. I've been anticipating this moment since you arrived in town."

Ashley knew of no way to say it plainer than to blurt it out. "I'm carrying a child. You can't possibly want me in that condition."

408

She'd played her trump card; now all she had to do was sit back and wait for Stark to express disgust and leave. After extracting his promise not to hurt Tanner, of course.

Ashley wasn't prepared for Stark's laughter. "Well, I'll be damned. So you're growing a brat. No wonder you decided to get hitched, or at least go through the motions again. You don't look pregnant. There is still plenty of time before you're too big to mount." At Ashley's appalled expression, he added, "You didn't think that little bombshell was going to change my mind, did you?" He laughed again. "Your condition will make bedding you more interesting. I've not had the pleasure of being inside a woman with child. I've heard that a woman is more passionate at that time."

Ashley felt gorge rise up in her throat and swallowed hard. It would take little to cause her to spew forth the contents of her stomach. She'd been so sure Stark would reject her once he was told about her condition. What kind of animal was he?

"Experiment on some other woman," Ashley said, backing toward the bureau.

"Ah, don't you see the irony of it, my dear? If you're already increasing you can't conceive my child. How fortunate for you and your husband." Ashley had slowly backed against the bureau, and she felt the satisfying pressure of the drawer handles poking her.

And inside the drawer was Tanner's gun.

Stark grinned and moved toward her.

Tanner rode through the dark streets of Oregon City, pleased with what he had accomplished but anxious to get home to Ashley. His business with Webber had taken less time than he'd anticipated; the deal had been signed and sealed this morning. Tanner was now a full partner in Webber-MacTavish Enterprises. Webber was to handle the leasing of land and the shipping end of the business, and Tanner would take care of hiring lumberjacks and felling trees. After losing everything to the war, Tanner had never expected a second chance at love and prosperity. And he had Ashley to thank for it. The little Yank had burrowed her way into his heart and refused to let him give up on life.

Exhausted from his long ride from Portland, Tanner reined his horse down Second Street. It was past midnight. He knew Ashley would be sleeping but he couldn't wait to slip into bed beside her and hold her in his arms. He had turned down Webber's offer to stay another night in Portland and had started home before the ink was dry on the partnership agreement. A full moon had guided him as he pressed on through the dark night.

He rode his horse around to the rear of the house, dismounted and removed the saddle from the animal's back. Then he walked around to the front door and was searching through his pockets for his key when he noted that the door was slightly ajar. Alarm shuddered through him. He drew his weapon and slowly pushed the door open.

Stark hovered over Ashley, his face taut with grim purpose. He had already dropped his gun belt, shed his coat and was wrestling now with the buttons on the placket of his trousers.

"Don't be shy, honey. I'll make sure you get pleasure out of this. I don't want to hurt your child, but if I have to force you, one never knows what will happen. New life is so fragile, is it not?"

Ashley blanched. His implied threat made her furious. The man was an animal. She heard him curse and saw him look down as he fumbled with the placket of his trousers. In his eagerness to free his straining manhood, his fingers didn't move fast enough to suit him and he began tearing at the buttons. A small window of opportunity opened and Ashley seized it. Whirling, she pulled open the bureau drawer, found the gun and drew a bead on Stark.

"Get out of here!" Her demand brought Stark's head shooting upward. His gaze narrowed on the gun in her hand. His own weapons were some distance away, and he

411

wondered if he could lunge for them before Ashley pulled the trigger. In his lust to possess Ashley he had thoughtlessly dropped his gun belt.

"I'm a tolerable shot, Mr. Stark. At this close range I could easily blow your brains out. Make one move toward those guns and you're a dead man. You're an intruder in my home. I have every right to defend myself."

"You're making a big mistake," Stark warned.

"No, you're making a mistake, Mr. Stark. Get out of here. Now!" She cocked the pistol.

Stark started to reach for his coat but Ashley didn't trust him. "Leave it. I'll see that it's returned to you, along with your guns."

Stark recognized Ashley's desperation and decided that retreat was the better part of valor. Not bothering to close the gap in his pants, he whirled on his heel, his face mottled with rage. He wasn't going to get himself killed for a trigger-happy slut. Ashley leaned against the open bedroom door, the cocked gun still aimed at Stark as he stomped through the parlor. Light from the lamp in the bedroom spilled into the parlor, giving her a clear view of Stark's back. She didn't relax her vigilance until she saw him reach for the front doorknob.

Suddenly the front door flew inward and Tanner stepped into the opening. He was so

412

stunned at the sight of Sam Stark, his coat missing, his trousers gaping open, that he was slow in reacting.

Stark, a master at keeping his wits, gave Tanner a slow smile. "You almost arrived too soon, MacTavish. But fortunately I was able to enjoy your slut of a wife before your arrival. Next time don't be so inconsiderate as to appear before you're expected." He made a great show of closing the flap of his pants and buckling his belt. Then he walked out the door and disappeared into the night.

The gun slid from Ashley's numb fingers as she slumped against the bedroom door. She couldn't have moved if she'd wanted to. She was still reeling from her close call with Stark.

"Tanner." His name slipped past her lips on a shaky sigh.

Tanner heard but gave no reply. He was still peering into the darkness, as if unable to comprehend the scene he'd just stumbled into. When it finally dawned on him that he'd just seen Stark emerge from Ashley's bedroom in a state of undress, and that Ashley wore only a nightgown, he slowly swung his gaze around to Ashley. Had he given his heart only to have it broken by a lying Yank? It hurt; dear God, it hurt. How long had this affair been going on? he wondered. Was the child Ashley carried even his?

Tanner moved toward her, his gait jerky, his face dark and dangerous, his body coiled

413

taut. For a moment Ashley thought he meant to strike her, and she shrank back in fear.

"What in the hell was Stark doing in your bedroom?" Tanner all but shouted. His gaze swept the room, coming to rest on Stark's discarded holster and jacket. "Your lover must have been in one helluva hurry. I hope he didn't leave you wanting. I know how you value your pleasure."

Ashley blanched. "What? You can't believe that I . . . Oh God, Tanner, how could you?"

His voice was as frosty as the air outside. "What am I supposed to think when I find another man in my wife's bedroom, missing most of his clothes? He all but admitted he'd been in your bed."

"And you believed him?" she asked incredulously.

"What was he doing here if you didn't invite him? I should have known better than to fall in love with a damn Yankee."

When she had first seen Tanner's face she'd felt fear, but now she was furious. How dare he accuse her of having an affair with Stark? She couldn't stand the man. She knew now how foolishly naive she'd been to agree to see Stark while Tanner was away, but she had done it for Tanner's sake. At the time she'd felt capable of handling Stark, and she *had* succeeded in routing him from her bedroom, hadn't she?

"How dare you!" she shouted in a fit of

414

rage. "How dare you accuse me of something so vile. I did agree to see Sam Stark, but it was for your sake, not for some tawdry affair. I admit he tried to take advantage of me, but as you noted, I sent him fleeing. I had him in my sights and would have pulled the trigger if he'd hadn't left when he did. Sam Stark is an opportunist. When he saw you he found a perfect chance to make trouble. Go away," she choked out. "I can't love a man who doesn't trust me."

"I'm not going anywhere. What did you mean, you asked Stark here for my sake?"

Sick with despair, Ashley turned on shaky legs and walked to the bed. She sat down and stared at him blankly. "Are you still here?"

"Tell me what happened tonight," he said more reasonably. Now that he'd had time to cool off, he realized he had jumped to conclusions without giving Ashley the benefit of the doubt. He should have known better than to believe a bastard like Stark. But when he'd seen Stark coming out of the bedroom, his mind shut down. "Did you let Stark in the house tonight, knowing I wasn't here to protect you?"

Ashley cast about for an answer. She knew she'd have to tell Tanner about Stark sometime, had even decided earlier that she would, but after he accused her of vile things he didn't deserve an answer. Her chin raised belligerently and she glared at him.

"I want an answer, Yank. If you don't want me to think the worst, I suggest you tell the truth."

"The truth is, I didn't let Sam Stark in the house tonight."

Tanner spit out an oath. "I told you to lock the doors."

"I did. He had a key."

Tanner sent her a skeptical look. "Did you encourage him?"

Ashley refused to meet his eyes. "If you must know, I told him you were going to be gone and agreed to see him."

Tanner's fists clenched at his sides and he visibly paled. How could Ashley do such a thing?

"I had to talk with him, Tanner. Just talk, nothing more. I had to convince him not to . . ." Her mouth clamped shut.

He grasped her shoulders and gave her a rough shake. "Not to what? Don't stop now, Yank."

The words came tumbling out in a rush. "He said if I . . . if I didn't give in to him he'd kill you. Not personally, it's not his way, but he has plenty of hirelings to do the job."

"So you invited him here, hoping to talk him out of killing me," he said through gritted teeth. "Tell me, Yank, how far would you have gone to save my life? Would you have welcomed him inside you?"

"I would do anything to save your life,

Tanner, anything but that. I was going to tell him I'm pregnant and hope he'd change his mind about . . . about wanting me. If he no longer wanted me then he'd have no reason to hurt you."

"And did you? Tell him you're pregnant, I mean."

Ashley flushed but her gaze did not waver from his. "I told him but it didn't seem to make any difference. He said he'd never had a pregnant woman before. He acted as if . . . he was looking forward to it. He came at me, discarding his guns and clothing on the way. He was distracted a moment and I managed to get the gun you'd left in the bureau drawer. I ordered him to leave and said I'd shoot him if he didn't. He must have believed me, for he was leaving when you ran into him at the door. That's what happened. I don't care if you believe me or not."

Tanner stared at Stark's guns and jacket lying on the floor and realized it could have happened just the way Ashley described. Then he saw his own gun where it had fallen near the bedroom door and cursed himself for a fool. He picked up the weapon and checked its chambers. Then he put it back in the drawer and slammed it shut. His face was suffused with cold fury as he headed for the front door.

"Tanner, where are you going?"

"To kill Stark."

Ashley ran after him, trying to pull him back into the bedroom. "No! You can't. Forget it, Tanner. The man isn't worth your life. Nothing happened. It was foolish of me to agree to see him alone. I knew what he wanted but thought I could convince him to spare your life."

"Dammit, Yank, when will you learn to let me fight my own battles? Stark can threaten me all he likes; I'm more than capable of defending myself. If you trusted me you would have told me about Stark's lewd proposal right away and let me end it once and for all."

"How? By killing him?"

"If that's what it takes."

"That's your answer to everything, isn't it? First Slater, then Stark. Think of our child, Tanner. I haven't seen a doctor, but all the signs lead me to believe I am indeed pregnant. I know I acted foolishly, but now Stark knows I have no interest in him. That doesn't mean you still don't need to be careful. Stark is a man who usually gets his way, and when he doesn't he turns mean."

Tanner mulled over Ashley's words. He was poised on the horns of a dilemma. He wanted to kill the man who'd dared to lay hands on his wife, yet he didn't want to jeopardize the new start in life he'd been given. He was excited about his partnership with Curtis Webber and looked forward to making

418

the venture work. And he was surprised at how eagerly he was looking forward to the birth of their child.

"What do you want me to do?"

"Lock the doors and come to bed. Tomorrow you can change the locks."

Suddenly Tanner turned and pulled her into his arms. She was surprised and humbled by the sheen of tears in his eyes. He tried to blink them back but they kept falling.

"Forgive me, sweetheart. I was blind with jealousy when I saw Stark coming out of your bedroom. I wouldn't hurt you for the world. Those terrible accusations . . . they spewed out before common sense returned. I know you'd never want a rat like Stark. But he's rich and I have nothing. You deserve so much more than I can give you. Please say you forgive me."

"I should let you suffer for even thinking I could want Sam Stark," Ashley said, still miffed. She pushed him backward onto the bed and stood over him, hands on hips, glaring daggers at him. "When will you get it through your head that it's you I want? Wealth means nothing to me. We'll get by. And I know we'll find a way to be happy however much Slater and Stark interfere in our lives." She gave him a confident smile. "I have faith in us, Reb."

"I know I've said this before and I'll say it again. I don't deserve you, Yank. I believe you're right. We'll get out of this muddle somehow. But you have to promise not to interfere again. Next time you could get hurt."

Ashley stretched out on the bed beside him. "I promise," she said, "unless you get in trouble and need my help."

He opened his mouth to protest and she pressed her lips to his. Tanner's response was instant and unashamedly erotic as he thrust his tongue into her mouth and deepened the kiss. Ashley moaned into his mouth, feeling his heat, his hunger . . . his love.

"I love you, Yank. Until I met you I had forgotten how to feel." His voice stroked her, rough-soft, rich, like the finest whiskey. "If I don't get these damn clothes off soon I won't be responsible for their condition."

Ashley laughed. Her hands slipped beneath his vest and raked it off his shoulders. His shirt followed. He raised himself slightly so she could ease them down his arms. By the time she worked his gun belt off and moved down to his trousers, his erection was straining against the placket. Then the buttons gave and she stared at him, awed by the strength of his need for her. Driven by the irresistible need to taste him, she took him in her hands and kissed his distended tip.

Moments of sheer stunning ecstasy gripped him. Then the pleasure became an unbearable agony of needing her as her tongue flickered over the length of him.

"God!"

He wrenched her away and into his arms, wild now to possess her. "I don't want to hurt you or the babe. If you keep this up I'll lose the ability to restrain my passion. Let me finish undressing. By then I should be more in control of myself."

Ashley watched hungrily as he removed his boots, stockings and trousers, pleased with this man she had married. When his clothes and her nightgown lay in a pile on the floor, he turned back to her and began slowly to touch her, to stroke her, his tongue and fingertips teasing, adoring, leaving no spot on her flushed skin unattended.

"God, Reb, you're driving me crazy. No more, please."

He laughed then against the softness of her breast, the sound husky and raw with excitement. "I love it when you beg."

Knowing exactly when she'd had enough, Tanner grasped her hips and slowly penetrated her. A shudder seized her body and she arched upward against him. He began moving in and out of her, deeply, frantically. His hands found her bottom, kneading, stroking. The hair on his chest scraped her sensitive nipples, and the stroking within her and the outer abrasion against her breasts were both incredibly arousing. Fever rose to an unbearable pitch, and then she screamed as her climax sent her over the edge into a fiery torrent of sensation. Tanner's hoarse cries of ecstasy followed her into the inferno. A long time passed before he found the strength to withdraw from the warmth of her body and roll onto his side.

"Do you know how much you please me?"

"I'm beginning to," Ashley replied. "Ask me again in fifty years."

Tanner grinned. "At this rate I'll be worn out in fifty years."

Suddenly Ashley grew pensive.

"What is it, sweetheart? Did I say something to make you sad?"

"I was just thinking about Ellen. For a long time I thought you couldn't love me because you loved your dead wife so much you couldn't accept another woman in your life."

"I'm going to say this once, Yank; then we won't ever talk about it again. I did love Ellen. She was sweet and vulnerable and far too frail for a man of my lusty appetites. I tried not to overburden her, and had she lived I'm sure our life would have been adequate, even happy.

"But Ellen didn't live. She's dead and I found you. I have something with you I could never have had with Ellen. You're nothing like Ellen, thank God. You're strong and vital, resourceful and passionate. You healed that aching wound deep within me that had been bleeding incessantly since Ellen's death.

Your caring pulled me from the darkest, deepest pit of hell. Never doubt that I love you, sweetheart."

Ashley's eyes grew misty with tears. That was the most beautiful, sincere speech she had ever heard. She loved Tanner with a depth and intensity that approached madness. She looked forward with relish to the next fifty years or so.

Tanner was nearly asleep when Ashley nudged him awake. "Are you sleeping?"

Tanner sighed. "Not anymore. Do you want to . . ."

"No, I just want your promise to be careful. Sam Stark doesn't strike me as a man who gives up easily."

In the darkness, Ashley couldn't see his face harden or his eyes darken with determination. "I'll be careful; you can depend on it."

Tanner's words seemed to satisfy Ashley. Tanner sighed gratefully. He didn't want her to suspect that he intended to call on Sam Stark first thing tomorrow.

Chapter Twenty

The following morning Ashley went off to school, forcing herself not to think about Sam Stark, or what a man with his vindictive nature might do to her and Tanner. Tanner had said he would handle it, and she tried to make herself believe it. They had parted at the schoolhouse after Tanner told her he was off to place an ad in the newspaper for experienced lumberjacks. Webber was doing the same in the Portland paper. They hoped to get a crew together within a month.

Tanner's first stop was the newspaper office. The second was Sam Stark's office. He barged through the door without being announced. Stark looked up, saw Tanner and reached for his gun. Tanner was faster. His gun literally flew into his hand.

"I didn't come for a shootout, Stark."

"Why did you come?"

"You know why. I want you to leave my wife alone. We're going to have a baby. She wants nothing to do with you. Your threats might frighten her but they don't me. I can take care of myself. Find a woman who will return your regard. You're not stupid, Stark. Most men wouldn't want a woman who doesn't want them."

Stark's lips thinned against his white teeth. "What makes you think your wife doesn't want me? She was willing enough last night. She was pure flame in my arms. She . . ."

"Knock it off! Tell me one more lie and I'll close your mouth permanently."

"Now see here, MacTavish, you can't just barge into my office and threaten my life."

"I just did. Now I'll give you a piece of advice. Nell is a good woman. She loves you, though God only knows why. You could do worse. Set your sights on a woman who doesn't have a husband to protect her."

"Don't tell me . . ."

A knock on the door interrupted Stark's reply. It was Nell.

"Burks is here, Sam. He says it's urgent."

Stark's attention shifted abruptly from Tanner. Burks was the man he had sent to Portland to glean information about Bernard Culp. "Send him in," he called out. He turned to Tanner. "You'll have to leave, MacTavish. This is important. We'll settle our differences later."

"Everything is settled," Tanner said as he headed for the door. It opened before he reached it, admitting a scruffy-looking man in desperate need of a shave and haircut. Tanner paid him little heed as he continued out the door.

"Shut the door," Stark ordered gruffly.

425

"What did you find out? It took you long enough."

Burks pushed the door shut but wasn't aware that it hadn't latched properly. "I was checking out leads, boss. I think you'll be pleased with what I learned."

"Well, spit it out. I'm not in the best of moods today. I can use a little good news."

"This news ain't good. Your friend Culp got off the ship, all right. And he left with Pratt Slater. When I reached Portland I learned that the ship Culp was supposed to have sailed on to Alaska was due back soon. I waited and spoke to the captain myself when he returned. He told me he never took Culp to Alaska."

Stark's eyes glinted dangerously. "So Slater was lying. That double-crossing son of a bitch. I suspected as much. Culp would never have cheated me. Our friendship goes way back."

"What do you think happened to Culp, boss?"

"He's dead," Stark said with certainty. "And if I'm not mistaken we'll find the missing money with Slater."

Slater stood listening outside Stark's door. He had been on his way to ask if Stark had any orders for him when he overheard the conversation taking place inside the room. No one was in the saloon this time of day, so he pressed his ear to the door. What he heard sent fear racing through him. He didn't wait around long enough to find out Stark's plans for him. Neither Slater nor the occupants of the room were aware that Nell had seen Slater eavesdropping outside the door, and curiosity made her put her own ear to the door and listen after Slater had gone.

Racing up the stairs and into his room, Slater pulled out the greenbacks and gold from beneath the mattress, stuffed them into his saddlebags along with a few personal items, and hightailed it out of the saloon. Within minutes he had saddled his horse and was heading north out of town. Portland was too close to Oregon City for comfort, he decided, but Seattle was just far enough to put him out of Stark's reach.

Back at the saloon, Stark and Burks left the office and approached Slater's room with guns drawn. Stark kicked open the door and spit out a curse at the sight of the empty room. The mattress had been shoved aside, and it appeared as if Slater had left in a hurry. If Stark had had any doubt about Slater having stolen his money, the gleaming gold coin he saw caught between the mattress and bedding dispelled that notion.

"He's gone," Stark snarled. "And he took my money with him."

"I'll get him, boss."

"Damn right, you will. Find Stumpy and Pete. Follow Slater and don't come back without my money."

"What should we do with Slater when we find him?"

"Take care of him. I don't care how or where. Go on, get out of here; you're wasting time."

Slater was several miles north of town when he realized he was being trailed. He left the road he'd been following and plunged into the woods. He heard his pursuers crashing through the trees behind him. Raw panic seized him. He should have known better than to think he could escape the long arm of Stark's vengeance. They might get him, he thought, but he damn sure wasn't going to let them have the money.

Slater was convinced that Stark's men hadn't yet seen him and that he had a few precious minutes to locate what he'd been searching for. Ahead he spotted a rotted tree with a large hole halfway up its trunk. Reining in his horse, he removed his saddlebags and stuffed them inside the hole. Then with his knife he carefully carved an arrow into the trunk so he'd be able to identify the tree when he came back for his money. That done, he leaped into the saddle and spurred his mount. Moments later Stark's men caught up with him. Ignoring their order to stop, Slater plunged onward, still hopeful of escaping.

Three bullets put an end to his hopes. One caught him in the back, another in the head, and the third in the neck. Any one of them could have killed him. He was dead before he hit the ground.

"Search him," Burks ordered as he turned Slater over to check for a pulse. There was none.

Stumpy went through Slater's pockets, finding nothing but a few dollars and change. "Nothing here," Stumpy reported.

"Dammit. Find his horse. The money is probably in his saddlebags."

A short time later Pete returned with Slater's horse. The animal carried no saddlebags. "What in the hell could he have done with the money?" Pete wondered.

"I don't know, but we damn well better find it. Slater probably got rid of it when he heard us behind him. Spread out and search. Stark ain't gonna be happy about this."

"What about Slater?" Stumpy asked, poking at the dead man with the toe of his boot. "We gonna leave him here?"

Burks thought about that a moment, then said, "Naw, we'd better hide the body." Casting about, he spied a ravine nearby. "Roll him down that ravine. Ain't nobody gonna find him down there."

They worked together to carry Slater's body to the ravine, tossing him over the edge with little ceremony. "Now let's start looking for that money," Burks said as he dusted his hands on his stained vest. The three men searched until darkness made it impossible to continue. They found nothing. They returned to town, arguing over which one of them would tell Stark. Burks lost.

"You what?" Stark leaped to his feet, his face mottled with rage and his neck veins corded. "What a bunch of inept idiots. Can't you do anything right? What do you mean, you didn't find the money?"

"It wasn't on Slater, boss. And his saddlebags were missing. We searched everywhere. Do you have any idea how vast those damn woods are north of town? He could have hidden the money anywhere. Or maybe he hid it before he left town. He could have given it to someone to keep for him. There are all kinds of possibilities. It ain't our fault, boss. We took care of Slater. Ain't no one gonna find his body for a long time."

"I don't give a damn about Slater. It's the money I want!" Stark shouted. "Tomorrow, round up the men and make a thorough search of the area. That money has to be somewhere."

The money was gone for good. It wasn't easy to accept the loss of five thousand dollars, but after a week of heavy snows Stark called a halt to the search. He had to content himself with the knowledge that the man responsible for its loss was dead.

Christmas vacation arrived and Ashley dismissed school for a two-week hiatus. They'd had no more problems with Sam Stark, but Ashley wasn't convinced he was out of their hair for good. Truth to tell, neither was Tanner.

Ashley was Christmas shopping one day when Nell approached her in the mercantile after making certain no one was around to see them. She didn't want to cause Ashley trouble by being seen conversing with her in public.

"Do you know who I am?" Nell asked, startling Ashley, who had been looking over a selection of knives she was considering buying for Tanner for Christmas.

"We've never met but I know who you are," Ashley said.

"If you're embarrassed to be seen talking to me, I'll leave."

"No, don't go, Nell. It must be important if you took the trouble to search me out."

"I just want to tell you that you have a good man in Tanner."

Ashley smiled. "I've known that for a long time."

"I'm ashamed to admit that I tried to tempt Tanner a time or two, but he told me in no uncertain terms that he was married and loved his wife."

"Tanner told you that?" Ashley was stunned, yet pleased beyond measure.

"Tanner told me all about you. I don't know why you and Tanner were living apart and I don't want to know, but I believe you and Tanner belong together. I just wanted you to know that I'll do everything in my power to keep Sam Stark from making a fool of himself over you. I know he hasn't acted like a gentleman where you're concerned."

You don't know the half of it, Ashley thought but did not say. "Why do you care what Sam Stark does?"

Nell stared down at her hands. "I love Sam," she admitted. "I've loved him for a long time. We were lovers once and I hoped he'd propose, but Sam decided I wasn't good enough for him. He wanted to become a respected citizen in town, and in his opinion I was an obstacle to that goal."

"I've heard he owns half the town. What more could he want?"

"He owns property, not loyalty. The townspeople respect his money but they don't trust him enough to let him court their daughters. Sam and I are alike in many ways. I thought we might get together again until you came along."

"I'm sorry. I did nothing to attract Mr. Stark. I love Tanner. I'm going to have his child."

Nell's face glowed with pleasure on

432

Ashley's behalf. "A baby. How I envy you. I've always wanted a child, Sam's child. Sam isn't a bad man. He's just power-hungry."

"I think you'd be very good for Mr. Stark, Nell. What are you going to do about it?"

"What? I don't think . . . that is . . . what can I do about it?"

"Things weren't always good between Tanner and me. We've had more ups and downs than the Rocky Mountains, some quite explosive. But through it all one constant in our lives remained: I wanted Tanner and he wanted me. I refused to give up on him despite the obstacles in our path."

"You're saying I shouldn't give up on Sam, is that it?"

"That's for you to decide. Personally, I think you're too good for Sam Stark."

"That's because you've only seen one side of him. I'd better go now, before we're seen talking." She turned to leave.

"Good luck, Nell." Ashley watched Nell duck out of the store, thinking that if Sam Stark had a good side she wasn't aware of it.

Nell mulled over Ashley's words all the way back to the saloon. She recalled the conversation she'd overheard several days before between Sam and Burks, and decided the information gave her enough leverage to make Sam at least consider her suggestion.

Stark was alone when she walked into the

433

office without knocking. "Can I talk to you, Sam?"

"Sure thing, Nell, I've always got time for you. Is there a problem with the saloon? Are the girls giving you trouble?"

Nell settled in a chair, fiddling with her skirts until she gained the courage to speak. "No problem, it's just time we had a serious talk about us."

"Us? There is no 'us' that I am aware of."

"That's the point. I want us to be together again. You know I've always loved you."

Stark fingered his mustache as he searched Nell's face. They had enjoyed one another for several delightful years, and Stark was truly fond of her. Despite her years her face was still youthful, still beautiful, and he realized she would age gracefully. Her body had grown somewhat more voluptuous throughout the years, but he didn't mind that in a woman. His main problem with Nell was that she wasn't good enough for him. He was going places and needed a woman who knew her way around society.

"Now, Nell, you know we can't go back to the way we were. What about your other lovers? Aren't they keeping you satisfied?"

"There have been no other men since we broke up," Nell admitted. "I had a brief flirtation with Tanner MacTavish but nothing came of it. He's one of those rare men who love their wives and don't cheat on them."

Nell's admission took the wind out of Stark's sails. He found it difficult to believe that a lusty woman like Nell had remained celibate since their breakup. It was also very flattering to his ego.

"Nell, I —"

"No, Sam, don't say anything, not until you've heard me out." She paused to take a reinforcing breath, then said, "I want us to get married. I'm not getting any younger and I want a family."

Stark's sudden intake of breath betrayed his shock. He stared at Nell with something akin to horror. "Are you loco? You must be if you think I'd marry you. We were an item once, but marriage between us has never been an issue."

"I'm making it one. We *are* going to marry, Sam, even if I have to use blackmail. And you're not going to bother Mrs. MacTavish again, not if I have anything to say about it."

Stark stared at her through narrowed lids. "What in the hell are you talking about? How can you blackmail me?"

"I know you had Slater killed."

"You don't know a damn thing!"

"Don't I? Let me refresh your memory. You thought Slater had stolen something from you and sent Burks out to track him down and kill him. I believe his body can be found at the bottom of a ravine in the woods north of town. I reckon Sheriff Dingus will

435

be interested in hearing what I have to tell him."

Stark gave a bark of laughter. "Dingus is my man. He won't do a damn thing."

"You may have helped get him elected, but the sheriff is an honest man. You own property, not loyalty. Sheriff Dingus will uphold the law and you know it. He'll get a posse together and scour the area until he finds Slater's body."

"I'm shocked that you'd stoop to eavesdropping, Nell. I suppose you heard what MacTavish said too."

Nell nodded. "I did and I'm ashamed of you. I don't know what happened between you and Mrs. MacTavish, but I know Tanner wouldn't have confronted you if it hadn't been serious."

"And you think marriage will tame me?" Stark scoffed.

"I want you to sell the saloon and build a house for us. I'm sick of fending off men. Once we're both out of the gambling and whoring business you'll gain the respect you've always craved. You said you were once a lawyer in New York. You can hang out your shingle if your other businesses aren't enough to keep you occupied."

Stark had been a lawyer at one time, and had made a damn good living at it. He had been raised on the wrong side of the tracks, and no matter how high he advanced in life

436

he'd never gained the respect he wanted. A wrongheaded decision had cost him his career in New York. He had gotten greedy and begun fleecing some of his wealthy clients whose families looked down their noses at him because of his background. He had amassed a small fortune before being disbarred from practicing in New York. He had escaped the scandal by migrating west, all the way to Oregon. The opportunities he found in this new land, not all of them legal, had made it unnecessary for him to resume his law practice. He had used his ill-gotten gains to buy property and quickly became obsessed with power. Power was a frightening thing. The more one had the more one wanted.

"Well, Sam, what do you say? Are you willing to risk everything you own in addition to your standing in town when I go to the sheriff, or do we get married?"

"I could deny everything."

"You could, but I suspect none of your hirelings will hold up under questioning. They'll tell the truth to save their own skins."

"Do you really want me that bad?"

Nell gave him a wistful smile. "There's a lot of good in you, Sam. I know you can become obsessive when you want something badly, but I truly believe I can cure you of that flaw. If you still have designs on Tanner's wife, forget them. Make one overt move in her direction and I'll go to the sheriff with what I know."

"Why are you being so protective toward someone you don't even know?"

"It's not Tanner's wife I'm protecting; it's you. I don't want to see you dead, and that's how you'll end up if you mess with Tanner MacTavish or his wife."

"Damn, I believe you really do love me," Sam said, grinning. "We did make beautiful music together, didn't we, honey?" He searched her face. "Are you sure there has been no other man since we stopped sleeping together?"

"No one, Sam, and it's been one helluva dry spell."

He gave her a speculative look. "Lock the door and come over here."

"Does that mean we're gonna get hitched, Sam?"

"It's what you want, isn't it?"

"More than anything. And the saloon? Will you sell it?"

"I'm tired of it, anyway. Stop jawing and get over here."

"One more thing. I want you to apologize to the MacTavishes."

Sam gave her a startled look. "Now I know you're loco."

"I want us to start this marriage out right. I'll forget what you did to Slater because the bastard deserved to die, but I won't have you

438

obsessed with or pestering another man's wife."

She stood abruptly and removed her jacket, revealing an extremely low-cut gown that displayed her full breasts to perfection. "What's your answer, Sam?" Her hips swayed seductively beneath her clinging skirts. She knew for a fact that Sam hadn't had one of her girls in ages, and she was determined to use her feminine wiles to lure him back into her life. She'd been a fool to have given up on him so easily.

Sam's mouth went dry. His memory wasn't so short that he'd forgotten how good it was between him and Nell. He supposed marriage to her wouldn't be all that bad.

"Did you lock the door, honey? I agree to everything you said; just get over here so I can put out those fires I've left smoldering too damn long."

Nell sighed with pleasure. "I do love you, Sam. I aim to show you how much every day of our lives."

"This damn well better be worth it, honey. I'm giving up a lot for you."

It was.

Meanwhile, Ashley told Tanner about her encounter with Nell in the mercantile.

"I hope Nell succeeds in getting Sam to marry her," Ashley said.

"I'll put my money on Nell. She can be

439

pretty damn persuasive."

"I suppose you know that for a fact," Ashley teased.

"As a matter of fact, I do."

Ashley gave him a saucy smile. "Nell said you told her you loved your wife."

"I do love my wife. What's so unusual about that?"

"You could have told me first."

"I didn't think you wanted to hear it."

"Every day wouldn't be often enough."

Tanner laughed. "I'll try to remember that. How is our baby today?"

"We're both fine, Reb; don't worry about us."

"I do, you know. It's going to be touch-and-go financially until this logging operation gets under way. It's your money financing this venture — you can pull out now, before we get in too deeply."

"Not on your life. We'll get by. How are things going so far?"

"I've hired a crew and we're waiting for the weather to improve before felling trees on land the company has leased. One day I'll be able to buy you everything you deserve."

"Shut up, Tanner, and kiss me."

Their kiss was interrupted by a knock on the door.

"Damn, just when things were getting interesting," Tanner complained. "I'll tell whoever it is to come back later."

Ashley followed him out into the hall. When Tanner saw who was standing on the doorstep, his hand went for his gun. He cursed himself for a fool when he recalled he had shed his guns upon entering the house.

"What do you want, Stark?"

"A word with you and your wife. I didn't come to make trouble."

"I didn't think you knew anything but trouble." Ashley nudged Tanner in warning. "Oh, very well, have your say and get out of here."

"May I come in? It's raining, if you hadn't noticed."

Curiosity got the best of Tanner and he stepped aside so Stark could enter.

"I won't stay long. I owe your wife an apology. And I guess I owe you one too."

Ashley's shocked gasp drew his attention.

"You're an attractive woman, Mrs. MacTavish. I shouldn't have pursued you once I learned you were married. Sometimes I become obsessive about things and can't help myself. It won't happen again."

Tanner couldn't believe what he was hearing, but decided to take Stark's words at face value. He didn't want Stark for an enemy but he certainly wasn't going to embrace him as a friend. It would be a long time before he'd learn to trust Sam Stark, if ever. He knew Ashley felt the same way.

"You've had your say, Stark; now get out of

441

here. It won't be easy to forget that you broke into my house with the intention of raping my wife. And even harder to forgive. You keep out of my way and I'll keep out of yours."

Stark nodded. "That's fair enough." He glanced at Ashley. "You might be interested to know that Nell and I are getting married next month. She wants a big wedding, so I'm inviting the whole town."

"Don't count on us attending," Tanner said. "I'm sure we're going to be busy that day."

Stark turned to leave. "Wait a minute," Ashley called after him. "Tell Nell I'm happy she decided to take the bull by the horns. She'll know what I mean."

"Poor Nell," Tanner said after Stark left. "She doesn't know what she's letting herself in for."

"I think she does," Ashley remarked. "She loves him. You probably know better than anyone that love can work miracles."

"I wish her joy of him. I just hope she'll keep him out of our hair for good. Now, where were we before being interrupted? In the middle of a kiss, I think. Come here, wife. Let's see if I can kindle that flame that burns just for me."

He held out his arms and Ashley walked into them, lifting her face to his kiss. Their kiss was long and sweet and not nearly enough to quench the passion that burst into flame the moment they touched.

"You're going to have to get used to this," Tanner said as he urged her into the bedroom. "I can't seem to get enough of you."

"Nor I you. You make me happy, Tanner. There is only one other thing that I would wish for."

"Name it and it's yours, within reason," he added dryly.

"Cole. We haven't heard a word from him and it worries me. There is still so much unrest and bloodshed on the plains. I wonder if he and Morning Mist are safe and happy."

"Try not to worry, sweetheart. I'm sure we'll hear from Cole one day soon." His eyes touched her like a physical caress, so potent Ashley could almost taste it. "Meanwhile, let me take your mind off of things you can do nothing about."

He kissed her again, his mouth hot and hungry. When she went limp in his arms, he picked her up and carried her to the bed. He undressed himself and then her, lavishing adoration on every part of her body, rendering her incoherent with need. Ashley tasted the rough saltiness of his skin, touching him in all the places she knew he loved. When neither could stand another moment of torment, Tanner grasped her hips and entered her.

It was a wild coming together — like being

caught in a turbulent storm and tossed upon churning, swirling winds. One sensation upon another pelted them. Like a violent thunderstorm, passion rose to a roaring crescendo; desire crested and struck like a lightning bolt.

Ashley cried out Tanner's name as he drove into her, seeking the ultimate depths of intimacy. Tanner felt as if he were going to break apart as he strained to bring Ashley pleasure while withholding his own. Maddening hunger had swept him into the eye of the virulent storm, and he feared he'd leave her behind.

"Come with me, love. I can't wait any longer."

"I'm with you," Ashley sobbed against his lips. "Forever, my love."

Then passion released its full fury, spilling rapture from his body to hers. They soared together above the storm, then began a slow, lazy journey back to earth.

Long minutes later, Tanner raised up on his elbow and grinned down at her.

"What's so funny?" Ashley wanted to know. "I thought this was supposed to be a tender moment."

"I was just thinking, Yank. If our child is anything like you, I'm never going to be bored."

Ashley sighed in mock annoyance. "And if our child is like you, I'll probably never get a full night's rest." She reached up and gave him a quick kiss.

He kissed her back, then sighed in perfect contentment. "I'm a lucky man. If I had to marry a Yank I'm glad it was one with the gumption to lead me to the altar like a sacrificial lamb. Now go to sleep before I decide to love you again."

She didn't.

He did.

Chapter Twenty-one

June, 1872

Tanner trudged through the woods, marking trees for the logger's axes. It was the first time he'd been through this particular area, and he carefully skirted rotted trees that had fallen throughout the years. They would have to be cleared out first, he thought as he bent to mark a large pine tree lying in his path.

He noted with curiosity the strange marking that had been carved into the trunk and wondered if it had been put there by Indians years before. The carving resembled an arrow. It appeared as if the tree had lain in that spot for a long time, possibly years.

Tanner moved on, but something about the fallen pine kept nagging at him. He turned back, his gaze strangely drawn to the carving. Then he saw it. He hadn't noticed it at first because the tree had fallen in such a way that the large hole in its trunk was partly obscured. But it wasn't the hole that drew Tanner's attention; it was the object poking out of the hole. Dropping to his knees, he used his shoulder to roll the trunk a few inches, until he was able to insert his hands into the hole and pull out the object.

Though intact, the saddlebags he had removed were covered with mold and starting to decay. He stared at them curiously for several long minutes before opening the flaps. Greenbacks and gold coins spilled into his hands. He sat back in shock and disbelief. He didn't bother to count the money, but it looked like a substantial amount, more than he'd ever seen at one time.

There was no identification, just a few personal items — a comb, a brush and a change of clothes. Tanner sat on his haunches for a long time, contemplating the windfall. He could build Ashley the kind of home she deserved with this money, and have some left over to sink into the business. The money didn't belong to him, he told himself. His logging business was healthy, but he'd had to sink nearly every penny of profit back into it. He and Ashley were getting by, but he wanted more for her and their little girl.

In the end, he stuffed the money back into the saddlebags and slung it over his horse. Then he cast about for an explanation. Who could have hidden the money in the tree, and why? And what should he do with it? The money didn't belong to him, regardless of the fact that he had no idea where to find the owner. Curiosity pushed him to search the area for clues. When he came to the ravine, something prompted him to look down.

"Well, I'll be damned," he muttered aloud.

The elements had reduced the body at the bottom to pale, gleaming bones and snippets of clothing, but it was still recognizable as human.

Climbing and sliding down the ravine, Tanner grimaced in revulsion as he poked the gruesome skull and collection of bones with the toe of his boot. Could this be the man who had hidden the money? he wondered as he hunkered down to search for identification. He found none. Scrambling back up the ravine, Tanner mounted his horse and rode back to town.

Sheriff Dingus stared at the greenbacks and gold that Tanner had produced from the decaying saddlebags and whistled softly.

"Damn, Tanner, where did you find that?" During the years Tanner had resided in Oregon City, he and Sheriff Dingus had become friends. Tanner had found the sheriff to be nothing like he'd expected. Dingus was his own man and dedicated to upholding the law and protecting the citizens of Oregon City.

"On my property north of town. I had gone there to mark trees for the lumberjacks when I found the saddlebags in a rotted trunk. As you can see, there is no identification. I found a body as well. Not really a body," he amended, "just a pile of bones at the bottom of a ravine. No identification there, either.

448

Has anyone reported money missing in the past few months? Or a robbery hereabouts?"

Sheriff Dingus carefully counted the money and gave another low whistle. "Five thousand dollars, give or take a few dollars. I can't recall any robberies involving that kind of money. Let me look through my posters."

Fifteen minutes later Dingus sat back in his chair and grinned. "Just like I thought, nothing."

"What happens next?" Tanner wanted to know. "Who does the money belong to?"

"Why, I reckon it's yours, Tanner. And I couldn't be happier. One day your business is going to be a mainstay of our community. Of course I'll have to go out and take a look at the remains, but if there is no identification like you said, then I see no reason why you can't claim the money. Even if there were identification, we can't prove the dead man is the one who hid the money."

Tanner left the sheriff's office in a daze. So much money, it was like a miracle. He couldn't wait to tell Ashley. She deserved so much more than he'd been able to give her.

Tanner stopped first at the bank, where he deposited the money into his personal account. Then he hurried through the streets, anxious to reach the rented house he and Ashley shared with their daughter. He couldn't wait to tell Ashley about his find. It was a miracle that he remembered to stop by the post office to pick up their mail. It had become a daily ritual, one that usually led to disappointment for Ashley. During their four and a half years in Oregon City they had received no word from Cole, and Ashley worried terribly about her brother.

Two letters awaited Tanner at the post office, but he was still too elated over his good luck to do more than glance at them, stuff them in his vest pocket and promptly forget them. A few minutes later he bounded into the house, calling Ashley's name.

"Tanner, do be quiet. Lily is taking a nap."

Tanner sent her a besotted grin. Lily, their redheaded daughter, was so like her mother it was uncanny. Her fiery temper often tried their patience, and there were times when Tanner referred to her as his Flame, but she had inherited the best of both of them. He loved her beyond reason, just as he loved Lily's mother.

"Sorry, love, but I have some wonderful news. You'll never guess. . . ."

"So do I."

Tanner paused. "So do you what?"

"Have some wonderful news. You first," Ashley said, patting the seat beside her on the sofa. "What is your news?"

Tanner paced, too exhilarated to sit. "I found something while marking trees in the woods north of town."

His excitement was catching. Ashley loved

the way his gray eyes changed to pure silver when he became animated . . . or made love. "Well, are you going to tell me what you found?"

Tanner stopped in front of her and hunkered down on his knees. He grasped her hands and held them tightly. "Money, sweetheart. Five thousand dollars stuffed in the trunk of a rotted tree. And it's ours. The sheriff has no record of anyone reporting a robbery or missing money. He told me it was mine to claim. Do you know what that means, Yank? You no longer have to do without those things you've always wanted."

Ashley was properly impressed but clearly not as excited as Tanner. "I already have everything I want. I have you and Lily and now . . ."

"Just think," Tanner enthused, "we can build that house we've always dreamed about."

"Are you sure you don't know who the money belongs to?"

"As sure as I can be. I didn't tell you about the body I found at the bottom of the ravine. Not exactly a body, more like a pile of bones. No identification there, either. The sheriff is going out to take a look at it tomorrow."

"Do you think there is a connection between the body and the money?"

"It's hard to say. There's no telling how long the body and money have been out there

451

in the woods." Tanner was disappointed as well as puzzled by her lack of enthusiasm. "You don't seem as thrilled as I am about this."

Ashley gave him a dazzling smile. "Oh, I am; it's just that my news —".

"Oh, I almost forgot," Tanner interrupted. "I stopped by the post office on my way home. There were two letters waiting for us." He reached into his pocket and pulled out two badly wrinkled envelopes.

"Two letters," Ashley whispered, almost afraid to open the missives. "Do you think either of them is from Cole? Oh, Tanner, I've been so worried about him."

"You'll never know until you open them."

Ashley tore open one of the letters, and her face fell in disappointment. "It's from Nell. She reports that moving to San Francisco has been good for her and Sam. She says Sam is practicing law again and they have been accepted by society there, unlike in Oregon City, where everyone associated her with the Red Garter.

"You know, Tanner, I think Nell convinced Stark to move to San Francisco in order to get him out of our hair. She's a good woman."

She read the second page, then exclaimed, "Nell is expecting a child! She's ecstatic and says that Sam is getting used to the idea."

"Sam Stark will never change," Tanner

predicted. "I wish Nell the best but I have grave doubts. I must admit, however, I feel more comfortable with Stark hundreds of miles away."

Ashley folded the letter and set it aside. "So do I. I wish I could be just as certain that Pratt Slater will never return to town. It's strange the way he just up and disappeared, without a word to anyone. Are you sure you didn't have anything to do with it?"

"I can't take credit for Slater's disappearance," Tanner said. "Who knows why men like him do things? I just count my blessings, sweetheart. Who is the other letter from?"

Ashley's hands trembled as she carefully opened the second letter. Intuition told her it was from Cole, and a frisson of fear made her hesitate before reading it. Despite not hearing from him in four and a half long years, Ashley had refused to believe Cole was dead. She and Cole were twins; she would have felt it in her heart if Cole no longer walked the earth.

"Read it," Tanner gently urged. "Is it from Cole?"

Ashley gave Tanner a wobbly smile and began to read Cole's letter. Halfway through she gave a strangled cry, clearly disturbed by the contents of the letter.

"What is it, sweetheart? Has something happened to Cole? Does he give an excuse for not writing or contacting us in all this time?"

453

"Morning Mist is dead." Tears streamed down her cheeks. "When Cole returned to Running Elk's village after testifying at Harger's trial, he found the village destroyed and half the People dead. Morning Mist was among those who perished. Running Elk survived and invited Cole to go with the survivors deep into the mountains where the pony soldiers couldn't find them. Cole agreed, knowing he needed time to heal and renew himself."

"Is that why he hasn't contacted us before now?" Tanner could well imagine Cole's heartbreak. He wouldn't want to go on living without Ashley.

Ashley nodded. "He's been with Running Elk all this time." She read further. Suddenly she squealed and turned to Tanner, excitement shimmering in her eyes. "Cole is coming for a visit! He should be arriving soon."

Tanner smiled in reply. "It's about time. I'm glad he decided to return to his own kind. Does he say what he's going to do with his life?"

Ashley gave a negative shake of her head. "The letter was brief. I'm sure he'll answer all our questions once he gets here. I'm curious, though, why he didn't come to us sooner."

"Some people prefer to grieve in private," Tanner replied, thinking of Ellen and the

454

length of time he'd held his grief bottled up inside himself.

"I hope Cole finds someone to love," Ashley said wistfully. "He can't grieve for Morning Mist forever."

"Where is the letter posted from?"

"Denver. He says he is well and we shouldn't worry about him."

Tanner kissed away her tears and hugged her fiercely. "We've had all kinds of wonderful news today. I found a small fortune, Nell wrote with good tidings, your brother is coming for a visit, and on top of all that, we have our daughter to be thankful for."

"There's more," Ashley said, sending him a misty smile.

"I don't think I could stand any more good news," Tanner teased. "Maybe you should save it for tomorrow."

"This won't keep." She took a deep breath and plunged ahead. "I saw Doctor Kirk today. I'm going to have another child."

Tanner paled. "Sweet Lord! I barely survived Lily's birth. I don't think I can go through it again."

Ashley gave a delighted laugh. "You don't have to go through it, Reb; I do."

"You know damn well I felt every childbirth pain you suffered. If your pain was half as severe as mine I don't know how you can be happy about having another child. I'm a selfish bastard. I should have been

455

more careful with you."

"I want this baby, Tanner. After living as a spinster for so many years, giving you children makes me gloriously happy."

Her enthusiasm was catching. Tanner gave her a crooked grin. "Just don't go overboard. Two children seems a perfect number. Shall we celebrate our good news, love? How long before Lily awakens from her nap?"

She returned his smile, adding a wink for good measure. "Plenty of time for a celebration."